I Remember You

Yrsa Sigurdardóttir

Translated from the Icelandic by Philip Roughton

HODDER

First published in Great Britain in 2012 by Hodder & Stoughton
An Hachette UK company

First published in paperback in 2013

2

A CIP catalogue record for this title is available from the British Library.

Paperback ISBN 978 1 444 72926 9
eBook ISBN 978 1 444 72927 6

Typeset by Palimpsest Book Production Ltd, Falkirk, Stirlingshire
Printed and bound by Clays Ltd, St Ives plc

Hodder & Stoughton policy is to use papers that are natural, renewable and recyclable products and made from wood grown in sustainable forests. The logging and manufacturing processes are expected to conform to the environmental regulations of the country of origin.

Hodder & Stoughton Ltd
338 Euston Road
London NW1 3BH

www.hodder.co.uk

This book is dedicated to my wonderful parents-in-law,
Ásrún Ólafsdóttir and Þorhallur Jónsson.

Special thanks for information on traditions in the Westfjords and the history of Hesteyri go to my colleague Ingólfur Arnarson, my cherished friends Halldóra Hreinsdóttir and Jón Reynir Sigurvinsson, and of course Mrs Birna Pálsdóttir, caretaker and landlord of the Doctor's House.

—*Yrsa*

Chapter 1

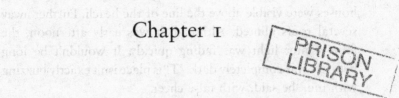

The waves rolled the boat to and fro in a constantly changing rhythm. The prow bobbed gently up and down as sharper movements shook the vessel, rocking it fiercely from side to side. The skipper struggled to fasten the little boat to a narrow steel post, but the weathered floating dock kept retreating, as if it were part of a game. He patiently repeated the same movements over and over, pulling the frayed rope in the direction of the post, but each time the coarse loop was about to fall into place, it seemed to be yanked away. It was as though the sea were playing with them, showing them who was in charge. In the end the man managed to secure the boat, but it was unclear whether the waves had grown bored of teasing him or whether the captain's experience and patience had got the better of them. He turned to the three passengers, his expression serious, and said: 'There you go, but be careful stepping up.' Then he jerked his chin at the boxes, bags and other things that they'd brought with them. 'I'll help you move this off the boat, but I can't help you take it to the house, unfortunately.' He squinted at the surface of the sea. 'It looks like I'd better get back as quick as I can. You'll have time to sort all this stuff out once I'm gone. There should be a wheelbarrow around here somewhere.'

'No problem.' Garðar smiled faintly at the man but made no move to start unloading the boat. He shuffled his feet and exhaled loudly, then turned his gaze inland, where several houses were visible above the line of the beach. Further away several roofs glinted. Although it was early afternoon, the faint winter light was fading quickly. It wouldn't be long before it was completely dark. 'This place isn't exactly buzzing with life,' he said, with false cheer.

'Well, no. Were you expecting it to?' The skipper didn't hide his surprise. 'I thought you'd been here before. You might want to reconsider your plan. You're welcome to come back with me; free of charge, of course.'

Garðar shook his head, studiously avoiding looking at Katrín who was trying to make eye contact with him so she could nod, or indicate in some other way that she really didn't mind going back. She'd never been as excited as him about this adventure, though neither had she opposed it outright. Instead she'd gone along with it, letting herself be carried along by his enthusiasm and his certainty that it would all go according to plan, but now that he seemed to be wavering, her own confidence in it had ebbed away. Suddenly she felt quite sure that total failure was the best they could hope for, but chose not to imagine the worst case scenario. She glanced at Líf, who was supporting herself on the gunwale, trying to regain the balance she'd left behind on the pier in Ísafjörður. After battling seasickness for most of the voyage, Líf looked utterly wretched, bearing only a passing resemblance to the perky woman who'd been so keen to come with them that she'd ignored Katrín's words of caution. Even Garðar didn't seem himself; as they'd drawn closer to shore, the bravado he'd shown as they prepared for the trip had faded. Of course, Katrín could hardly talk; she was sitting on a sack of firewood, doggedly refusing to stand up. The only difference between her and the other two was that she'd never been looking forward to the trip. The only passenger who seemed excited to disembark was Putti, Líf's little dog, who – in defiance of all their assumptions to the contrary – had turned out to have excellent sea-legs.

Apart from the lapping of the waves, the silence was absolute. How had she ever imagined this could work? The three of them, all alone in the dead of winter in a deserted village way up north in the middle of nowhere, without electricity or heat, and the only way back by sea. If something happened, they had no one to rely on but themselves. And now that Katrín was facing the facts she admitted to herself that their resourcefulness was decidedly limited. None of them was particularly outdoorsy, and almost any other task you could name would suit them better than renovating old houses. She opened her mouth to make the decision for them and accept the captain's offer, but then shut it without saying a word, sighing quietly to herself. The moment had passed, there was no going back, and it was far too late to protest now. She had no one to blame but herself for getting involved in this nonsense, because she'd let numerous opportunities to raise objections or change direction go by. At any point since the house project had first been raised she could have suggested that they decline the offer to buy a share in it, for example, or that the renovations could wait until summer, when there was a regular ferry schedule. Katrín suddenly felt a cold breeze and pulled the zip of her jacket higher. This whole thing was ridiculous.

But what if it wasn't really her passivity that was to blame, but the eagerness of Einar, now deceased, who'd been Garðar's best friend and Líf's husband? It was hard to be angry with him now, when he was six feet under; nonetheless it seemed clear to Katrín that he bore the greatest responsibility for this absurd situation. Einar had hiked in Hornstrandir two summers ago and so was familiar with Hesteyri, where the house was located. He had spun them the story of a village at the end of the world, beauty and peace and endless hiking trails in an unforgettable setting. Garðar had been inspired – not by the lure of nature, but by the fact that Einar hadn't been able to rent a room in Hesteyri, since the only guesthouse there had been full. Katrín couldn't remember which of them had gone on to suggest they see if any of the other houses there were for sale and transform one into a guesthouse, but it didn't matter; once the idea had been mooted there was no going back. Garðar had been unemployed for eight months and he was completely gripped by the idea of finally doing something useful. It was hardly going to dampen his interest when Einar expressed a keen desire to take part, offering to contribute both labour and capital. Then Líf had stoked the fire with extravagant praise for the brilliance of the idea and characteristically effusive encouragement. Katrín remembered now how much Líf's eagerness had got on her nerves; she'd suspected it was partly motivated by the prospect of time apart from her husband, as the renovations would require him to spend long periods of time up north. At that time their marriage had appeared to be falling apart, but when Einar died, Líf's grief had seemed bottomless. An ugly thought stirred in Katrín's mind: it would have been better if Einar had died before the purchase of the house had been completed. But unfortunately that wasn't how it had happened: now they were stuck with the property, and only one man excited about the renovation project where there had been two. The fact that Líf was so keen to take on her husband's role and press on with the repairs probably had something to do with the grieving process; she had neither skill nor interest in that kind of work, that much was certain. If she'd wanted to pull out, the house would have gone back on the market and they'd probably be sitting at home watching TV now, in the comforting arms of the city where night was never as black as here in Hesteyri.

When it became clear that the project hadn't died with Einar, Líf and Garðar had gone west one weekend and sailed from Ísafjörður to Hesteyri to take a look at the house. It had certainly been in poor condition, but that did nothing to diminish Garðar and Líf's excitement. They returned with a pile of photographs of every nook and cranny of the house and Garðar went straight to work planning what needed to be done before the start of the tourist season. From the photos, Katrín would have said that the house was held together by its paint, despite Garðar's insistence that the previous owner had carried out all the major repairs needed. For her part, Líf added flowery descriptions of Hesteyri's incredible natural beauty. Before long Garðar was making in-depth calculations, raising the price of an overnight stay and increasing the number of guests that could fit into the little two-storey house every time he opened his Excel spreadsheet. At least it would be interesting to see the place with her own eyes and work out how exactly Garðar intended to accommodate all these people.

Katrín got to her feet but couldn't see the house from where she stood on deck. From one of the panoramic shots that Garðar had taken of the area it had looked as if it was located at the edge of the settlement, but rather high up, so it should be visible. What if it had simply collapsed after Garðar and Líf had been on their reconnaissance trip? Nearly two months had passed since then, and the area was subject to no small amount of foul weather. She was about to suggest that they verify this before the boat sailed away when the skipper, doubtless starting to worry that he might have to carry them off the boat, said: 'Well, at least you're lucky with the weather.' He looked up at the sky. 'It could still change despite the forecast, so you should be prepared for anything.'

'We are. Just look at all this stuff.' Garðar smiled, a trace of his previous conviction returning to his voice. 'I think the only thing we have to fear is pulled muscles.'

'If you say so.' The captain didn't elaborate on this, and instead lifted a box onto the pier. 'I hope you have fully charged phones; if you climb up to the top of that hill you can get a connection. There's no point trying down here.'

Garðar and Katrín both looked towards the hill, which seemed more like a mountain to them. Líf was still staring back at the eddying black surface of the sea. 'That's good to know.' Garðar patted his coat pocket. 'Hopefully we won't have any need for them. We should be able to make it through the week; we'll wait for you here at the pier, like we discussed.'

'Bear in mind that I can't make it out here if the weather is bad. But if that's the case, I'll come as soon as it clears up. If it's a bit rough, obviously you don't need to stand here waiting on the pier; I'll come up to the house to get you. You can't hang around here in the cold and wind.' The man turned and looked over the fjord. 'The forecast is fair, but a lot can change in a week. It doesn't take much to make the boat bob like a cork, so we'll have to hope it's not too rough.'

'How bad does the weather have to be to stop you from

coming?' Katrín tried to hide her irritation at this pronouncement. Why hadn't he told them this before they made arrangements with him? Maybe they would have hired a bigger boat. But as soon as the thought entered her mind, she realized that they wouldn't; a bigger boat would have cost far more.

'If the waves are high on the open sea it's not likely I'd attempt it.' He looked back over the fjord again and nodded at the water. 'I won't sail if they're much worse than this.' Then he turned to face them. 'I need to get going.' He went to the stack of supplies on deck and passed Garðar the mattress that was lying on top. They formed an assembly line to move the boxes, paint pots, firewood, tools and black bin bags stuffed with non-breakable items onto the floating pier. While Katrín arranged the items along the pier to keep the end of it free, Líf was allowed to rest. She was in a bad way; it was all she could do just to hobble onto land and lie down near the top of the beach. Putti followed her, jumping about on the sand, obviously delighted to have solid ground under his feet and blind to the sorry condition of his owner. It took all Katrín's strength to keep up with the men, and sometimes they were forced to jump onto the pier to help her. Finally the cargo stood in a long line on the dock, a kind of guard of honour for the visitors. The skipper started shuffling his feet impatiently. He seemed more eager than them to part company. His presence provided a sense of security that would disappear with his little boat over the horizon; unlike them, he had dealt with the forces of nature before and would be prepared for whatever might befall him. Both Garðar and Katrín flirted with the idea of asking him to stay and give them a helping hand, but neither of them expressed it. Finally the man brought things to a close. 'Well, all you need to do now is get ashore, and you're on your way.' He directed his words at Garðar, who smiled half-heartedly, then clambered onto the floating pier. He and Katrín stood there, staring down at the man with bewildered expressions. He looked away, half embarrassed.

'You'll be fine. I just hope your friend feels better.' He nodded towards Líf, who was now sitting up. Her white jacket stood out sharply, a reflection of how poorly the new visitors fitted into these surroundings. 'See, the poor love seems to be feeling better already.' His words failed to cheer them up – if that had been his intention – and Katrín wondered how they looked to him: a couple from Reykjavík, a teacher and a graduate in business administration, both barely over thirty and neither of them cut out for any great physical exertion; not to mention the third wheel, who could barely lift her head. 'I'm sure everything will be all right,' the captain repeated gruffly, but without much conviction. 'But you shouldn't wait too long to get your gear up to the house; it'll be dark soon.'

A heavy, tangled lock of hair blew across Katrín's eyes. In all the rush not to forget anything on the list of necessary building materials and supplies, she had forgotten to bring hair-bands. Líf claimed she'd only brought one with her and had had to use it during the sea crossing to keep her hair out of her face as she vomited. Katrín tried to push the hair back with her fingers, but the wind immediately ruffled it again. Garðar's hair wasn't faring much better, though it was a lot shorter than hers. Their hiking shoes looked like they'd been bought specifically for this trip, and although their windproof trousers and jackets weren't brand new, they might just as well have been – they'd been given them as wedding presents by Garðar's siblings, but this was the first time they'd had a chance to use them. Líf had bought her white ski-suit for a skiing trip to Italy and it was about as appropriate to their current environment as a bathrobe. It was also clear from their pale skin that they weren't big on outdoor pursuits. At least they were all in good shape from spending hours at the gym, although Katrín suspected that whatever strength they'd managed to build up was unlikely to be sufficient for the work they'd be doing here.

'Do you know if any other visitors are expected to come here this week?' Katrín crossed her fingers behind her back. If so, there would still be hope that they could get a ride home earlier if everything went badly for them.

The skipper shook his head. 'You don't know much about this place, do you?' They hadn't been able to talk much on the way due to the noise of the engine.

'No. Not really.'

'No one comes here except during the summer, since there's no real reason to be here in the dead of winter. People stay in one of the houses over the New Year, and one or two house-owners pop over sometimes to make sure that everything's in order, but otherwise it's empty here during the winter months.' The man stopped and looked over what was visible of the settlement. 'Which house was it you bought?'

'The one furthest back. I think it must have been the priest's residence.' Garðar's voice betrayed a hint of pride. 'You actually can't see it from here in the dark, but otherwise it's quite prominent.'

'What? Are you sure?' The skipper looked surprised. 'No priest lived in this village. When there was still a church here, it was served from Aðalvík. I think you must have been given the wrong information.' Garðar hesitated and various thoughts crossed Katrín's mind, among them the hopeful notion that this was all a misunderstanding: there was no house, and they could turn right round and go home.

'No, I've had a look at it and it clearly used to be a priest's house. At least, there's a rather nice cross carved into the front door.'

The skipper seemed to have trouble believing Garðar. 'Who else owns the house with you?' His brow had furrowed slightly; it was as if he suspected them of having come into possession of the house by some criminal means.

'No one,' replied Garðar, frowning. 'We bought the house from the estate of someone who died before he could renovate it.'

The captain tugged on the rope and then jumped up to join them on the pier. 'I think I'd better find out what's going on here. I know all the houses in the village and generally each of them has several owners, usually siblings or descendants of the previous inhabitants. I don't know of any house that could have belonged to one individual.' He wiped his palms on his trousers. 'I can't leave you here unless I can be certain that you've got some shelter and that you haven't been fed a load of nonsense.' He set off down the pier. 'Point me to the house when we get to the top of the beach; we'll be far enough there from the boat for its lights not to blind our view.'

He strode off and they followed, forced to take larger steps than they were used to in order to keep up with the man, who walked with a fast, loping gait that belied his short stature. Then he stopped as suddenly as he'd started, and they barely avoided knocking into him: they'd come to where

Líf was sitting miserably. It looked to Katrín as if the colour was returning to her cheeks. 'I think I've stopped vomiting.' She tried to smile at them, without much success. 'I'm frozen. When can we get inside?'

'Soon.' Garðar was unusually curt but then obviously regretted it, since he added in a much gentler tone: 'Just try to bear up.'

He pushed Putti aside as the dog greeted their arrival by fawning over him. Irritated, he brushed sand off his trouser leg.

The skipper turned to Garðar. 'Where did you say the house was? Can you see it from here?'

Katrín positioned herself next to the men and watched as anxiously as the old captain. Although Garðar's description of the village was vivid in her mind's eye, it was difficult to reconcile it with what she saw now. The little cluster of ten houses and their accompanying storage sheds was more spread out than she'd expected, and it struck her how much distance there was between them. She would have thought that in such an isolated community people would have wanted to live closer together, to draw strength from each other in times of trouble or hardship. But what did she know? She actually had no idea how old the village was. Maybe the people there needed large gardens for keeping livestock or to plant vegetables. There could hardly be a shop there. Garðar finally spotted what he was looking for and pointed. 'There, furthest out, on the other side of the stream. Of course, you can only see the roof – on the other side of the hill with the spruce trees, which block the view a bit.' He dropped his hand. 'You don't think a priest lived there?'

The old man clicked his tongue, and stared up at the

innocuous-looking roof where it rose over the yellowed vegetation on the slope. 'I'd forgotten that place. But no, it's not the priest's house. The cross on the door doesn't have anything to do with a priest. The person who lived there was a follower of the Heavenly Father and his Son and thought it was a fitting tribute.' He pondered for a moment and appeared to be about to say something, but stopped. 'For years the house has gone by the name of Final Sight. It's visible from the sea.' The man looked as if he wanted to add something, but again did not.

'Final Sight. Okay.' Garðar tried to look nonchalant but Katrín could see through him. One of the things he had found most attractive about the house was that it had once been inhabited by one of the most important figures in the village. 'I guess it would have been a lot to ask to have a rectory in a place this size.' Garðar looked over the houses, most of which were fully visible from where they were standing, unlike the partially hidden one they now owned. 'But weren't there more houses here at one time? Some of them must have been torn down over the years.'

'Yes, yes, quite right.' The old man still hadn't turned back to face them and appeared distracted. 'There were more houses here. Of course there were never many people living here, but some took their houses with them when they left. Only the foundations remain.'

'Have you ever been in there? In our house?' Katrín had the feeling that something odd was going on, but that the man couldn't express it for some reason. 'Is the roof about to collapse or something like that?' She lacked the imagination to come up with anything else. 'Will it be safe for us in there?'

'I haven't been in there, but the roof is probably all right.

The previous owners were quite enthusiastic at first about patching the place up. Everyone starts off well.'

'Starts off?' Garðar winked at Katrín conspiratorially and grinned. 'So it's high time someone got down to business and completed the repairs.'

The man ignored Garðar's attempt to lighten the mood; instead he turned away from the little cluster of houses that could hardly be called a village and prepared to head back down to the pier. 'I'm going to get something from the boat.' Katrín and Garðar hesitated, taken aback, not knowing whether they should wait there for him or follow; finally they decided on the latter.

'Where are you going? You're not leaving me here alone!' Líf scrambled to her feet.

Katrín turned back towards her. 'We'll be right back. You've been sitting there for over half an hour, so a few minutes more won't make a difference. Just rest.' Before Líf had a chance to object, Katrín hurried to catch up with Garðar and the skipper.

The skipper disappeared into the boat, then reappeared a moment later with an open plastic box containing various items she couldn't make out. From it he pulled out a key ring holding an ordinary house key, and another that was much more old-fashioned and grand-looking. 'Just to be sure, take these keys to the guesthouse in the doctor's residence.' He pointed at one of the most respectable-looking houses, clearly visible from the pier. 'I'll let the owners know I've loaned them to you. The woman who looks after it is my wife's sister; she'll probably be glad to know that you have somewhere else to go if anything should come up. You don't need to worry about staying there.'

Something unspoken hovered in the air between Garðar and Katrín: they hadn't told the man about their plans to create competition for the guesthouse to which they were being given the keys. Neither said anything. Katrín held out her hand and took the key ring. 'Thank you.'

'You should also keep your phone batteries charged, and don't hesitate to call if you have any trouble. In decent weather I can make it here in under two hours.'

'That's very kind of you.' Garðar put his arm around Katrín's shoulder. 'We're not quite as hopeless as we look, so I doubt it will come to that.'

'It's nothing to do with you. The house doesn't have a great reputation and although I'm not superstitious, I'll feel better knowing that you have somewhere else to go and that you're aware you can call for help. The weather here can be dangerous sometimes, that's all.' When neither of them responded he wished them good luck and said goodbye. They muttered farewells in return and stood rooted to the spot, waving, as the man steered the boat carefully off the pier and sailed out into the fjord.

When they were alone, anxiety overwhelmed Katrín. 'What did he mean by "the house doesn't have a great reputation"?'

Garðar shook his head slowly. 'No idea. I suspect he knows more about our plan than he was willing to admit. Didn't he say his sister-in-law runs the guesthouse? He was just trying to scare us. I hope he doesn't start spreading rumours about the house.'

Katrín said nothing. She was sure Garðar was wrong. Apart from Líf, no one knew about their plans. Neither she nor Garðar had discussed them with their families for fear of jinxing the project. It was bad enough that their families pitied them because of Garðar's unemployment. Their relatives thought they were taking a trip out west for Katrín's winter holiday from school. No, the old man hadn't said what he did to scare them; there was something else behind it. Katrín sorely regretted not having pressed him for more details in order to prevent her imagination from running wild. The boat receded into the distance faster than she recalled it arriving, and in an incredibly short amount of time appeared only as big as her fist.

'It's awfully quiet here.' Garðar broke the silence that the boat had left behind. 'I don't think I've ever been in such an isolated spot.' He bent down and kissed Katrín's salty cheek. 'But the company here is good, that's for sure.'

Katrín smiled at him and asked whether he'd forgotten their Lazarus, Líf. She turned away from the sea, not wanting to see the boat disappear completely, and looked along the beach and up towards the land. Líf was on her feet, waving at them frantically. Katrín raised her hand to wave back but dropped it when she saw something move quickly behind their white-clad friend. It was a pitch-black shadow, much darker than their dim surroundings. It disappeared as soon as it appeared, making it impossible for Katrín to distinguish what it was, but it looked a bit like a person, a short one. She gripped Garðar's upper arm tightly. 'What was that?'

'What?' Garðar peered towards where Katrín was pointing. 'Do you mean Líf?'

'No. Something moved behind her.'

'Really?' Garðar gave her a puzzled look. 'There's nothing there. Just a seasick woman in a ski outfit. Wasn't it just the dog?'

Katrín tried to appear calm. It could well be that her eyes

had deceived her. But it wasn't Putti, she was certain of that; he was standing in front of Líf, sniffing the air. Maybe the wind had blown something loose. But that didn't explain how quickly it seemed to have gone by, although there could have been a sharp gust. She let go of Garðar's arm and focused on breathing calmly for what was left of the walk down the pier. Nor did she say anything after they'd reached Líf. There was a rustling noise and a cracking in the dry, yellowed vegetation behind them, as if someone were walking through it. Neither Garðar nor Líf seemed to notice anything, but Katrín couldn't avoid the thought that they weren't alone there in Hesteyri.

Chapter 2

'I don't know who could have done this, but I doubt it was kids or teenagers. Although it's certainly possible.' Freyr stuck his hands in his pockets and stared at the destruction in front of him once more. Tattered teddy bears and rag dolls were strewn across the floor, the limbs torn from most of them and the eyes pulled out. 'My first hunch is that we have every reason to be concerned about this person or persons, although it's difficult to make a complete diagnosis based on this mess. If it helps, I'm leaning more towards the idea that whoever did this worked alone. I'm sorry I can't be more precise.' He stared at the yellow wall and the remnants of the drawings made by the Ísafjörður schoolchildren, which consisted only of the corners where they had been fastened to the wall with Blu-tack. The remainder of the drawings lay on the floor, torn and tattered; thick white paper covered with brightly coloured pictures. At first glance it appeared that the vandal had torn them down hastily in order to make room for his message. Upon closer inspection, it was clear that he'd taken time to tear the pictures up. Clumsy letters covered the wall. He had gone over each one repeatedly, scrawling them in violent strokes with crayons, which lay in pieces among the shredded drawings. There was no way of guessing the age of the person who had written the message on the wall, if it were in fact a message: DIRTY.

The wall was illuminated for a moment and Freyr was blinded by the flash. 'Have you got anything to say about this graffiti?' Dagný removed the bulky camera from her face without turning towards him, and instead continued to inspect the inscription.

'No, nothing.' Freyr studied her profile. Although it conveyed a particular kind of toughness, her short, messy hair brought out the femininity in her face – which was no doubt the opposite of what she intended. He hadn't worked out whether it was her role as a policewoman that made her try to conceal her sex appeal, or whether it was down to her lifestyle. Dagný was unusual in this regard; generally he could read people like a book, and this uniqueness of hers attracted him, even though he received little or no response to his feeble attempts to deepen their relationship. She seemed comfortable in his presence on the rare occasions that they met, yet their friendship never seemed to have a chance to intensify. Either he was ready for it and she wasn't, or else the few times she had shown some interest, he was immediately racked by doubt and backed off. His doubts had nothing to do with her, but with himself; deep within him dwelt the suspicion that he wasn't worthy of her, that he was too broken and burned to make a connection with her or with any other person. But then his doubts would evaporate and she would retreat, leaving them permanently caught in this ridiculous vicious circle.

This was the first time for many years that he hadn't known how to go about handling a relationship with someone, and it had awakened in him memories of his life before he'd become a specialist in human behaviour. These memories were probably the root of his attraction to Dagný, but he made a point of not wondering about this or drawing conclusions for fear of obliterating his feelings and ending up all alone, as he had been before. He turned away from her and focused on the word scribbled on the wall. He shook his head and blew out slowly, as he always did when he was thinking. 'Of course, various things come to mind, though none of them are particularly helpful.'

'For example?' Her voice was devoid of feeling, reminding him of the bored girls who worked in his local bakery when they asked whether he wanted them to slice his bread.

'Well, dirty money, dirty laundry, dirty politicians, dirty cops, dirty movies. Something along those lines, though I don't see how they could possibly be connected to the vandalism.' Dagný's expression didn't change. She raised the camera to her eyes again and snapped a photo. It was hard to see what that one photo would add. After taking a photo she always examined the image in the little screen to make sure she'd captured what she'd intended, so she could hardly be worried she'd messed up the ones she'd already taken. He wondered if she used the camera as a mask to hide behind.

'I thought psychologists studied these things. Don't you need to know the motivation behind what people write when they're in an agitated mental state?'

'Yes, but usually we have more to go on than a single word. Maybe I missed the class on people who break into schools, go berserk and write mysterious messages on the wall.' As soon as he said this, Freyr regretted it. Why was he letting her sarcasm get on his nerves? It wasn't as if he was trying to be a comedian, or making light of the situation. 'I recommend you try to find the culprit the traditional way, then if you do, I'll speak to him and give you my opinion as to what might have made him do this. For the moment I can't add much to your investigation.' In fact, he didn't know why she'd called him out; his job description at the Regional Hospital in Ísafjörður didn't include giving advice to the police, and she hadn't behaved as though she expected his opinion to mark a turning point in the investigation. 'Unless you want me to look up similar incidents elsewhere and see what conclusions I can draw from them? I don't know if that would be useful.'

'No, no.' Dagný's tone was brusque, but softened when she hurriedly added: 'Thanks, but that won't be necessary.'

The sound of children's voices carried in through the window. Under normal circumstances they would probably have been in this room, playing or drawing more pictures to adorn its walls, but this morning was far from ordinary. The teacher who had turned up first had been stunned, and had immediately called the police to report the break-in. Dagný and an older officer had been sent to the scene; Freyr supposed she'd been sent because she reported for work early. The normal day shift for police officers didn't start until eight, but Dagný habitually woke around six, regardless of whether she was working. The only difference was that she was generally out of the door at seven o'clock on work days, apparently too restless to hang around at home any longer. This he knew only because she lived across the road from him, and his morning routine was much the same. In this respect they had something in common: neither of them liked wasting time doing nothing. This appealed to him; in the few relationships he'd had in his life, the women had always wanted to cuddle in bed for as long as possible and hadn't understood his urge to jump out of bed as soon as he opened his eyes, preferably before the paper came through the letterbox. He could happily imagine a relationship in which he would have company in the kitchen while it was dark and quiet outside and others slept. He had no other ideas as to what he was looking for in a life companion; too little time had passed since his divorce. He couldn't work out whether his memories of his previous relationship before everything went wrong were a realistic reflection of what he was looking for, or whether he was viewing them in a rosy light. In fact he knew the answer; he just didn't want to face it.

Freyr went over to the window and at first saw only his own reflection in the glass. He looked younger than his age but that was doubtless because he kept himself in shape, thus avoiding the extra pounds that had started to weigh down his former classmates from medical school. Still, this was only fair, since he hadn't enjoyed as much female attention as they had during his university years. These days, luckily, women seemed to appreciate his strong facial features; and, given that he remembered what it was like to have to clear his throat to get a woman's attention, he was planning on holding onto his looks for a while. Naturally they would start declining at some point, but he still had several years to go until he hit forty, so it wasn't like he had one foot in the grave just yet.

The children were scattered around the playground, their snowsuits making them look stiff and almost spherical. Although the winter had been unusually mild, it was still cold outside and their fiery red cheeks glowed beneath multi-coloured bobble hats. Freyr could well imagine that this incident would result in a spate of visits to the health clinic; the flu was going round and ear infections were on the increase. If the children weren't going to be allowed back in until things were cleaned up here, they might have to stay outdoors for the rest of the day. 'When can the poor things come back inside?' Freyr watched a girl topple onto her head after walking straight into a sandpit.

'When we're finished.' Dagný took more photos. The flash in the window indicated that she'd moved over to the basic-looking bookshelves lying on top of their former contents. 'It shouldn't take too much longer; we've already taken fingerprints from most of what the vandal might conceivably have touched, but I don't expect anything to come of it. It's my understanding that every square centimetre in here is covered with fingerprints. It's going to be nearly impossible to determine whether any of them belong to him.'

Freyr said nothing as he continued to watch the children. If he squinted, he could imagine that he'd gone back in time several years and that this was his son's playground. One of the children could then be his son; there were several boys who moved like he had as a toddler, and when they were this bundled up it was easy for Freyr to deceive himself. However, he wouldn't allow himself to indulge in the fantasy. It would be too painful to abandon the dream world and return to the cold reality in which there was no longer any place for his son.

The door opened to admit Veigar, the older police officer who had responded to the call with Dagný. 'How's it going here?' He looked around and shook his head. 'What a fucking abomination.' He was accustomed to working with Dagný, so it didn't bother him when she didn't reply. Instead of repeating the question or taking offence, he turned to Freyr. 'Have you solved the case for us, mate?'

Freyr pulled himself away from the window and smiled in reply. 'No, I haven't pieced it together yet; but, from the evidence, I'd say a pretty sick person was at work here.'

'Yes, it doesn't take an expert from the south to see that.'

Veigar bent down to pick up a broken chair leg. 'How could anyone do this? I have no interest in understanding what drove this idiot to it, I just want to know *how* he actually did it.'

'Was nothing spared?' Freyr had only managed to glance over the place but of course he'd noticed various things on his way in: the children's coat rack in the lobby had been destroyed, the hooks and the shelves above them all torn down from the walls.

'Very little. The kitchen, for example, was in a right bloody state.'

'But was this the only message?'

Veigar scratched his head. 'Yes. Maybe he meant to write more but didn't have time for it. He was probably exhausted after making all this mess.'

'We don't know whether it was a man or a woman.' Dagný didn't look up, busying herself instead with putting the camera into a black bag. 'It could even have been a couple or a group of people. It barely seems possible for one man to do all this alone, even if he did have the entire weekend.'

'He certainly didn't hold back.' Freyr nudged a pile of track sections from a wrecked wooden train set with his foot. 'Didn't anyone notice anything? Neighbours, or passers-by? All this must have made quite a racket.'

'Not that we know of. We haven't contacted all the residents of the adjacent buildings but the ones we spoke to didn't notice anything, or at least nothing clicked if they did hear something. There's quite a distance between the buildings,' replied Veigar.

A red plastic bucket bounced off the window where Freyr had just been standing and they all looked round in surprise. 'The poor kids must be getting bored out there,' said Veigar.

'Something's got to be done if they can't come in. It's only an hour until lunch and the only toilet they've got access to has a permanent queue outside.'

'Have you spoken to the headmistress?' Dagný pushed down hard on the camera in order to close the bag.

'Yes, and she's not too pleased with the situation; I mean, she understands, but she's still annoyed. The children must be getting cold.'

Freyr waited for Dagný to snap that they would just have to grin and bear it, but she didn't. On the contrary, she displayed an unusual amount of consideration, for her: 'They should be able to have the smaller room in fifteen minutes or so. It was empty, so it wasn't damaged much. They'll have to eat with their plates in their laps, though; I still haven't come across any undamaged furniture.'

'I'll let the headmistress know. She'll be relieved.' Veigar walked out and left the door open, giving them a clear view of the devastation.

'I'd better get going. I don't think I can be of much more use here – if I was of any use to start with.' Freyr looked back towards the window and the children playing outside. They seemed even more restless than before. They were probably starting to get hungry. His attention was caught by a boy of three or four, not because he reminded him of his son but because unlike the others he stood stock-still, staring at Freyr as he stood there at the window. Although an attempt had been made to shield the children from what had happened they had sensed that everything wasn't as it should be, and this boy's expression suggested that he believed Freyr to be the evildoer who had destroyed the schoolroom. The child appeared fearless, in fact, his stare and frozen expression suggestive of pent-up rage, which seemed to be directed at Freyr. Freyr tried to smile and waved at the child to let him know that he wasn't the bad guy, but it had no effect. There was not a flicker in the child's stony face.

'Are you making faces at that kid there?' Dagný had come up beside him and was now pointing at the boy in the green snowsuit. 'Weird kid.' She rubbed her upper arms as if she felt cold, even within the warmth of the school.

'It looks to me like he thinks I'm the vandal. At least he's glaring at me like I am. Maybe he's scared.'

Dagný nodded slowly. 'It's strange that more of the kids don't seem scared.'

'I'm sure some of them are worried, but hopefully they've shrugged it off and got lost in playing games instead. Most children have an incredible ability to block out bad feelings, but this little boy clearly isn't that type.' Freyr couldn't take his eyes off him. The other children had obeyed a staff member and gone inside to eat. The boy must have heard her too, but he hadn't moved a muscle and didn't take his eyes from the window. Suddenly the headmistress came out and pulled the boy away. As they walked off he turned back so as not to lose sight of Freyr. It wasn't until he'd gone around the corner that they broke eye contact.

'Well, well!' Dagný raised an eyebrow at him. 'If I hadn't seen you this weekend I might have reason to question you about your movements.' She smiled, which was rare; a real shame considering how beautiful and genuine her smile was. His ex-wife had smiled often and it had been a lovely sight, until life deprived her of any reason to do so. Freyr smiled back, delighted that she had paid him any attention at all. But Dagný's expression immediately resumed its usual seriousness. 'I don't know why, but all of this is making me feel kind of uncomfortable.'

Freyr surveyed the destruction in the classroom again. 'I'm not surprised. You have every reason to be concerned, and even to wonder what this individual is going to do next.'

'No, I don't mean uncomfortable about that. I mean I've got a strange feeling, as though I'm forgetting or have overlooked something, as though there's more to this than just someone giving in to their destructive urges. I was hoping you could explain it.'

Freyr was silent for a moment as he considered his reply. He didn't want to interact with her as a psychiatrist; it was one thing to examine the weekend's evidence as a participant in a police investigation, but quite another to approach her personally in his clinical capacity. One of the main reasons he had taken the job in Ísafjörður was that it gave him the opportunity to practise general medicine alongside his specialism. There was no need for a full-time psychiatrist here, and that suited him well. He had enough on his plate dealing with his own mental state, without having to immerse himself in others' every day of the week. He noticed that Dagný was fidgeting, impatient at his lack of response to her question, so he hurriedly replied: 'I expect it's a combination of things – this dreadful scene, which would leave a bad taste in anyone's mouth, and the urge to find the guilty party. You're under pressure to tie up the investigation of the crime scene, so you're also concerned about missing something that might matter. And to top it all off, your mind is trying to process all of this. The outcome is the feeling you describe.' He stopped there, although he could easily have gone on for much longer.

'I see.' She didn't seem very convinced but said nothing

further, since Veigar had stuck his head round the door. 'Dagný, we need to get going. Gunni and Stefán have come to finish up here, because we're needed elsewhere.' He gave her a look meant to convey that something even more serious than the desecration of a children's classroom had taken place.

Dagný hurriedly said goodbye and rushed off with Veigar, leaving Freyr standing there. He had to content himself with calling goodbye to them before the door banged shut.

He stood in the lobby, surrounded by children, and by teachers who were deftly removing the youngsters' snowsuits. One of them bundled four children into the corridor, telling them that now they would get to eat in the little gym, what fun! Freyr winked and waved at several of the children on his way past, then bid farewell to the staff, who responded in kind without looking up from their work. As he took hold of the front door handle, he felt a tug at his trouser leg and looked down with a smile. It was the boy who'd been standing outside. He was still wearing his green snowsuit. The boy stared silently up at Freyr without releasing his trouser leg. For some reason Freyr felt slightly uncomfortable in the child's presence, although he was used to odd behaviour in his dealings with his patients. He bent down to the boy. 'Did you see the police here before? I'm helping them catch the bad guy.' The boy carried on staring, still not saying a word. 'The police always catch the bad guy.' The boy muttered something that Freyr didn't catch properly, but before he could ask the boy to repeat it one of the teachers called the child over. Freyr straightened up and went outside. Apparently the child wasn't immune to the effects of the mess and destruction inside after all – he thought he'd whispered '*Dirty*.'

Chapter 3

Katrín sat on the edge of the porch behind the house, closed her eyes and relished breathing in the clean air. The wood had sunk into the ground in one corner, meaning she had to lean in to the house to keep her balance. The sun was already up, hanging low in the sky as if it had turned up sick for work and didn't expect to make it through the whole day. Its rays didn't feel hot, but rather lukewarm, although Katrín had no complaints after having been inside the cold house. Anyway, you couldn't make demands of the sun this far north in the dead of winter; you simply took what little sunshine you were given and were grateful. Gentle gusts of wind blew over her face and the fresh breeze carried away the paint smell that had settled in her clothing and hair. The feeling was profoundly satisfying and she breathed as deeply as her lungs allowed. The smell of chemicals always made her feel uncomfortable, since each inhalation reminded her of the toll the toxic vapour was taking on her limited number of brain cells. No doubt today's painting frenzy had killed a good number of them.

Katrín opened her eyes and stretched. If you ignored the babble of the stream separating the house from the abandoned village, the silence was absolute. Finding it a little uncomfortable, she listened harder, but nothing changed. She and Garðar had both had trouble sleeping in the silence the night before, even though they were exhausted by the seemingly endless conveyance of things from the pier. Líf, on the other hand, who couldn't help much after being so sick, had slept like a rock. They could have used her help; the wheelbarrow the skipper had mentioned had been nowhere to be found, meaning they had to carry everything themselves. Katrín had resolved to count the number of trips but lost count as exhaustion took over, so she didn't know whether it had been twenty, fifty, or even a hundred. Her aches and pains told her all she needed to know; her upper arms hurt at the mere thought of last night's travails. She rubbed her sore muscles. Frustratingly, as she'd suspected, all the hard grind at the gym in recent years appeared to have been no help.

Katrín shifted position on the porch and tried to spot Garðar and Líf on the slope west of the village, but it was hard to detect anything much through all the angelica, dry and dead since last summer, and downright impossible to see all the way to the top. Garðar had said that the slope seemed gentle most of the way up, then there was level ground that reached almost to the next fjord to the north. Katrín suspected Garðar hadn't had much to go on when he described the conditions there. She felt too comfortable to stand up and try to see them, and she was sure they'd be back soon anyway. She wasn't entirely certain how long ago they'd left; it had been many years since she had worn a wristwatch, contenting herself with the clock on her mobile phone. But the phone's battery was too precious to leave it turned on. One thing was certain – they'd been away for so long that she was utterly relieved not to have gone with them. The skipper had said there was mobile phone reception on top of the hill, but that information might be about as reliable as his tale about the wheelbarrow. Maybe they'd have to walk much further in search of a good connection once they were up on the summit. It would have killed her to have to tramp around up there, and in any case, Garðar didn't need her there just to ask the estate agent whether some boxes they'd found in the house belonged to them or to the estate. Katrín didn't see why he was wasting time on this, especially given that they depended on the phone being charged if the weather were to turn bad or they needed emergency assistance, but once he'd decided on something he was immovable, so she hadn't objected. Even when Líf, who was too unwell to help out with the renovations, said that she would accompany him, Katrín had held her tongue, though she longed to say that Líf really should be trying to paint something. She guessed the reason Líf was so keen on going off with Garðar was because she knew Katrín would find work for her to do as soon as the two of them were left alone. Katrín wasn't quite as compassionate as Garðar, who had told Líf that morning that she should just rest until she felt better.

She peered again through the yellowed sea of vegetation in the hope of locating them. Maybe something had happened; neither of them was used to hiking in the mountains, and Líf was quite accident-prone to boot. She smiled. Of course they were all right. What could possibly happen? The three of them were the only people here, and apart from the birds, a grey fox appeared to be the only other living thing in the area. The animal had watched them from afar as they moved their materials the night before, but it hadn't appeared today; Putti's presence had probably frightened it away. Once Garðar and Líf had set off, Katrín was virtually alone in the world, since the blessed dog had let itself be persuaded to go with them even though its short legs hardly looked sturdy enough to climb mountains. This was the first time she'd experienced such total isolation and she found the surroundings and the empty house behind her oppressive. She would gladly have welcomed the company of the fox, if it made an appearance. Katrín had no idea whether foxes were mostly nocturnal, or if they came out during the day. She hoped that the animal would show its face, but she primarily wanted Garðar to come back – and Líf, of course. She struggled to her feet, but although she could now see most of the slope, she still couldn't catch the slightest glimpse of them – though that meant almost nothing, since both of them were wearing clothing in earth tones that would blend into the snowless winter landscape. She was searching for signs of movement along the path they'd taken when she heard a sudden creak in the house behind her. A chill ran down her spine and she instinctively moved a little further away. She longed to run up the slope to where Garðar and Líf must be.

Then she relaxed. She could be such a wuss. This was an old house – there was nothing unnatural about a noise or two. It was only thermal expansion of the wood in the sun. She was just so unused to this oppressive silence. Still, she yelled out when a hand gripped her firmly by the shoulder and someone shouted, 'Boo!'

'Idiot!' Katrín shoved Garðar's hand away and stamped her foot, furious. 'I could have had a heart attack.' She'd never liked sudden shocks, ever since childhood, and her anger at Garðar was also directed at all those who had played this same trick on her through the years. 'I hate it when you do that.'

Garðar pulled back his hand in surprise. 'Sorry. I didn't mean to scare you.' His expression, full of remorse, made

Katrín think of all the painters who had captured that same expression in their immortal works of art.

'You just really startled me.' She smiled apologetically. 'You're not an idiot. It was just a knee-jerk reaction.' Garðar looked like a hurt child and she felt a sting of remorse as she remembered how sensitive he'd become after months of unemployment. 'I'd just been trying to catch sight of you on the slope, and I really didn't expect you to sneak up on me from behind like that.' It must have been Garðar making the creaking noise as he walked through the house. They had all noticed the large number of loose and worn-down floorboards that loudly reminded you of their presence every time you stepped on them. 'But I'm so glad you're back. Where's Líf?'

Garðar looked as if he were trying to decide whether he should hold her little outburst against her or let it go, and in the end he seemed to decide to be his old cheerful self. He smiled and stroked her hair and she could see a flash of the good old Garðar reappearing: the Garðar who was rising rapidly through the ranks of one of the country's biggest investment companies; the Garðar who got the most out of life; the Garðar she'd fallen in love with. 'She went inside. She was going to find some food for us.' He kissed her on the cheek. 'I didn't mean to creep up on you, I just didn't realize how fast you can move.'

'What? I'm like a snail; I can hardly move an inch for my aching muscles.'

'A snail? A cheetah, more like – we could see you out at the front of the house, but when I was nearly here you shot inside so fast that I thought the house had caught fire.' Garðar kissed her other cheek. 'So I followed, and found you standing behind the house. What's going on?'

Katrín frowned. 'I was never in front of the house. I finished the wall I was painting and came out here on the porch to get some fresh air and look out for you. Maybe your eyes were playing tricks on you.'

Garðar shrugged, but appeared as surprised by Katrín's explanation as she was by his story. 'I guess so. Has anyone else come here since we left? Was there a boat, or something?'

She shook her head. 'Did we drop something yesterday that the wind could have picked up? Could it have been a piece of clothing or some carpet? The sun's so low that it's hard to make out anything properly. It was probably just some litter. Maybe it was the fox.'

'Maybe.' He nudged the sagging porch with his foot. 'I need to repair this. No matter where I look, there's some sort of project.'

'At least you don't have to do anything more to my wall.' Katrín grinned proudly. 'It's ready for the first guests, all white and beautiful.' She was glad he wanted to change the subject. She didn't want to wonder any more about what Garðar and Líf had seen or not seen. The idea that there was someone else in the area was ridiculous, and made her feel uncomfortable. They were just unused to the silence and the empty environment. 'I guess I'd better start the next wall while there's still some light.' Then she remembered Garðar's reason for going up the hill. 'What did the estate agent say? Could you get reception?'

'He didn't answer. It might be better to try at the end of the day; he could be somewhere in town showing a property, or just busy.' Garðar looked back at the house. 'We'll just look in the boxes and if it's clearly junk, we'll leave it. Otherwise we'll take it back with us if we don't get hold of the agent. I can't be bothered to keep going up there just to try and get hold of him. It would be a lot less hassle just to carry the stuff down to the pier when we leave.'

Katrín sighed. 'I never want to hear the word "carry" again.' She leaned up against Garðar, wrapped her arms around his waist and shifted her body weight over to him. 'Maybe you'll have to carry *me*. I'm worse than I was this morning.'

'You'll be lucky, today. You're not the only one with aching muscles.' He kissed her on the head, somewhat distractedly, before straightening up. 'I'm starving. Shall we go and have some of the delicious provisions Líf's preparing?'

The thought of the tinned food, bread and other things that they'd bought for their trip didn't whet her appetite much. 'I'd kill for a pizza.'

Garðar smiled faintly. 'Not on the menu.' He unwound himself from her embrace and prepared to go inside. 'And even if we could get some, I don't feel like climbing back up the mountain to order it. Come on; let's have something to eat while it's still fresh. I don't know what we'll have left by the time we get to our last few days, so we may as well enjoy eating something besides instant noodles.' Through the kitchen window they could see Líf chopping something, her lips moving as she spoke either to herself or to the dog. Katrín wondered if this was why Líf had decided to get a pet: after Einar died, obviously Líf had no one to talk to at home, which must have been difficult for her. Katrín slipped her hand into Garðar's palm and entwined her slender fingers in his strong, stubby ones. Although they'd been together for over five years now, there were still moments when she found herself wondering how it had happened. During their time as schoolmates – through half of primary school and all of secondary school – he had never shown any interest in her, so she'd settled for admiring him from afar and letting herself dream. He'd been part of a clique to which she would never belong; the good-looking, clever kids on their way up had little in common with a young woman who was neither a beauty queen nor particularly brainy. That was the world of Garðar, Líf, Einar and others whom life had spoiled in every way imaginable. But despite the fact that she was very average-looking, constantly struggling to lose a few pounds, and always had her head buried in a book, Garðar had made a beeline for her at a club downtown two years after graduating and they'd never looked back. That same evening Líf and Einar had paired up, and it was precisely because of this parallel that Katrín always got goose bumps at the thought that Einar was now dead and Líf a widow. She had to remind herself regularly that she wasn't going to suffer the same fate just because her relationship with Garðar had started on the same day.

Garðar freed his hand from her grip and sat down on the porch. As he was taking off his shoes, which he declared were grafted onto his feet, Katrín went in to check on Líf. She found her still in the kitchen, where they were keeping their food even though there was no refrigerator or running water. There was a sink, which Garðar said he thought could be fed from the stream, but none of them had any idea how to hook it up. Líf had her back to Katrín as she cut bread on a warped chopping board they'd found in a drawer, the board rattling against the countertop with every stroke of the knife. Katrín stopped in the doorway and had to raise her voice to make herself heard. 'How was it?'

Now it was Líf's turn to be startled. She gave a little cry

and straightened up abruptly as the chopping board clattered on the counter. Then she turned around with the knife flat against her chest, where her hand had moved reflexively in fright. 'Jesus.'

Katrín regretted not being more careful in approaching her. All her irritation at Líf for having dragged her feet when it came to the renovation work drifted away. 'God, sorry. I thought you'd noticed me.'

Líf paused to catch her breath before speaking. 'It's not your fault.' She let the knife fall and exhaled. 'I've been sort of highly strung since Einar died. First I couldn't be alone, and now I can't be in others' company.' She smiled. 'It's kind of frustrating.'

'I can imagine.' Katrín had no idea how she should react. Líf was much more open than she was and had repeatedly tried to discuss Einar's death with her, but Katrín never knew how to respond for fear of coming across as too cold, overly solicitous, or somehow stupid. It was unbearable, in fact, and Líf couldn't have failed to notice how nimbly she generally managed to avoid discussing Einar's death. Garðar, on the other hand, was brilliant; it had surprised her to see how naturally he interacted with the tear-sodden Líf during the worst of the trauma. Maybe it was because of how close he and Einar had been, best friends since primary school, which meant Einar's death was a huge loss for him too. Katrín made a rapid decision not to act like a coward. They were going to live together for the next week and it would be impossible to skirt around the topic completely or leave it up to Garðar to do the sympathizing when Einar's death came up. 'It must have been terribly difficult for you. It must still be.'

'Yes, it is.' Líf turned back to the bread and began cutting again. 'Did you know that a woman in Hesteyri watched her husband and son drown out there in the fjord?'

'No.' Katrín knew nothing about the area and if all the local folklore was like this, she didn't really want to know any more. At least not while they were there.

'She remarried, and the new husband drowned as well.' Líf turned back to Katrín, holding the plate of sliced bread. 'It makes my sorrows pale in comparison.'

'But you don't feel any better just because other people have suffered worse.'

'No. It just helps to know that people have dealt with harder things and survived.' She laid the bread on the little kitchen table, then placed her hands on her hips and looked over the spread, apparently satisfied with the results. 'I don't understand what happened to the ham. I'm sure we bought several packets.' She looked at Katrín. 'It looks like a lovely meal, anyway. Don't you think?' She reached for a packet of sliced cheese and placed it next to the bread.

Katrín nodded, smiling. 'Delicious. I wonder if we should add a cafeteria to this guesthouse idea.'

Garðar hobbled in. 'My feet are killing me. These shoes are rubbish. No wonder they were on sale.'

'You've got to break in walking shoes before you go climbing mountains, you idiot.' Líf shook her head. 'Even I knew that.' She handed Putti a little slice of liver sausage, which he took in his mouth and carried to a corner before lying down and tucking into it.

'Now you tell me.' Gingerly, Garðar sat down on a worn chair and the women watched nervously to see whether the rickety thing would support him. They exchanged a smile when he didn't fall to the floor.

A tired-looking kettle belonging to the former owner stood on a plate on an old-fashioned wood stove. 'I wonder if it's possible to burn angelica in this contraption?' said Katrín, opening the hatch beneath the plate. She stared into the black emptiness, which smelled of ashes. 'I could really do with a coffee, but we probably shouldn't be using up our firewood for that.'

'I don't really know. Maybe if you squash it down.' Garðar stretched out his bare feet and wiggled his toes. 'Maybe it would burn up too fast to get the pot boiling. We can always try.' He spread butter on a slice of bread. 'But there's no way I'm getting back into those shoes to collect fuel. Not now.' He stared at a patch of floor at the back of the kitchen. 'What's that on the floor there?'

They looked at the spot that had attracted his attention and Líf shrugged. 'A stain, that's all. This is an old house, remember?' A large, irregular blemish coloured the wooden floor where it joined the wall.

'But the floor is new. The previous owner laid this parquet, since the old floor was probably in such bad shape it was unsalvageable. It's not completely finished, though.' Garðar frowned. 'Yet another thing we need to fix. Maybe we'll put a border over it.'

Katrín looked away from the stain, uninterested for the moment in further repairs. 'I'll go. I want coffee more than something to eat.' She pulled her long, thick jumper tighter around herself. 'There's angelica all over the place here, so it won't take me any time at all.' She grabbed the kettle to take with her. There was actually still water in the tub they'd filled the night before and carried together up to the house, but it was better to rinse out the kettle before they started using it.

Just in case, she asked Garðar to look inside it and check whether there was a dead mouse or something equally disgusting in there.

Katrín walked down the dark, narrow hallway to the back door. The sun was still hanging in the sky but it seemed to have grown colder outside, probably because the wind had picked up. She considered simply abandoning the expedition, but her longing for coffee won out.

It was even colder at the stream. Her fingers stung as she dipped the kettle repeatedly into the stream. She squatted with one foot on a stone in the middle of the stream and the other on the sodden bank. She could easily lose her balance and fall backwards into the water, and that thought alone was enough for her to pronounce the kettle clean enough. She filled it, at the same time admiring the beauty of the water flowing past her. It was impossible to imagine anything purer than its sparkling surface, as if the stream were made of liquid precious metal. She saw her reflection in the bubbling water and thanked God for its ripples; she wasn't particularly keen to admire the paint splotches on her face and in her hair. When the kettle was full, Katrín straightened up. As she concentrated on not spilling it, she thought she saw, reflected in the water, someone standing behind her.

'Líf? Garðar?' Katrín turned her head carefully so as not to lose her balance, but could see only the long slope that the stream bisected on its way out to sea. She shook her head; what nonsense. Of course Líf was still in the kitchen looking for the ham and Garðar was barefoot, lamenting his chafed heel. Besides, he wasn't stupid enough to try to scare her again. She looked back down into the stream and saw the same as before: her own distorted, crooked outline, but also the silhouette of someone right behind her. There was no way of discerning what was causing this illusion. She looked back behind her but there was nothing more to see than the first time. It must be the sun messing with her perception in some strange way that she was too tired to understand. Maybe it was something in the stream and not behind her; some pebbles on the bottom or vegetation moving around. She dragged herself away from the riddle; she would never get her coffee if she kept this up.

On returning to the house she put the kettle down gently on the crooked porch so as not to tip it over, then turned to the angelica in the tangle of faded vegetation around the house. As she uprooted the first dried-up plant she suddenly recalled a student who had said goodbye to her rather dolefully at the end of the last school day before the winter break. The boy was small for his age and had a difficult time in class. He was an extremely attractive child, with a bright complexion and wide eyes, and when he came into the classroom, dressed in his winter coat with a too-large rucksack on his narrow back, it was precisely his eyes that captured her attention. From them shone a sadness that seemed so profound it surely couldn't be connected to the uneventful school day. 'Don't go, Katrín.' She'd put her pen down on top of the clumsy alphabet in the workbook she was going over, and gave him a friendly smile. 'What do you mean? I'm not going home straight away. I still have a bit of work to do.' The boy stood there, his small hands clutching the shoulder straps of his rucksack. 'Don't go to the bad place. You won't come back.' Katrín had wondered whether he was ill and delirious, but his pale cheeks didn't suggest that he had a temperature. 'I'm not going to a bad place, not at all!

I don't like bad places, I only go to places where everything is nice.' The boy had stood there, rooted to the spot, half opening his mouth to reveal the two pearly-white, over-sized adult incisors in his upper jaw. Then he repeated, with the same sadness in his voice: 'Don't go to the house. You won't come back.' After this he had turned on his heel and left the room, before Katrín could think of anything clever to say. It was long after he'd closed the door behind him that she realized she hadn't once mentioned the trip she had planned to the class. Perhaps this brief but peculiar conversation had had more of an effect on her than she was willing to admit, and perhaps it was also the reason why she was having such a hard time adjusting to the place.

Katrín focused on the angelica. She wasn't going to let her imagination run wild. This was Garðar's dream, at least for the moment, and there was no need to upset either him or herself with any silliness. She tore out one dead plant after another, filling her arms in no time. It wouldn't amount to much if they packed it down, though, so she put the pile next to the kettle and began pulling out more. She moved further and further from the house, following what appeared to be a path leading through the brush. She'd gathered quite a bit more when something white caught her attention at the bottom of a deep hollow. The undergrowth in the hollow was even denser than everywhere else and to get a better look Katrín had to bend down and push the withered grasses and dead weeds aside. Suddenly she jerked back, dropping the angelica she'd already gathered. What the hell..? 'Garðar! Líf!' she called. 'Come here! You've got to see this!'

Chapter 4

'I need to discuss this later, Sara.' Freyr wanted more than anything to hang up, to pretend the connection was bad. He'd been paged to the duty station and the last thing he needed on a long workday was to have to talk to his ex. Least of all there, with people coming and going all around him. There was no denying that the topic would cause anyone within earshot to listen harder. For the moment no one was about but him, and he had every intention of ending the conversation before the next person walked in. 'You know how I feel about taking calls during working hours.' He could have added that he found her calls horrendous at any time of day, but she was fragile and he preferred not to say goodbye to her when she was in an agitated state.

Her rapid breathing came through the receiver. 'But you're not listening to me. If you listened I wouldn't need to keep saying it.' She sounded utterly, miserable and her voice was shriller than usual.

Freyr shut his eyes and pinched the bridge of his nose. He could feel the onset of the headache that had characterized their last year together, an oppressive throb at his temple that no painkiller seemed able to cure. 'I do hear everything you're saying, Sara. I just don't believe in these things, you know that. But thanks for telling me.' The latter statement was the opposite of how he actually felt. He would have preferred her to keep her dream about their son and his messages from beyond the grave entirely to herself.

'He feels bad where he is.' She was clearly about to start sobbing.

'Sara.' Freyr scrubbed at his eyes. 'You've got to stop this. There's nothing we can do and nothing we left undone back then. You've got to face reality. Benni's not coming back.' His own voice finally cracked a tiny bit as he let his hand drop and opened his eyes. This obsession of hers had reopened the poorly healed wound in his heart so often that it was nearly gangrenous. Had he not made the decision to leave her, he would most likely have ended up drinking himself to death or destroying himself by some other means. All he wanted was to be able to go through the grieving process on his own terms, without constant interference from the delirium that gripped Sara. Before moving out, he had never looked forward to going home and had eked out his work as much as he possibly could. He still did, in fact, which said a lot about his pathetic little apartment which he was barely familiar with even after living there for six months. 'You've got to accept it, for your sake and everyone else's. And now I've got to say goodbye.'

'He came to me in a dream. Benni feels bad where he is and he wants you to find him,' she repeated.

Freyr wanted to shout, but suppressed it. 'Thanks. Talk to you later.' He hung up, the same questions that kept him awake most nights running through his head. How could a six-year-old boy vanish without trace in broad daylight? Where was he? Why couldn't he be found? Freyr stood up and stared for a moment at the ugly, awkward handset as if it held the answer.

* * *

The old man's frail body jerked spasmodically. 'Would you like something for your cough?' Freyr put down the patient's chart.

'Would one more pill make any difference?' said the man in the white hospital gown, stretching his purple lips into a ghastly smile. As his gums had receded, his false teeth had long since become one size too large and they overwhelmed his face when they appeared like this in all their glory. 'All right, then.' He laid his trembling hand gently on his own chest as it moved up and down to the rhythm of his feeble breathing. 'I swallow everything I'm given, my good man. But I think I've almost had enough.'

'So you've said.' Freyr knew as well as the old man that his days were numbered. He was in his late nineties and suffering from bowel cancer. Freyr, however, was too tired to discuss life and death with him today. 'What a beautiful girl.' He lifted a framed photo of a girl with dark plaits from the bedside table. 'Is this your great-granddaughter, who was here earlier?' As soon as he'd said it he realized this couldn't be the case. The child in the photo was older than the little girl who had led her mother out of the room earlier that day.

The man gave a short, rattling laugh. 'Almost. You're quite perceptive. The photo was taken of my granddaughter, Svana, twenty years ago. And now she has a little girl herself. Both of them are wonderful, they often come in to see me.' The man's watery eyes squinted as he looked at Freyr's hands. 'You're not married?' Another coughing fit prevented him from continuing his interrogation.

'Divorced.' Freyr grabbed his stethoscope. 'I'd like to take a quick listen. That cough doesn't sound so great.'

'Does any cough sound great?' The old man didn't wait for a reply, but continued, 'That's a big mistake you're making, my good man, if you plan to spend your life alone instead of remarrying. A big mistake.'

Freyr nodded in agreement. 'Well, hopefully I'll put that right. I just need a woman. I'm not exactly beating them off with a stick.' He pulled the covers off the man's chest and unbuttoned his gown. 'It'll be a bit cold, but I expect you're used to that by now.'

'Svana, my granddaughter who was here earlier, she's single.' The man looked into Freyr's eyes. 'She's a good and beautiful girl. And so is her daughter.'

Freyr smiled at him. 'I don't doubt it. They're probably too good for me.' He looked at the big wall clock above the door. 'I'm always working.' He placed the stethoscope on the man's speckled chest. 'How old is the little girl?'

'Three. Speaks perfectly.' The old man stopped to cough, as Freyr instructed. 'Her preschool was closed this morning, so our little cherub had the day off and wanted to visit her grandfather. Someone vandalized the place last night. A damned shame.' The man stopped again and concentrated on breathing deeply, in and out, as Freyr asked. As soon as Freyr stuck the stethoscope back in his pocket he continued, 'Unfortunately, some things never change. There will always be scumbags who get a kick out of spoiling things for others. There's something particularly unpleasant about that kind of destruction. When I taught primary school here, the school was vandalized once. That was such a horrible day – I feel for the staff at the preschool if it was anything like that.'

'I was called out there this morning and I saw the state of

the place. I know what you mean.' Freyr buttoned up the man's gown and spread the blanket back over him. 'We just have to hope they find the perpetrator.'

'I don't hold out much hope of that. They never found the one who wrecked our primary school all those years ago; no one's ever cracked the case.' The old man shook his head sadly. 'Damn it, I can hardly remember anything nowadays, but I'll never forget it. Everything that could possibly be damaged had been. In those days things weren't so replaceable; you couldn't just stroll to the shops and upgrade things as soon as they showed any sign of wear, so the damage wasn't just emotional. The school and its staff bore the marks of the incident for several years afterwards.' The old man succumbed to another violent coughing fit, then continued in a slightly hoarser voice, 'They had to be sparing with the paint, so the graffiti showed through for a long time after. It wasn't until the entire school was repainted that the letters disappeared.'

Freyr was waiting patiently for the man to finish so he could move on to his next patient, but his story sounded uncomfortably familiar. He had tried to reach Dagný at lunch to ask whether there was any news, but without success. There was no way of knowing whether the investigation was making any progress or whether everyone was just as clueless as they had been that morning. Of course Dagný might have returned his call, but Freyr kept his mobile phone in his locker to avoid interruptions at work. Unfortunately Sara had figured this out and found a way to call the department directly. 'Did you say something was written on the walls?'

'Yes. It was completely incomprehensible. The vandal must

have thought his message was clear, but he can't have been in his right mind.'

'What had he written?'

'Just a few words, but the same ones repeated throughout the building.' The old man cleared his throat but didn't cough, much to Freyr's relief. '*Ugly* was written on the wall of my classroom. Whatever that was supposed to mean.'

'Ugly?' Freyr exclaimed. The old man focused his watery blue eyes on Freyr. 'Yes. I chose to interpret it as the man referring to himself and what he'd done. That helped me, having to look at it for all those years, even if you could only see a faint shadow of the word through the paint.' The man pulled the cover all the way up to his chin. 'I had a harder time coming to terms with what was written in the assembly hall.'

'And what was that?' Freyr was determined to end the conversation so that he could finish his shift, go home, take an ibuprofen for his headache and lie down. Still, he couldn't resist asking; the events of the morning had had a deeper effect than he'd realized or was willing to admit to himself.

'*Dirty*.' The old man's voice sounded stronger than before, as if the low baritone of his former years had returned. The old man seemed to notice this himself, and he struggled to sit up in bed. 'In the assembly hall, of all places. No child should have to sit and look at that.'

'Did you say "dirty"?' Freyr thought he must have misheard the man. 'Are you sure you're not confusing this with what your granddaughter told you this morning about the preschool?'

The old man gave Freyr a displeased, even indignant look. 'Of course not. I was going to tell you that I remember this as if it happened yesterday, not this morning. Scribbled on the wall was this one word. Dirty.'

Dagný's expression when he told her was not unlike the old man's, except that her displeasure seemed grafted onto her face. 'What are you saying? That there's a vandal who breaks into schools at sixty-year intervals?' She shook her head slowly. 'I don't buy it. If that were the case, whoever was in the school last night would have to be at least seventy years old. That doesn't fit. The old man must have heard about the "dirty" graffiti during the girl's visit this morning.'

'That's not what he believed.' Freyr tried to hide his irritation. As soon as he'd told Dagný the story, he'd realized how ridiculous it sounded. Still, he'd insisted, even though logic was on her side. It felt odd to be the one insisting on a story that was difficult to justify. That was usually Sara's role.

'No, but isn't he in his nineties?' Dagný allowed herself a rare smile. 'I'd say he's just a bit confused.'

Freyr let his eyes wander over the packed bookshelves in the office. 'Would you be willing to check whether there are records of the old case? It would remove any doubt about whether the man is confused or not. He seemed absolutely convinced that he was remembering things correctly.'

'Do you have any idea how much work we have to do here? It isn't just the healthcare system that's suffered cutbacks. We have far too few employees and for the moment the break-in at the preschool isn't a priority.' Dagný lifted the stack of papers on the desk and let it thud back into place. 'We're investigating more cases than just this one. There isn't much more we can do in this situation than speak to the people who seem the likeliest candidates, and if we're lucky, someone will confess or we'll nail him by his fingerprints. If that fails, we'll have to hope that whoever did it will be arrested for something else entirely, and that his fingerprints will give him away. Either that or we might find he's already on record. In any case, it'll take quite some time to find out.' She shrugged sadly. 'There was such a mess of fingerprints in the preschool.'

Freyr was sweating in his thick coat, but didn't want to ask her to open a window for fear that the wind would blow the pile of papers onto the floor. 'How much time are you talking about?'

'One or two weeks. We'll see how it goes.' There was a note of surrender in her voice. 'If the government had insured its property, this would be a matter for the insurance company and it would take over the investigation. But since that isn't the case, it looks as though we'll soon have to conclude our own investigation, unless new evidence turns up or we hear any rumours about the vandalism. As you can imagine, no one goes through old files in search of . . .' She stopped for a moment, trying to work out what she wanted to say. 'Well, I don't really know what.'

Freyr said nothing. He personally had no idea how sixty-year-old police reports could help them now. As he sat there on his hard, uncomfortable chair, he realized that Dagný was right; the crime wasn't so serious that it necessitated a complex police investigation. The graffiti would doubtless be painted over, the damage repaired, and the case would be history. He decided to stop worrying about it; he wouldn't take it too well if Dagný started lecturing him about medicine. He'd let her know what he heard – there was nothing else he could do. 'Did something bad come up this morning? You left in such a rush.'

Dagný frowned automatically and stroked her chin, as she did when she was pondering something or facing a difficult decision. 'Oh, I might as well tell you. You'll hear about it at work tomorrow morning anyway. I actually thought you knew already.'

'What? I haven't heard anything.' Freyr had purposely buried himself in his work in order to shut out the lingering feelings his conversation with Sara had provoked, which meant he had completely missed the day's gossip. The hospital might have been abuzz from one end to the other with stories without him being aware of it.

'Someone committed suicide in Súðavík last night. The body was found in the church this morning when the priest arrived. We had to get there quickly.'

'Was it a kid?' Freyr hoped not, especially because young people's suicides occasionally came in waves. In the eyes of some teenagers, there was something heroic about surrendering your life in the battle of adolescence. It only took one of them to sow the first seed of tragedy before others began to follow.

'No, it was an older woman.' Dagný took the topmost paper from the pile on the desk and read from it. 'She was sixty-nine years old.' She looked at Freyr. 'Maybe she had trouble accepting the fact that she was a pensioner. Some people live for work. Or else she'd become seriously ill and didn't want to deal with it.'

Freyr nodded thoughtfully; ridiculously, it hadn't immediately occurred to him that it might be a woman. Although only a quarter of suicides in Iceland were committed by women, there was nothing odd about such a thing occurring in the Westfjords, any more than anywhere else. There were between seventy and eighty suicides a year throughout the country, most of them in Reykjavík and its suburbs, but perhaps statistically it was the turn of women in the west. 'Suicides more commonly involve older people, but although I obviously haven't looked into this case, I'd say it was unlikely that the end of her career had anything to do with it. In general, it's men who have difficulty accepting that. The woman's relatives might know the reason behind it.' Freyr slipped off his jacket. 'Mind you, I would be interested to know why she picked a church. Generally, people choose to do it at home, or out in the wild when they want to protect their families from the additional shock of finding them dead. That location is fairly unusual.'

'Maybe she was a devout Christian and wanted to be nearer to God when she died. Although she wasn't a religious fanatic or anything like that; we learned that much from her husband. Of course, he could have been lying to us; if he were a fanatic himself, he might have a different definition of the term.'

'So she was married?'

Dagný nodded. 'Yes. With three children and five grandchildren. Of course some of them have moved south, but they're all alive. She wasn't recently bereaved and grieving.'

'But couldn't the husband suggest any likely explanation? Did it take him completely by surprise?'

'Apparently so. He was very shocked and seemed not to have had the slightest suspicion that something like this might happen. If he knew about any underlying depression or other illness, he didn't share it with us. He did mention that she'd been a bit stressed and unsociable recently, but not enough to make a big deal about it. It was just a phase some people go through, which eventually passes – that's what he seemed to think, anyway.' Dagný looked Freyr in the eye. 'But not this time.'

'How did she die?' Freyr didn't know whether Dagný would tell him, though it didn't actually matter since an autopsy would be performed on the corpse tomorrow.

'She hanged herself.' Dagný studied Freyr's reaction. 'And it can't have been easy. The roof is quite high in that church.'

'Right.' Freyr knew that dying this way was ugly, recalling that those who chose this method to end their lives more often than not ended up with deep scratch-marks on their necks. They realized too late that while life might be no picnic, it was much kinder than death. 'Did she leave a letter or a note?' he asked, although he already knew only a quarter of those who chose to go down this road left behind goodbyes, since it wasn't easy to explain such a decision – and probably sometimes there was nothing to say.

'I'm not at liberty to discuss that.' Dagný looked away.

'I understand. I'll stop asking questions. I just wanted to let you know what the old man told me; I thought it might matter.' He began to put his jacket back on.

Dagný leaned back in her grand office chair, which looked far more comfortable than the rickety thing that Freyr was sitting on. 'You didn't mention if anything else was written on the walls of the old man's primary school. Was there anything besides the word "dirty"?'

'Yes. There was more. I don't know precisely how many words there were, but the old man did specifically mention one that was written on the wall of his classroom: "ugly". There might have been other words scribbled on the walls elsewhere in the school. I can ask him for more details if you want.'

Dagný's computer signalled that she'd received an e-mail, but she seemed not to notice. Her cheeks appeared redder than before, but when she spoke again after an awkward silence it was as if nothing had occurred. Maybe the room was just getting warmer. 'Yes, yes. Go ahead and do that. It can't hurt to hear what he has to say.'

After Freyr had shut the door behind him, Dagný reached for a plastic file holder that had been lying next to the computer, upside down. She lifted the plastic and stared at the paper inside. Delicate feminine handwriting filled every inch of the page, scarcely leaving room for even one more letter. Dagný stared at the text as she picked up the phone, but glanced away from it briefly to select a number. 'Veigar. Where are the old police reports stored?'

Chapter 5

The faded white wooden crosses lay side by side on the little kitchen table, their melancholy appearance contrasting with the spotted, tablecloth that was trying its best to make things look more cheerful. 'They have nothing to do with the house,' said Garðar, who hadn't seemed too annoyed about having to put his shoes on again when he'd heard Katrín shouting from outside, but was now clearly tired of this topic. He would have chucked the crosses onto the pile of timber outside long ago if Katrín hadn't objected. 'You can see for yourself that the crosses have broken or been broken off graves somewhere and then brought here. If the graves had been where you found the crosses, the stumps would have been sticking out of the grass.'

'Why would anyone remove crosses from graves and throw them out here?' Katrín couldn't take her eyes off the weathered wood and peeling white paint.

'I agree.' Líf was standing in the corner, as far from the table as possible. Her arms were crossed on her chest and her face was full of displeasure at Katrín's discovery. At her feet lay Putti, sound asleep after his meal of liverwurst and assorted other delicacies. Now and again he twitched, as if involved in some great adventure in dreamland. 'Who would do such a thing?'

'Shouldn't we be asking why a child and a woman, maybe

its mother, would have been buried here behind the house? I find that much more difficult to comprehend than the fact that the crosses were thrown out there. And they would have been in a much worse state if they'd been left there untouched for more than half a century. Someone must have maintained them over the years, yet this house has been more or less empty.' Garðar read the faint inscription on the bronze plates attached to the crosses: '"Hugi b. 1946 – d. 1951" and "Bergdís b. 1919 – d. 1951".' He rubbed his eyes. 'Forget this. Let's put the crosses back where we found them and ask someone who might know something about it when we're back in Ísafjörður. It's my guess that headstones replaced the crosses and whoever was responsible was uncomfortable about getting rid of them. Whether that person or those persons had ties to this house, I have no idea, but there's no reason to make a big deal out of it.'

Katrín gnawed her upper lip thoughtfully. 'Yeah, maybe.' She stared out through the dirty kitchen window. 'I can't do anything about it, but it still makes me feel uncomfortable. Even though you might think it's silly, there's something unnatural about this. I had a very strong feeling that something bad was going on here when I saw the crosses poking up out of the weeds. That's how they were, not just thrown haphazardly into the hollow.'

'But why?' Líf pressed herself back even further into the corner. 'I'm absolutely certain those people are buried there.'

'I have no idea how they got there, but if I were going to bury just one person, let alone two, on this site, I'd choose flat ground over that hollow. Maybe whoever it was wanted to hide the graves.' Katrín was unhappy with how whiny she sounded.

'And then put crosses on them?' Garðar gave her a tired

smile. 'Believe me, these crosses come from somewhere else. There are no graves in that depression.'

'Should we try digging a bit?' Katrín looked at Garðar, hoping he would say no. She didn't want to find coffins or skeletons a mere hundred metres from the house. 'Maybe the graves are somewhere else around here.'

'We should check it out. If there are graves here, I'm off.' Líf's voice grew more agitated with each word. Her reaction had surprised Katrín, because even though Líf was generally highly strung, she was never this much of a nervous wreck. Maybe it was too soon after Einar's death for her to tolerate hearing about people dying in strange circumstances. 'I'll swim if I have to.'

'That's enough nonsense.' Garðar bristled. 'No one's going anywhere and we're not searching for graves around the house. Do you really want me to start digging the place up?' He didn't wait for a reply, but added: 'No way. Firstly, we won't find anything, and secondly, we'd end up wasting all our time on it.' He stood up, grimacing slightly. 'Things are going to go slowly enough after that bloody hike – my legs are killing me.' He moved over to the wall by the door and stretched one calf muscle. 'We've got to work hard if we want to get things finished on time. And that's hardly going to happen if I'm limping around out there with stiff muscles and blisters, searching for old graves with you screaming over my shoulder every time my shovel hits a rock.'

Katrín knew he was right, though he could have worded it more tactfully. But she refrained from pointing out his lack of tact; the last thing they needed in this lonely place was to end up pissed off with each other. 'Okay. But it's pretty strange, you must admit.'

'Strange? It's not just strange,' cried Líf. 'It's *weird.*' She seemed to regret her choice of words and hurriedly added: 'Was the guy who owned the house not quite right in the head? Can we expect more of this kind of thing?'

Garðar had never properly told Katrín the story of the house – he must have received some information when he purchased it – but she knew this was partly down to her. She had shown limited interest in the project and allowed him to prattle on about renovations, timber, countersinks, et cetera, without joining in. She turned to Garðar. 'Could he have had something to do with these crosses? What sort of man was the previous owner, anyway?'

Garðar relaxed his right calf and started stretching his left. This seemed more effective, since it made him scowl even harder. 'There's only what I've already told you. He was just some guy, and no, I don't think these crosses can be connected to him in any way. He acquired the place long after the crosses were put on the graves, judging by the dates on them.' He relaxed his calf and moved away from the wall. 'He was also a bit of a loner, unmarried and childless, so I don't think he'd have brought the crosses with him from Reykjavík. He never lived here or in Ísafjörður.'

'Could he have had a wife that he never told anyone about?' Líf's voice trembled slightly. 'Have had a child with her and then killed them?'

Garðar looked at the ceiling in exasperation. 'Somehow I doubt it. He would have had to have been an extremely early starter; the guy would hardly have been more than ten years old when this Hugi was born.' He sighed. 'The crosses have nothing to do with the house, and they were probably put there by some tourist or God knows who.'

'I woke up to the sound of someone talking last night.' Líf pursed her lips until they went white. 'I don't know why I didn't tell you about it this morning, but it seemed to be coming from the ground floor. There's something wrong with this house.'

'That's enough.' Garðar seemed unhappy about the way the conversation was developing. No doubt he missed having Einar there, or simply any other man who he could roll his eyes at. 'You dreamt it. It's true that there's plenty wrong with this house, but it all has to do with maintenance, which is why we're here.' He shook his head and muttered: 'Voices. Jesus.'

'I know what I heard. And it was just one voice. A child's voice.' The house's woodwork cracked loudly just as Líf said this, and she jumped.

'See.' Garðar sounded triumphant. 'That's what you heard. Houses make all sorts of noises, especially old wooden shacks like this. You're just more aware of it at night when everything's quiet.'

'It wasn't a creak like that. It was a voice.'

Katrín didn't want to hear any more about Líf's dreams. She didn't want to fuel her own imagination with the idea that every crack or creak of the house was a voice speaking or whispering. 'I agree with Garðar, Líf; you dreamt it. You know how it is when you're drowsy, you start imagining all sorts of nonsense.' Before Líf could reply, she turned to Garðar. 'But even if the guy didn't have any children, he must have had heirs. Why didn't they want to keep the house?' In a way this was an odd question; the house was dilapidated, yet according to the skipper who had sailed them to the area, property here was sought after.

'How would I know? Maybe they're all old and have no

interest in making the trip out here. There's no electricity and the house is in need of repairs, which is something not everyone is willing to deal with. Maybe the people needed their money more than some shack in the middle of nowhere. There are probably a million reasons. I didn't want to start asking the estate agent about some dead guy, even if you wouldn't have hesitated.'

'Well, I wouldn't.' Though Líf said this, Katrín knew better. Líf wasn't much given to verbosity; things were either wonderful or rubbish, and decisions were made without much reflection. Her and Einar's strong financial situation had perhaps inspired her response; the consequences of blundering into some sort of badly thought out plan were never so awful that it made much difference one way or another. Katrín found the discussion of the house's previous owner a welcome distraction and she regretted having made a big deal about the crosses; she particularly regretted having made Garðar hobble out on his sore feet, and having startled Líf. She was embarrassed that she hadn't simply grabbed the crosses and brought them in, but it was too late now. She would have to fix this by shaking off the unpleasant feeling their isolation seemed to inspire in her and make sure that Líf didn't sense it – she seemed to be in such a state that the slightest sign of anxiety on Katrín's part would fuel her fear. Katrín stood up and went over to Garðar. 'Aren't you glad we weren't with you? The estate agent would probably have cancelled the sale.' She put her arms around him. Through his thick clothes she could feel warmth emanating from him and hoped that it was mutual, though he seemed distant and didn't return the embrace. He was probably uncomfortable in front of Líf, since he was never one for public displays of affection. Yet

Katrín had the sneaking suspicion that there was more to it, and that Garðar knew more about the house's owner than he was willing to admit.

'I am, very glad.' Garðar pushed a curl that had detached itself from the rest of Katrín's tangled mess of hair out of her eyes. He looked past her and winked and smiled at Líf. Katrín couldn't see Líf's reaction, but she hoped that this friendly display would calm her down. Garðar turned back to his wife and put his arms around her. 'Shall we stop chattering and get back to work?'

Katrín sighed. 'I've hardly got the energy to paint any more today; isn't there something that we can do with our eyes shut?' She felt too content in Garðar's arms to tear herself away from him and resume working. The sun had sunk even lower in the sky since the food had been put on the table and all at once it was as if darkness was descending. Suddenly the kitchen didn't seem as ugly; the yellowed paint on the walls looked less patchy and the stains of years gone by faded into the background.

Garðar squeezed Katrín slightly awkwardly before loosening his grip. 'We can take better advantage of the rest of the light if we do something outside. We could start ripping out the rotten planks from the porch. It'll warm us up as well. Come on, Líf, some fresh air will perk you up.'

'Well I'm not going to stay in here by myself.' Líf's voice seemed to have regained its former assurance and she sounded normal again. She smiled at them and emerged from the corner. 'It's probably warmer outside than in. I'm freezing to death.' She nudged Putti with her toe and he woke with a start, looking embarrassed at not having remained on the alert. He stood up and stretched with a yawn.

As soon as Líf said this, Katrín felt the cold that had crept over them like the dusk. She automatically zipped her fleece all the way up her neck and pulled its sleeves over her fingers. They would certainly warm up working outside. 'Me neither. We're definitely lighting the stove as soon as we come back in. Screw sparing the firewood.' Still, the longer they waited to light the fire, the better. The amount of firewood had seemed endless as they carried it from the pier, but last night when they'd fetched some logs to fire up the stove before they went to bed for the night, the stack had looked worryingly low. None of them wanted to spend their final evenings shivering, so they had agreed to light the stove as little as possible.

'I'll work like the devil himself is driving me if you put those crosses back where you found them. I can't imagine having them in the house tonight,' said Líf. It was a reasonable enough proposition, but no matter how much Katrín tried to pluck up her courage to go and return the crosses, she couldn't shrug off the profound unease that prevented her from actually doing so.

'Agreed,' she said at last.

Líf seemed to cheer up again at Katrín's assent. 'Good. I wouldn't sleep a wink with these things in the house.'

Garðar opened his mouth as if he were planning to say something; maybe to ask when they'd become so neurotic, but he stopped and merely nodded. He grabbed the crosses and took them to a little space between the kitchen and the back door, where someone had put up some makeshift shelves for provisions. The shelves were mostly empty; they'd arranged their tools on the bottom one, but otherwise the only things on them were some dusty, empty wooden crates, as well as the cardboard boxes containing the things whose ownership they'd been puzzling over. They managed to put on their outerwear in the narrow space without bumping into each other too much. Garðar took the crosses with him, Katrín a crowbar and hammer, while Líf settled for a can of fizzy drink that she'd grabbed from the kitchen. The air outside was pleasantly clean and fresh and Katrín couldn't help but stand there and enjoy the feeling of filling her lungs again, allowing her sore muscles to rest for the final push in the day's repairs. In the meantime, Garðar set off for the hollow to return the crosses, with Putti at his heels, while Líf sat on the porch sipping her drink. They watched Garðar in silence as he inched his way through the angelica that swallowed Putti as soon as they stepped into it, then vanished when he bent down to replace the crosses in the clump of weeds. Katrín's heart beat faster when he didn't reappear immediately. What would she do if he vanished entirely? Líf would certainly lose her mind and she wasn't sure that she herself wouldn't do the same.

But Katrín didn't need to wonder about this for long, because suddenly from the brush emerged the dark blue jacket for which she'd paid a large sum as his Christmas present two years earlier. Then Garðar swept his hat off his head, smiled at them and held up his other hand, thumb raised. Katrín was relieved but still felt uneasy inside. Her discomfort at being alone in this place refused to slacken its grip, just as the last withered leaves on the branches beside the house stubbornly refused to fall. She smiled back and waved, determined to go with him next time he and Líf climbed the hill in search of a mobile phone signal; the hike could hardly be any more unbearable than how she would feel if something happened to them or they got lost up there.

'Well, then. That's that out of the way.' Garðar's breath was visible, as was Putti's, though less so. 'Shall we work on the porch while there's still enough light to see?' He kicked at the corner of the porch, jolting Líf, who was sitting on the edge of it just next to him. 'This is probably all completely rotten.'

'Then should we tear it up, if it is?' Katrín stepped from the porch onto the grass. Líf was jolted again, and this time a little bit of her drink splashed from the can. 'We don't have the wood to replace it.'

'If we'd brought along everything we needed, we'd still be carting stuff up from the pier now. I guess we'll have to come back later, maybe even bring a carpenter with us.' He put his hand out for the crowbar Katrín was holding.

'A carpenter?' Katrín stopped kicking at the porch. 'We can't afford a carpenter. I thought the material and the things we've already bought would be enough.' She felt a sudden flush of panic. They were a whisker away from going bankrupt; all the money Garðar had scraped together from securities trading had vanished in the form of worthless stocks, leaving behind nothing but debts. In fact, they *were* technically bankrupt, but the banking system kept them afloat thanks to some tricks that Katrín didn't completely understand and left Garðar to deal with. But these solutions were only superficial; the clock was clearly ticking, and soon the life raft would be set adrift. Her income and Garðar's unemployment benefit might have sufficed if they'd been debt-free and got around by bicycle. But they'd spent the money that was supposed to ease their payments over the next few months on renovations to this house, and there wasn't a króna remaining. The notion that they could afford to hire a carpenter to work so far from civilisation, on a full-time wage plus special location allowance, was about as realistic as them tearing down the house and building a new one. 'We can't afford it. You know that.'

As so often during their conversations on this topic, Garðar ignored her protests, since there was more to it than simply not being able to hire a skilled worker. No less than their entire future was at risk; their hopes and dreams would come to nothing, even though their plans hadn't been particularly ambitious: a house, two cars and, later, children – no more than the usual. Though it might prove painful, Katrín could just as well live without these things, but Garðar seemed incapable of dealing with the reality. She was starting to think that he felt everything would be doomed if he said a single word about their situation now.

'Let's just try tearing up one damaged corner and we'll see,' he suggested. He stuck the crowbar beneath a worn-out plank and stepped on the shaft. Creaking and cracking sounds hindered further conversation as he struggled with the wood.

Katrín stood at a distance and watched, too angry to participate in this demolition project. She was cold again.

'Don't worry about the money,' Líf, who had stood up, whispered in her ear. 'If we need to hire a carpenter, I can see to that. We're all in this together and I have plenty of money.' She placed her hand on Katrín's shoulder, but then let it fall again awkwardly. 'Einar converted most of our assets into euros just before the crash and he had life insurance, too, so I'm doing okay. And I don't fritter it away, do I?' Katrín looked at her and smiled. She could think of few women who spent as much as Líf did on clothes, haircuts, bags, shoes and other necessities. And although Líf might be well off at the moment, Katrín doubted that her resources would be enough to maintain the lifestyle to which Líf had accustomed herself while Einar was alive. At least not for long. As the CEO of one of the biggest companies in Iceland, Einar had had a very good income before the crash, and when the company had changed hands he was given a handsome severance payment, no doubt leaving him potentially worry-free for the rest of his life as far as money was concerned. But brokerage accounts were one thing; a steady income quite another. The former could take some serious hits if investments weren't managed properly, and she couldn't envision Líf paying attention to such things – any more than she could envision her getting a job. 'Thanks for the kind offer. But it's better if we try to manage these repairs ourselves. It's good for us. For you, too.' She smiled warmly at Líf, since her offer had been gracious. But Katrín had no interest in taking money from her, even if the gesture was well intended, unless they were able to match Líf's contribution. She had even less faith in the idea that Garðar could live with accepting charity from Einar's widow.

'Well, let's see. If it all goes pear-shaped, you know the offer still stands.' Líf took a sip of her drink, looking fairly relaxed. She watched as Garðar worked relentlessly away at his demolition project. 'I'm so happy that I get to be here with you. I hate always being alone.'

'Well of course.' An icy wind blew around the house and Katrín felt the cold air slip in beneath her jacket. The chill it gave her, however, was quickly forgotten when a long plank that Garðar was working on came free, providing a glimpse of the earth that had lain untouched beneath the porch for decades, maybe even an entire century. At first glance it was unremarkable, merely dark and indistinguishable, but after a moment she noticed yellowish stripes in the black soil. 'What's that?'

Garðar put down the broken plank and looked into the gap. 'I don't know.' He bent down and poked at the soil. 'These are bones. Bird bones, it looks like.' He brushed away the dry soil and pulled out two little bones, the size of fingers.

'No, that doesn't make sense.' Katrín bent down to Garðar. The bones looked old and dirty. 'They're far too chunky. They must be from a sheep. But what are bones doing here?' The same anxiety the crosses had awakened in her appeared again. She knew little or nothing about bones, but she knew enough to realize that these were too thick to belong to a bird. It suddenly crossed her mind that they were human. It would certainly put an interesting spin on things if the graves she feared were near the house were literally underneath it.

'Ugh, that's disgusting. Are you joking?' Líf put down her drink can and peered over Katrín's shoulder into the darkness.

'It must be the remains of some food that fell under the porch, or else a fox dragged the bones here. Maybe there was a den here once. The house is old and the bones don't look recent.' Garðar continued to brush the soil away carefully and found more bones, now the entire skeleton of an animal which did in fact appear to be a fox. 'See. Look. What did I tell you?'

'Why is there a dead fox under the porch?' Katrín looked as far beneath the porch as she could, but saw nothing except darkness. 'Don't they usually die in their dens?'

'Probably they're just as likely to die anywhere. Maybe the poor thing starved here during a spell of bad weather.' He shrugged. 'And I'd guess these two bones we found first are from the fox as well.' Garðar held up the bones in question, which didn't actually appear to fit anywhere in the seemingly intact skeleton lying in the soil beneath them. But none of them said anything. The only sound that emerged from the group into the twilight was Putti's whine as he sniffed hopefully at the bones in Garðar's hand then backed away, thwarted.

It wasn't until they were snuggled up close to each other in their zipped-together sleeping bags that Katrín realized Garðar's explanation didn't really fit. In rural areas, foxes keep themselves far from human habitations and would never make a den under a house like this. But Garðar was asleep and Katrín refrained from nudging him awake to share her revelation with him. She was even less keen on disturbing Líf, who also lay fast asleep beside them, the dog curled up but alert on top of her sleeping bag. Instead she pondered how the bones had ended up beneath this rickety porch, falling asleep before she reached any conclusion.

Katrín's breathing had long since become regular when a vague human voice drifted up from downstairs; a soft child's voice, which seemed to repeat the same indistinguishable words over and over. They were too exhausted to be woken up by it, or to let Putti's low growl disrupt their sleep.

Chapter 6

The woman was doing a little better, and seemed less agitated than during Freyr's last visit. Otherwise everything was precisely the same as it had been the day before, so that the two visits seemed to merge into one. The woman sat in the same chair, staring out of the same window; in the air hung the same cinnamon smell, as if the same rice pudding were always being served. The worn, crocheted shawl was draped slightly further to the left over her shoulder and she'd forgotten to do up the top button on her blouse, revealing her bra's beige shoulder strap. Otherwise, all identical: even the ladder in her thick nylon stockings showing beneath the hem of her skirt was in place. 'I understand you didn't want to go out yesterday. Do you remember that you didn't think it was such a bad suggestion when I mentioned it to you? It's good to take advantage of the nice weather while it lasts.' Freyr spoke louder than usual. The woman wore a hearing aid and had a tendency to lose the thread. 'And you remember what I told you about the importance of going out for regular walks? They don't need to be long ones if you're tired or a bit under the weather, but you'll feel better if you get some fresh air, even if it's only for a short time, Úrsúla.'

'I don't want to go out.' The woman's voice was lifeless and piteous, as if each breath could be her last. 'Not now. I don't want to be here.'

Freyr didn't quite know how to reply. Úrsúla had had nearly a year to become accustomed to her new surroundings, but she appeared to be adjusting very slowly. They didn't actually expect her to adapt fully to her new circumstances – the move to this nursing home had occurred rather quickly; when no other solutions were available, the decision had been made to bring her here – but Freyr had originally hoped for significant progress.

She was something of a loner; born in 1940, she had no close relatives besides a decrepit older brother who was living in Ísafjörður, which had most likely influenced the decision to move her here, along with the fact that the woman's last legal residence had been in Ísafjörður before she fell ill at an early age and was sent to a hospital in Reykjavík. She hadn't set eyes on the town for more than half a century; when she went to Reykjavík she was a teenager with a serious mental disorder, experiencing hallucinations and constantly plagued by fear and anxiety, and when she returned home her life was more or less over; she had grown old and there was little ahead.

In light of the woman's condition it was unclear whether she would ever feel comfortable in her new home. She'd been an outsider as a child and had a difficult upbringing; her illness had probably started to manifest itself without anyone really noticing, and she was written off as an antisocial and rather boring kid, which meant she didn't even have any happy childhood memories to comfort herself with. Yet she had still been sent here. This kind of decision was one of the reasons why Freyr didn't want to have to concentrate only on his specialism, psychiatry; conventional general medicine was freer from the red tape and endless compromises of the psychiatric set-up. Úrsúla was a clear example of the system's ruthlessness and lack of compassion, which grated against Freyr's professional ambition. She was among the twelve residents who were forced to find refuge elsewhere when Department 7 of Kleppur Mental Hospital was closed. For decades the department had been run as a specialized treatment facility for people with chronic mental illness and severe behavioural disturbances; some of the patients, including Úrsúla, had been housed there for years, even decades. Freyr struggled to accept the argument that permanent residence in hospitals didn't accord with modern healthcare practices or humanitarian considerations. No doubt that was true for some, but not for those who were in their advanced years and viewed the department as their home. He suspected that the nearly thirty full-time salaries saved by the closure of the department had weighed heavier than humanitarian considerations. 'There's nothing unusual about you taking a bit of time to get used to a new place. But hopefully it won't take long for you to come to terms with being in Ísafjörður.'

'No.'

The woman's reply was so categorical that Freyr chose not to argue. 'Of course you know I'm never far away and you can send for me if you feel you need to. The nurses are always here as well, so you just let us know if you're feeling bad.' He turned to the nurse. 'But I think that's enough for today.' He placed his hand on the woman's and felt how she stiffened at his touch. Her dry skin was ice-cold. It was quite depressing to think how low a percentage of those who suffered from serious mental illnesses had any hope of a reasonable recovery. For example, Úrsúla had had to live her life with the unshakable belief that she was in danger; that someone was after her and wanted to harm her. No common sense or explanation could remedy this delusion, and without medication she constantly feared that some mysterious entity was on the verge of sinking its claws into her. Her medical records ran to hundreds of pages and they made for sad reading; a more oppressive life was hard to imagine. She had a major birthday this year: she was turning seventy, but that milestone would doubtless pass as quietly as everything else in her life: a slice of cake from the staff, who might also sing her 'Happy Birthday'. Freyr resolved to remember to bring her a beautiful gift when the day arrived; he was sure it would please her. Several times he had heard her lament that she hadn't been confirmed – four months before her confirmation was due to take place, she'd been admitted for the first time, and despite being ill and not entirely herself, she had clearly hoped to go through with the ceremony, having no doubt been looking forward to it for some time, like most adolescents. It had always struck Freyr as sad that no one had arranged for her wish to be fulfilled, but perhaps it would make amends to do something for the woman now, when another festive occasion was imminent.

'She doesn't refuse her medication.' The nurse had followed Freyr out. 'I think it'll all work out. As long as she doesn't have a serious attack. Of course, we can't monitor her twenty-four hours a day, but we do look in on her and sit with her as much as we can. We'd feel better if there were a night shift here, but as long as she takes her sleeping pills before bed we can manage without it.'

Freyr nodded. In Ísafjörður there was no communal residence where the woman could live and the nursing home was the only appropriate place for her. Its staff also looked after home care in Ísafjörður and its neighbouring towns, so they had enough on their plates even before taking on a woman who had spent so many years in a psychiatric ward. He knew these regional transfers were a significant factor in his being hired by the Regional Hospital; there was no psychiatrist in Ísafjörður or in this region of the country and it was difficult for general practitioners to provide the woman and others like her with the proper care. Upon coming to Ísafjörður, Freyr had been assigned the task of holding a course for the few staff members of the nursing home on the care of the mentally ill, and although it wasn't as good as a specialized training course of several years' duration, it had proved useful. This wasn't necessarily all down to him, either – the staff had worked hard and shown a great deal of interest in what he'd had to say.

After specifying what time he would come the next day and saying goodbye, Freyr went out to his car. Before getting in, he looked up at the building and saw Úrsúla's face in the window where she always sat. It was devoid of any emotion. She stared at him, following his every move. Freyr halted, surprised, and they caught each other's eye. He raised his eyebrows when she opened her mouth and started speaking to him through the double glazing. The fact that he couldn't hear her didn't appear to stop the woman; she was still absorbed in her monologue when he looked away and got into his car. Until now Úrsúla had always been almost silent in his presence, communicating only in very short sentences, and certainly never making speeches such as the one he'd just witnessed. He couldn't work out what had prompted it, but knew from previous experience that a variation in behaviour wasn't a good sign. It could indicate that she was starting to go downhill. As he left the car park he called the nurse to express his concern to her and ask that they keep an eye on her. He didn't want these conscientious staff to end up in a situation like the one when Úrsúla had lost the hearing in one ear after sticking a knitting needle into it. This had occurred several years ago and Freyr had only read about it in reports, but that was enough. She had wanted to silence a voice in her ear which was threatening her, a voice that was entirely imaginary and could therefore just as easily have started plaguing her from her belly or her toes. An attempt to silence it in one of those parts of her anatomy would have been even bloodier. In any case, they had every reason to remain alert.

Freyr's next visit was also for monitoring purposes. He'd been asked to look in on the husband of the woman who had killed herself in Súðavík. The man's local GP had contacted Freyr the previous evening and expressed concerns about his condition, saying that he was grateful to be able to turn to a specialist who had more experience with psychological problems than he himself did. Freyr had made several of these house calls in the south, treating people who were having difficulty coping with bereavement, although he'd encountered no suicides since moving west. So he knew what to expect, as well as the most appropriate ways to assist the grieving and bewildered spouse. According to information from the hospital, the woman had never been diagnosed with depression or any other serious disease, nor shown any signs of mental disturbance. In other words, there was nothing obvious to explain her last, desperate act. In cases like these, family members would usually start by saying that they had noticed no changes in the deceased's behaviour, and that the suicide had hit them like lightning out of a clear blue sky.

But more often than not the truth would turn out to be a different story: the person who'd chosen to put an end to their life had in fact gradually sunk so low that death had been welcome. Because this process could develop slowly, family members didn't notice the decline or simply didn't recognize the warning bells that rang with increasing intensity.

There was no traffic in the tunnel and Freyr allowed himself to drive faster than normal. He was well aware that the structure was safe and the mountain wasn't about to flatten him, yet he was always glad to see the opening on the other side. The lighting wasn't strong enough to overcome the night-blindness that always hit him when he drove into the tunnel in daylight. He had never got used to the light on this six-kilometre long journey, but thought it more likely that his discomfort had a psychological rather than a physical origin. The thought of being in a place where man was not originally intended to travel aroused in him a primitive fear that he couldn't handle. But this time it wasn't the thickness of the rock above him or the unnatural light that bothered him.

The image of Úrsúla speaking silently to him through the window troubled him, as well as the nagging feeling that he had failed, that he should have postponed his trip to the widower in Flateyri, turned round in the car park and gone back in to hear what she wanted to tell him. He had no idea what that might possibly be, but it increased his curiosity and regret at failing to investigate the matter while he'd had the opportunity. He would probably never know what she had on her mind. A ridiculous idea nestled deep in his brain: that the woman had meant to tell him something concerning his son. But he was well aware that she couldn't possibly know a single thing about his situation, and that this feeling was most likely a result of the phone call from his ex-wife, which was still bothering him.

The tunnel finally came to an end and as soon as Freyr was no longer surrounded by the silent rock he felt relieved. His thoughts about what Úrsúla had muttered through the glass took on a more sensible air. It would have changed nothing if he had gone back up to her; she would probably have withdrawn into her shell as soon as he appeared at her bedside again. The GPS tracker beeped cheerfully as it came back into contact with its satellites, and began directing him to the widower's home in a sparsely populated village jutting out into the sea beneath the slopes of Eyrarfjall Mountain.

Huge avalanche barriers stretched up along the slope, silently recalling the horror of the time, fifteen years ago, when the houses and their sleeping residents had been swept away. There was an unusually small amount of snow on the slopes, and the dark barriers could be seen clearly beneath the thin dusting. Freyr let his eyes wander up along them. Maybe the woman, who was called Halla, had lost someone she cared about in the avalanche and never recovered afterwards. Many people took these shocks very badly; it was unbearable to be constantly reminded of such a loss. He knew that more than anyone.

But this turned out not to be the case. With the help of the GPS tracker, Freyr drove straight to the grieving widower's home. He parked the car, slowly unbuckled his seatbelt and looked over the house and its garden: an unassuming, single-storey concrete abode, considerably smaller than the palaces in the newer neighbourhoods of Reykjavík. The house appeared to be decently maintained, with clean curtains and several thriving plants in flowerpots in the windows. The hedges, at present no more than naked branches, looked as if they'd been trimmed in the autumn. In other words, there was no evidence of serious depression on the part of the homemaker. Of course it was possible that the deceased woman's husband had seen to keeping the house and garden tidy in the hope that if everything looked fine on the surface, the situation would improve; order and control would be infectious. This would be resolved in his conversation with the man, although it was difficult to know whether he would answer honestly questions concerning the division of the household tasks; some men his age felt it beneath their dignity to put on rubber gloves.

While Freyr waited for the door to be answered, he scrutinized the copper doorplate bearing the couple's names: Halla and Bjarni. Below them were the names of their grown-up children: Unnsteinn, Lárus and Petra, whose names were still engraved on the plate even though they had long since left home. This wasn't the only copper ornamentation at the entrance; on each side of the door hung crosses that were far less weathered than the nameplate beneath the doorbell. A third cross had been attached to the front door itself. These symbols seemed to indicate that they were people of faith, and perhaps tied in with the place where the dead woman had chosen to end her life. However, it didn't tally with religious devotion – or the decree of the Bible – to take matters into one's own hands in the way the woman had, rather than entrusting oneself to God. Freyr himself was no believer, and he hoped the widower would avoid going into the subject of religion.

It was so calm and quiet outside that Freyr could hear footsteps approaching from within the house. The door opened slowly and silently. The man who appeared in the doorway was dressed in clothes that hung off him loosely, as if he had put them on out of long-standing habit and not bothered to adjust them properly on his body. His thin white hair was wiry and hadn't been combed for some time. His eyes were swollen. 'Are you the doctor?' His voice was hoarse, as if he were speaking for the first time that day.

Freyr affirmed that he was and extended his hand. At first the old man looked at it in surprise, or so it seemed, before taking it. His handshake was weak and he muttered something about Freyr coming in. He didn't need to take off his shoes. In the lobby, Jesus Christ, a crown of thorns on his head, stared upwards, the very picture of melancholy. The image was in an impressive frame, considering that it was a reproduction, and although Freyr was no art expert he came to the conclusion that the picture and frame were rather new. As he followed Bjarni into the house he spotted a sturdy candle with a golden cross and an inscription from the Bible, a carved wooden plaque praising the Lord, and several crosses similar to those hanging at the entrance. Apart from the image of Jesus, the objects seemed to have been placed quite haphazardly. Perhaps the couple had come across a clearance sale at a Christian bookshop and had had trouble arranging their purchases. Otherwise it was an extremely normal-looking home, apart from the little pile of newspapers and mail lying on the mat beneath the letterbox.

'Are you a man of faith?' Freyr sat down on the sofa opposite the widower, who had taken a seat in a tired old easy chair.

The man stared distantly at the coffee table between them, then said: 'Yes. No. Maybe not right now.' His voice was devoid of all emotion. Freyr recognized this hollow sound very well from his job, and he'd lost count of the number of times he'd watched people knead their hands together as the defeated widower did now.

'But Halla? Was she a believer?'

'No. Yes. The opposite of me. Wasn't so, but became so.'

'I ask because your home seems to indicate as much – or at least it gives the impression that Christian folk live here. That's not too common these days.' This was a white lie; Freyr wanted to know whether Halla had been gripped by strong religious extremism, which in some cases could be a sign of underlying psychological problems or even illness. Mental illnesses could usually be characterized by changes in thinking, behaviour or mood, or a combination of all three, and Freyr was fairly certain that one or more of these changes must have applied to Bjarni's deceased wife. He just needed to find out which ones.

'Halla's interest in religion resurfaced a short time ago. I didn't give it much thought, and it didn't bother me. The only difference was that she started reading the Bible instead of trashy novels.'

'It looks to me as if her renewed religious interest went a bit deeper than that.' Freyr let his eyes wander over the Christian decorations. 'When did you start noticing it?'

The man looked up at the ceiling, as if a calendar were hanging there. 'Three, four years ago. I don't remember precisely.'

Freyr changed tack. 'As far as I understand, your wife didn't have any obvious difficulties, wasn't struggling with alcoholism and hadn't been physically ill. Is that right?' The old man nodded, apparently sincerely.

'Was there anything in your relationship or your circumstances that might possibly have deprived her of the will to live?'

'No. We got along fine. We were happy, even. Or so I thought.' The man paused. 'We weren't in any financial trouble – we'd never been rich, or particularly poor, and we were happy with what we had, which wasn't likely to change. Although my expenses have been cut in half now, I suppose.'

This final addendum indicated that although the man was crossing an emotional minefield, he did have a mental map of the area and would probably make it through unscathed. He was able to view his circumstances from a neutral perspective; although his black humour wasn't particularly funny, it was a sign that he wasn't completely overwhelmed by the gloom of his current situation.

'I've come to help you, as you know,' said Freyr. 'There must be a lot going on in your head and hopefully I'm better than nothing if you have any questions. Or I can do the talking, if you find it more comfortable.'

The man snorted. 'I just want to know why she did it. You can hardly answer that, can you?'

'No, maybe not, but I think it's likely she was ill. Mental illness can cause people unbearable pain and they can see no way to relieve their suffering other than suicide. When that's the case, there's no one to blame; there's nothing that you or anyone else could have done. You should keep that firmly in mind.'

The man gave Freyr a sceptical look. 'Halla wasn't in any pain. I would have known.'

'Maybe her faith eased her discomfort, or else she concealed it out of consideration for you.'

The man shook his head, but no longer seemed quite so convinced. 'I've been thinking about it almost constantly since it happened, trying to remember something in her behaviour that I should have noticed. Something that could have helped me prevent her from doing what she did. But I can't recall anything.'

Freyr decided not to reel off all the principal manifestations of suicidal tendencies. One of the clearest warning signs was a similar earlier attempt. But this was certainly not the case here. Right now it would be unhealthy for the man to become filled with regret; if Freyr were to name some of the signs, it could cause the widower even more distress if it turned out that any of them applied to Halla's behaviour. Instead Freyr directed the conversation to how Bjarni might best arrange things to help him come to terms with the loss of his wife. The man seemed to listen and take note, and even asked a question or two, which was a good sign. Freyr was heartened to hear that the couple's daughter, Petra, still lived in town, although the sons had long since left for the south. So the old man wasn't left entirely alone, and Freyr urged him to have his daughter come and visit as often as possible, to go to her place for supper and accept all the companionship that she and the family had to offer. When asked, Bjarni said that he wasn't considering following the same path as his wife, which was also a good sign, although his saying it didn't mean they could assume it was true. Freyr was feeling reasonably satisfied with the way things were going when he realized that he had to get home. Bjarni also looked a bit tired and seemed to have stopped taking in what he was being told.

'I'm going to look in on you tomorrow, if you don't mind; and you can call me any time.' Freyr handed him a business card and watched the man squint at the small lettering. Again Freyr was reassured by the widower's reaction, since the man showed a sign of interest.

After saying goodbye, Freyr walked to his car. As he reached for the keys in his jacket pocket, he noticed a steeple that he hadn't seen on his way through the village. Surprised, he returned to the house. 'One final question: didn't Halla attend church here in Flateyri?' he said when the man reappeared in the doorway.

'Yes.' Clearly he understood precisely what Freyr was asking. 'She didn't belong to the parish in Súðavík, or attend mass or do anything else at that church.' His voice hardened as he added: 'She just chose to die there, but I don't understand why she did it or why she chose that as the location.' He fell silent, letting his eyes wander past Freyr to the town behind him. 'Like many of us, her interest in the past grew over the years. She had recently taken to visiting old friends quite often, and she developed an increasing fascination with genealogy.' He noticed that Freyr found this interesting and clearly wanted to make sure his words weren't misunderstood, or that anything more could be read into them than he originally intended. 'But I've felt the same, and I didn't take my own life. It was all perfectly normal.'

On his way to Ísafjörður, Freyr couldn't help but wonder why the woman had gone to another community's church to kill herself. She'd doubtless wanted to protect her friends and relatives from finding her dead, but she could have chosen the church in Suðureyri, Þingeyri, or Ísafjörður, all of which were much closer. There must have been a reason for her choice, but Freyr found it impossible to guess it. He knew that it mattered; he just couldn't figure out why.

Chapter 7

The temperature had dropped, yet Katrín's back was clammy with sweat. The cotton T-shirt felt as if it were glued to her skin and it clung uncomfortably each time she moved. The chill that stung her bare cheeks even though she was burning hot everywhere else was particularly unpleasant. She could endure heat or cold but they didn't go together at all; it was like eating salted sugar. She stretched, planted her hands on her hips and looked at what she'd accomplished in the last hour or so. When she'd been within a hair's breadth of getting a thundering headache, she'd given up on the stinking paint smell inside and gone out for fresh air. There she took up where they'd left off in their repairs to the porch the day before. Their progress was nothing to be proud of; so far it had been extremely limited and, if anything, it looked like they had made matters worse. Boards lay strewn about and the irregular edges of the part of the porch that Garðar had decided didn't need fixing had become even more irregular. In one place Katrín had broken a long plank that reached some way into the undamaged part of the porch. Garðar would be over the moon about that when he turned up again. Líf, on the other hand, would see the funny side. She'd smiled many times during their work today, not least at her own clumsiness. This wasn't the only example of repairs that had gone haywire. Everywhere inside were half-completed tasks;

improvements that they'd begun but quickly given up on or put on hold. No one brought up the topic of when they were planning to complete these difficult projects; Líf had no interest in anything other than what she was doing at any given moment and Katrín and Garðar were both careful not to say a word about their working methods. This wasn't the first time that they had resorted to denial to try to avoid their problems. Of course they knew that this didn't work, that it just made things worse; it would probably all come to a chaotic head just before they left and then they'd rush around madly trying to quick-fix everything.

The whole situation just made Katrín want to sigh deeply but she restrained herself, not wanting to break the profound silence to which she was becoming accustomed, and which seemed to be gaining in intensity. Instead she let her hands drop and exhaled silently. Things would sort themselves out one way or the other. The porch spread out beneath her feet, gaping at the world as if it were terribly surprised at all this commotion after being allowed to rot in peace and quiet for decades. Through the large gap she could see the dark soil beneath. Apart from the animal bones that they'd found there, this murky place appeared to be as devoid of vegetation and about as fertile as the moon. Katrín found herself disgusted by the musty odour that arose from beneath the porch, although it wasn't particularly pungent or even that unpleasant. Perhaps it was the discovery of the bones that still bothered her. In truth she had trouble understanding why the thought of them made her tremble; she wasn't a vegetarian, so there was no reason why the bones should have awakened any particular emotions in her. Nonetheless she avoided looking under the untouched planks. Perhaps she was afraid of uncovering human bones; the earthly remains of the woman and the boy for whom the crosses had been erected.

'Ugh.' Garðar appeared in the doorway, a hideous sight. His face and clothing were covered with splotches of white paint. The dark stubble on his chin no longer looked like a shadow, but instead resembled patchy, poorly groomed feathers. He looked either hung-over or ill and in fact when Katrín squinted, he almost seemed half dead. His bloodshot eyes did nothing to diminish this effect. 'I was this far from suffocating.' Garðar showed her a tiny space between his thumb and index finger. 'I'd forgotten how awful paint thinner is.' The last time they'd needed to do some decorating at home they'd hired a painter, since money had not been an issue and it had seemed pointless to get their own hands dirty. If someone had suggested that within a few months they'd be on the verge of bankruptcy, they would have smiled sympathetically and reminded that individual to take his medication. 'I don't know how long Líf will last. She's finishing up the door and window frames in the attic.' Garðar leaned lazily in the doorway. 'Of course I've rarely seen such a poor paint job; in the summer sun it'll look ridiculous.' He stepped outside. 'What happened here?' Garðar had spotted the damage to the porch. He didn't sound particularly annoyed.

'I didn't know my own strength,' grinned Katrín. 'To be honest, I have no idea what I'm doing. I just had to get outside, and this was the obvious task to get on with.'

'I should have come with you. Too late now; this stink is stuck in my clothes, and probably grafted to my skin, too.' Garðar ran his hands through his hair and ruffled it to try and get rid of the smell. 'I was thinking of going for a short hike; I need to air myself out a bit. Do you want to come along?'

'Absolutely.' Katrín stood up, relieved not to have to work out the best way to save the porch. She'd prefer to fill in the space beneath the wood with sand or pebbles and then lay new planks over the gap, but something told her that porches weren't built on frames for nothing. 'I'm going to get Líf. It'll do her good to come along.'

'It'll also do the house good for her to take a break.' The porch groaned as Garðar bent down and poked at the edges of the damage. 'And it looks to me like it'll do the porch good, too, if we stop for a bit.' He stood up and followed Katrín inside. 'Did you go down to the beach earlier?' he added as he put on his coat in the front entrance and Katrín went upstairs to call Líf. His hand hit a shelf as he pulled on one sleeve and he swore vigorously.

Katrín turned on the stairs and waited until he'd stopped swearing. 'Down to the beach?'

'Yes, I saw wet shoeprints and shells on the floor in the living room. I hope you're not planning on decorating the house with them. I've got enough on my hands with the basic renovations, never mind messing about with seashells.'

Katrín smiled quizzically. 'I didn't go gathering seashells. I got stuck straight into wrecking the porch.' She unzipped her jacket. The cold air cooled her, but she soon felt a chill and zipped it back up again. 'It must just be some rubbish that was here when we came.'

'I doubt it. I don't remember seeing it there.'

'I didn't bring any shells in here and if you didn't either, then they must have been here already. Either that or Líf went and got them.'

Garðar looked puzzled. 'She hasn't been anywhere. I was working in the room next to hers and I had to listen to her constant racket.'

Katrín shrugged. 'Well, I hardly think the fox could have brought them in. Or Putti.'

'No, I suppose not. He's been lounging around all morning. Anyway, the shells have been lined up to form letters, and to my knowledge dogs aren't generally fantastic spellers.'

'What did they spell?'

'They said "Goodbye".' Garðar zipped up his jacket briskly. 'They must have been there before and I'm just misremembering. Maybe the paint thinner's going to my head.'

'Goodbye?' Katrín frowned. 'It'll do you good to get out of the house for a bit.'

The three of them set off, Putti following reluctantly behind them, without discussing where they were headed. None of them wanted to go uphill, and they were all in such a sorry state that they didn't need to say as much. The sun was as high in the sky as it would get for the time of year, casting long shadows and creating distorted images wherever it shone. The crunching of the pebbles on the path was a familiar sound after they had tramped back and forth along it with the supplies on the first day. Garðar walked unusually slowly, apparently taking each step carefully. He paused at the first house and pretended to be looking at how the downpipes from the roof were set up. Katrín, however, knew that he was stopping to rest his sore heel.

'Why are all the windows boarded up?' Líf pressed her face against the panels covering the window beside the front door. The windows of all the houses had been given the same treatment, making them look as if they'd been blinded. Their house was the only exception – its dirty panes had been left unprotected against storms and wind, but luckily they had held.

'No doubt to prevent interior damage, if the panes should break.' Garðar took hold of the downpipe from the rain gutter and shook it.

'Why should a windowpane break? There's no one here.' Líf leaned away from the house.

'I don't know, maybe they can get damaged in bad storms or something. Or birds could fly into them.' Garðar seemed pleased to have come up with an answer for Líf; since neither she nor Katrín knew anything about the matter, neither of them could challenge him. He inspected the downpipe even more carefully and now began examining its fastenings.

'This is so weird.' Katrín looked out over the village.

'The pipe?' asked Garðar in surprise.

'No, the settlement here. What must it have been like to live in such a small, isolated place? And how do you think the residents felt moving to Reykjavík after being accustomed to this?' She gazed at the renovated buildings. Having now experienced for herself how much work was involved in restoring a house in such a place, she was finally able to appreciate how the others might have managed. 'How must the people have felt, leaving their homes for the last time?'

'Awful, I expect.' Katrín heard the sadness in Garðar's voice. Unless a miracle was about to occur, they would be in the same boat as these people in the middle of last century; they would lose their home in Reykjavík and be forced to shut its door behind them for the final time. The only difference was that she and Garðar would have to see their old home when they drove through the area, whereas the people in Hesteyri had moved far away and therefore were seldom reminded of what they had lost. Some time ago Katrín had resolved to avoid her old area when the time came for them to have to leave it. She didn't want to see another family's car in the driveway, other curtains in the kitchen windows, other furniture in the garden, and she knew that Garðar felt the same.

Líf came and stood next to Katrín and looked around. 'But what were they supposed to do? There were no jobs to be had after the factory was closed and then it was pointless to try to go on living here, even though some of them might have been resisted the inevitable for a while.'

Just like her and Garðar. Katrín said nothing, but the words echoed in her mind. The miracle they needed to keep the property wasn't going to happen; if they were really lucky they'd be able to hold on until the so-called 'Key Bill' was passed and they could return their house keys to the bank without any further financial consequences, unless the bank found a loophole in the new bill.

'What's that?' Katrín pointed at the slope south of the settlement. On it was a large rock or pile of stones jutting towards the sky, apparently placed there by human hands.

Garðar turned to look where Katrín was pointing. He shrugged. 'No idea. Should we wander over there? We can take a look at the houses on the way; maybe we'll see something that might be useful.'

'What I'd find useful is a nice spa,' Líf grumbled. 'I'd give anything for a massage right about now.'

'There's no danger of that.' Katrín, too, would have given her right arm for just a warm bubble bath. She had long since stopped allowing herself to dream of expensive spas.

They walked gently down the path but had to keep stopping for Garðar either to pull up his sock on his sore foot or fold it over to try to cover the wound on his heel. Neither seemed to help for more than a few steps, and Garðar had started to limp by the time they finally reached the place that had drawn Katrín's attention. They looked at the houses along the way without picking up any useful tips on how to restore their own house. If it hadn't been for Garðar's sore heel they would have gone up to each of them to get a better look, but that would have made the hike too long. The organization of the settlement suggested that it had had sufficient space, with some distance between the houses. On the other hand, it couldn't have been expanded much before running out of habitable land.

'We don't need to go any further if it's killing you.' Katrín grimaced as Garðar pulled down his sock to reveal a blood-red blister. He winced when the curious Putti sniffed at the wound. Katrín tried to remember whether they'd packed bandages or analgesic sprays from the car, but could only recall having planned to take such things with her, not actually having done so. 'Your foot looks awful.'

'It'll be all right tomorrow. I have other shoes that don't come so high up the ankle.' Garðar pulled his sock all the way down to the middle of his instep as he rested his foot on top of his shoe. 'It was stupid of me not to have worn them now.'

'That's absolutely disgusting.' Líf made a face, but then smiled. 'I think amputation is the only cure. It's a tragedy.'

Garðar didn't seem amused, though he tried to force a smile. He was going to reply but Katrín beat him to it. 'Just wait here. Líf and I will head over there and have a look at it. You can rest your leg in the meantime and we'll take our time coming back.'

Garðar couldn't hide his relief at a chance to sit down. 'Good idea. I doubt I'd make it back if I took one more step.' He plonked himself down on a grassy bank that appeared specially designed to allow people to rest their weary bones. 'It wouldn't hurt to cool down my heel a bit.' He stretched out his leg to allow the wind to soothe his half-bare foot, and it was as if the wind took this as a cue to blow colder.

'I'm going to wait here too.' Líf sat down by his side. 'I've actually had enough walking to last me a lifetime.' She let herself fall backwards and lay staring up at the sky. 'Don't be too long.'

On her way up the hollow Katrín had to keep pushing her hair out of her face, since the wind seemed to be trying its best to blow it constantly into her eyes. She automatically stuck her hand into her pocket to see if she had a hair-band before remembering that of course she hadn't brought any. As a result, she could see little or nothing and couldn't get a good idea of the area until she'd nearly reached her destination. She stopped, turned back and shouted to Garðar and Líf: 'It's a cemetery. Maybe the crosses are from here.' She wasn't certain whether they'd heard her over the breeze, but Garðar waved at her. Instead of shouting louder she walked all the way up to a level area containing several rather elegant but weatherworn graves. She could tell them about this on the way back to the house. The man-made structure that had caught Katrín's attention, a memorial made of stacked-up stones, was located in the centre of the area. Not many people had lived and died around here, judging by the number of graves, which seemed to be only several dozen. Most of them looked as if winter had repeatedly been allowed to run roughshod over them; by the skipper's account, no one visited the area from the end of August until the spring. It was likely that some of the graves had never been tended. Many of the dead had lost their offspring to the south or to distant places, and then there were those who had lived and died alone. It was clear, at least, that in some places the brush had been allowed to grow undisturbed, and it now lay withered and dry among the graves. Weathered crosses and crooked headstones were the only indication that the previous residents of the village were resting there. Katrín knew she was starting to let her imagination run away with her, but she thought the vegetation looked even more lifeless here than elsewhere in the area, and the stalks and dried-out plants appeared to snap more loudly beneath her feet. The wind also felt colder and seemed to carry a whisper that her ears couldn't quite make out. She suddenly felt chillier, as though she would never warm up again. After zipping her jacket all the way up she felt slightly better, even if she still wasn't warm. She took several steps to a fenced-off plot with an impressive iron cross that had broken and now stood with its head tilted. The fence around the area must have been unusually elegant in its time, but its delicate ironwork was now just as rusted as the cross. The effect was tragic.

She turned abruptly to see whether Garðar and Líf were still where she'd left them. They were, of course, and seemed to be in intense discussion. She suddenly longed to turn around and run back to them; let the cemetery wait until they returned with her to have a look at it. But she knew she would be annoyed at herself as soon as she went back down the path if she didn't investigate whether the crosses were from the cemetery, so she turned and walked quickly over to the first grave. On it was an impressive headstone with the names of a couple who had died in 1949. Neither the date nor the names matched those on the crosses, which Katrín recalled were 'Hugi' and 'Bergdís', and although she wasn't entirely certain, she thought that both had died in 1951. She was quite surprised that she should remember this, since she was usually particularly bad with dates and numbers. She turned to the next grave, but the inscription on its headstone was so faded that there was no way of telling what was on it. The same went for the next two headstones. As she stood and wondered whether she should check all the graves, Katrín noticed that a panel of text was affixed to the memorial.

She walked up to the modest but attractive pile of stones. On top of it stood a cross and within a hollow space on its front was a handsome bell, as well as the panel containing the text that Katrín had noticed. When she got closer she was pleased to see that it was a map showing the position of the graves, along with a list of the names of those resting in the cemetery. Also on it was a black and white picture of a little church, with general information stating that a church had stood just inside the village; it had been built in 1899 and was a gift from the Norwegian M.C. Bull, who ran the whaling station Hekla in Stekkseyri. A chapel had served the settlement for several centuries before the church was built. The church had been moved to Súðavík in 1960, but the text explained that the bell in the memorial was from the church, and had been cast in 1691. Katrín found that interesting, particularly given that it hung there unprotected, accessible to everyone. The summary ended with some exceptionally brief information about Hesteyri, considering how many people had lived their lives there, experiencing all the pain, tribulations and joyous moments that fate would have dealt them. Perhaps history didn't offer any detailed information, so the marker made do with stating that Hesteyri had become a certified commercial town in 1881; around 420 people had resided there permanently at the settlement's height; it had had a telegram station, then later a telephone exchange, as well as a physician. Concerning the end of the settlement, all that was stated was that around 1940 its population had started to dwindle and the last residents moved away in 1952.

There was more information to be gleaned from the list of names. Two groups were described: those who were known to have been buried there but whose exact location was unknown, and those who rested in marked graves. The unidentified graves were mostly from the turn of the century, 1900. Katrín found herself thinking that at that time the residents hadn't had the resources or reason to put up hard-wearing markers and the graves had therefore vanished into oblivion when weather and vegetation levelled the mounds or other signs of them. The known graves were more recent, the majority of them dating from the 1920s. It surprised Katrín that the newest graves in the cemetery were made in 1989; there were also three individuals buried here whose nationality was the only information still readable: two Norwegians and one German. It was a sad fate to be buried in a distant land that over time forgot a man's name, his date of birth, and even date of death, which at least must have been known.

But it wasn't the foreigners that Katrín was most interested in. The names on the crosses that they'd found turned out to be among those buried in known graves. Hugi Pjetursson and Bergdís Jónsdóttir, both died in 1951, she at thirty-two years old and he at five. Katrín stared at the names while pondering their poignantly short lives. Bergdís was most likely the boy's mother, and the boy's surname told her his father was called Pjetur; but no father was to be found in their plot, nor was any Pjetur named in the two lists. She was happy that Líf had decided to wait with Garðar; she would have found it embarrassing and uncomfortable to have her there, considering how recently Einar had died. His death had been easy and silent; he had fallen asleep never to wake up again, while here this mother and her son had probably bid farewell to this world through an accident or disease, since they had died in the same year, if not on the same day. Of the two evils, Einar's path was surely more desirable, even though it wasn't in one's power to decide such a thing. Líf would probably disagree with this, however; she had woken with her husband cold and dead by her side. Katrín felt a deeper chill.

The map of the cemetery pointed her to the grave of Hugi and Bergdís, a fenced-off but unmarked plot. If she hadn't had the map to rely on, she would have assumed that these were reserved plots that hadn't been used after the village was abandoned. Unlike other plots, there was no overgrowth present here; instead the ground was covered with black, dusty soil. Oval-shaped white stones lay here and there on the surface but no remains of weeds or grass were to be seen anywhere. The outlines of the graves were marked with a low pile of stones that was falling down. The wind blew harder when Katrín walked over to the plot and the unpleasant whispering grew louder, though she still couldn't quite hear what it was saying. She had to grab her hair and hold it back tightly in order to see anything properly. Although she didn't really need to see anything – she knew the crosses were from here. Her confirmation came after she'd got a grip on her hair and could see a bit better: two broken wooden stumps stuck out of the ground at the end of the graves. Bingo. Although there was no clear explanation as to why the crosses had been removed and put next to their house, Katrín was at least very relieved to know where they had come from. Maybe crazy – or drunk? – tourists had vandalized the graves and thrown away the crosses by their house, although that explanation sounded ridiculous as soon as it crossed her mind. Her relief then evaporated completely when she saw that the round white stones weren't stones at all, but shells.

Katrín picked one of them up and inspected it thoroughly. It was pale and damp and had been scraped out, or the creature that had occupied it had been removed some other way. Katrín looked around in search of more shells that might be hidden in the grass next to the grave. She saw none. It occurred to her that birds might have been responsible, but then the shells should have been lying all over the place. Besides that, it was too much of a coincidence for birds to have arranged the shells in the dirt – they all faced the same way, with the convex side up. The wind blew the soil and the shells were no longer as distinctly white. The next gust went one better and covered some of them completely. Katrín squeezed the shell she was holding, turned on her heel and hurried back to Garðar and Líf. It was inconceivable that the shells had been there since the autumn. They could hardly have been there much longer than since that morning, considering how quickly the wind was blowing dirt over them now. But who had put them there? She would have to investigate whether the shells were similar to the ones Garðar had found in the living room of their house. Maybe there was someone else in the village, trying to avoid making his presence known.

She felt relieved when she finally left the cemetery and spotted Garðar and Líf. At precisely that moment she thought that at last she could hear what the wind had been constantly whispering.

Run, Kata.

Chapter 8

The photo of his son stood on his desk in the simple office that he hadn't been interested in making his own in any other way. Similar photos could be seen everywhere he was in the habit of stopping; at home, one on the kitchen counter next to the coffee maker, another on the bedside table, a third on the little table next to the armchair where he watched television. The pictures were all over the place; he'd lost count of them, indeed he didn't want to know how many there were. Most of the frames were the same: inexpensive and not able to withstand much handling. Some of them had fallen apart and been traded in for sturdier ones. He'd originally bought all the frames in the same shop after picking up enlarged photos of his son. He'd chosen the photos as haphazardly as the frames, having been pressed for time. He remembered the day clearly; when he woke he couldn't recall his son's face, no matter how he tried to imagine it. The face was always just out of reach, just on the verge of appearing, but needing one last effort to recall it. The framed photos were intended for such moments, but Freyr had immediately realized that they would constantly increase in number, and in the end his inability to picture his son would become inescapable.

'Who's in the photo?' Dagný nodded her chin at the picture. She was unusually tired-looking, but that made her no less attractive in Freyr's eyes, merely more human. Her short hair wasn't as wild as usual and lay a bit flat at the end of the long working day. Her sofa at home was probably a more attractive prospect than dropping in on him, but Freyr wasn't to blame for that – she'd asked to see him. 'Anyone I know?'

'It's a photo of my son. Benni.' It suddenly occurred to Freyr to turn the photo round for her to see it, but he didn't.

'He was never found, was he?' Dagný reddened slightly as soon as she said this. 'I heard the story just after you moved here. It didn't need to be described to me in any detail; I still remember the news vividly. Children don't often disappear in Iceland.'

'No. Thankfully not. But it's not the only example. Two teenage boys disappeared from Keflavík fifteen years ago. They've never been found.' Freyr watched Dagný shift awkwardly in the chair at the topic of conversation, even though her desire to know more about what had happened was clearly stronger than her politeness. It didn't bother him; it was much better when people asked him straight out instead of tiptoeing around it every time anything vaguely connected to the incident came up. In the worst instances, people blushed deeply if a child were mentioned, and then tried whatever they could to direct the conversation onto another topic. On those occasions he usually stopped them and told them that it was OK, but that he didn't want to talk about his painful loss. 'The way things stand, I don't expect him to be found now; it's been three years and every little patch of ground where he might conceivably be has been gone over with a fine-toothed comb.'

Dagný appeared relieved that he was able to discuss the subject. She looked into his eyes instead of allowing them to roam the walls of the office and asked her next question more boldly than the previous one. 'What do you think actually happened? It's strange that nothing should have come to light.'

Freyr nodded; apart from his ex, no one could have pondered this question more than he had. But his speculation hadn't led him to any conclusions. 'I simply don't know. It doesn't help that he went missing while playing hide-and-seek with his friends. Maybe he crawled into a well or a hole that somehow closed behind him, but of course all those possibilities were investigated. They searched garages, houses, cars, camper vans, and everything else in the neighbourhood that could possibly have accommodated a child. The police think that he must have ended up in the sea; still, it's quite a distance from Ártúnsholt, where we lived, down to the beach, so I've always doubted that explanation. Of course it's possible that he went all that way, but it doesn't tally with the game of hide-and-seek; the kids said they never went far to hide, and the purpose is to be found in the end. You know that from your own childhood; you didn't go off to another neighbourhood to find yourself a good hiding place. In any case, they weren't allowed to go near Ártúnsbrekka because of the traffic, and they stuck to that. I don't think Benni would have broken that rule.' Freyr folded his arms across his chest. 'But I don't know that for certain.'

'But dogs? They must have been used. Didn't they find any trail?'

'Yes, but it didn't lead anywhere. The trail ended at Straumur Street, which is north of the Ártúnsbrekka area. There's a large petrol station a short distance away and there was a huge amount of traffic heading out of town at the time. From what I understood, the exhaust from the cars ruined the scent for the tracker dogs. And it didn't help that it started pouring with rain that evening.'

'Could he have been kidnapped? If there was a lot of traffic it's conceivable that he was grabbed by someone in a car. At the petrol station, perhaps.'

'It's not impossible, but that was also investigated in depth. There are numerous CCTV cameras at the petrol station and none of them showed anything suspicious. Of course they don't cover the entire area, but they almost do, and they did show every single car that drove out of the station. The licence-plate numbers of all the cars that passed through there from approximately the time that Benni disappeared were taken down and their owners were contacted, but it led to nothing, just like everything else.'

Dagný looked at Freyr thoughtfully. 'But he could still be alive. Couldn't he?'

Freyr paused for a moment before answering. He knew that her intentions were good; to awaken some hope in his heart. But the reality was another thing. The most appalling scenario he could imagine was that his son was still alive in the hands of some monster, because no normal person would have taken an unknown child like that. Freyr had had enormous trouble accepting the most reasonable yet most unbearable conclusion – that Benni was dead. His ex-wife, Sara, was still struggling to accept their child's fate, and was slowly but surely sinking deeper into a psychological quagmire. 'No. He's dead. Benni had congenital diabetes, type one. He couldn't have survived for long without receiving insulin, since he was due to have an injection around an hour after he went missing. During the investigation they checked on whether any abnormal purchases of insulin had taken place.

All the doctors and pharmacies were on alert, so I'm fairly certain that it was checked thoroughly, and nothing unusual came to light. The disease probably played a part in what happened; if Benni suffered insulin shock in his hiding place, down at the seaside or wherever he was, there's no question of what the outcome would have been. Without any hope of assistance, he'd have gone into a coma.' Freyr smiled dully at Dagný. 'Although it might sound silly, that possibility gives me a tiny bit of consolation. It would have been a completely painless way to die.'

'I understand.' Dagný crossed her legs. 'It's devastating and you have my condolences. I've always meant to tell you that, but I couldn't quite bring myself to. It's not something I have any experience of – fortunately, I know.'

'Thank you,' Freyr replied sincerely. Sara felt that other people's empathy was superficial, that no one could put themselves in her shoes and understand her feelings. Freyr was of a different opinion. For him, you didn't need to go through hell yourself in order to sympathize with those who ended up there. 'It's all so terrible, but it's getting better. The worst is behind me.'

'Was the questioning a hard thing to go through?' Dagný's cheeks flushed and she added hurriedly: 'I mean, was it more difficult for you than it needed to be? I've often wondered how people experience the police, whether we come across as colder than we really are.'

Freyr took a moment to think this over, since he'd never considered it. 'God, I don't know. I suppose the hardest thing to swallow was the fact that me and Sara, Benni's mother, were the first suspects. Of course I understood that they couldn't rule out any possibilities, but that doesn't change the fact that it was incredibly painful while the investigation was going on.'

Dagný frowned. 'It couldn't have gone on for long. Did it?'

Freyr shook his head. 'No, not really. I could prove that I'd been down at the hospital getting Benni's medicine and running some errands, and Sara's sister had been visiting her since that morning, helping to prepare a birthday party for their mother. Our stories were corroborated and we were treated much more kindly once we were no longer under suspicion.' He smiled to show that he bore no ill will towards the police.

He didn't know whether it was because she thought it inappropriate, but she didn't return his smile before speaking again. 'I suppose I should get to the business at hand.' She placed a little salmon-coloured cardboard box on the table. 'I've gathered evidence from the break-in at the preschool, and I'd appreciate it if you would look it over. I know I didn't take it particularly well when you suggested looking into the older break-in at the primary school, but I changed my mind and had the old reports dug out.' She cleared her throat, but politely. 'There are striking similarities between the events, but you'll see that yourself when you take a look at this. My supervisor has authorized me to hand over the files to you, considering that the break-in appears to display some kind of mental disturbance and wasn't carried out for financial gain. Most of the material is photocopied, but of course you'll make sure that it doesn't get around.'

Freyr stared at the pink box. The colour seemed garishly at odds with the contents and he wondered who had chosen it. A large white sticky label had been fixed to the lid; it was crooked but its message was clear: *The contents of this box are the possession of the Ísafjörður Police. Confidential.* 'What are you expecting from me? Am I meant to solve the case?'

Dagný huffed. 'Not exactly.' She looked down. 'There's more in the box. Evidence concerning Halla, the woman who committed suicide in Súðavík.'

'Oh?' Freyr pulled the box towards him. 'Has anything come to light in her case? Do you think it's possible it wasn't suicide?'

'No, there's nothing to suggest that. But there are other things that raise questions.'

'Questions are an inevitable by-product of suicides, but there are seldom any answers. For example, it surprised me that she chose the church in Súðavík and not a closer one, but I couldn't work out why. I read on the Internet that the church was moved there from Hesteyri when the village was deserted, despite significant opposition from its former residents. It crossed my mind that those objections might have played a part in Halla's choice of location, but we'll never know one way or the other. Maybe she had some entirely different connection to Súðavík. Or possibly Hesteyri.'

Dagný said nothing and stared at the box. 'That isn't what was bothering me.' Then she looked up and into his eyes. 'Did this woman know you?'

'What?' Freyr hadn't expected this and couldn't hide his surprise. 'Do you mean, was she a patient of mine? I would have said so when this came up.'

'I didn't necessarily mean that, but was she possibly connected to you or your ex-wife – was she related to you or something of that sort?'

'No.' Freyr knew that Dagný would eventually tell him what she was getting at, but nonetheless he couldn't hide his impatience. 'I'd never heard of this woman until the day before yesterday. Did her husband suggest otherwise? He didn't mention a word of it to me.'

'No, he says the same thing as you; he doesn't think there's any connection. I called him before coming here.' She waited for Freyr to say something before continuing: 'These two cases – the break-in and the suicide – also appear to be connected. However, it's impossible for me to determine the connection. I want to say as little as possible, so I don't negatively influence your own reading of the evidence.'

'Maybe you could tell me how you came up with the idea that I knew the woman.' Freyr had had enough training in reading people to be well aware that Dagný had deliberately omitted this detail.

A clattering in the corridor gave her a moment to think. Food trolleys were being pushed to the wards for dinner. The rattling of the dishes and crockery momentarily overwhelmed everything else but then quickly faded into silence. 'Could she have taken part in the search for your son? Were searches conducted in Flateyri or Ísafjörður?'

Freyr suddenly found his office intolerably hot. He loosened the knot in his tie and undid the top button on his shirt. 'The answer to your second question is no. The search wasn't countrywide, although the public was asked to stay on the lookout for Benni and photos of him circulated in the media. I don't know the names of all the people who searched in Reykjavík, but I don't think Halla can have been among them. Police and rescue teams handled the search; she wasn't a policewoman, and I doubt she'd have belonged to a rescue team because of her age.' Before he had a chance to ask what had prompted her to make such an enquiry, Dagný turned to her next question, which was equally incomprehensible.

'Does the name Bernódus ring any bells?'

'No.' Freyr's fingers were itching to get to the contents of the box. Judging by Dagný's questions, they were obviously quite remarkable. 'I'd remember it. It's an unusual name.'

Dagný nodded; apparently she'd been expecting a different answer. 'I understand.'

Freyr laid his hands on top of the box, smiled at Dagný and said, 'Well, I can't say the same. I can't make head or tail of what you're getting at.'

'Open the box and have a look at what's in it. As I said, it appears to me that the old and the new break-ins – and Halla's suicide – are connected.' She hesitated before continuing, now in a voice so low that it was nearly a whisper. Yet she was reluctant to look him in the eye. 'As well as the disappearance of your son.'

Freyr's jaw dropped in astonishment, but no sound emerged from his throat. He seemed to have lost the ability to breathe. But he recovered quickly. 'That can't be right.' He could hear that his voice sounded anything but friendly, contrary to how he had tried to train it for his job. 'How did you work that out?'

'As I said, it's best if you take a look for yourself.' She stood up and removed her jacket from the back of the chair. 'Maybe come and talk to me after you've formed an opinion. I'm sorry if this seems ridiculous, but it can't be helped.' He stared at her as she went to the door. After opening it she turned back. 'I should mention that I didn't know it was your son in that photo when I asked about it before. I hope you don't think I've been trying to pry. It's not like that at all.' She shut the door behind her without giving him time to reply or say goodbye. The room's temperature still seemed to be climbing and Freyr took off his tie. He tossed it over the desk, onto the chair where Dagný had been sitting. Then he removed his white coat and did the same with that. The garment landed where he'd aimed it, but then slipped down the back of the chair onto the floor.

Around half an hour later, Freyr had finished going through the evidence. He had settled for skimming over the bulk of the data, which was enough to allow him to understand why Dagný thought she'd found a connection between the two break-ins, as well as to Halla. Black and white photocopies of photographs taken after the earlier break-in were eerily similar to the scene at the preschool. The images were relatively unclear, but the main similarities could be made out. In comparison with the vast number of photos that Dagný had taken of the damage while he was present, the old photos were incredibly few. Of course he might only have got to see some of them, but he suspected that the small number was indicative of how expensive it was to develop film all those years ago. The most striking photo was of the graffiti on the wall of the school's assembly hall. Dagný had included an equivalent photograph taken at the preschool. Freyr knew that the same word had been scribbled on both walls, so he wasn't surprised by that. What he was taken aback by was how similar the graffiti was. Disregarding the different backgrounds in the photos, it was almost as if the writing were the same. He would have liked to have enlarged both images and viewed the words in higher resolution side by side, but that was impossible, at least right now. Maybe Dagný could help him with that later.

The two break-ins had other things in common; in neither

case had the police managed to determine how the vandal had got in. All the windows were fastened from the inside and all the panes were undamaged, in addition to the fact that no door appeared to have been forced open. In the older case, the police had checked on who had master keys to the school and subsequently concluded that none of those people was connected to the break-in; nor had any keys been lost or passed around. The police report on the break-in at the preschool described a very similar situation: it seemed almost impossible that keys had been used to get in. It was thus unclear as to how access had been gained to either the primary school in 1953 or the preschool now. Freyr had neither the imagination nor the expertise to enable him to speculate about this.

Other elements gave him pause for thought; for instance, a photocopy of an old class photo, which, according to the files, might possibly shed light on who was responsible for the first break-in. The reason for this was stated, but in any case it was obvious: the faces of several of the children had been obliterated by repeated jabs with a sharp object. The frame's glass had been broken out and the photo hung back up in its place in the group's classroom after it had been vandalized. No other class photo had received the same treatment; they'd merely been thrown into a corner like old rubbish. It therefore seemed likely that the perpetrator had something against the children in the photo. Freyr couldn't see from the case files whether this theory had led to anything, and given the ages of the children in the photo, all of them appearing to be between eleven and twelve years old, that was perhaps understandable. It was difficult to imagine that such young kids could prompt anyone to do such a thing. On the other hand, Freyr knew that children this age could be quite brutal with their peers, although victims of childish nastiness seldom resorted to vandalism such as had been wreaked on the school.

At the bottom of the photograph were the names of the children in the class, but it was impossible for Freyr to make them out on the blurry photocopy. However, among the files he'd found a list of the six children who had provoked the vandal's strongest ire and was surprised to see Halla's name among them. Next to the names, their dates of death had been written in, according to what was written next to Halla's name. Nothing was written next to one of the names, Lárus Helgason, so Freyr assumed that he was still alive. The five whom he knew or presumed to be dead – Halla, two men, and two other women – all seemed to have passed away before their time during the past three years, if Freyr were correct in his assessment. He wasn't familiar with any of them apart from Halla. He wasn't quite sure what this ought to tell him, but it was clearly unusual, statistically speaking, how this group had all perished within such a short period of time – apart from the one still living. Of course, such a thing wasn't entirely unlikely; these people had been between sixty and seventy years of age when they'd died, so the fact of their death was not a huge surprise. But still. It would be interesting to learn how each of them had died. If it were a case of multiple suicide it would certainly be worthy of investigation, since such a thing was nearly unheard of except when it involved teenagers.

What struck Freyr most was the copy of the letter that Halla had left behind when she'd killed herself. The letter was identified by a yellow Post-it note stuck to the paper, since it was entirely unclear from the contents that it was a farewell letter. It looked as if the photocopier hadn't been able to copy it entirely, since the beginnings and ends of words at the edges of the page had been cut off. Halla had apparently used the entire page, leaving no margins – although that didn't really matter, since what she had written made no sense anyway. The text was very much in the spirit of what Freyr had witnessed from those who had completely lost their grip on reality. The thread tying together their thoughts and perceptions had frayed. The message that Halla clearly wished more than anything else to leave behind was perfectly incomprehensible to anyone other than herself, and with her suicide she'd ruled out the possibility that it would ever be understood. Judging by the letter, Halla had either suffered trauma the same day that she committed suicide, causing the psychosis that ended with her terrible deed, or else her husband had lied to Freyr about her mental health. It was very clear from what she had written that everything was not as it should be. But there was something else that gave Freyr even more cause for concern after reading the letter: the repeated references to his son.

Got to find Benni, got to find Benedikt Freysson, got to find Benni, got to find Benedikt. Can't find Benni, can't find Benni, where is Benni? Forgive me, Bernódus, forgive me, forgive me, forgive me. Can't find Benni, can't find him, can't find him. Forgive me, Bernódus, forgive me, forgive me, forgive me. Forgive me, Bernódus.

Freyr put the paper down, rested his elbows on the table and covered his face with his hands. He stared at the text without blinking, until his eyes stung and he was forced to close them. And when he saw nothing but darkness, he finally felt better.

Chapter 9

The moon cast a dim light through the windows. The white, newly painted walls helped brighten the room and Katrín thanked her stars that Garðar had had his way and the purple colour she'd suggested had been rejected. Anything that could possibly counter the effects of the darkness was useful. They'd decided to spend the night in this room because it was so much brighter than all the others in the house, being the only living space they'd finished painting. It was useless to complain about the paint smell or the toxic fumes, despite the fact that they'd all suffered from the headaches that it caused. Having one light room was worth it, though the light diminished for a second as Líf went over to stare out of the window. 'I'd be happy to go home.' She turned to Katrín and Garðar as they tried to make themselves comfortable on the mattresses that were serving as a sofa. Putti lay curled up at Katrín's feet and she felt the warmth emanate from his little body through her thick woollen socks. 'Tonight, I mean.' Líf's blonde hair fell loosely around her neck and despite the fact that any trace of make-up had long since vanished from her face, she looked incredibly good, seeming more like she'd just come from a massage at the spa she was constantly talking about than from a shift doing construction work out in the wilderness. 'If that person who's around here somewhere were all right, he would come and say hello, not scatter shells all over the floor and make a giant mess on it in his dripping wet boots.'

Garðar sipped from the can he was holding. 'Come on. There must be some explanation for this, even though we might not be able to see it at the moment. It's pointless getting all worked up about it; the shells were probably there to begin with without us noticing them, and the water could have just leaked onto the floor. As you may have noticed, this house is somewhat lacking on the maintenance front.'

'Oh, wake up. It needs to rain in order for water to leak in. No, there's a crazy person around here and he's hiding in one of these houses. I get goose bumps at the thought of what this message is supposed to mean.' Líf rubbed her upper arm. '"Goodbye"? What's that supposed to mean? Does he want us to go, or is he planning to kill us and wants to say goodbye before he does?' She turned back to the window and stared out. 'Would we have noticed if a boat had sailed here in the night, or even in the morning?' She stared at the shore, which was about a hundred metres below the house, and out at the sea. 'I don't see any boats, but maybe the man left it further up the fjord.'

'Of course we would have heard a boat. Do you remember how noisy that tub was that brought us here?' Garðar took another sip of his drink. 'There's no one here but us.'

Katrín wasn't quite as convinced as Garðar, although she didn't agree with Líf. They'd been so exhausted the night before that helicopters could have landed outside the house without them noticing. She felt that Líf's theory might well hold up, but it hadn't crossed her mind that a boat could have landed somewhere other than at the pier. Of course that was possible; the skipper had said that even here people often had to be ferried to land in rubber rafts. Meaning it was probably possible to sail past Hesteyri, drop anchor out of sight further up the fjord, then row to land in a rubber raft that would be easy to drag under cover. Using that method, someone could arrive here without anyone else noticing. 'Let me have a sip.' She took the can and drank from it. Despite the cold in the house, the drink was lukewarm. They hadn't yet lit the stove downstairs, which was connected only to a radiator in the room they had slept in until now. That did little for the room in which they now sat, in their thick sweaters and woolly socks. 'Shouldn't we worry about this tomorrow? Everything seems much more manageable in the daytime than in the evening and at night. I'm not sure I'm in the mood to talk about this any more.'

'I can't sleep with some nutter on the loose out there.' Líf looked back at them, leaving a frosty haze on the windowpane. 'What if he comes tonight? The lock downstairs wouldn't keep out a child. It was probably him that I heard when I woke up.'

Garðar heaved himself up to standing. Putti looked up but stuck his muzzle immediately back under his tail and went back to sleep. 'There's no one here but us, believe me. There's nothing to fear – I'll even prove it to you by going down and fetching the beer. Maybe a little alcohol in your blood will help cheer you up again.' Katrín gulped down the drink. She couldn't imagine that he would really abandon them and go out into the night. When they'd come home from their hike earlier, she'd gone straight to the living room to have a look at the shells that Garðar had mentioned. As they walked slowly home she'd held so tightly to the shell that she'd brought with her from the grave that deep, coarse stripes had formed in the palm of her hand. She didn't release her grip until she was standing looking at the white shells, exactly the same as hers, on the floor of the living room, irregularly forming the letters of the word *Goodbye*. So it was a farewell. None of the three of them would confess to having done this. Katrín had the feeling that Garðar suspected Líf, although he seemed to believe her when she denied it – her stunned expression when she'd looked at the unevenly formed word had no doubt helped her credibility on this front. Katrín was convinced that someone besides the three of them was responsible for these shells, and she still hadn't managed to get rid of the unease that had gripped her in the living room. She would never let Garðar go out alone into the night, at least not while it was still unclear whether someone else might be waiting for him outside. Líf's nutter, for example. 'You're not going out alone.' Katrín wiped drops of the fizzy drink off her chin and chest. 'You either forget about getting the beer or I'm coming with you.' She didn't want any beer, and wanted even less to go out into the darkness. The dog looked up again and stared sorrowfully at her, as if he agreed with her completely.

'You're not leaving me here alone.' The tone of Líf's voice made it clear how serious she was. 'I'm going with you.' The white walls seemed to pale and the yellowish moonlight faded as soon as Líf spoke. The one cloud in the sky had drifted in front of the moon. It seemed to be up to a coin-toss: either Garðar went nowhere or they would go with him. If Líf had suggested that they forget about the beer because she was afraid of remaining behind alone, doubtless Garðar would have given in and they wouldn't have gone anywhere. But Katrín had never been a lucky person and could pretty much blame herself for having offered two options. If you wanted a specific outcome, you should only suggest one.

The moonlight appeared duller after they'd come out into the twilight, despite the disappearance of the cloud that had temporarily covered the moon. Fortunately it was a short walk to the stream where Garðar had put the beer. Putti trotted along lightly behind them, stopping to urinate against the wall of the house before scampering to catch up with them. At some point a narrow but fairly level path from the porch to the riverbank had formed, and they followed this. It was set to drop below freezing that night and their breath was frosty. There was a melancholy feel to the atmosphere, as if something bad – yet anticipated – had finally taken place; something of which nature alone was aware.

Garðar tried to brighten the mood, though without much success. 'Let's make a deal. If you stop talking about the shells, tomorrow I'll focus on connecting the septic tank so that we can get the toilet running.' In a little cubby-hole next to the front entrance one of the previous owners had installed a toilet and sink that they couldn't use, since it wasn't actually connected, as if the man had given up before completing the project. Similarly, a lot of work had clearly gone into installing a green plastic septic tank in an open pit outside, but that too was unconnected.

'Any ideas on how to get it in working order would be very welcome.' Katrín had seen Garðar scratching his head over the septic tank as he tried to work out where this and that pipe ought to connect to the tank and where they were supposed to lead. 'I think we're going to have to settle for continuing to pee outside.' As soon as she said this she regretted not simply having taken him up on his offer. Maybe that would have encouraged him to throw himself into the project and fix the toilet. It wasn't a thrilling prospect to have to go outside alone, in the middle of the night if necessary.

Garðar didn't seem too pleased, which just went to show what kind of state they were all in. Usually it took a lot more than that to irritate him. 'What do you know about what I can or can't do about these things?'

'Stop bickering, get the beer and let's go back inside.' Líf hopped from foot to foot on the bank above the stream as Garðar inched his way down, very carefully. Katrín moved closer to Líf, while Putti pushed between them so as not to miss anything, apparently having trouble deciding whether he should follow Garðar or remain with the women. Visibility was poor and the ground around the stream might already be frozen. Judging by how carefully he was proceeding, Garðar was obviously keen not to slip on an icy patch and end up in the freezing water. And it can't have helped that they had discovered they hadn't brought along any bandages. Smirking, Líf nudged Katrín and called out to Garðar: 'Wouldn't it be funny if you fell in?'

'Ha ha.' He'd reached the stream and now wiped his dirty hand on a dry tuft of grass dangling over the stream-bed. He turned to the dark water in search of the beer. 'You've got to be joking!'

'What?' Katrín tried to see what had caused the renewed frustration in his voice, but she couldn't see anything except his back and the running water.

'The beer isn't here.' Garðar looked up at them. 'Did you take it?'

Both swore that they hadn't. 'It probably is there. Didn't

you just put it further up or down the stream?' Katrín looked up and down the channel but caught no glimpse at all of a white plastic bag beneath the vibrant surface of the water.

'Someone's taken it.' Líf whispered this, but in Garðar's earshot. 'Do you believe me now?' She grasped Katrín's arm tightly.

Putti seemed to sense Líf's agitation and growled softly. He turned in a circle and barked once into the darkness between the stream and the house. Katrín felt agitated. 'Come on, Garðar.' She wanted to know whether someone was standing behind them, but couldn't bring herself to turn around. 'We'll find it tomorrow.' Líf's grip was hurting her arm. 'That's enough.'

Garðar walked purposefully downstream. 'The bag's there.' He gave them what appeared to be a victorious look. Katrín couldn't see anything from where she was standing. 'It's floated off. I should have put a heavier rock on top of it.' He stopped, bent down to the stream and lifted the sodden bag. 'Fuck.' Garðar held the bag as far from him as he could to keep the water from dripping on him. When the bag had finished emptying itself Garðar turned back and handed it to the two women. 'I'm going to walk along the bank and see if I can find the cans.'

Katrín could barely stifle a screech. But instead she took the bag and let it drop between her and Líf. Only then did Líf release her grip on her, and Katrín set off to follow Garðar. 'I'm coming with you. You're not going alone. What if you fall in?' As soon as she tried to gain a secure foothold she understood why Garðar had stepped so slowly down the slope; it was saturated with water.

'Are you two nuts?' Líf had stopped whispering now and

didn't wait for a reply, but instead hurried after Katrín. She was in such a rush that they both nearly lost their balance when she reached her. But Líf appeared not to notice and said breathlessly:

'Let's go back inside. This may be a trap. Whoever it might be out here has taken the beer because he knew that we'd go looking for it, like idiots.' Realizing the group was on the move, Putti stopped growling and followed the women. He didn't let the unstable ground bother him, but shot past them on steady paws. He sniffed at the bank and started growling again. 'See.' Líf waved in Putti's direction with her free hand. 'He senses there's someone here. Did you see? He was sniffing at the place where the beer was.'

'He's always barking at nothing, Líf. Even in town. It doesn't take anything special.' Garðar moved just enough to make room for the two women on the narrow bank. 'We'll walk from here the little way down to the shore and along it for a bit. Nothing's going to happen and it'll do you both good to see that there's nothing bad hidden behind the next rock. Maybe then I'll get a break from all your nonsense.' Putti stared at Garðar and barked when he said nothing more. It was hard to say whether he agreed with him or not.

They set off silently, and it wasn't until Katrín spotted a can stranded at the mouth of the stream that the silence was broken. They all sped up and even Putti seemed to recover his good mood, lifting his tail, which had hung down since they left the house. Triumphantly, Garðar fished the can out of the water and they continued their walk along the beach, much more cheerful than before. The smell of the sea was refreshing, too, and Putti ran happily ahead only to turn around, run back and then repeat the game immediately. But

Garðar was the most noticeably chipper of all of them, holding his head high with satisfaction at having been right about the fate of the beer. His happiness seemed to have spread all the way down to his feet, since he'd nearly stopped limping. He was the first to spot the next can, lying in a clump of weed a short distance from the mouth of the stream, and grabbed it saying that they should have brought the bag with them; carrying ten cans home would be harder in practice than in theory. The next two were also lying a little way away, but they had to walk a short distance more before coming upon the fifth. Líf found it and in her delight she momentarily forgot her fear and ran ahead to fetch the gold-coloured can that gleamed in the moonlight. When she turned around triumphantly, holding the can in the air, Katrín couldn't help but smile; all her concerns had blown out to sea on the cold breeze. It was then that Putti stopped abruptly and started growling again. Although Katrín couldn't work out how it was different from the previous growl, it was, seemingly loaded with gravity and fear, as if the dog sensed something threatening it. Or them.

Katrín stopped and grabbed Garðar. She shushed Putti, who whined as he snuggled up close to her legs. Then he stopped. At first nothing could be heard but the crunching of the pebbly beach beneath Líf's feet, but then Katrín heard a low weeping with no obvious place of origin. She held onto Garðar even tighter and whispered: 'Did you hear that?'

Líf was still a short distance from them but near enough to realize that not everything was right, and she stopped. 'What? What's wrong?'

'Come here, Líf. Don't stop.' Garðar tried to appear calm but Katrín could tell that he was alarmed. Although he hadn't answered her, it was clear he'd heard the sound as well. 'Get over here.' Líf didn't move. The beer can in her hand looked slightly bizarre, as if she were at a festival in high summer. 'Don't stand there like a lemon, hurry up!' He had to shout to make himself heard over Putti, who was now barking as loudly as his little body could manage. The weeping was no longer audible through the noise.

When Líf finally came to her senses and started running towards them, Katrín saw what had elicited this reaction in Garðar; not the low sound of someone crying, but a person standing at the top of the beach just behind where the can had been lying. Katrín gasped. Despite the uncomfortable near-certainty that there was someone else in the area, the tiny bit of scepticism that she'd still harboured had kept most of her fear in check. But now there was no longer any room for the slightest doubt. The twilight prevented Katrín from seeing clearly, yet she grasped that the person stood with his cap-covered head hanging down to his chest and his arms dangling; she'd never seen anyone stand like that before. It was as if the person had surrendered to the injustice of the world. Without pondering this any further, she realized that the weeping had come from this pitiful figure. However, it was impossible to understand why it stood there alone, crying. The vague outline of a raincoat made it hard to tell whether it was a man or a woman, but suddenly the person moved, causing Katrín to realize that they were standing even closer than she'd first thought. 'Jesus.' She squeezed Garðar's arm with all her might. 'It's a child.'

Garðar freed himself from her grasp, walked over to Líf, grabbed her shoulder and positioned her forcefully next to Katrín. She was still holding the beer can. 'Stay here.' He didn't wait for an answer, but ran towards the child as fast as the loose pebbles allowed, paying no heed to his sore foot. Katrín was too late to stop him and could only watch him tear off in the direction of the top of the beach where the child was standing. But as he drew nearer it turned on its heel and disappeared into the darkness – with Garðar behind it. The sound of footsteps above the beach faded as the pursuit grew distant. Instead the only sound was Líf's whimpering. Putti was unusually silent as he lay meekly on his stomach between them.

She had to do something, so Katrín raised her hands to her mouth and desperately shouted Garðar's name. But the wind carried her cry out to sea. 'Come on!' Katrín let her hands drop. It was useless yelling her lungs out; they had no other choice but to wait on the cold beach for Garðar to return. Despite the fact that she got along well with children, and was generally a kind-hearted person, she sincerely hoped that he would be alone.

There was something more than a little wrong with this child. And whatever it was, they couldn't possibly be capable of solving it.

Chapter 10

Contrary to all forecasts, the weather deteriorated. This didn't surprise Freyr; in fact it was remarkable how mild it had been recently. He had thought a lot about the weather before finally deciding to move west. He had never been much of a one for winter sports, but he knew that Ísafjörður was a true skiers' paradise; after the króna crashed his friends in the south had suggested going for a holiday there instead of Austria or the Italian Alps. But because of the unusual warm spell, these friends still hadn't shown their faces, even though they'd made plans for their visit before Freyr had headed west in the autumn. He hadn't decided whether he was disappointed or relieved at their postponing the trip. Immediately after moving he'd looked forward to their visit, but over time he'd started to fear being reminded of his former life and stirring up memories that he wanted to leave behind, some for good. Regular phone conversations with these friends in the south always featured uncomfortable questions about his future and his life over the next few years. On bad days they conjured up mental images of himself still in Ísafjörður in the hospital's forlorn single-family residence, watching television far into the night. Alone.

The sleet hit the windscreen with increased force and the windscreen wipers were nearly powerless against it, no matter how fast they moved. Freyr held unnecessarily tightly to the steering wheel but consciously relaxed his grip after entering the town limits. The car was old and inexpensive, since it had been all Freyr could afford after his divorce, when he had left to Sara whatever they'd managed to acquire. He had started off with a clean slate and over time would scrape together what he needed, while it was unlikely that Sara would ever be in a condition to work full-time again. In any case, leaving her almost everything freed her from most financial problems, though she still had plenty to deal with. The only condition that he'd set when they divided their possessions was that the house be sold; he knew it wasn't healthy for Sara to roam about the empty house where she would be constantly reminded of Benni and the past. Sara had invested in a decent apartment downtown, although he'd recently heard from a concerned friend of hers that Sara was planning to put the apartment up for sale and buy another one in Ártúnsholt – closer to their old home, no doubt to continue her endless search for their son in the neighbourhood. But as far as that was concerned, he had little say, things being as they were.

The discussion on the radio seemed to be drawing to a close; the entire way over he'd been listening to a depressing interview with an economist who offered an extremely bleak outlook on the nation's financial state. When, by chance, the conversation took a more positive turn, it seemed to surprise the speakers completely, and they nearly shouted each other down trying to get the conversation back on course. Freyr had no idea why he was putting up with this depressing exchange; it wasn't as if there were a shortage of radio stations. However, there was no need to change stations at this point; the hospital was just around the corner. Freyr hadn't intended to end his journey there; he'd only gone for a drive in order to clear his mind, but he'd decided to head there after driving aimlessly up and down the fjord. The television hadn't captured his attention, and he didn't want to go to bed early and take the risk of waking in the middle of the night and lying there, sleepless, worrying about things.

The drive around the fjord had helped him focus his thoughts. The files from Dagný had made him more upset than he'd been in a long time and he felt himself creeping uncomfortably closer to the precipice that Sara had already plunged off. Apart from during the first weeks after Benni's disappearance, Freyr had managed to ignore his most disturbing thoughts; perhaps he had given them free rein now and then, but never for very long. There was nothing either he or Sara could have done to change what had happened. He had to keep that firmly in mind when he started blaming himself for having stayed too long in his office after fetching the insulin the morning that Benni disappeared. It wouldn't have changed anything if he'd come home an hour earlier. Not a thing. Or would it? Naturally, doubt assailed him quite often, but he always packed it away carefully in a suitable place somewhere in his head before turning to other things, usually long before obsession managed to sow its seeds. Sara wasn't as good at this as he was, and he couldn't blame her for that. Few people knew better than he did how difficult it was to rein in such painful thoughts and, unlike him, Sara had never been tough. Now he'd managed to overcome despair once again, forced himself to look the problem in the eye and determine to solve it.

The question that he now faced was undeniably unusual: why had a complete stranger in Flateyri mentioned Benni by name in her suicide note? It didn't look as if there would be any straightforward answer, but he would find it. There was always an explanation, no matter how strange, and he just had to go ahead and search for it. Therefore, in the end he'd decided to go back to the hospital, get the files from Dagný and try to work this out immediately, rather than letting it hang over him until tomorrow. It was out of the question that he'd be able to sit back down in front of the television or do anything else – not tonight, and probably not any time soon.

He took off his jacket and checked if Halla's medical files had been sent over. Freyr had been given the job of going over her medical history for the autopsy report, and all the files were kept at the healthcare clinic in her home town, Flateyri. Amid the day's bustle he'd forgotten to check whether they'd been sent over to Ísafjörður, although they must have been, considering how close the two places were. And indeed they had; a thick envelope marked with his name waited on the secretary's abandoned desk, and he grabbed it after leaving behind a message on a little slip of paper saying that he'd taken the records. He didn't want a tongue-lashing from the grouchy secretary, so he hoped she would be satisfied with the message.

The administrative wing of the hospital was like a graveyard. He met no one on his way to his office and felt relieved; he wouldn't have to explain what he was up to so late in the evening, especially given that he wasn't on duty. Just to be sure, he shut the door behind him so that the room's light wasn't visible if anyone passed by. When he finally sat down behind his desk, he felt like a burglar.

Halla had lived her whole life in Flateyri, meaning her entire medical history came from one place. Apart from the death certificate that was yet to be issued, the records covered the woman's life from the cradle to the grave. If she'd ever suffered from any mental problems, that kind of information would be found here; that is, if her doctor had noticed and recorded it. He decided to start at the beginning and read each page carefully so as not to miss anything. He wanted to find out whether her mental health had been defective and search for an explanation for her strange note. His best theory was that a possible mental disorder had started to manifest itself around the time that Benni had gone missing, and that media coverage of the disappearance had merged with her delusions. It wouldn't be unusual. He also recalled Halla's husband mentioning that it had been around three years since Halla's increased religious interest had started to become noticeable. That also fitted in with this time frame. Benni had disappeared a little over three years ago.

But no such information could be found in the endless list of ordinary ailments and annual flu jabs that marked the milestones in Halla's medical history. Her tonsils were removed when she was eleven, she broke her arm once on a skiing trip, went through three normal pregnancies and had her children, had one stillbirth, cut herself on a knife, and more along those lines. During the past five years her visits to the doctor had increased, but all of them were related to high blood pressure and cholesterol issues for which she was being treated. There was nothing that could be associated in any way with mental illness. The one entry connected with mental health was from when she was thirteen. Her mother had taken her to the doctor because she thought her daughter was behaving peculiarly; she was frightened and unsociable and not entirely herself. The doctor's conclusion was that her condition had to do with puberty, which had just begun, and although Freyr read the report several times over there was nothing to indicate that there was anything unusual about the diagnosis, though these days this kind of thing would be followed up more thoroughly than it had been then. It did catch his attention, however, that this visit had occurred in the same year and at the same time as the break-in at the primary school; the doctor's report was dated December 1953. In order to confirm this he looked in the old police report from Dagný's files, and he was right: the break-in had occurred at the end of November the same year. He couldn't see any connection, but the coincidence was interesting nonetheless. A break-in at the primary school and Halla suffers from depression; a break-in at the preschool under very similar circumstances and Halla kills herself. The connection wasn't exactly crystal clear, but it was still something to ponder.

When it became obvious that there was nothing more to learn from the medical files, Freyr ran through the papers from Dagný again. These had much more substance, as they were formal police reports and other files that had been written in the knowledge that others would be reading them later. He ran his eyes over Dagný's summary of the contents of Halla's handbag, which had been lying on the floor of the church, but which she'd overlooked the first time she'd been at the scene. The bag contained nothing unusual: a make-up bag, a wallet, a little hairbrush, a packet of ibuprofen, some chewing gum, keys, and a mobile phone. However, a note concerning the mobile phone stood out. Its memory was full of messages that all said the same thing: *Find me. Find Benni.* The sender's number was blocked and Dagný's attempts to find it out had been fruitless. The newest messages in the inbox were three months old, which made it difficult to know whether the sender had stopped their harassment or whether the inbox was simply full up and refused to accept any more. Freyr read this information over and over again but only became more confused each time; there was a particular accord between these words and the letter that Halla had left behind. Yet it was difficult to base such a connection on four words. Freyr felt his heart beat faster at seeing his son's name a second time in connection with this suicide, and his headache flared. He put the paper down and tried to compose himself.

He turned to the class photograph that had been damaged during the break-in. The children were arranged in three rows; they stared straight ahead, all with rather befuddled expressions, as if the photographer had snapped the photo by surprise. Naturally, the expressions of the children whose faces the vandal had obliterated weren't visible, but Freyr didn't imagine they'd have been any more unusual in appearance or their smiles any bigger than those of their classmates. Most of the children were dressed in their best clothes; the boys in shirts and ties and the girls in skirts and cardigans. The only exception was a short boy standing at the end of the middle row. He was neither dressed up nor wearing a look of surprise. He seemed extremely sad; his big black eyes weren't staring straight ahead, but away from the group, and as a result he seemed out of place and isolated. He also stood a bit apart from the others, not shoulder to shoulder with everyone else, like the rest, strengthening Freyr's hunch that he was either new to the class or was an outsider to the group for different reasons. His clothes looked scruffy; his trousers were too short and his jumper frayed, worn and badly fitting.

Again Freyr felt irritated at having just a photocopy to hand, since the names of the children beneath the picture were unreadable. He only had a handwritten list of the names of the ones whose faces the vandal had obliterated from the photo. Since he was familiar with none of them but Halla, he wanted to know who the others in this class were, since hopefully some of them still lived in Ísafjörður. He didn't think it was entirely impossible that a former student might provide him with information that hadn't found its way into the police reports. Maybe the children knew who had done the deed back then, even if they hadn't informed the police or the school.

Freyr leaned back in his chair and looked at the messy files, which didn't come anywhere near providing him with a better insight into how Halla was connected with the disappearance of his son. If anything, they'd confused him even more. Maybe the explanation was simply that there was no explanation. For the moment it was difficult to conclude otherwise. All the same, he didn't have to give up immediately. This would haunt him like a nightmare if he stopped now, no matter how little hope he had of finding an explanation. He noticed that it was too late to call Dagný. It was possible that she had further information about the case, and just as likely that she hadn't let him have all the files. She also had the original version of the class photo, where the names of the students could be found. He decided to send her an e-mail, which would be waiting for her the next morning.

As he turned on his computer the door of the office creaked loudly and he looked up. The door opened slowly, as if the visitor had his arms full and were pushing it open with his shoulder. But before it opened wide enough for someone to step through the gap, the door stopped.

'Hello.' Freyr sat motionless. 'Who is it?'

No answer. Only the clicking sound of a defective fluorescent bulb out in the corridor. 'Hello?'

Freyr stood up, annoyed, and opened the door. There was no one there. He looked down the corridor. Nothing. He probably hadn't shut the door properly earlier. He shrugged and shut it behind him, but pulled the knob hard to be certain that the latch fell into place. Then he sat back down at his computer and opened his e-mail. Waiting for him was a message from a colleague of his at the National Hospital. The subject of the message was the name Halla, so Freyr opened the e-mail, doubting whether anything could surprise him in this matter. The message turned out to be quite down to earth compared to everything else. The sender was a doctor at the Research Clinic in Pathology, the man responsible for performing the autopsy on Halla. He wanted Freyr to let him know where he should send the report on the woman's condition, and asked at the end of the message to be sent information on any psychiatric drugs and other medication that Halla had been taking as quickly as possible, as if he assumed that the woman had been undergoing treatment for mental illness. He went on to ask whether Freyr would also compile a general medical history on the woman, especially concerning the formation of scars on her back. Freyr raised his eyebrows, reached for the medical files and flipped quickly through them in search of information on injuries that might have left behind these scars, in case he'd overlooked it. He hadn't. No accidents, illnesses, or anything else suggested such a thing. Freyr replied to the message, informing the doctor that he had the files and would be quick in compiling the information. He then added, after brief deliberation, that he would probably ring him tomorrow morning. It would be easiest to speak to the man directly about the scars, as well as to let him know that Halla hadn't been taking any medication except for high blood pressure and cholesterol.

Before closing his e-mail program he opened another message, this one from Sara. His first reaction had been to leave it unread until tomorrow morning, but he decided it was better to get unwelcome news out of the way. He regretted it as soon as he read the short text. Sara was still stuck in the same rut, asking him to call her since she didn't want to bother him at work again. She desperately needed to talk to him, since she had the feeling that Benni was planning to go after him and she wanted to prepare him for the experience. Freyr sighed. From time to time Sara had said she'd seen and heard Benni, and of all the nonsense that had taken place he found these hallucinations of hers the most difficult to deal with. His patients were one thing and he could deal with their problems; it was another thing altogether when his ex-wife displayed the same behaviour. He closed the message, determined to call her neither tonight nor tomorrow. Over the course of the week Sara would forget about these delusions, and they would be replaced by others that he would be better equipped to deal with.

Freyr started slightly when a click suggested that someone had grabbed the doorknob. Again the door opened as slowly as before, and stopped once there was a small gap. The fluorescent bulb could he heard clicking once more, now with apparently greater frequency.

'Hello?' Freyr leaned over the desk to try to see through

the gap. There was nothing but the blinking of the faulty ceiling light. 'Hello?' A chill passed over him when a familiar voice whispered in response to his call. A voice that had always been lively, contented and joyful, but that now sounded cold and lifeless. A voice that seemed so near, yet at the same time so infinitely far away.

'Daddy.'

Chapter 11

There seemed to be no end to the sleet. Through the bedroom window on the second floor they'd watched the storm move in north from the sea. It appeared like a black, vertical curtain, against which the feeble moonlight was powerless. Just before the sleet hit the house, it was as if a blind were being pulled down over the little light coming from outside, and it took their eyes several moments to become accustomed to the near total darkness. Now, apart from each other's outlines, they could see only the window and the storm pounding it. Although in fact they were lying so close together that none of them needed to wonder where the other two were. Which was good.

'I'll never be able to sleep,' Líf muttered through a thick sleeping bag that she'd pulled up over her head. 'Why did we come here?'

Katrín didn't answer, since there was little to be gained from reminding Líf that it was she and Garðar who were responsible for this nonsense. He was silent too, but she hoped that wasn't a sign he was asleep. It was only fair for him to be the last to enter dreamland; even if he was troubled by the events of the evening, they'd affected Katrín and Líf more. She nudged him with her elbow and was relieved when he winced. So he was awake. The sleet hammered the windowpanes even more forcefully and the draughty window let in a cold gust of wind. 'Does anyone know whether the radiator is still warm?' Katrín asked, though there was only one answer she wanted to hear: that it was still boiling hot and that the firewood in the stove would last all night. There was no way any of them would be persuaded to go down to stoke it. Though she did seem to be the best off: Putti had lain down on her feet, making her toes quite warm.

'I think so.' Garðar's voice was uncomfortably sleepy. 'But that'll hardly last much longer.'

'Then we'll just freeze. I'd rather freeze to death than be stabbed by some crazy child wandering around the countryside here for God knows what sort of crappy reason.' Líf stuck her head out of the sleeping bag to make her opinion on this situation absolutely clear. 'The locks on the doors are useless.'

'There's nothing wrong with the locks, either on the front or the back door. No one's getting in here unless they force them open.' Garðar didn't sound particularly convincing. However, there was more determination in his voice when he went on: 'And that strange child isn't going to turn up here. I don't know where the hell he went, but if he didn't go into one of the houses then I'd say he's on the verge of perishing in the storm.'

'Don't say that!' Katrín hadn't yet been able to form an opinion about the child's presence in this deserted place, but she hoped that he was in the company of adults. Although she'd only seen him from a distance, and for a short time, she knew children well enough from teaching them to realize that this particular one wasn't in his right mind. The thought that a mentally ill child had somehow made his way to the abandoned village, and was now out wandering alone in the storm, was deeply disturbing. 'Is there definitely no point in searching for him?'

'Are you sure it's a boy? I'm not sure, and I chased the kid for a long time.' Garðar yawned. 'But whether it's a girl or a boy, there's absolutely no way I'm going out into this weather to look for them. The child doesn't want anything to do with us, and he or she will be able to get in somewhere if it's cold enough. They'd have to be a total wimp if they couldn't manage to tear a board off a window somewhere.'

Líf had stuck her head back down in the sleeping bag and had to raise her voice in order to be heard. 'Don't even think of feeling sorry for this child, Katrín. I don't care whether you're a teacher or not; that is not a viable option.'

Sometimes life could be simplified by rules and regulations, and this was one such example. Katrín listened to what Líf was saying and suppressed the waves of emotion that rose and fell inside her, as though she were riding on a boat. Now Líf only had to ban her from being afraid and Katrín would be just fine. She shut her eyes and for the first time since they had lain down she thought she might be able to fall asleep.

But then Putti started and gave a low growl. Katrín's toes quivered along with the dog's chest. She couldn't resist the urge to sit up, even though it was dark and she didn't want to see a single thing. 'Why is he growling? Did you hear anything?'

Líf sunk herself deeper into her sleeping bag, emitting a low cry that the down filling muffled even further. Garðar sighed. 'This dog is hopeless. He's just growling because he wants something to eat. Or needs to pee. He's never needed to hear anything to make noise.' In Putti's defence, the wooden floor on the lower storey was creaking loudly. They'd all got to know this noise, which came from loose boards in the kitchen. Now Garðar reacted and sat up next to Katrín. 'What the hell . . .?' Again Líf cried out inside her sleeping bag.

Katrín gripped Garðar's upper arm tightly. 'Could the wood in the house be contracting because of the weather?' She could hear how shrill her voice sounded, but she couldn't care less. 'We'd have heard if someone had come in. Wouldn't we?'

Garðar answered neither question directly. 'Where's the torch?' He felt around on the floorboards next to the mattress and found what he was looking for. 'This is absolutely . . .' He wriggled out of his sleeping bag and looked around for his clothes. 'I'm going to take a look downstairs. It's probably nothing, and I can add some wood to the stove at the same time. I can't guarantee the temperature up here tonight if the weather continues like this.' From the sound of it, he seemed to be having a few problems putting on something over his thick pyjamas. Putti's growl had turned into a pitiful whine, as if he felt as unhappy about Garðar's plan as Katrín did. Líf, however, was silent and motionless in her sleeping bag, so still that it was as if she'd lost consciousness. Katrín longed to follow her example, dig herself further into her own sleeping bag, squeeze her eyes shut and count down the minutes remaining of the night. But she couldn't bring herself to do so. The thought of lying in the darkness and having only Líf and Putti to rely on if Garðar didn't return was far more intolerable than going down with him and maybe running the risk of meeting the child. And what could happen, actually? Children had never made her feel uncomfortable before now, and it was pointless to give in to this kind of hysteria. So she stood up, pushing Putti to his feet at the same time. He stopped whining, so only his breathless panting could be heard.

'Would you mind turning on the torch? I can't find my jumper.' She was pleased to hear how calm she sounded. 'I can help with the stove.' The floor was ice-cold under her bare soles.

Garðar didn't protest, clearly happy with the company. A bright beam of torchlight lit up the room and it took them a few moments to accustom their eyes to the dazzle. Katrín threw on her jumper and slippers and once she'd escaped the iciness beneath her feet and could finally see something, her courage grew and she felt bold enough to go downstairs. 'I'm ready.' Putti moved right up to her and rubbed his side against her legs. This was his way of indicating that he too was ready. She looked at the oblong hump on the floor. 'You wait here, Líf; we'll just be a moment and we have a torch, so nothing will happen.' How a torch, even a powerful one, was supposed to protect them against all misfortune was unclear, but Líf neither said anything nor gave any indication whatsoever that she'd heard Katrín. So Katrín just shrugged and followed Garðar to the landing.

Even with the torch on they had to inch their way carefully down the steep staircase to ground level. It would be easy to hurt oneself very badly on these steps. The beam from the torch seemed less powerful here than it had in the narrow room upstairs. The conical light created long shadows that swayed in rhythm with Garðar's rapid hand movements. It was as if everything were in motion and Katrín stayed close behind Garðar in order to lessen the discomfort she was feeling. 'There's no one here.' Garðar stopped in the living room doorway. The beam was reflected in the window opposite. He was briefly blinded by the glare and had to cover his eyes. 'I'm going to check on the front and back doors, but it was obviously just the weather.' He pulled Katrín up next to him so she could see for herself that there was no one in the living room, but he was careful not to point the torch at the window again. 'This is getting ridiculous.' Having dwindled as they came downstairs, the storm whipped itself up once more. The house creaked and Katrín instinctively wrapped her long jumper tighter around herself.

'Let's check the doors and then throw some wood in the stove. I'm freezing; I can't wait to go back up again.' She looked down at Putti, who seemed to tremble as he stood between them with his tail between his legs. 'See Putti? Poor thing – he looks like he's about to croak.'

Garðar looked at the dog and his scowl became even more exaggerated in the strange light of the torch. More than anything he resembled an actor in a silent movie, interpreting a very surprised man. 'He looks more scared than cold, to me.' Garðar reached down to pat Putti on the head. The dog cowered, avoiding his touch. 'Yes, he's terrified.' Garðar stood up straight. 'He's not used to this weather, poor little thing. Back home we've never seen him freak out, have we, on the rare occasions that it gets stormy?'

Katrín hoped that he was right, that Putti was just frightened by the intensity of the storm. The other possibility was that he sensed the presence of an unfamiliar person, which she found a far more disturbing thought. 'Maybe he needs the toilet.' She wanted to add her own down-to-earth explanation, just for a change.

'He's out of luck, then.' Garðar pointed the beam at the

floor, illuminating the way to the front door. 'He's not going out in this weather, so you can blame me if he pisses in here.' He walked away slowly. They had stacked all sorts of building materials along the walls in the hallway and Garðar took some time to check in all the places where a child might conceal itself. Because of this it took quite a while to cover the short distance, but Katrín felt a sense of relief every time it turned out that there was nothing hidden behind the stuff. She cheered up even more when they got all the way to the door, which turned out to be locked. 'You see? I told you.' Garðar tugged at the doorknob to reassure himself that it was secure. Then he let go, and pointed the torch at the floor. 'What the hell?' He was standing in a puddle. 'Did the damn dog piss on the floor?'

Putti had stayed right up close to Katrín the entire time, shadowing her almost as if they shared one body. 'He hasn't left my side; that's not his doing.'

Garðar squatted down and aimed the torch at the puddle. 'No, it's just water.' He shone the torch along the floor of the hallway leading to the kitchen. More puddles were reflected in the light. Garðar stood up so quickly that Katrín barely managed to move aside. 'Jesus.' His voice was a whisper now, and Katrín's heart began pounding in her chest like never before. Putti sensed that something was wrong and whined again.

'What?' Katrín whispered back. She desperately longed to shut her eyes, throw her arms around Garðar and let him guide her, preferably upstairs and all the way into her sleeping bag. They had heard nothing from Líf and she envied her terribly for not being downstairs with them. Now it appeared that the other option had been better: to hide in the sleeping bag, let Garðar deal with this and hope for the best.

'These are footprints. Someone's come in.' Garðar changed the torch's setting, dulling the light. 'They lead into the kitchen.' This last thing he said in such a low voice that Katrín barely managed to make out the words.

'Let's go upstairs.' She tugged at Garðar, although she knew full well that he would never listen, since there was no sense in going back upstairs if some stranger were there downstairs. It wouldn't stop that person from visiting them upstairs if he so desired. 'What should we do if there's someone there?'

Garðar would probably have replied if the same noisy plank in the kitchen floor hadn't creaked again. Katrín was so startled that she lost her breath and hid her face in Garðar's fleece. She felt the tension in every single muscle in his back and how his heart was beating just as fast as hers. 'Who's there?' Garðar's voice sounded deep and confident, despite everything. 'Will you please show yourself? We can provide you with shelter, but we don't want you here if you don't let us know who you are.'

No reply. The silence in the hallway seemed heavy and dense, as if they were at the bottom of a deep hole. Nevertheless, Katrín wanted to cover her ears; if she heard another creak she would scream with every fibre of her being. Suddenly the silence was broken, but the sound came from an entirely different direction. Líf had heard Garðar and had started to wail something incomprehensible, most likely ordering them to get back upstairs to her. Her shouts broke the trance that had been slowly paralysing them and Garðar headed into the hallway. 'Will you please come out?' As before, no one replied.

'What if he has a knife?' Katrín whispered in Garðar's ear as she stood close behind him, holding onto him tightly. It was either follow him or fall behind, and under no circumstances did she want to be left standing alone in the darkness. 'We left both the bread knife and the meat knife lying there on the table.'

Garðar was silent and took a few determined steps forward. When he suddenly stopped, Katrín realized that they were now standing in front of the kitchen door. She wondered whether she should open her eyes or keep them closed. Yet another creak in the floor, from a distinct direction, helped her decide and she squeezed her eyes shut even tighter. The sound came from the kitchen and the only thing separating them and what caused it was the old, worn-out door. Maybe the person was drawing closer, brandishing two knives. Katrín had to force herself to breathe, so much did this thought unsettle her. Putti growled, quietly but angrily. 'Don't open it.' She couldn't bring herself to stretch to speak into Garðar's ear, but instead spoke directly into the nubby texture of his fleece. Her words didn't have the intended result, because she felt his right arm move in the direction of the door. The floor creaked again, but this time the drawn-out, unbearable sound stopped almost mid-creak as the doorknob and the hinges squeaked.

At first Garðar said nothing and Katrín didn't dare open her mouth to ask what he could see. Then he took two steps forward and she felt the threshold beneath her feet. 'What the hell is going on?' Garðar seemed both surprised and angry. But not afraid.

'What?' Katrín could barely sigh this word. She absolutely did not want to hear the answer, but asked anyway. Maybe the unwelcome visitor had stabbed himself with the knife, since Garðar sounded somewhat relieved.

'There's no one here.' Garðar walked so quickly into the

kitchen that Katrín lost her grip on him and was left behind on the threshold. She opened her eyes and saw him pulling open the only cupboard that could possibly conceal a person, but it turned out to hold nothing but a broom, which fell out towards him. Next he checked the window, but it was closed and latched from the inside. 'What the fuck is going on?' He turned to her. 'Didn't you hear the creak before I opened the door? Someone was in here.'

'Yes.' Katrín wrapped her arms around her body to protect herself from the cold that she now felt more intensely, deprived as she was of Garðar's warmth. Incredulous, she tried to understand the situation. She walked into the kitchen to take a better look, and was aware that Putti wasn't following her. He stood on the threshold, small and pitiful. He was trembling and his short brown fur quivered. She bent down to him and tried to get him to come over, but the dog wouldn't budge. Katrín stood up and turned back to Garðar. Putti would recover as soon as they went back upstairs. 'Could it have been a rat?'

'More like a big, fat person. The floor wouldn't creak under such a small animal. Even Putti walks around here completely silently, and although he's not exactly big, I'd like to see a rat his size.' Nonetheless, Garðar opened the few drawers in the sparse kitchen fittings and shone the torch into each of them. 'And in any case, I don't know where one might hide.' He bent down on one knee and shone the light beneath the cupboard, the stove, and along the entire floor. It gleamed on the same kind of puddles as in the hallway. 'Nothing here.' The torch beam stopped at the back wall of the kitchen. 'What's that?' He stood up and walked closer. 'This wasn't like this before. Was it?'

Katrín went over to him and stared at the black spot on the floor, which had grown larger. 'Is this damp? Maybe that's the explanation for these puddles. It might just be coincidence that they look like footprints.' Garðar knelt back down and shone the light over the edge of the stain. 'It looks like mould.' He stood back up. 'It looks more green than black to me. But I'm no damp specialist. Maybe it comes in all sorts of colours.' He sniffed the air. 'But there's no mouldy smell here. It smells more like the sea.'

Now it was Katrín's turn to bend down and examine the watery footprints on the floor. She inhaled carefully through her nose, perceiving a smell that reminded her of the beach. 'The puddles smell of the sea too, Garðar. It's probably seawater. That doesn't leak into a house.'

Garðar came over to her and sniffed one of the puddles. Not stopping there, he stuck his finger into it and tasted the water before Katrín had a chance to stop him. Then he spat on the floor and pushed Putti away when the dog looked as if it was going to lick up what he'd spat out. 'It's seawater.' The torchlight moved up and down as he stood upright once more. 'I don't get this; someone must have come in here. I just don't understand how.'

Katrín was so uncomfortable looking at the wet footprints that she glanced up from the floor and stared at the kitchen table where they'd had hot cocoa before going to bed. A brown ring from Líf's cup, where the cocoa had splashed out, was still there. But there were other things on the table too: a newspaper that, on closer inspection, appeared to be covering something. 'Garðar.' Katrín was rigid with fear, and quite proud of herself for being able to speak at all. 'Garðar,' she repeated. 'Why are the crosses in here again?'

Before he could answer, the sound of a chunk of wood falling in the stove startled them. Garðar's unsteady hand immediately aimed the torch at the stove and now the wavering beam illuminated the cinder-coloured steel. Katrín was thankful that neither of them had a weak heart and imagined that even if Einar had been alive, he would have suffered heart palpitations that would have led to his death right then and there. 'Jesus, what a shock.' Katrín sighed heavily, then gasped when a scruffy old ball Líf had brought along for Putti came rolling slowly out from under the stove. She threw herself back into Garðar's arms. Through his fleece she once again felt his heart hammering just as fast as her own. 'Is there something under there?' She noticed that Putti had retreated into a corner, where he stared at the toy and gave a low growl. Generally the ball made him happy.

'The floor just shook a bit when the wood in the stove shifted.' Garðar had rarely sounded so unconvincing. 'You'll have to let go of me if you want me to look under the stove. Just to be sure. Nothing living could be under there; it's too hot.' Katrín did as he suggested, though she had to push herself to free her clenched fingers. Garðar's head nearly touched the floor as he bent down on his hands and knees to see under the stove. 'There's nothing there. Actually, that's strange – the floor seems to tilt backwards under there, not forwards.' He stood up and wiped his palms on his trousers.

'I have to go upstairs.' Katrín's voice trembled. 'I can't take any more.' She called to Putti in a croaky voice. He came over to them but seemed cautious, which was unlike him. 'Please, come on.' Garðar opened his mouth to say something but decided against it. He probably had no great desire to stay there any longer than her. They could hear Líf calling to them from upstairs, wanting to know what was going on.

'We're coming.' Because of how she felt, Katrín's voice was hardly loud enough to carry between floors, but since there was no further sound from Líf, she must have heard her.

Garðar shone the torch along the entire length of the room, back and forth, until at last he seemed convinced that there was nothing there. Then he turned back to Katrín and made her walk ahead of him out of the room. He steered her down the hallway towards the stairs. 'Go up. I'll wait here in the meantime.' Katrín didn't have the energy to ask why he wanted to wait downstairs. 'Hold onto the rail, because I need the light down here. I just want to make sure there's no one here who could follow us up.'

He didn't need to say anything more; Katrín hurried into the darkness above her. With one step to go, she got a strange feeling and slowed down. There was nothing to see but the shadowy, empty hallway. Of course she was just confused; nevertheless, she felt the hair rise on her arms as soon as she took the last step and entered the hallway itself. Before she realized what was happening, a door to the side of the landing swung forcefully open and the blow that landed on her knocked her backwards. She felt herself fall and the stairs disappeared beneath her feet.

Chapter 12

The storm had left Ísafjörður that night and continued north to the abandoned settlements in Jökulfirðir. Freyr could time when the storm had subsided almost to the minute; he hadn't slept a wink, and at first the constant pounding on his bedroom window had helped to keep him calm until he stuck the headphones from his iPod in his ears and allowed the music to take over. It was quite clear to him that he was losing his grip on reality; in fact he already had, according to all the traditional definitions that he applied to his patients. He'd heard voices and seen things, had lost all connection to his real surroundings, as he'd always feared would happen. It was awful to think that he'd left Sara so that he wouldn't end up like this, when perhaps it was inevitable after all. Perhaps he hadn't split up with her in time; the seeds of mental illness had already managed to sprout roots when he packed into cardboard boxes the little that he took with him. In fact he wasn't particularly surprised at this development; what surprised him more was how realistic unreality felt. Now he understood better all those patients who had sat before him and described the most extraordinary things without blinking, convinced that their fantasies were part of ordinary life. It was incredible, really. All his life he'd thought that people experienced these kinds of delusions like a high; they were like a hazy reality that would be easy to distinguish from what was considered normal, at least when they came back down. But this had proved not to be the case. He'd heard Benni's voice in precisely the same way as he did the voices of his colleagues on ordinary workdays.

Nor were the visual hallucinations any less powerful. When he'd finally forced himself to look into the corridor the night before, he'd seen his son running away, in the same clothing as he'd worn on the day he disappeared, and exactly the same height. Although common sense told Freyr that this was impossible, he was convinced his eyes hadn't deceived him. It was no use reminding himself that Benni was dead, there could be no doubt, and that even if he were still alive, he would have grown much taller in the three years that had passed since his disappearance. The best that Freyr could come up with was that it had been an entirely different child, a child with the same hair as his son's and wearing the same kind of clothing. But he knew how absurd such a coincidence would be, and was confused by the way the boy had vanished. After a long chase, during which the boy had passed through one door after another, always well out of reach, he ran into the medical ward and vanished. When Freyr ran in panting, out of breath, no one there had seen anyone. Two nurses whom Freyr had nearly knocked over when he went around a corner had shaken their heads, unable to conceal their shock at Freyr's appearance and his visible agitation. He was gasping for breath, his hair all messed up, and had difficulty explaining what was going on. It didn't help that according to the roster, he was off duty and didn't have any actual business being at the hospital that evening. When the glances exchanged by the nurses became uncomfortable, Freyr had excused himself and left. That was when he first became dimly aware that he was losing it. There had been no child there, let alone his long-dead son.

Now he was back at work again, standing in front of the mirror in the staff toilets. He pulled himself away from it and drew a deep breath. The glossy yellow wall tiles had always got on his nerves, but now he found the way they framed his haggard face particularly unbearable. His eyes were bloodshot and his face puffy after his sleepless night. In addition, before leaving for work he'd been too pre-occupied about whether he'd lost his mind to remember to shave, so he was also sporting a dark six o'clock shadow. He was fairly certain that both patients and co-workers suspected he'd been drinking the night before. But there was nothing he could do about it except hope that the day would be gentle with him; he was perfectly used to working for forty-eight hours straight, so that held no fear. It was a lot better than lying at home and letting his mind wander in circles. Here he could concentrate on work, and while he did that there was no time to be chasing after hallucinations. However, one thought kept creeping into his head again and again, despite his pushing it aside just as quickly: his conscience gnawed at him. Of course he should let his boss know that he was worried about his own mental state. But Freyr knew how that would turn out; he would be sent home for a ten-day break to recover, which meant an increased workload for his colleagues. So it wasn't just the idea of hanging around at home with his thoughts that made him shudder. However, he did resolve to go straight to his supervisor as soon as he thought he could no longer do his job and the safety of his patients was compromised.

But so far, there didn't appear to be any danger of that.

Things seemed to be going perfectly normally and he neither saw nor heard anything that might be considered unusual. However, this all led him back to the same conundrum: if he *were* suffering from a serious mental disturbance, he would be ill-equipped to judge what was normal. But despite all his specialized education in the field of psychiatry and his experience of helping those who had a confused sense of reality, he was convinced deep down that this was not the case. It couldn't be. It simply mustn't be. Freyr had paid particular attention to the nurse who'd gone on rounds with him, and she showed no sign of thinking that he was behaving unusually. To check, he'd deliberately made a ridiculous remark about a patient's condition and felt relieved when the woman furrowed her brow and shot him an inquisitive look. It gave him hope that the events of yesterday evening had been an isolated occurrence and now all was right in his head again.

Now Freyr hurried to his office to see whether he could reach the doctor who was to perform the autopsy on Halla. He had already called twice that morning, but reached a switchboard operator who suggested he try later; the man was in the building but apparently not in his office. In the empty corridor he hesitated slightly. Then he carried on, determined not to see or hear any sort of nonsense. The annoying squeaking of his work shoes suddenly grew distinct. The linoleum floor was uncomfortably shiny. The fluorescent light continued to blink erratically, making loud clicks. He would have to remember to chase up the caretaker and remind him to change it. He was actually thankful for the damn bulb when he grabbed the doorknob to his office with a clammy hand. Focusing on such an ordinary object and its maintenance was enough to keep the image of his son running down the corridor from entering his head, as he'd feared it might.

Freyr shut the door behind him but then stopped at the recollection of how it had opened twice, apparently on its own. Of course it was possible that there was something wrong with it – loose hinges or a broken knob had caused it to open, which had then triggered the hallucinations that had just been waiting to appear after such prolonged mental strain and general fatigue. This all seemed very rational to him as he walked over to his desk with the door wide open behind him. Until the door slammed shut with a loud bang. An icy chill passed over Freyr. He forced up some saliva, swallowed it and continued towards his desk as if nothing had happened. If the door were in need of maintenance, it could just as well shut on its own as open without warning. When he sat down he could only stare at the door, every nerve taut and every muscle tense, entirely prepared for his body to jerk if the door should open. But nothing happened. Without taking his eyes off the door he picked up the phone, dialled the switchboard and asked to be put through to the caretaker. He was relieved to hear his own voice sounding completely normal; he was in a bad enough state without his voice growing shrill as well.

The caretaker answered after six rings, just as Freyr was about to hang up. He was an older man, calm and easygoing. He seemed surprised when Freyr told him why he was calling and said that he'd changed the bulb that morning. It took Freyr a little while to convince the man that just a minute ago he'd watched it blink and in the end the caretaker reluctantly agreed to come and have a look. It didn't help when

Freyr asked whether he knew if there were anything wrong with the door to the corridor; if the building was crooked or something that could cause the door to open or close without warning. At first the man didn't understand the question. Freyr added that his office door had a tendency to open or shut without anyone appearing to come near it. The caretaker said that as far as he knew the building was pretty robustly built and right-angled. He added that if the building leaned, Freyr's door would either open or close, not both. Unless Freyr thought it was rocking from side to side?

Freyr said goodbye and hung up, his cheeks flushed, and turned to the next phone call. Although he knew that Dagný was probably waiting to hear from him regarding the files that she'd loaned him, he couldn't imagine speaking to her with things as they were. He was even less keen on meeting her, considering his current appearance. He would see how he felt at the end of the day, and then call, if he felt confident enough. Instead he dialled the direct number of the doctor at the Research Clinic in Reykjavík, who answered on the first ring. He introduced himself and they exchanged a few pleasantries before turning to the matter in hand: Halla, waiting ice-cold on a hard steel bench for her autopsy.

'It would actually be better if you could come down here.' The doctor, who was called Karl, was obviously surprised that Freyr hadn't seen any mention of the scars on Halla's back in her full medical history. 'Maybe they're from self-inflicted wounds, and possibly they're connected to her mental condition. I'm no specialist in that field and I'd welcome some assistance.'

'The morning flight has gone, so I can't come until around suppertime. Wouldn't that be too late?' Freyr felt an indescribable longing to get away for a bit. 'I could spend the night, of course, and come to you first thing in the morning, if that's more convenient for you.'

Karl thought for a moment but then said he preferred the second option. 'We're cutting back here, so the lab closes at five. We could always do the autopsy after hours, but I don't particularly want to work for the government for free these days.'

It was different for Freyr. He wasn't even planning on asking for his plane ticket to be reimbursed, in case it complicated things and lost him the opportunity to get a little break. He would pinch a day from his summer holidays instead if he needed his supervisor's permission to go. 'See you at eight tomorrow morning, then.'

'I'd better roll Halla back into the fridge.'

The old man had taken a turn for the worse. This didn't particularly surprise anyone, least of all him. The bags under his eyes were yellowish, and despite the fever that had settled into his body, his face was deathly pale. Even his cough couldn't inject colour into his cheeks; all the weak rattle did was interfere with what he was trying to say. 'Sorry.' He raised a bony hand to his nose and mouth and used a handkerchief to wipe a drop of saliva from his bluish lower lip. 'I remember these kids well; I taught their class the year after the photo was taken. Their class teacher was in an accident and I filled the position, since my previous class had gone on to secondary school in the spring.' He placed the photo in his lap and leaned back on his pillow. The hospital bed was in the upright position, meaning he was sitting up rather than lying down. 'There was a lot of speculation as to why the vandal chose this photo in particular. There were others hanging on the same wall, but he left all of them alone.'

'Did the children he picked out have something in common? The ones he defaced?' Freyr had brought the list with him and read out the names. 'Were they particular friends, a clique or anything like that?'

'We never knew that directly. At playtime it didn't look as if they'd formed a special group, although they were all good friends. Most of them had one specific friend, boy or girl, a kind of best friend. Of course, that sort of friendship you notice; kids who always want to sit next to each other and who stick together like glue outside class. In other respects we didn't know much about their social lives. There was more discipline in those days and the school tried to teach the poor things as much as possible in the shortest amount of time. There wasn't this emphasis on life skills or whatever it's called that's taken over education these days. They'd probably formed a group outside school but we teachers generally had our hands full with our own children, without having to worry about the others outside the school grounds. That was their parents' job.'

Freyr nodded. 'Do you think that any of these children are still living in Ísafjörður, or nearby? I'm particularly interested in speaking to Lárus Helgason.' He decided not to mention that of those whose picture had been subjected to the vandal's wrath, Helgason was the only one still alive. He probably had information up his sleeve that he hadn't previously shared.

The old man pondered this for a moment. 'As far as I know, he moved away from Ísafjörður long ago. He went south as a young man to study auto engineering and never returned. But I could well be remembering incorrectly.'

'I'll probably find him in the phone book.' Freyr smiled at the man. 'Do you remember Halla at all? She was in this class, but she lived all her adult life in Flateyri.'

Again the old man had to think for a moment before answering. 'Sure, sure. A chubby little dark-haired girl. Quite a rascal, as I recall.' He looked at Freyr. 'Her father was a drunk. Treated her mother and the kids badly. The girl coped incredibly well, given the circumstances. She was sharp, though you wouldn't say clever, exactly. Fortunately, none of his offspring inherited the sins of the father. Each of them was more good-tempered than the last.'

'That's a blessing.' From what the old man was saying, Halla's father might well have suffered from an untreated psychiatric disorder. In those situations it wasn't unusual for people to turn to the bottle. If this were the case, there was an increased likelihood that Halla had struggled with psychological difficulties, despite her managing to hide the symptoms from her family members. 'There have been some pretty bad alcoholics round here over the years. But it's growing less and less common, I think. People are more aware of the dangers of alcohol than they were in those days.' The old man picked up the photo again. 'The father of this little chap here had a great deal of trouble with alcohol. Loathsome man.'

Freyr looked at the photo and saw that the man's crooked finger pointed at the ragged boy standing just outside the group, at the end of the middle row. 'Did he turn out okay, the poor kid?'

'Bernódus? No, I can't say he did. A terrible business.'

Freyr's mouth suddenly went so dry that he was tempted to drink the glass of water that undoubtedly held the old man's dentures at night. 'Did you say Bernódus?'

'Yes, that was his name, poor thing. He wasn't in the class when I took over, so I never taught him, but I remember his name well. You don't easily forget someone who ends up like that.'

'Did he turn out to be a drunk, too?' The old man put down the photo and Freyr took it. The boy's eyes stared back at him from the poor copy; it looked as if the photocopier had taken particular care with his face. *Bernódus.*

'No, no. It didn't ever get that far. He disappeared.' The old man coughed again. 'Without a trace.'

Chapter 13

The storm had subsided but had left the house damp, making the cold unbearable. It had proved impossible for Líf to force herself into a fourth jumper, though she had struggled for some time to make it fit over the other three. She was restless and complained bitterly that she couldn't stand the itching from the wiry threads that managed to poke through from her woolly socks to her cotton ones. Of the two evils she still felt it better to scratch than to freeze to death, so she settled for the itchiness and simply scratched herself more often with an old knitting needle that Garðar had found between two loose floorboards. Katrín found it difficult to witness Líf's nervous agitation, as she herself shivered and shook on her kitchen stool; she couldn't work out whether it was from the cold or the shock she'd suffered the night before. She was bruised all over from the fall, but considering how much worse it could have been, she wasn't complaining.

It was impossible for her to recall how she'd fallen; which part of her body was hammered by which step and when it was that she'd hit her head so hard that she lost consciousness. Most likely it had occurred immediately after she lost her balance, judging by how little she remembered of the fall and Garðar's description of how she'd tumbled down like a rag doll. According to him, what had saved her was how flexible her body had been as she tumbled. After Katrín regained consciousness she lay at the bottom of the stairs and stared bewildered at the worried faces of Garðar and Líf. But before she opened her eyes, what they were saying had managed to slip through the fog in her head, which cleared quickly, and she thought their words were probably the reason why she'd taken the accident so well. Líf had thought that she was dead, and in her peculiar state of mind Katrín had thought so too, and felt sadness at her own demise wash over her. When Garðar said that he had found a pulse, an incredible sense of relief washed over Katrín and nothing else mattered any longer, neither pain nor the headache from which she was still suffering, although she'd more or less managed to get used to it.

'Are you sure you're not feeling ill?' Garðar looked at Katrín and she could read in his expression how bad she must look. 'If you have concussion, we have to do something about it.' He didn't elaborate any further, and Katrín doubted he had any idea how they should treat her if this was indeed the case. They'd agreed to call the skipper and ask him to come and get them, and in fact there was nothing else they could do for her until help arrived.

'No. That's probably the one thing I'm not suffering from at the moment.' Katrín's voice was hoarse; she hadn't said much since she'd woken up. She'd fallen asleep in the middle of speaking; the shock had overcome her after Garðar and Líf had helped her upstairs and into her sleeping bag. They hadn't understood anything of what she was saying, since the words had tumbled from her lips either in a torrent or one by one between sobs. This had tested Garðar and Líf's patience, as well as their interpretive abilities, but they tried as best they could to comfort her. Eventually sleep provided her with the solace that she so desired; one minute she was awake and whimpering about wanting to go home, and the next she was floating in a dreamland where she and Garðar were newlyweds once more and incredibly happy. Although she couldn't recall the dream in detail, she remembered that when she woke she'd expected a dejected little person to be standing over her, staring at her from beneath its cap, its face hidden in darkness. She dared not open her eyes, but when she finally did, no such thing met her gaze; the only thing she saw was the room's shabby, dirty ceiling.

Katrín rubbed her forehead. 'Do you have a mirror, Líf?' Curiosity plagued her, although she actually had no desire to see how she looked. But when she was handed the little cosmetic mirror, she swallowed twice before holding it up to her face. Fortunately, her appearance turned out to be better than she'd hoped: a scrape on one cheek and a bit of a bruise beneath one eye. She tilted the mirror upwards and held a finger to a large red mark extending outwards from beneath her hairline.

'None of it's permanent.' Líf stood over Katrín and smiled, her expression melancholy. 'You'll look lovely again.' She turned to Garðar. 'That is, if the boy doesn't manage to kill you.'

Garðar tried to conceal how annoyed he'd grown at Líf talking like this; ever since they'd woken up she had carried on a continual monologue of her concerns about recent developments, despite the fact that they'd already decided to abandon the place. She was convinced that the boy had been behind the accident, based on Katrín's description of how quickly and unexpectedly the door had slammed into her. Garðar, on the other hand, tried to maintain that it had been caused by a draught, even though all the windows had been closed.

Katrín wasn't willing to form an opinion on this, or at least not out loud. In her heart she knew that the wind hadn't opened the door. On the other hand, she admired Garðar's patience and his ability to rule out the more obvious, but less pleasant explanation. 'That's enough nonsense, Líf, just stop thinking about it. It's not helping, you going on and on.' He ran a box cutter along the brown tape on one of the boxes they thought the former owner had left behind. 'We'll go through this stuff while we wait for the light to get better, then we'll hike up the hill and call the skipper. I thought we were agreed on that.'

'Only if you tell us exactly what happened to the previous owner. I can't believe you kept it a secret.' Líf pouted. 'I would never have let you drag me here if I'd known about it.'

Katrín paid little attention to this. Líf was the sort of person who heard only what she wanted to hear in any given situation. Einar, God rest his soul, probably *had* told her about it when he bought the house. And although Katrín was furious at Garðar for having hidden it from her, she felt she had to defend him. Until now she'd been content to listen to them bicker about it, but she'd gained new strength after seeing her own face and realizing that the scrapes and bruises on it didn't make her look like the Elephant Man after all. 'Are you quite sure he was here when he disappeared? Couldn't he have been on a boat, or out hiking, or something like that?'

'According to Einar he vanished from here.' Garðar opened the box. 'He was on the same mission as we are, to fix up the house, but when they came to get him they found no one. Obviously I have no idea whether he died of exposure somewhere outside, I have no way of knowing precisely what happened. He was never found. I didn't want to bother you with it, but I think it matters in light of the bizarre break-in last night.'

'*He* killed him.' It was useless to argue with Líf; her words and tone of voice brooked no argument. 'He pushed him down the stairs, then strangled him.'

'Exactly how he died doesn't matter now. We'll go through this stuff and see if he left anything behind that could help us figure out what's going on.' Garðar didn't look directly at either of them as he spoke. 'You agreed that we would, remember?' Katrín had had no say in the decision, since it had been made before she regained the power of speech. Just coming down the stairs had proved difficult enough for her; she'd only just managed to inch her way down and into the kitchen, where, shivering, she took a seat and listened to the others' conversation. She'd refused to go down until Garðar had thrown the crosses out of the house and assured her that there were no new footprints.

'Didn't you say he disappeared three years ago?' Katrín was praying this wasn't linked to the incident last night, and the more she thought about it, the less likely it seemed. 'The child can't be older than eleven or twelve, so three years ago he would have been eight or nine. There's no way such a young child could have killed a man, let alone survived here all this time.'

'Not unless someone else is here with him.' Líf did have a point, and she couldn't conceal her satisfaction at having come up with such a clever theory.

Garðar didn't reply, but continued to rummage through the box. 'Maybe there's a radio in with this stuff. Who knows?

That would save us having to trek up the hill. I don't know about you, but I'm not really looking forward to that.'

Katrín looked out of the window, at a scene very different from before. In place of the dull earth colours of sleeping vegetation, everything was white. The sleet had turned into snow during the night, and a thin layer of it covered the ground. The snow had stopped falling, but she quaked nonetheless at the thought of schlepping up the hill; she was in no fit state for the walk and there might be icy patches concealed beneath the snow, plus they had no spikes for their shoes or anything like that. And since there were three of them, there was no way to split the group in half without one of them ending up alone, meaning she had no choice but to go along. She wasn't going to stay behind on her own, and she couldn't imagine Garðar making the journey by himself. A sudden gust of wind blew up the snow in front of the wrecked porch and tiny snowflakes danced in the air. Then, just as suddenly, everything went completely still. Katrín turned her attention back to the kitchen table and the dusty boxes. Garðar had taken several items from the first box, none of which appeared likely to tell them much: two books, a hammer, a wallet and a torch. She reached for the latter and tried to turn it on, but the batteries were dead.

'Doesn't a radio need electricity?' Líf went over to where Katrín sat and picked up the wallet.

'I don't know, but if there's one here, it probably runs on batteries. Otherwise it would have been pointless to lug it up here.' Garðar rearranged the things in the box in order to see deeper inside. 'What a pile of fucking junk.'

'Who do you suppose did this?' Katrín put down the torch and picked distractedly at the tape on the side of the box.

'He could hardly have packed all this up before he disappeared.'

'Maybe the rescue teams that came to search for him. Or someone connected to his estate.' Garðar pulled out two tea towels from the box and looked at them. 'The stuff seems to have just been thrown in, so I doubt it was him, or anyone close to him. I know *I* wouldn't pack my belongings this way. Everything's all mixed up.' He put the checked towels back and pulled out a brightly coloured plastic plate. 'There's no system at all.'

'His name was Haukur. Haukur Grétarsson.' Líf waved a credit card she'd found in the wallet.

'We don't know that's his.' Garðar grabbed the card and looked at it before handing it back to Líf and continuing with his rummaging.

'Whoever packed the boxes probably thought they'd be taken to town soon after. The wallet is full of credit cards, receipts and coins.' Líf flicked through the receipts. 'But if the man put these in the boxes himself, he must have committed suicide. No one packs away his own wallet.'

'What did he buy?' Katrín picked up the bits of paper Líf had already examined. The receipts were just over three years old and the amounts were all quite small: a few thousand krónur at Hagkaup supermarket, a haircut at a barber's near Hlemmur bus station, Domino's pizza, Subway, petrol. The next batch was much the same; faded slips of paper containing useless memories, records of trivial everyday purchases. Suddenly goose bumps sprang up on Katrín's arms. 'These receipts suggest that Haukur was a bit of a loner. Most of them are from supermarkets and fast food places, and he never spent much.'

'I guess they're from three years ago and everything's gone up since then, but he can't have had many people to invite round for dinner,' said Garðar. 'I know the fact that he didn't have any close relatives or a spouse made the sale of the estate much easier.' He pulled out some folded pieces of paper, opened them, read what was written on them and grinned. 'Awesome!' He turned the two pages towards the others; a receipt from Byko Hardware Store and a pencil drawing marked with dimensions. 'This is a drawing of the septic tank connections.' Katrín and Líf stared at him in bewilderment, clearly not sharing his excitement. 'Don't you get it? We can connect the toilet.' His joy faded slightly. 'Well, maybe not now, but on the next trip.'

'The next trip?' Líf shook her head and laughed mirthlessly. 'I'm about as likely to come back here to connect a septic tank as I am to take a bath in it once it's full.'

Garðar put the pages down. 'Okay. Maybe you won't come with me, but I can still come.' He seemed disappointed at their lack of reaction. 'We can raise the price of the rooms if there's a toilet here.' He closed the box and grabbed another. 'In the spring this will all seem like a bad dream. I promise you.' Neither Líf nor Katrín uttered a word, although Katrín had her own opinion. She would never let him come here alone, or even accompanied. This was an evil place, full of bad feelings. Garðar, who had opened the second box, was rummaging silently through it. All this produced was a pair of binoculars, which Líf was quick to grab. She went over to the window and inspected the view.

'There's one thing we could do.' Katrín watched as Garðar chose a third box and opened it. 'We could move over to the doctor's place. We could watch the house from there through the binoculars, and maybe we'll see how the child gets in while we wait for the boat.' Truth be told, Katrín was less interested in knowing how he got in than in getting out of this house and into alternative accommodation. Of course what she wanted most was to set sail immediately for Ísafjörður and fly home from there, but she knew the skipper would need time to get to them. He could hardly drop everything and come at a moment's notice. She felt around in the pocket of her outermost jumper and felt the comforting shape of her mobile phone. She took it out and the familiar object warmed her cold palms. Soon they would be standing on the hilltop with the skipper at the other end of the line. Out of habit she turned it on. Nothing happened.

'As I said before, it's best if we stick to our original plan.' Garðar took some notebooks out of the box and leafed through them. 'It'll soon be light enough for us to set off and go and call.'

Katrín stared at the grey screen. 'My phone's battery is dead. I must have turned it on by accident and the battery ran out.' She shook the phone frantically, not believing her own explanation.

'What?' Garðar wiped the dust from his palms and went over to her. 'That's weird.' He took out his own phone and turned it on. Holding it slightly away from him, he gawped at it in disbelief. 'You're kidding me,' he said to himself, before shaking the phone in the same way as Katrín had shaken hers. He pushed the power button again, much more firmly than before. It made no difference. The phone was dead. 'Oh, come *on*.' He turned to Líf, who was still gazing complacently out of the window through the binoculars.

'Líf. Try switching on your phone. There's something wrong with ours.'

Líf turned around slowly and let the binoculars drop. The look of fear on her face was a familiar one to them by now. 'No.' She shook her head fervently. 'I don't want to. Let's just go up the hill and try them there. I'm sure my phone is fine.'

'Give me your phone, Líf.' Garðar put out his hand. 'We're not going anywhere if we don't have a phone that works.' When he realized that Líf was once more on the verge of breaking down, he hurriedly added: 'If it's dead too, we'll figure something out. There's no reason to panic.'

Líf opened and closed her mouth twice without saying anything. Then she tentatively handed Garðar a bright pink clamshell phone, adorned with glittering rhinestone hearts. 'Don't tell me if it doesn't work. I don't want to know.' She squeezed her eyes shut, but couldn't resist the temptation to peek. Katrín realised she had crossed her fingers without meaning to.

'I don't fucking believe this.' Garðar hammered on the keys of the little pink phone so hard that one of the hearts fell off.

'How is this possible?' Katrín uncrossed her fingers and took the phone from Garðar to see for herself. The screen of the gaudy little thing was just as blank as hers had been. 'How can three phones that have been turned off the entire time be dead?'

Líf muttered something incomprehensible and let herself fall back against the wall. The dark blue of her irises stood out starkly in her pale face. 'Why did you try it? Maybe it would have worked if we'd just gone up and turned it on when we were up there. You jinxed it.'

Garðar covered his eyes with his hand and took a slow, deep breath. He stood motionless for a few moments, before letting his hand drop and sighing loudly. 'Okay. This isn't exactly what I had planned.' He tapped lightly with two fingers on the box. 'I can't deal with this right now. Unless you want me to punch a hole in the wall and add one more task to the list of renovations, I've got to pretend this thing with the phones isn't happening.' He looked at Líf and then at Katrín, who recognised this reaction all too well; he couldn't cope with this sort of crisis at all. Her headache had intensified and it felt as if it were crushing her brain. 'Maybe something will come out of these boxes to change things.'

Katrín could see Líf was stopping herself from saying something, obviously negative. Personally, she could think of nothing that would lighten the atmosphere, which at the moment she imagined was similar to that on board a submarine trapped under ice. So she followed Líf's example, sat back down on her stool and watched miserably as Garðar rummaged through the latest box. In the silence they could now hear sounds that had escaped them as they were talking – the low groan of the wind and some cracks and creaks in the house, which made Katrín's skin crawl. Líf twitched in fright at each sound. 'Look!' Garðar pulled a black zipped-up case out of the box. 'Isn't this a video camera?' He unzipped the bag quickly. 'It is!' A neat silver camera emerged. He leaned his head back and closed his eyes. 'Please let the battery in it fit one of the phones.'

'You're not telling me that still works.' Líf's voice was devoid of its usual agitation and anxiety. 'That would be ridiculous.'

After fiddling with the camera for a few moments, Garðar

discovered how to turn it on, only to find out that of course the battery was dead. It was also a chunky block that was far too large for their phones; the idea had been ludicrous to begin with, formed from desperation rather than ingenuity. However, instead of putting the camera down, he continued to examine it, eventually opening a little compartment in its side that held the memory card. 'I wonder if it's possible to view this on a camera?'

'It won't fit in mine,' said Líf. 'The card is too big.'

Katrín reached for the card. 'It's like the one in our camera.' They'd bought the camera five years ago when it was the latest model, but it looked rather lame now in comparison to Líf's shiny new one. 'Still, I don't know whether you can look at videos on it.'

Garðar hurried to the front entrance to fetch the camera, ignoring Líf's grumble that it wouldn't work, since their camera battery was probably dead as well. He came back with the camera and immediately replaced its memory card with the other, smiling from ear to ear when the camera switched itself on.

'There!' He turned the little screen towards them where they could see the first frame of each piece of footage on the card. Most of them showed the house or its surroundings, and seemed to have been taken to document repairs or construction. 'He probably wanted evidence of the work he put into the house. He must have had a lot to do.' Garðar flipped to the next screen, which showed more opening frames. 'These are completely black.' He raised his eyebrows and tried to play one of them. Líf and Katrín had taken up position on either side of him in order to see better. Katrín's headache eased off when she stood up, although other parts of her body moaned in pain with every movement.

They watched the dark screen and listened hard to catch the vague sound from the camera's little built-in speakers. They heard several of the house's familiar little creaks and groans, then the recording stopped without warning. Garðar tried the next one, which was also so dark that it seemed as if the screen were turned off. He was about to stop the playback and try another clip when a more rhythmic creaking, like footsteps on floorboards, came from the camera. It was only through sheer luck that he didn't drop the camera when the frightened voice of the cameraman could be heard whispering: 'He's in here.'

Chapter 14

On his way to the police station to meet Dagný, Freyr thought about coincidences. His shift had passed unbearably slowly, as if he were wading through treacle. Incredibly, Freyr had somehow managed to do his job without his colleagues and patients noticing how out of sorts he was. Still, he couldn't refrain from virtually running out of the hospital when his shift ended. When he got into his car he stuck the key in the ignition with a trembling hand. Dagný had promised to look into the disappearance of the boy in Ísafjörður nearly sixty years ago, and while Freyr was occupied with work he hadn't been thinking about how this tragedy could be linked to his son's case – it had taken all his energy to concentrate on the down-to-earth problems of his patients. Now that he'd had time to consider this question on the way to the police station, his feeble hope that there might finally be an explanation for Benni's disappearance had dwindled.

The two disappearances were strikingly similar, yet so far apart in time that there couldn't possibly be a connection between them. And yet. He didn't like coincidences, which more often than not turned out not to have any explanation at the end of the day. But what was a coincidence? Wasn't it when similar things occurred within a short interval? Could sixty years be considered a short interval? If two meteorites landed in the same place on Earth several centuries, or even millennia, apart, you'd call it a coincidence. But what about events in people's lives? Wasn't the occurrence of similar events with a break of several decades – spanning more than two generations, even – too long a time to merit the term coincidental? He wasn't sure. Children didn't often disappear without a trace, though it was unfortunately more common than rocks crashing down through the Earth's atmosphere. The less frequently something happened, the longer the amount of time there could be between events for them still to be coincidental. So was this coincidence, then? Freyr couldn't decide, and his mental turmoil was accompanied by a feeling of hopelessness, making it impossible for him to focus on anything.

He knew it would help to talk through this out loud, make sentences out of his ideas and see how they sounded. Another person's questions would also help him to get his thoughts on track, yet he still said nothing and couldn't bring himself to air them as he sat next to Dagný at the police station. Instead he tightened his grip on the edge of the sturdily built table in front of them, doubtless chosen for its durability, and flipped with his other hand through the old police reports he was forcing himself to concentrate on. Judging by the serious look on Dagný's face, there was no lack of focus on her part. Yet she must have been tired, with a long working day behind her. If she weren't being so obliging to him, she would have gone home long ago. 'I don't think we'll find out anything more about this.' Dagný placed the final piece of yellowed paper on the stack in front of her. The old-fashioned black lettering on the report made Freyr think vaguely of the sound of striking typewriter keys. 'Of course the boy might be mentioned in other reports, since his disappearance attracted some attention, but we can hardly go through all the reports made by the Ísafjörður police in search of it.' She smiled sadly at him. 'I enquired about this through a colleague of mine who's retiring from the department. He remembered it from his childhood and was absolutely certain that the boy was never found. So we haven't missed anything.'

'No.' Freyr re-read the final report that seemed to have been made about the case. It was dated to the feast of St Þorlákur, 23 December 1953, almost two months after the boy disappeared. A man thought he'd seen a shabbily dressed boy behaving oddly on the beach near the harbour late in the evening, in the blistering cold, and the description fitted Bernódus perfectly. The boy had stood there still as stone, staring down as icy seawater washed over his feet. When the man called to him and said that he was going to come down onto the beach himself, the boy had disappeared, making the man think he had probably fallen into the sea. His search of the beach proved fruitless, so he notified the police. The investigation was neither long nor detailed, since there was little that could be done about the situation. The child wasn't found and there were no signs of his whereabouts that evening, nor the next day when the search was renewed. The man was asked to describe the child in more detail, and it seems that a clear-sighted police officer had realized that the boy's tattered clothing fitted with the description of the boy who'd gone missing in the autumn. 'The investigation of the boy's disappearance seems to have come to a swift end. At least it was far more detailed in Benni's case. I hope this is a sign of changed times and doesn't reflect the difference in the two boys' social statuses.' Bernódus had been the son of a single father with a drinking problem and mental health issues, while Benni had had two reliable and concerned parents, who would never have settled for anything less than a full investigation.

'I suppose it's a bit of both. The police's working methods have changed, as they have in other professions.' Dagný took the papers they'd gathered and stood up to go and photocopy them. 'If you and your wife hadn't involved yourselves in the search for your son, it's entirely possible that it would have been called off earlier. The attention would probably have been directed more towards you if you'd seemed unnaturally interested in the details of the case, but in any case, the behaviour of family members always has an influence, one way or another.' She arranged the papers on the desk into a tidy pile. 'In fact, I looked over the files in your son's case in the light of his possible connection to these other cases, and I must say that the police considered you extremely suspicious for a time.' She studied him, obviously wondering how he'd react.

Freyr didn't try to evade it, since there was no reason to. 'I already told you that; I'm not trying to avoid discussing it. It was awful for a while; I was almost out of my mind with worry about my son, and on top of that I was afraid I'd be wrongfully arrested. Amazingly, though, I actually didn't give a damn about myself; it simply didn't occur to me to care, we were so busy grieving at Benni's disappearance.'

'I understand that.' Dagný was still staring at him. 'Did you ever find out what happened to the insulin? The stuff that was missing from the package?'

Freyr relaxed his grip on the edge of the table and rubbed his temple. 'No, it was never found. The drugs never left my sight and I'm well aware that it made the police suspicious at the time, but everything I said was true, and it was all corroborated. I hope there's nothing to the contrary in the reports, but I'm absolutely certain that the police believed me. I didn't take the insulin out of the box.' If he had a hundred krónur for every time he'd wondered about this, he would be a rich man, though unfortunately he had never come to any satisfactory conclusion. He was convinced he'd either been given an incomplete prescription at the hospital pharmacy, and that there'd never been more than one syringe pen in the box, or that the missing needles had fallen out of the box without his noticing it. He'd gone to the hospital to pick up the drug, been given it in a box inside a little bag, and hadn't given it another thought. He'd been in a hurry to get back to his office, where he'd stayed for around two hours before realizing he had to get home.

Even today his heart ached at the thought; what had he been thinking, not going straight home? Of course what awaited him at his office had appealed to him more than the idea of helping Sara and her sister bake and prepare for the birthday party. But still. He had never regretted anything more, though there was nothing he could do about it now; the best he could do was push the thought of it firmly aside.

'It was a terrible day in every way,' he said. On his way home he'd been delayed even more; he'd been in an accident with a trailer and become even more stressed about the frosty welcome he'd face from Sara. He hadn't noticed the trailer attached to the back of a car he needed to overtake at the exit from Ártúnsbrekka. His car wasn't badly damaged, though the trailer had been dented and its coupling rather bent out of shape. In fact the only time that he hadn't had the paper bag containing the prescription within reach was when he'd got out of his car at the petrol station to speak to the angry driver and fill out insurance papers while the man examined the damage to his trailer. The bag had been lying on the front passenger seat, and he had thought nothing of it. 'I think either the drug was missing from the box from the start, or else it was stolen at the petrol station, though that's less likely. Surely I would have noticed if someone had sneaked into the car while I was standing next to it.'

'Nothing showed up on the petrol station's security cameras?'

'No, I'm afraid not. We parked all the way at the end of the forecourt, since there wasn't enough space for two cars, and only the car with the trailer appears in the video. But as I said, I doubt very much that anyone could have got into the car without my knowledge, and even if they did manage to, they would probably have taken the bag and not bothered to get the syringes out of their box.'

'Yes. Probably.' Dagný's expression was unreadable. 'It's not really relevant now. I was just curious. It struck me when I read it.'

As Freyr watched Dagný leave the room he tried to imagine what sort of person could have treated the disappearance of his own child with the sort of disregard that Bernódus's father had shown. He couldn't understand it in the light of his own experience. The man hadn't even bothered to report his son missing; that task had fallen to the school nurse. She'd complained to the boy's teacher when he didn't turn up for a medical check-up and was told that the boy hadn't shown up for school that morning. The nurse then called his home and was informed by the father that he wasn't in his bed. It was then that he reported it to the police, who went straight to his house. In the first statement taken from the father, he said that he hadn't even noticed whether his son had come home from school the previous day: he'd fallen asleep over a bottle he'd managed to get his hands on and when he woke up he assumed the boy had gone to school. He'd only realized that something was wrong when the school called to ask whether his son was ill. He'd looked into the boy's room and noticed that the bed hadn't been slept in that night.

Although the officer who'd written the report had clearly put some effort into wording it carefully, without passing judgement, it was obvious how much the negligent father disgusted him. It would have been impossible to hide it completely, except by leaving out anything said by the man, who neither had any idea where his son might be nor appeared to be in any particular rush to find out. In the father's final statement, taken about two weeks after the disappearance, the police force's patience with him appeared to have worn thin. Among other things, he had said it might be for the best if his son wasn't found, as then he wouldn't have to pay for his funeral. Freyr was so flabbergasted that he had to read this again to be sure he hadn't misread it. He would personally give anything in the world to have the bones of his son returned and lay them to rest in consecrated ground.

Of course the man had been ill. As a psychiatrist, Freyr was interested in learning about his history, but he doubted any data on him was available. There was nothing in the reports about what had become of Bernódus's mother, or whether she'd been similarly unfortunate. Freyr could probably find out by asking some of the town's older residents, and he immediately thought of the old teacher who was his patient. However, the father and his son had only lived a short time in Ísafjörður and there was nothing in the files about where they'd moved from. Hopefully the old man would have a better recollection of the boy's story, which must have been a topic of conversation at the school after his disappearance. Freyr hadn't been interested in discussing this with him when he'd visited him that morning, but he would tomorrow.

The noise of the photocopier, which had carried into the meeting room, stopped. 'Would you like a coffee, maybe?' Dagný appeared in the doorway with two sets of paper, the yellowed originals and the bright white copies. 'I don't need to brew it or anything. We've got a coffee machine.'

Freyr shook his head. 'No thanks.' For the moment he wanted nothing. The memory of how Sara had wasted away after Benni's disappearance suddenly resurfaced. She'd only eaten when he ordered her to, and their sex life had evaporated completely. Her apathy was total. He felt his heart contract when he compared in his mind the old, curvy Sara, full of happiness and life, with the husk that remained, living only out of habit. Although his fears that he could end up on the same path might be unfounded, he had to remain conscious of the danger. Sara hadn't realized where she was heading when she declined her first cup of coffee.

Freyr stretched. 'Actually yes, I will.' He forced himself to watch Dagný turn in the doorway to go and fetch the coffee, and admired her slim hips and the shapely backside her loose-fitting police uniform didn't quite conceal. With that he felt a bit better, and relaxed even more when he took a sip of the strong coffee.

'It's not clear from this whether Halla had any ties to Bernódus other than being his classmate at the primary school.' Dagný sat back down next to him and started putting the old reports back into folders. 'Or if she did, it escaped the notice of the officers investigating the case.' She shook her head as if to jolt her brain into proper working order. 'Something caused Halla to become obsessed with the boy.' Dagný ran a hand through her cropped hair. 'But no matter how I try, I can't think of any sort of connection that might form between kids of that age that would last for decades after one of them had died. Even if they'd been best friends, which I find rather unlikely. According to the school's information, Bernódus was unsociable and mostly kept to himself. I'm sure someone would have mentioned if he'd had a close friend.'

Freyr agreed. He also knew that children like Bernódus, who had no support from relatives and were emotionally neglected, were usually social outcasts. They hardly ever had a 'best friend' and were lucky not to be constantly bullied. 'Of course it's possible that his disappearance traumatized her at the time and that the shock resurfaced when her mental health started to deteriorate. Children are sensitive at that age, and serious events in their formative years can leave permanent scars.' He looked at Dagný. 'And of course it's also possible that someone was responsible for Bernódus's death and that she witnessed it or knew about it.'

'No, that can't be it.' Dagný frowned. 'Why wouldn't she just have said something?'

'There could be many reasons. Maybe she was afraid of being next; maybe she didn't realize what she'd seen until afterwards, when it was too late; maybe she felt ashamed that she hadn't done anything to help Bernódus, or wanted to protect those who played a part in his disappearance.'

'Like who?' Dagný's initial doubts about Freyr's theory seemed to be dwindling.

'A close relative, for example. Apparently Halla's father was also a drunk. Perhaps he had a propensity for violence too.'

Dagný nodded thoughtfully. Her hair, sticking up where she had tousled it, echoed the movement a moment later, as if it had needed an instant to collect itself. 'That would explain a few things, I suppose. I wouldn't want to keep that kind of thing a secret all my life.' She rocked in her chair and crossed her legs. 'Do you think she might have suppressed her memory of it only to have it spring up in her head later and drive her to kill herself?'

Freyr smiled. 'It's extremely rare for that kind of thing to occur; in fact it's fiercely debated in the literature whether it happens at all, even though repressed memories are often discussed in the media – in connection with sex crimes against children, for example. It's never been proven either way. I'd be really surprised if that were the case here.'

'Have you given any more thought to how this could be connected to your son?' Dagný looked him in the eye. She seemed slightly nervous and as a result maintained the eye contact a little too long. Freyr felt a bit like he was taking an oral exam. 'I mean, have you come across anything that might explain Halla's interest in him? He seemed to be on her mind as much as Bernódus.'

'I didn't think of anything, and I don't believe she had anything at all to do with me, my son or my family.' Freyr pulled the photocopied reports towards him. 'Her relationship with Benni was only in her mind and it's anyone's guess why she imagined it.'

'It's still a bit weird. Don't you think?' Dagný continued to hold his gaze. 'Your son disappears, you move here, and then an old case turns up in which a boy disappears in a similar manner.'

It would have been simplest to deny it, write it off as an incredible coincidence and then steer the conversation onto something else. But instead he decided to take the opportunity, since Dagný had brought it up, to say what was on his mind. 'I think it's more than strange. It's crazy, in fact. If I weren't so freaked out by it I might be able to gather my thoughts and work it out. It's just so bizarre that I don't really know where to begin.' Freyr took a sip of his coffee, which was now lukewarm, and continued: 'My son and Bernódus don't seem to have anything in common except for their disappearances. There are decades between them. They don't appear to be related; I checked on it in the *Book of Icelanders* just now. It's been too long since Bernódus disappeared for the same person to have taken them away. Of course everything points to these cases being entirely unrelated, but I still can't bring myself to accept it. Especially given that the names Benni and Bernódus both appear in the letter that Halla left behind, and in the text messages filling her phone. Those two things can't be coincidence in my opinion, though I can't stretch my mind enough to connect them.'

Dagný gave him a faint smile. 'I couldn't agree with you more. Of course I was hoping you would notice something we'd missed in the files, but I'm not really surprised you didn't. I assure you, we've continued to investigate every angle concerning Halla: we've spoken to her widower, her children, her former colleagues, but no one knows anything and everyone is equally surprised when we bring up your son, let alone Bernódus.' She reached for some papers that she'd brought with her to the meeting room but hadn't touched since putting them down. 'Both her husband and her daughter say that she had little or no communication with her friends in recent years, so there's not much to be had from them. But she had been trying to rekindle childhood friendships. Some from that group had moved away, so she spent a lot of time on the phone and her husband complained bitterly of the high phone bill. One of the women lived in Ísafjörður, but she died shortly before all this started with Halla. The widower and his daughter are fairly certain that this woman's death was what prompted Halla to seek out her old friends – she realized that she didn't have that long. He also said, after you spoke to him about it, that he'd thought a lot about the religious reawakening she'd experienced and thought that the woman's death had inspired it as well. Halla had wanted to ensure a place for herself in heaven as death drew nearer.'

'And how does this all relate to her having sought out old friends?' Freyr hoped Dagný was just telling him details from the police investigation. The mystery was complicated enough without adding senior citizens from all over the country.

Dagný handed him two of the pages. One was a copy of the school photo that he was now all too familiar with, and the other was a list of the names that had been scribbled in. He went over it. Lárus Helgason, Védís Arngrímsdóttir, Silja Konráðsdóttir, Jón Ævarsson and Steinn Gunnbjörnsson. 'As you can see, Halla's old friends are the same as the ones defaced in the photo all those years ago. And as we know, most of them are now dead. After Halla started tracking them down they all passed away, one after another.'

Freyr pushed the list back over to Dagný. The photo remained there in front of him, Bernódus's pitiful face looking out at him. 'Did you speak to this Lárus, the one who's still alive?'

'Yes and no.' Dagný folded the paper. 'He hung up on us when we told him our business, and since he lives in Reykjavík we can't check whether he would give us a warmer welcome in person. I'd prefer not to get the police down south involved in this for the moment. I'm simply not sure how I could describe the case to them in a way that made sense.'

Freyr looked away from the photo, which was on the verge of hypnotizing him. 'How did the others die? It's not entirely unexpected when people are over seventy, but all the same, it's a pretty high mortality rate in such a short amount of time.'

Dagný cleared her throat. 'Well, none of them died of health issues – neither long nor short illnesses. Védís bled to death after an accident, Jón died from complications from burns, Silja died of exposure, Steinn was run over, and Halla was a clear case of suicide.'

Freyr let Dagný's words sink in as he tried to draw conclusions about the group based on these sad statistics. He wished he had a piece of paper and a pen to make some notes. 'Has anyone investigated these incidents? Found out whether there's reason to assume they're connected?'

'No, they haven't. You need a special warrant to ask for that kind of information, and since it involves a number of different police authorities, it would take ages. These people lived all over the country. I also don't think we can really pursue it. It would be difficult to explain why we need this information; nothing suggests that any crimes were committed and we've got no reason to be asking questions.' Dagný stopped for a second and took a deep breath. 'Plus there's one more thing.'

This didn't sound good, but he asked nonetheless. 'What?'

'The first person from the group to die, Védís . . .' Dagný didn't finish her sentence, instead handing Freyr yet another sheet of paper that appeared to be the preface to an autopsy report. 'She lived here in Ísafjörður, so I was able to find out how she died. As you can see, she died three years ago in an accident in her garden.' Dagný licked her dry lips. 'She fell onto some open garden shears, with the result that the major artery in her neck was cut, along with her oesophagus. Don't ask me how it's possible to be so unlucky, but it's all described in the report and no one disputed that it was an accident.'

'Stranger things have happened.' The coffee was too cold for Freyr to risk another sip, but he took one anyway. 'Did you know this woman?'

'Not exactly, but I remember her. She was very unusual; she sometimes held séances at her home. But that's irrelevant.' Dagný grimaced slightly. 'I wanted to draw your attention to something else – the date of the accident.'

Freyr looked for it in the summary. He had to read the date twice to be sure, though he'd seen this same numerical sequence more often than he could count. His mouth dry, he muttered: 'It's the day that Benni disappeared.'

'And there's this, too.' Dagný pointed to the line above the date of death. 'She lived in the same house as you do now. She died in your garden, in other words.' She looked at him even more intensely. 'Coincidence?'

Chapter 15

Putti seemed to realize that the night and the terrors it held were just around the corner. He was lying next to Katrín as she sat with her legs stretched out on a folded wool blanket alongside Líf and Garðar, staring into the darkness surrounding the house. Her entire body still hurt but she'd got used to the pain, and besides, her headache was gone, so relatively speaking she felt quite well. From time to time the dog became unusually alert, lifting his head off his short forelegs and baring his teeth for no reason. Nothing in particular appeared to provoke this reaction, and there was no way of getting him to calm down again until he realized there was nothing there. Under normal circumstances, the babbling of the stream and the lapping of the incoming tide would have been soothing, but now it was as if they harboured other, more threatening sounds. Now someone could sneak up behind the house, slink along it and inch their way silently to where the three of them were sitting without their ever being aware of it. Yet they found it preferable to sitting inside, waiting for the dead undergrowth outside to rustle and the floorboards to creak.

'Let me watch it one more time.' Líf reached over Katrín, trying to get the camera from Garðar. 'Please.'

'Not a chance.' Garðar checked to see whether his jacket pocket was zipped up so Líf couldn't get at it. 'You won't see any more than what we've already seen, and the battery's running low.'

'Why do we need the camera battery?' Katrín's voice was calm. It was as if she'd decided simply to accept the situation and whatever might occur. She didn't know how long this odd serenity would last, but she was going to enjoy it while she could. Yet it bothered her a little that the reason her fear had abandoned her was probably because she'd accepted the inevitable: the child would do to them whatever it had done to the house's previous owner; they would vanish off the face of the earth and no one would know their fate. 'I'm not going to take any photos.'

Garðar scowled at her. 'Of course not. But what if we find another memory card? There might be something on it that could help us. We still have two boxes to go through.'

'There's nothing on any memory card that could help us. If the last owner had known anything useful, don't you think he would have saved himself?' Katrín squinted and tried, unsuccessfully, to make out the flimsy washing lines she knew were there somewhere in the twilight.

'Don't be so negative.' Líf shifted slightly away from Katrín but then appeared to regret it and moved back to the same spot. She bumped into Putti, who looked up in irritation and shook his head, making his ears flap, and yawned widely before letting his head fall back down. He didn't close his shiny dark eyes, but stared from beneath his wispy eyebrows at the checked pattern on the rug. 'I can't cope with you being pessimistic on top of everything else. We've got enough to worry about.'

'I'm not being negative.' Katrín felt a little muscle cramp and stretched her sore legs. She had no idea whether the cold made the cramps worse, but her legs felt chilly despite her protective trousers. 'I'm just realistic. We all heard it; he experienced exactly the same things as we have, except he was alone. I reckon he was here at the same time of year, even. I saw snow in some of the shots.'

'That doesn't necessarily mean anything. It can snow here in August.' Garðar stretched his neck, obviously feeling stiff himself. 'We should be careful about comparing our situation to his. As you said yourself, there are three of us, whereas he was by himself.' Katrín held her tongue, though she longed to laugh out loud. They could certainly sleep in shifts, but otherwise they didn't appear to be in any better a position than the poor man who'd lost his life in this place, alone and abandoned. From the clips they had ascertained that his phone had also died without warning. He, like them, had seen a boy who seemed to stand there with his head bowed, within reach, but who disappeared when approached. The two crosses had turned up inside the house without explanation and Katrín could still feel the heaviness she'd felt in her chest when she saw them appear on the camera's little screen, the shaky voice of the man narrating their discovery. He didn't appear to understand what was happening any more than they did. Her discomfort wasn't eased when some shells appeared in another clip. But it was the last shot that had struck her most. Then even her fear had gone away, and a peculiar calm came over her. The man sounded defeated. He spoke so softly that it was difficult to distinguish his words, especially because he yawned constantly, clearly very tired. However, they understood that he was saying his final good-byes to various people, none of whose names they recognized. The man seemed to have accepted his fate. He wouldn't make it back to town. At least not alive.

They'd watched the video over and over again in the hope of hearing or understanding what the man was saying, draining the battery, though that hardly mattered. The man had then used the camera like a Dictaphone; it wasn't possible to see anything in the darkness surrounding him and talking was all he could do. His voice trembling, he said that he didn't have a torch, since it had disappeared, and that he felt as if something were about to happen. There was an unbearable stench in the house and he constantly came across wet footprints, not his own, on the floor. The air was charged with something repulsive, something alive, and it was after him, though he didn't know what he'd done to deserve it. Then he suddenly fell silent. At that moment another individual appeared for a second, but too briefly to get a clear glimpse of him, there being virtually no light. In fact it was no more than a black shadow against a slightly lighter background. They tried to play the video slowly, stop it and view it almost frame by frame, but their attempts were in vain; they could never hit the right moment. Nevertheless, none of them was in any doubt that it was the boy. Equally, none of them was willing to speak up and say that he weirdly appeared to be a similar age to what he was now, three years later. Meanwhile, they could hear the man gasping for breath. Then he began to speak again, but the video clip ended in mid-sentence. Either the camera had gone dead for a moment or something else, something worse, had happened. Then, although he whispered the words frantically, they had no trouble understanding him: 'He's coming. He's coming. Oh God, oh God, he's . . .' This was the final recording on the memory card.

Putti lifted his head and growled, longer and deeper than before. Garðar snorted. 'You can bet your life that what's really freaking us out is this bloody dog. If he'd just shut up we wouldn't be reacting like this. People can make up all sorts of nonsense and start imagining the most ridiculous things.'

'Don't talk about the poor thing like that. Come here, Putti, come to mummy.' Líf patted her thigh, but Putti didn't appear to be particularly impressed, though he did stop growling. He didn't move any closer to Líf, however, but stayed snuggled against Katrín. After her fall down the stairs he'd stuck close to her and was apparently determined not to leave her side. Garðar watched the dog, shook his head and yawned, then was clearly reminded of the video clip and the disjointed sentences of the sleep-deprived man, and quickly tried to swallow his yawn. 'Shouldn't we be getting inside? It's starting to get colder and we can't sit here all night.'

'I don't want to be in there.' Líf had started scratching Putti behind his ears, apparently jealous that the dog now seemed fonder of Katrín. 'I actually like the cold out here better.' She cuddled the dog, who appeared not to notice. 'Couldn't we just bring our sleeping bags out here?'

'No.' This reminded Katrín of her students. When the children were faced with something they didn't like, they came up with all sorts of unrealistic ways to avoid the inevitable or at least to postpone it. Líf must have known that eventually they'd have to go inside. Right now it seemed a bit more tolerable sitting there outdoors, but they were unlikely to still feel that way when it came to closing their eyes and going to sleep.

'But we could go and sleep in the doctor's house. We have the keys, of course.' Katrín didn't want to say it, but there might be a radio there or something that could put them in touch with the outside world. She was no better than Líf in her unrealistic expectations.

Líf was thrilled with this idea, but Garðar needed a bit more deliberation. 'Would we be any better off there?' He was still on his feet, peering out into the darkness at where the house stood. The night sky was overcast, and there was no light from either the moon or the stars. 'The child is just as likely to harass us there as here.'

'Maybe. Maybe not.' Katrín was also standing up now, despite her protesting muscles. Putti lay still but gazed up at her, looking sad somehow. She smiled at him, uncertain whether dogs understood different facial expressions. 'Well, I'd feel better about going there than staying here tonight, at least. What about you?'

Nothing else needed to be said; none of them was particularly interested in bedding down on the first floor again, in the room that the previous owner also appeared to have chosen to sleep in. Putti watched their every move, always staying close to Katrín, who had to endure piercing pain with each step. It had become embarrassingly clear that he preferred her to his owner. Perhaps there was nothing particularly strange about the poor creature realizing that it had limited support from Líf, but Katrín was surprised that the dog wasn't focusing its attention on Garðar. He was the one who was at least attempting to pretend that everything was fine.

'I think I felt a snowflake.' Líf adjusted her sleeping bag in her arms and stroked her cheek. 'Wouldn't it be good if it snowed more? Then maybe we'd see footprints.'

'Would you follow them?' Garðar was behind Katrín and Líf, who had just enough room to walk side by side on the narrow trail. Garðar's walk was barely faster than Katrín's, as his foot had barely healed. 'I don't really see that happening.'

'I'm not talking about going out tonight, but maybe

tomorrow when it's light. It's not as if there are so many people here that the place would be covered in footprints. Just imagine if we could find the little bastard, tie him up and finally have some peace. Maybe we get to kill him, since he obviously killed the man who used to own the house?'

Katrín raised her eyebrows, which made the sore spot on her scalp ache. Líf wasn't quite right in the head. But she left it to Garðar to respond to this nonsense and the two of them continued to bicker back and forth about it on the way over. Although Katrín generally found it boring to listen to quarrelling, she found it comfortable now. There was something so mundane and familiar about it, almost like standing between an old couple who couldn't agree on anything. When they tiptoed carefully across the dilapidated bridge over a branch of the stream, Katrín didn't even feel her heart beating rapidly, as it had done before now, at the thought of falling into the icy water. She was too busy listening to Garðar talk irritably about how tracks could be covered over by snow in a surprisingly short amount of time. Líf didn't believe this for a second and the issue was still unresolved when they suddenly came to the pale yellow two-storey house that had previously housed the village physician.

'God, I hate how they've boarded up the windows. It's as if the house's eyes have been poked out and bandages slapped on.' Líf shuddered.

They stood silently, staring at the house. Líf's description was unnervingly accurate. Garðar was the first to break the silence. 'At least it's obvious that no one's gone in there except with a key. The door's the only thing that hasn't been nailed shut. However good this child is at hiding, I doubt he's *that* good at break-ins. It doesn't look as if the door's been messed with.' Although Garðar sounded confident, none of them seemed keen to be first to try the door.

Putti was hopping around between Katrín and Líf, apparently agitated by something – the cold, perhaps. He looked miserable. The prospect of the poor thing freezing to death prompted Katrín to cut to the chase. 'Who has the key?' As soon as she said it, she realized none of them had thought to bring it.

'I'll shoot back over. I'll be no time at all.' Garðar didn't listen to their feeble protests. Neither of them was keen on turning back, nor did they want him to go. But someone had to get the key, and it was pointless to make a big fuss over who should go when someone had already volunteered. They watched him jog rather awkwardly, due to his heel, out into the darkness and he seemed to disappear from sight incredibly fast. When they'd stood staring at the darkness for an uncomfortably long time, Katrín walked up to the house and put her sleeping bag down by the door. Líf followed her example. Then they sat down on the porch, which was far sturdier than the one attached to their own house, and waited for Garðar and the key. Putti stood at the base of the porch, sniffing the air.

'Please. Don't growl.' Líf wrapped her jacket tighter. 'I can't take any more.' The dog made no sound but turned quickly towards the house and stopped abruptly. This house stood much closer to the sea than theirs and here the sound of the waves was louder, as they hit the beach more vigorously than earlier in the evening. From time to time there also came a more forceful splashing sound, as if someone were kicking around in the shallows. 'How long is it since Garðar left? Shouldn't he be back by now?' Líf didn't look at Katrín, since she herself knew how silly the question was. 'I can't wait to get inside and into my sleeping bag.'

'Me neither.' The fatigue that had built up during the day was starting to take effect. Katrín felt once again how tiring psychological stress could be, no less so than physical labour. When she and Garðar were having problems she often felt as if she were on the verge of collapsing in the evenings, and it was precisely then that the issues seemed insurmountable and everything felt hopeless. 'I think we've done the right thing coming over here.' In fact she'd remembered that they hadn't brought any firewood with them and that it would be extremely cold inside, but it helped that Líf had been wrong to predict further snowfall. 'We don't have anything to heat the house with.'

Líf moaned, but immediately regained her composure. 'Oh, who cares? If I can just get into the house I'll be happy.'

'Agreed.' Katrín began to yawn, but stopped midway when Putti started growling where he stood, staring towards the side of the house. When he stopped, they could clearly hear a crunching sound. Líf grabbed Katrín's arm tightly with both hands and squeezed. 'What was that?'

Katrín shushed her and listened more carefully. It was as if someone were walking just around the corner of the house. All of the odd calm she had enjoyed disappeared, and her racing heartbeat was back, faster than ever. She'd heard that animals were sensitive to the emotions of the people around them, and this appeared to be the case for Putti. He growled even louder and barked sharply several times. The crunching sound stopped.

'What should we do?' Líf sounded as though she desperately wanted to clamp her eyes shut and hope this would all go away by itself, and Katrín felt the same. But she shushed Líf once more and tried to think of something. There was no way she was going to stand up and look around the corner, no matter what might be there. The only thing she could think of was to pull Líf to her feet and run off after Garðar. They'd been idiots to think it would make any difference coming to this house.

Putti was still barking frantically, lifting off the ground slightly each time. Then he stopped abruptly and whined piteously, which was even worse. His bark had at least implied that he thought he could handle whatever was around the corner. The whine suggested entirely the opposite. Katrín stood up carefully and motioned to Líf to do the same. She whispered in her ear: 'Let's walk slowly in the direction of the steps and then run as fast as we possibly can when we reach them. We'll just leave the stuff behind.' How she intended to run remained to be seen; in her condition she had enough trouble walking.

Maybe whatever awaited them had overheard Katrín's plan, because the sound started up again. It seemed to be approaching with uncomfortable speed. Katrín stared helplessly at the corner of the house. She was convinced that now they would see the face of whoever was lying in wait for them, but she was far from prepared for it. The only thing she could do was fix her gaze on the sharp edge of the wall. Líf also seemed hypnotized. They screamed as loudly as each other when a small hand reached around the corner. Four pale, yellowish fingers appeared, gripping the wood, then disappeared just as quickly. The next thing they knew, a voice was coming from whoever was standing around the corner. They couldn't understand the words, but it was clear that it was a monologue not intended for others' ears. There was no way to determine whether it was a girl or a boy speaking. Katrín felt the hairs on her arms rise when the possibility crossed her mind that this was a clinically insane adult, putting on a child's voice. There was nothing innocent or joyful in its tone, as you'd expect from a child, although the size of the hand did not suggest an adult. The high-pitched voice fell silent.

'What did he say?' Líf squeezed Katrín's bruised body so hard that it made her dizzy with pain. 'What did he say?'

'Shh!' The crunching noise had resumed, now accompanied by a disgusting, indefinable smell. It could best be described as a blend of kelp and rotten meat. The voice spoke again, now slightly louder and clearer: *Don't go. Don't go yet. I'm not finished.*

Katrín heard nothing more over Líf's screams as she threw herself towards the steps without so much as a backwards glance to check whether Katrín was following her. Katrín was left alone on the porch, too numb even to shush Putti, who was barking even more hysterically than before. Yet he couldn't drown out the terrifying voice, now raised in anger:

I said I'm not finished.

Chapter 16

Freyr had actually never given the house in which he lived much thought. For him it was just a stopping point, not a place he wanted to become tied to. Most of the furniture had come with the house and would remain there when he moved, either back to Reykjavík or to other accommodation in the west. Perhaps he might even end up buying. As a result he lived there as if it were a hotel: folding his clothes and placing them all together on one shelf in the wardrobe, where he also hung his shirts and suit jackets. He used other storage spaces in the house just as sparingly, like a guest who shouldn't be opening doors or drawers unnecessarily. He even kept his food in one corner of the refrigerator. His only personal effects were the photos of his son, which he could gather into a box in under five minutes. It wasn't as if there were any limitations on how he might use the house; when the hospital's personnel director had given him the keys, they were accompanied by the warmest wishes for his stay there; he was to make himself at home. Freyr had thanked him and asked nothing further, having not felt inspired to ask how the hospital came to own the house.

Now that he had some idea of the identity of its former owner, he looked at it in a new light, indoors and out. He'd gone from room to room and examined the books and other items on the shelves, the furnishings and everything else that had awaited him when he first set foot inside the house. Until now he hadn't paid any attention to any of it, let alone wondered where the things had come from. But at the end of his investigation of the house he felt sure that very little of it had belonged to the woman who'd died in the garden. There was no consistency to anything, either in period or style. The photos on the wall were colour reproductions, the furniture shabby and poor quality. The lavishly patterned curtains were the only thing he thought might have belonged to Védís, as they looked like they had been chosen with thought and care, though they weren't to his taste. Considering that Védís must have been born around 1940, like Halla and the others in the class, the furnishings should mainly have been from the seventies, not a mishmash of various time periods during the past century. The dinner service, glasses and tableware, pots and pans all looked as if they'd come from a show kitchen at Ikea. It was inconceivable that an elderly woman during all her years as a householder hadn't acquired so much as one spoon that would remain in her home. The hospital must have found itself with an empty residence and furnished it, buying most of the items from the charity shops or Kolaport Flea Market and the rest from Ikea. The furnishings told him nothing about Védís, in other words. Dagný had called him at his office and told him the entire story of the circumstances leading to the hospital's purchase of the house. He'd avoided contacting her; she must already think he was strange enough after his behaviour of the previous few days. According to the information Dagný had obtained, the former owner had left the hospital her possessions in her will. The woman she spoke to had made a point of saying that the bequest had taken people completely by surprise, since Védís had had absolutely no ties to the hospital. She had never been admitted for long-term patient care or needed the hospital's services beyond the usual sort of requirements. Still, something had inspired her to do this, because approximately a week before her death she'd drawn up her will and made these arrangements for her one significant asset. Although it was unclear what had motivated her, her charitable gesture had certainly come in handy; quite a lot of the staff moved to Ísafjörður from out of town and needed a place to stay.

And this is how Freyr came to be living in this house. A single, elderly woman had decided to bequeath her home to his future workplace. Shortly afterwards, she had fallen onto a pair of sharp garden shears. Freyr found this almost too explicable a coincidence compared to the conspiracy theories that had run through his head when Dagný first told him about it. He was ashamed at how quick he'd been to over-interpret something that was nothing, thereby falling into the same mindset as his patients, which had lately become a disturbingly common occurrence. He let the heavy curtain fall and watched the pale pink material swing slowly back and forth a few times. There was no reason to stare any longer at the garden and the scrubby undergrowth that no doubt missed the care of its former owner. Freyr thought he knew where the accident must have occurred, though this wasn't due to any kind of epiphany, but to a hunch based on a few things he'd been thinking about.

There was a little spot at the edge of the garden, directly across from the large living room window, where a concrete wall separated the garden from the pavement. Next to it was a handsome bush that had dropped its leaves before Freyr moved in. He had no idea what type it was. If pressed, he would guess that it was a rosebush, based on the thorns hidden in the dark mess of branches. They couldn't be seen from where Freyr stood at the living room window, but he remembered them from when he'd fetched a ball there for some neighbourhood children. For some reason they hadn't wanted to get the ball themselves, but had instead knocked on Freyr's door and asked him if he would. When he thought about it, only one boy had stood on his doorstep. The others had hung back on the pavement and watched from a safe distance. At the time, Freyr had thought that they didn't want to walk on the pale yellow grass without permission, or were afraid the house owner would give them an earful, but now he had the sneaking suspicion that the garden's sinister history had been the reason. They were old enough to remember the accident and probably little else had been discussed in the area in the months after Védis's sudden death. Freyr couldn't be sure he wasn't making things up to fill in the gaps, but now he recalled that when he'd gone over to the bush to reach for the colourful plastic ball, he'd experienced an uneasiness he couldn't explain. In retrospect, he'd felt as if silence and darkness dwelt at the roots of the bush, and that a jaunty, colourful plastic ball had no business being there.

No doubt this memory had got scrambled in his mind, but that was irrelevant. In front of the bush was a dark spot, a dark brown area of bare earth in an otherwise tidy patch of grass that the winter had treated relatively mildly. Nothing had been there that could explain the absence of grass, and although Freyr had had little interest in the garden, he would probably have noticed if a rock or some other large thing had disappeared from the spot, not least because it was visible from the living room window. No, he was convinced that it was there the woman had bled to death, and that if he looked into it, a sensible explanation would be found for the absence of grass there. Maybe the saltiness of Védís's blood had affected the soil, or neighbours or the clean-up team had unwittingly spilt toxic cleaning solution over the area. The woman must have bled copiously.

Freyr fidgeted irritably. He'd already eaten, and packed the few things that he wanted to take with him to Reykjavík the next morning, and although the late news was about to start he couldn't bring himself to turn on the television. He felt ill at ease enough already without the state of the nation making things worse. Without consciously deciding to do so, he put on his tracksuit. At the front door he stopped and stared at his key ring, stamped with the emblem of the town of Ísafjörður. On it were four keys: two identical ones to the house, one to the garage and the fourth to a storage room in the basement, which he'd had no use for. He remembered feeling that the once-over he'd given it when he moved in was all he needed. He gnawed thoughtfully at the inside of his cheek before sticking the key in his pocket and strolling out into the cool winter evening. He would jog his usual circuit and no doubt feel better afterwards; at least he would be physically tired, which should make it easier for him to fall asleep. Then he resolved not to think of anything other than what he saw on his run.

When he got outside, however, he couldn't resist the temptation to look at the spot where he now thought Védís had died. On this mild winter evening there was no particular smell of plants or flowers, yet Freyr could detect a faint scent of drowsing nature as he breathed deeply through his nose.

However, when he stood over the dark spot, that scent gave way to a heavier, more powerful odour. Freyr felt a burning sensation in his nose and mouth as he inhaled the rank air, and he covered them with his hand. He bent down and picked up a thin branch from beneath the bush and poked a bit at the dark brown earth. It was moist and seemed warmer than it should have been, although Freyr couldn't bring himself to place his palm on the spot. If it was a toxic material that prevented anything from growing there, he had no interest in getting it on his hands. He stood up halfway before stiffening as a grating metallic sound came from under the shrub.

At the same moment, an image of garden shears appeared in his mind.

Freyr took a deep breath and again smelled the powerful odour that emerged when he poked at the soil. He felt nauseous but forced himself to bend back down and peer beneath the overgrown, ragged bush. Of course there were no shears, and in fact it was remarkable how little he could see. It was dark outside now, certainly, but beneath the bush it was as if the darkness were even blacker, not even allowing a glimpse of the wall two metres behind it. Even without leaves the branches were dense enough to prevent the dull glow of nearby streetlights from penetrating them. Freyr shook his head, annoyed at himself for letting his imagination mess with his mind like that. He stood back up and walked determinedly towards the gate, acting as if he couldn't hear the grating sound that followed him. He felt very relieved when he emerged from the garden and started running down the street.

Although he ran quickly, he hadn't gone far before he heard another jogger approaching from behind at even greater speed.

The jogger ran rhythmically, much lighter on his or her feet than Freyr. When the footsteps sounded as if the jogger were on the verge of catching him, he slowed down slightly to let this keen athlete go past. He felt a clumsy grip on his shoulder and Dagný asked him breathlessly to relax a bit. 'Are you in a hurry?' She stood with her hands on her thighs and exhaled. 'I saw you start off just as I was finishing and I was going to say hello to you, but you ran off so fast that I started to think you were trying to get away from me.'

Jogging on the spot so as not to lose his pace, Freyr smiled at Dagný. It felt great to see her; she was the opposite of everything that he'd been mulling over and imagining in the past few hours. Her red cheeks and rapid breathing were a connection to life and everything the future had to offer, while the horrible furnishings and unkempt garden belonged to the past and a history that nothing could change. 'Sorry. I would have stopped if I'd seen you.'

Dagný straightened up. 'I'd be happy to jog a bit more with you if you promise to go just a bit slower.'

Freyr would have agreed to run backwards if she'd asked. 'Absolutely. You have no idea how starved I am for some company.' In fact, he would have been happy just to continue jogging on the spot there on the pavement, staring into Dagný's grey-blue eyes. They weren't entirely identical; one was set at a tiny bit more of an angle than the other, which was precisely what made her face irresistible.

'I followed you because I was thinking of looking in on you,' said Dagný after they'd set off again. 'I figured you were probably wondering about all of this and I thought maybe I could help. I remember Védís well, which maybe isn't saying much.'

'Were you living round here when she died?'

'No, I bought my house two years ago, after she'd already passed away. But she was certainly enough of a character to attract attention, even if you weren't her next-door neighbour.' Dagný stopped to catch her breath before continuing. 'Is there anything in the house that could conceivably provide clues about her connection to the other cases? I must confess that I don't understand what it's all about.'

'It doesn't look to me as if any of her belongings are still there. They might have gone to her relatives, though the hospital inherited the house itself.' Freyr lessened his speed slightly; he mustn't forget that she'd already done her share of jogging for the day.

Dagný seemed happy to be able to slow down a bit. 'The hospital got everything, naturally, but after the assessor went over the household inventory it turned out that it had some value, since a lot of it came from her parents' estate, including some antiques. I was told that the bulk of it was sold in Reykjavík, but that her most personal effects were kept back in case a relative came looking for them later. And of course a lot of stuff was thrown out.'

'I still haven't had a proper look at the storage room in the basement. Maybe the stuff they kept is there. At least I know it's not anywhere else in the house, or in the garage. I've never given much thought to the house's former residents until now; I don't even know much about the guy who lived there before I moved in. I just know he was a doctor from Reykjavík, like me.'

'Yes, he moved out a few months before you arrived.'

Freyr knew nothing more about the man than what he'd heard at the hospital, which was that he hadn't completed his contract and that he didn't seem to have been very popular – possibly as a result, although it might also have been down to his personality. 'But if the things are in the storeroom now, is it okay to look through them, or open boxes? Obviously I don't own the stuff, though it is in the house I live in.'

Dagný slowed down even more. 'I can promise you that no one here in Ísafjörður is going to start snooping around to find out what you've been up to in your house. You were given a key and if it opens the storeroom containing some of the deceased owner's things, then it's entirely up to you if you take a look at it.'

They jogged in silence for another short stretch before Freyr noticed that Dagný was really starting to tire and suggested they turn back. He could have carried on running for a good while longer but preferred to jog back with her rather than continue on alone. When they got to the house he decided to invite her in for a glass of red wine, soft drink, tea, beer, coffee, or whatever she wanted. She looked down, exhaled, and then accepted his offer, on the condition that she first be allowed to go home and shower; she would come back in half an hour or so. Four minutes later he had finished showering himself, having invented a quick method of doing so during his student years, when he was always in a rush and it felt as though every minute could make a difference. He dried himself and dressed with the same speed, and in order to shorten his wait for Dagný he decided to go and have a look in the storeroom. The evening was so tranquil and the neighbourhood so still that he would no doubt hear her when she opened the old steel gate.

It was darker in the back garden than the front. He was very careful to support himself with his hand on the wall as he went down the basement stairs. Visibility was poor and he didn't want to fall or trip up, especially not when he was expecting a visitor. The hinges creaked loudly as he opened the door. He reached for the light switch inside and looked around at the nearly empty basement.

There was as little to see as there had been last time. Dust danced in the beam of light. Freyr decided to look behind the little partition towards the back of the basement, something he hadn't done before when he'd merely peeked in. There he found a cardboard box, upon which was written in large letters, with a black marker: *Védís Arngrímsdóttir*. Without thinking about it too much, he lifted the box, worrying that he might not hear Dagný.

He was going to wait to open it until Dagný was gone, but he couldn't contain his curiosity and looked inside. The box contained mainly books, and on top was an old, worn-out notebook with a handwritten title: *Dream Diary 2001–*

Chapter 17

The clouds all seemed to have given up at the same moment, probably from the weight of their burden; one minute everything was calm, and the next the night air was filled with heavy, gusting snow. It swallowed every sound, muting the babbling of the stream and the rush of waves at the seashore. This transformation didn't make them feel any better, although initially it had been a definite relief to lose the surrounding sounds and the need to start in alarm every time they heard a creak in the rickety house. It didn't help that the windows were all boarded up, meaning they were now entirely deprived of two of their five senses, making it difficult to know whether someone was outside.

'I want another cigarette.' Líf was restless, passing her index finger through the flame of a candle standing on the old dining room table where they sat. She'd found an open pack of Winstons in the kitchen and taken one, to the noisy protests of Katrín, who didn't want to steal anything from strangers. It was bad enough that they were burning down one of the candles that stood in low copper holders here and there throughout the house, and there was an overwhelming likelihood that they would continue to do so until only the stumps were left. Their urgent need, however, might justify the thievery – unlike Líf's smoking, a bad habit that she should long since have given up. 'Do you want to go and have a look with me again?'

'No.' Katrín certainly wasn't going to start doing Líf any favours after she'd run off and left her alone to face what was hidden around the corner of the house. In fact, nothing had happened; after making his threats the owner of the voice had disappeared, leaving Katrín sitting there trembling to her marrow in the silence of the evening, Putti next to her, until Garðar came running to her with Líf at his heels. Líf had stumbled into his arms as she fled up the path, meeting him on his way back to them with the keys. Panting and breathless, she'd told him what they'd encountered and he ran ahead immediately to find Katrín, unsure what he would encounter at the doctor's house after hearing Líf's description. When it became apparent that Katrín was unhurt he strode angrily and resolutely round the corner in the hope of finally catching the delinquent child and giving him a thrashing. But there was no one there, which was no surprise to Katrín; the boy had left some minutes before and since he knew the area a thousand times better than they did, it was useless to try to go after him. Nor did the darkness offer much opportunity for heroic deeds.

'I don't understand how we managed to forget to bring candles.' Garðar had been muttering this same sentence at regular intervals ever since Líf had set eyes on them. 'I swear I must have forgotten candles even existed when we were buying supplies.'

'Please, come with me. I can't go alone.' Líf jerked back her hand after forgetting what she was doing and passing her finger too slowly through the flame. She shook her finger and stuck it in her mouth to cool it down. 'It's definitely warmer there than here.'

It was ice-cold in the house. After Garðar had satisfied himself that no one was hiding along the side of it they'd been so frantic to shut themselves in that all of his suggestions that they make one trip together to fetch firewood fell onto stony ground. With the snow falling it was pointless to talk about dashing there and back, even now that they'd calmed down a bit, because none of them was particularly good with directions and there was a risk of them getting lost and dying of exposure. Now they sat there in their jackets and sweaters with sleeping bags round their shoulders, patting themselves to keep warm. Katrín actually found this difficult, since her body was so sore it could barely stand the abuse. 'I don't want you to take any more of those cigarettes. How would you like it if someone broke into your place and stole your fags?'

'I wouldn't give a damn if I were coming home after being away as long as these people. Cigarettes get ruined when they're left like this with the packet open. They're barely smokeable now, let alone in the spring. I'm actually doing them a favour.' Líf reached for the pack lying on the table between them, took a cigarette out and acted as if she were smoking it, without lighting up. 'If there weren't so few in the pack, I'd encourage you to take up smoking with me.'

Katrín didn't feel like replying to this and Garðar seemed absorbed in a stack of books standing on a shelf on a nice-looking sideboard. They were mainly about the region: the history, geography, people and traditions of the Westfjords; Garðar had wondered aloud whether they should put together a similar collection for their guests in the future. Katrín had clamped her mouth shut but had longed to shout that it would never happen; they would never return here to complete these renovations – if they made it home at all. She watched him as he peered at the small print, trying to keep out of the little light they had to see by. He turned the page. 'Anything useful there?' she asked.

Garðar looked up from the book. 'Yes and no. I was hoping to find something about the houses here, preferably something about our little place, but I haven't come across anything. This is mainly about hiking trails and the like.'

'Is there anything about a trail leading to town?' Líf had started poking at the candle flame again, now more careful about the speed of her finger. 'We could maybe walk from here.'

'Are you nuts?' Katrín didn't need to see out of the window to recall the storm they'd been met with when they let themselves be persuaded to accompany Líf outside so she could smoke her stolen cigarette. 'It'd probably take days. We're much better off waiting here for the boat. After tomorrow we'll only have two nights left, and then the skipper will come and fetch us.' She didn't mention that this was subject to the whims of the sea.

Líf shrugged. 'I'm not talking about hiking non-stop all the way to Ísafjörður – if we had a map that pointed out some houses along the way we could stay in them. Hike from one to another, something like that. There are a lot of houses here in Hornstrandir. We would only need to know where they are, so we wouldn't miss them.' She picked up Putti's ball from the floor and threw it to him. He looked at it and moved away, giving it a very wide berth. Líf had brought the ball with her from the other house, but the dog now seemed to avoid it like the plague, despite having played with it a lot in the first few days. Neither Katrín nor Garðar had told her how the ball had rolled out of its own accord from under the stove the night before, and they'd awkwardly watched her attempts to get the animal to take it. 'I don't understand why he doesn't want to play with the ball any more. Until now he never let it out of his sight.' Líf looked surprised and hurt. She obviously felt that the dog had completely turned its back on her.

'Stop worrying about the dog.' Garðar sounded angry, but Katrín knew that he probably found it just as uncomfortable as she did to watch the dog's reaction to the ball. They had suggested to Líf that the toy must be giving off a weird smell that had got into the plastic somehow. 'And Katrín's right. There's no way we're walking from here. I bet it was precisely that idea that caused Haukur, the former owner, to disappear. He wandered off and died of exposure. There's no chance of us finding our way – in the dead of winter, to the few human habitations still standing here – without a GPS tracker, which we don't have; and if we were to get lost, no one would think of looking for us until it was too late. We don't have working phones, remember?'

'Of course I remember; if we had a phone we would call the captain and have him come and get us.' Líf was starting to grow more despondent; her nicotine urge might have been irritating her, but she didn't dare go out alone to satisfy it. 'I'm just trying to come up with a solution. Unlike some people.'

Garðar's expression was far from friendly as he glared into Líf's defiant eyes. Katrín sighed to herself. Now they would start quarrelling again, just as they had when they were making their way over here, but now it felt angrier, more serious. She might have found it oddly comforting on the way, but there was nothing appealing about it now. 'Come on, Líf.' She pushed the chair back from the heavy wooden dining table and stood up. 'I'll go outside with you for your fag. We'll just buy a pack in Ísafjörður and return it to the people, along with the candles that we have to replace anyway.' Líf smiled gratefully at her. At first she seemed a bit surprised, as if she'd hardly been expecting a friendly gesture on her part. Katrín, however, had no interest in taking sides in these silly arguments and felt the only thing for it was to try to nip them in the bud from the outset. If Líf got to smoke and Garðar got to flip through the book in peace, the atmosphere might lighten and Líf would forget her idea about walking to town.

'Thanks, you're a star.' Líf was still smiling as she lit up. They stood close together in the frame of the open back door. It opened onto a sun porch, like their own house, although this one was in far better shape. 'I would never have had the guts to stand out here alone.' The snow continued to fall, covering everything with a thick white blanket.

'No problem.' Katrín moved over a bit so that the smoke wouldn't drift straight into her face. 'But be prepared to move quick smart if we hear any noises out here. I'll slam the door so fast you'll risk being squashed.'

'Don't worry.' Líf blew out smoke and looked in surprise at the cigarette. 'Funny.' She rolled it a bit in front of her face and stared as if in a trance at the glowing tip. 'I haven't smoked since Einar died.'

Katrín had often wondered how Líf had managed to stop smoking at the time. It couldn't have been easy grieving for her dead spouse at the same time as battling her addiction. 'Wasn't it difficult to stop then?'

Líf took another drag and shook her head slowly. 'No, it was no problem. I was in so much shock afterwards that I couldn't eat for several days, let alone smoke. When I pulled myself together a bit it was as if the urge had been taken away from me. Very strange, but that's how it was.'

Although Katrín generally got completely flustered whenever Einar's death came up in conversation, there was something about the stillness and silence of the snowfall that loosened her tongue. Suddenly she wasn't afraid she might say something that would come across as insincere or tacky. 'Of course it must have been horrible. I've often tried to imagine how things have been for you, but I just can't.'

'It was what it was.' The snow seemed to have the opposite effect on Líf. Generally she was open, but now she seemed distracted. 'It was what it was.'

Katrín wasn't sure what she should say next. She hugged herself tighter to ward off the cold.

'Of course it's too late to say it now, but I've never told you just how terribly sorry I am. I would have liked to console you, but I never dared offer, I just hoped that you knew you could always turn to me. It was so, so terrible for you that I felt as if anything I said or did would just be trivial in comparison with what you were going through. I was such a late addition to your group of friends that I still feel a bit like a gatecrasher. Not that you've made me feel like that, it's just a kind of innate insecurity I have.' Katrín breathed deeply. The air that filled her lungs was fresh and satisfying, although it was tinged with a slight smell of smoke. Maybe it was just contentment at having finally said what was on her mind that was making her feel so relaxed. 'Well, I hope that one day you'll find another man you can love as much as you loved Einar.'

Líf had been amusing herself by puckering her lips and blowing out big clouds of smoke. She seemed to be flustered when Katrín finished talking, and it was as if the smoke was going back into her lungs. She coughed slightly, but then laughed a desolate laugh. 'Hopefully I'll find someone I can love *more* than I loved him.'

'What?' Katrín didn't know whether Líf was joking. Líf smiled at her, her expression sincere. 'Things weren't going very well for me and Einar; you and Garðar must have noticed it. We would probably have divorced if he'd lived. The last four years of our marriage were a complete disaster, and I'd had enough.'

Katrín did her best to hide her astonishment. 'We knew you'd gone through some rough patches, but I just thought you'd got over them by the time Einar died. You were absolutely devastated, and I know that was no act.'

'I was mourning for what had been. The Einar that I first met and the Einar that I married. Not the man I lived with in the last few years. We couldn't stand being in each other's presence any more. That's why I had no idea he'd been undergoing medical tests for his heart; I'd noticed a bottle of pills in the medicine cabinet but we spoke so little to each other that I never asked about them. When we went to sleep on the night he died, we didn't even say goodnight to each other. Of course we couldn't have known that we would never see each other again, at least not in this life. I would have liked to have said goodnight, at least. But that's how it was. We both got what we wanted, though in different ways. We parted company.'

Katrín was still too shocked to be able to respond to this. No doubt she would have learned about this if she'd opened herself up to Líf earlier. 'Shit,' was all she could think of to say.

'Yes. Exactly. Shit.' Líf knocked ash off her cigarette and a large grey fleck drifted slowly down among the snowflakes. 'It was almost worse than losing someone you loved. Of course I mourned him, but I also felt a little bit like the world's biggest hypocrite, having previously wished he'd go to hell.'

She took her last drag on the cigarette and the tip burned into the filter. 'Remember that girl at the funeral who cried and cried – really pretty, dark-haired, wearing a grey outfit?'

'No, I can't say I do.' Katrín hadn't paid much attention to anyone but Garðar, who'd had a very difficult time saying farewell to his best friend.

'Doesn't matter.' Líf tossed the butt out into the night. 'She was his assistant. He had an affair with her for years, I think.' She turned to Katrín. 'Actually, I don't think, I know.'

Katrín's eyes were so wide that her eyelids ached. 'Did Garðar know about this?'

Líf shrugged. 'I suppose not. I think Einar was more interested in keeping it from him than from me. They were still friends. Not like us.' Líf moved away from the door and Katrín followed her example.

'Didn't you try to patch things up at all? Our marriage hasn't been a bed of roses but it's always been fixable.' Katrín decided to let it all out, just like Líf. 'Actually, the onus always ends up being on me. I'm the one who compromises when it becomes clear that he's not going to try.'

Líf nodded. 'Yes, I know. Einar was the same. Of course I tried everything I could at first. I made appointments for marriage counselling, but he never turned up. The sessions just changed into my own personal therapy, which actually helped me a lot. I became angry instead of being sad and it's a much, much better feeling.' She smiled conspiratorially, stretched towards Katrín's ear and whispered: 'I even cheated on him in revenge. To even the score. One all.' She leaned away from Katrín again and her expression returned to normal. 'But then I broke it off, since it was pointless and my motives were all fucked-up. Einar never realized; he was too busy with his own infidelity to notice what I was doing behind his back. In fact, I'm really happy things happened the way they did, but sometimes I wish I'd told him before he died. I almost did once, just to get back at him.'

'Who was it, anyone I know?' Katrín was fairly familiar with the close-knit group of Einar, Líf and Garðar's friends, to which she'd been graciously admitted after she and Garðar had started seeing each other. Although Líf and Einar had made her feel quite welcome, the others were a different story, deigning to talk to her only out of loyalty to Garðar. Katrín felt she could always read in their eyes, especially the women, that he was far too good for the likes of her – a non-entity, a teacher who wasn't particularly stylish or beautiful. She had no trouble imagining that some of the people in that happy little group would have had few qualms about stealing each other's boyfriends or girlfriends.

'You don't know him. He's older than we are and we weren't at all well-suited. It was a mistake on my part.' Líf smiled sadly at Katrín. 'I think I'm better off with someone closer to my own age.'

'Okay.' Katrín had no idea what else to say. She felt slightly ashamed of her own curiosity, though it didn't seem to bother Líf at all. In any case, she felt relieved when Líf said nothing further. Her news had caught Katrín completely off guard. They walked silently back inside to Garðar, and Katrín prayed he wouldn't start quarrelling with Líf again. She needed peace and quiet to take in what Líf had said. Her worries proved unfounded.

'Guess what?' Garðar had got further into the book, which he'd moved closer to the candle's flickering flame. 'I've found a short section about our house.' He placed his finger on the middle of the page. 'Here's a little bit about the woman and the boy whose names are on the crosses.' He didn't seem to notice their silence in his own excitement. 'They drowned just out there.' He turned and pointed at the living room window, through which nothing could be seen. It didn't make any difference; they knew perfectly well in what direction the sea lay, and it was hard to drown on dry land.

'Did their boat sink?' Katrín tried to appear interested, though Líf and Einar's toxic relationship was occupying her mind entirely.

'No, no. The ice broke beneath them.' Garðar shuddered with a sudden chill as he said this. 'It was winter and the fjord was iced over. It says here that the boy had gone out onto the ice, which wasn't strong enough to hold him though he was just a short distance from land. His brother saw and went to get their mother, who tried desperately to save her child, but the ice broke beneath her as well. The two of them were already dead by the time rescuers managed to scramble out onto the ice on some boards. They were buried in the cemetery. It was the last funeral in Hesteyri while people still lived here.'

Just as he said the last word, the house was struck by a huge blow that even the storm couldn't deaden.

Chapter 18

Although man has pondered the meaning and purpose of dreams for ages, no definite conclusions have yet been reached. It makes no difference whether it's scientists who try to find physiological explanations, religious groups who read divine messages in dreams, or New Ageists who believe that dreams provide insight into the indefinite future. Some progress has been made, however: for example, scientists have been able to identify which neurotransmitters populate the brain in a dream state and prevent the limbs from moving in conjunction with what the dream tells the body is happening. They have also determined the stage of sleep in which dreams take over. Psychiatrists flirted with dream interpretation in the mid-twentieth century, but their theories had long since been put aside when Freyr began his specialized studies and were taught only for their historical significance. Dreams, after all, are dissimulators; their contents are distorted and reports of them merely patchy recollections that give no indication of what is missing – if anything – from the story, or whether something was fabricated to fill in the gaps. There are no independent witnesses to dreams, making them, as factors in psychoanalysis, at best crutches to use when all other options have been exhausted.

Now for the first time Freyr regretted not being more familiar with the most recent theories on dream interpretation. He knew that many clinical studies were being conducted on dreams, but very few of the articles published in the journals appealed to him. He had thus merely skimmed through them. He owned an excellent book on the subject, in which more than fifty thousand dreams were investigated, but it was somewhere in storage. Actually, Freyr recalled that the result of this extensive investigation had been something along the lines that people throughout the world generally dreamed the same things and that the dreams depended to a large degree on events in their daily lives. Firemen dreamed more often of fires than divers did, and so on. It was difficult to tell whether this conclusion fitted in Védís's case, except perhaps that if her dreams reflected her everyday reality, that reality was considerably different to what Freyr was used to.

Freyr had read through every single dream in her diary, since they were neither numerous nor long. He read some twice, some three times. He wanted to try to understand what these strange descriptions and interpretations said about the woman; what she saw in her dreams, how she reported them and what she thought most interesting about them. He even scrutinized Védís's handwriting in the hope that it would shed some light on her condition at the time of writing down each dream. But there was little to be discovered from it. The delicate script was nearly always the same, with nothing to indicate that any unusual agitation was controlling her hand. Every single letter was crisp and clear; the script slanted slightly to the right and the capital letters were more elaborate than Freyr was used to. Yet although the handwriting said nothing about the woman, her dreams were a different story. Freyr believed that the descriptions were realistic and that the woman hadn't made up anything that she described; he based this, among other things, on how irregular the entries were. If she'd written about her dreams day after day, Freyr would have been suspicious, since no cases existed of people being able to recall their subconscious adventures every single morning.

It wasn't until 2007 that her dreams became significantly interesting. Prior to that they'd been very normal, describing banalities that sleep distorted and changed into adventure or horror. Védís either ended up in situations characterized by overabundance and positivity, or else she was trapped in a world in which her arm fell off, the earth swallowed her home, she wound up in jail or something in that vein. Her interpretation of these dreams was extremely simple: bad events were omens of good things and vice versa. If her friends or relatives appeared in her dreams, she would write about them particularly, often noting to herself at the conclusion of her interpretation to contact them and warn them of this or that or ask about prospective heirs who proclaimed their arrival in one way or another. Twice, dead relatives of prospective parents had come to give names for the children and, according to her entries, she wanted to pass this information on. These were the extremely ordinary dreams of an extremely ordinary woman.

But as if someone had clicked their fingers, the descriptions took on a completely different form in February 2007.

When her dreams had first taken an odd turn, Védís seemed rather reluctant in her interpretations. Now they no longer centred on family and friends or anything else she was familiar with, but instead she entered a world characterized by darkness, danger and evil, from which she repeatedly woke terrified and drenched with sweat. At first she tried to interpret this as a positive omen: soon she would win the lottery, if she could just manage to count how often specific things that appeared repeatedly in these dreams turned up, but this soon stopped and Védís approached her dreams with increasing fear and tension. Freyr wasn't surprised. The woman now seemed to be prevented from sleeping peacefully and getting enough rest, and that alone created fertile ground for psychological difficulties, anxiety and depression. It was impossible to say which came first, the chicken or the egg, but after these dreams had been going on for around six months, it was difficult to follow the thread of the woman's readings of them; her language and references grew ever vaguer, making it harder to grasp their significance without further information about the woman and her circumstances.

But he didn't need to know anything more about Védís to connect one specific detail to her life. Or rather, her death. During the last two months before she died, garden shears started appearing more and more often in her dreams. They were bloody, and they frightened Védís. As she described them, the shears were either lying on the ground or in the hands of a boy who was the main character in these unsettling dreams, from the very first one to the last. Védís never saw his face, and she woke with a start every time he seemed to be on the verge of showing it. He generally appeared in the distance or turned his back to her as he stood, head bowed, at the edge of the dream. Védís didn't give any indication of who this boy was, but in her dreams her task was to get to him and speak to him. But she never accomplished this. He was always out of reach, no matter how fast she ran or how kindly she spoke to him. Freyr was fairly certain that Védís thought she knew who this boy was, but she never put his name to paper; she only hinted that he seemed familiar to her, but she could never be entirely sure of who he was – besides not being certain that she wanted to know. Freyr felt that this suggested Védís could have had something on her conscience that she pushed aside, and that by doing so she was depriving herself of the healing or comfort that could be found in coming to terms with a painful experience. If she refused to deal with her problems in her waking state, it was no surprise that they invaded her dreams.

The last dream she recorded was from the night before she died. The night before Freyr's son disappeared. He read over the description of this dream particularly carefully but discovered little to shed light on this strange coincidence. The dream was essentially the same, a hopeless chase of this unknown boy through dark corridors and fog, past crying children. They leaned up against the walls of the maze through which Védís wandered and refused to show their faces when she bent down to them. The children were covered with cuts, sores and bruises, which were visible when they reached out to grab her legs. In fact, the only significant difference between this dream and the others was that now there was a green lustre to everything, and Védís felt she couldn't breathe properly because of this green air. For further clarification she'd written that she felt as if she were in a submarine that had run out of air. The dream ended differently as well. This time she managed to approach the boy from behind and touch him. As soon as she placed her hand on his bony shoulder she regretted it and realized that it was a terrible mistake, as she wrote clearly in her dream diary. Then she heard the boy say: 'You shouldn't have done that.' The voice was much more like that of an elderly man than of a child, but the worst thing was that it seemed as if the voice came from behind her. The boy she was holding onto wasn't the same one she was always chasing. He stood behind Védís, and when she turned around slowly she woke up, her chest heavy.

'The only connection that I can see to Benni is so random that it hardly deserves a mention.' Freyr had just told Dagný all the details of Védís's dreams. 'One of the boys playing hide-and-seek with Benni said that Benni was going to hide in a submarine, but then he immediately took it back.' Freyr's eyes stung from all the reading, and he blinked several times to moisten them. 'This suggested what the police always considered most likely – that he'd gone down to the sea – but there was nothing there that could have been described as a submarine, even as viewed through a child's eyes.'

'But why would the boy have said something like that out of the blue and then taken it back?' Dagný sat opposite Freyr at the kitchen table, the dregs of some red wine in one of the two wine glasses that had come with the house. It was nearly midnight.

'Children are extremely poor witnesses. The boy was probably chuffed that the police were talking to him and wanted to add something. Maybe his childish imagination told him that a submarine had taken Benni and sailed away with him. His parents said he'd recently watched a film involving a submarine. It doesn't make much of a difference anyway, because it turned out that this boy had left the game to go to his cousin's birthday party before Benni went missing, so he couldn't have seen or heard anything that mattered. His parents confirmed it.'

Dagný nodded and changed the subject. 'I'm wondering whether Védís's death would have been investigated differently if they'd had this dream diary.' Her cheeks reddened slightly. 'You know – all this with the garden shears.'

Freyr emptied the wine bottle into her glass. He had enough wine in his, and didn't expect to finish it. He found the idea of being tipsy uncomfortable under these circumstances. 'I suppose so. It could very well be that there's a connection between the dreams and the accident, but not a criminal one. The two things could be connected easily if we suppose that Védís handled the shears clumsily precisely because of her dreams – she'd been stressed about handling them and thereby wasn't careful enough. But I have no idea why she dreamed about garden shears in the first place; there could be a thousand reasons for it and none of them particularly noteworthy. It's not possible that anyone planted it in her mind, which somehow led to her death, if that's what you mean.'

'No, not at all.' Dagný pulled one leg underneath her. 'There was clearly no one else involved. I was wondering more whether it was suicide.'

Freyr shrugged and placed the bottle on the counter 'I think that's rather unlikely, although suicide of course takes a variety of forms.'

'But don't you find it strange that she also dreamed about Halla, sitting and weeping, her face purple and her tongue sticking out, in a church that resembled the one in Súðavík?'

'Yes, of course that's striking, in the light of what happened to her. I also think it's interesting that the only people she mentions by name in the book after the dreams become so bizarre are her childhood friends from the class picture.'

'Why would that be?' Dagný's teeth were stained from the wine, but to Freyr this just increased her charm. 'I'm not one for prophecies and dreams, but I don't see what logical explanation there could be for this. Védís died before these people started popping off. It's out of the question that she could have been connected to their deaths in any way, even though she seems to have predicted all of them.' Dagný paged through the dream diary quickly until she found what she was looking for. 'Here, look. Jón appears here with a black face and no eyelashes. He's missing half his fingers, and the others are black and burned.' She turned to the next page. 'Silja is blue and frosted, lying on a snow bank and speaking to her without blinking, while snowflakes gradually fill her eyes. You remember that she froze to death?' She flipped rapidly through more pages. 'Here. Steinn. Lying at her feet, broken and shattered, and Védís writes, and I quote, that some of the injuries are so bad that nothing can heal them; precisely what happened to him. He lay there *like a doll thrown off a high-rise* and stared at her unable to speak, let alone anything else. The only thing he could do was blink his glazed eyes.' Dagný looked up from the book. 'I read the police report that was compiled after he was run over, and her description fits it pretty well. The same thing can be said of all of them; Védís appears to have dreamed how they would die.'

Freyr took care over what he said next, since the topic had taken a strange turn and it would be easy to jump to unrealistic conclusions. 'It's stated clearly that Védís got in touch with all of these people, and even though they didn't all take her overtures well, none of them hung up on her. So they heard her descriptions, and who knows, maybe they had some effect. Although I don't believe in that kind of thing, I'm afraid I'd be concerned if an old friend called me and told me sadly that she was always dreaming that I'd drowned or something like that. I might actually start behaving differently on lakes or out at sea, which might cause me to fall in and drown. That's what I think happened in each of these cases, as well as where Védís herself is concerned. Perhaps there's nothing that mysterious about it.'

Dagný ran her fingers over the book. 'I'm not completely convinced, sorry. But you get marks for trying.' She stared at the blue lettering as if searching for a hidden meaning that could explain all of this. 'Do you think this might be forged? That it wasn't written by her at all, but by someone else after her death – and therefore after the others had all died too?'

This hadn't crossed Freyr's mind. 'Interesting idea.' He reached for the book and turned to the first page. 'I doubt it, but we would need to compare the handwriting with hers to eliminate the possibility completely. Otherwise, the handwriting might not be the main issue. This fits with what Halla's widower said in his conversation with you, that Halla had started calling these childhood friends of hers around three years earlier – after Védís got in touch with her. It says in the book that Védís was thinking of speaking to Halla around the same time that she first appeared in her dreams. So, she seems to have rekindled her relationship with this old friend of hers, although it didn't last long because she died a short time later.'

'I wonder what they talked about? The meaning of the dreams, or how they might take advantage of these omens to avoid the danger?'

'I guess they'd have just talked about everything. The dreams were the trigger for their renewed acquaintance, but then they discovered that they had things in common and sought out each other's company.'

'That doesn't explain why Halla turned to the others when Védís slipped and cut herself to death on the garden shears.' Dagný took a tiny sip of wine. 'Védís probably told her all her dreams about the group, and when she died the way she did, Halla probably wanted to spread the message and continue to warn the others. It actually begs the question why the others continued to answer her phone calls and get in touch with her. According to Halla's widower, there were a lot of long telephone conversations over an extended period of time.'

Freyr paused for a moment before replying as he tried to remember the name of the childhood friend who was still alive. 'Obviously, the most direct course of action would be to ask the only one of them left about what actually went on.' Freyr flipped through the book a bit in search of entries concerning the man. 'Lárus. The one who appeared to Védís with his guts hanging out.'

'What sort of death do you suppose awaits him?' Dagný rested her glass on her leg and swirled the wine in it like an experienced wine taster preparing to sip and spit.

'No idea. Maybe stomach cancer.' Freyr pushed back thoughts of accidents and illnesses that could do serious damage to one's abdomen. 'Perhaps I'll try to find him tomorrow, since I'll be in town. He lives in Reykjavík.'

Dagný looked at the kitchen clock. 'I'd forgotten that you're heading south in the morning. I'd better get going.' She put down her glass and stood up. 'I like the idea of you trying to reach Lárus; I'd prefer this not to get mixed into the investigation with things as they are. I don't want to have to explain all this spooky stuff to my boss or the police down south. It can wait.'

When they were at the front door Freyr wished he could ask her to stay the night, but was afraid she would say no. Dagný herself seemed unsure how to say goodnight, and she appeared relieved to remember a detail that she'd forgotten to ask him about in their conversation concerning the diary. 'Do you remember how Védís wrote near the end that she'd started being woken by noises in the basement and that it disturbed her dreams, so that she couldn't finish them?' Freyr nodded. 'Have you noticed anything, heard a knocking like she describes or any other noises?'

'No, not that I recall.'

'Too bad.' Dagný smiled. 'Not that I want you to be haunted or anything. I was just hoping that if the noises were still occurring, they might be coming from broken pipes or something in the house itself, and that way we could solve at least one part of the puzzle.'

Once Freyr was under the covers he listened for noises from the house, instead of falling asleep to music on his iPod as he usually did. It wasn't long before he regretted it.

Chapter 19

The night had passed without any trauma; either they'd been too tired to notice anything, or their move to the doctor's house had had the desired effect. The hammering sound, which had nearly frightened them to death, had stopped just as abruptly as it had begun, and Katrín and Líf had managed to persuade Garðar not to rush outside. They'd subsequently checked all the windows and doors to reassure themselves that no one could get in, and propped chairs under the knobs of the front and back doors for added security. Reasonably satisfied with this arrangement, the three of them had then settled themselves on the upper floor and huddled together on the biggest bunk they could find in the hope of keeping warm. Nevertheless, Katrín was so cold when she woke up that she doubted the situation could have been worse, even if she'd slept out on the porch, alone. At first she found it difficult to use her hands, but then returning circulation slowly worked its way out to her extremities. Her joints were stiff and her entire body ached from her injuries, and the few bruises that weren't covered by clothing were larger and darker than they'd been the day before. She didn't dare look beneath her clothing and examine the rest because of the cold. Every breath and every word left behind a little white cloud and magnified the chill that seemed to have settled into her battered body. In the faint light that came in through the loose window shutters she could see Líf and Garðar's deathly pale faces, their eyes swollen and their noses bright red. Their hair was oily and dirty, since they'd given little thought to washing themselves in the confusion of these past days.

It was as if Líf read from Katrín's expression how she looked. She scratched her scalp, which only served to mess up her hair and make her look even scruffier. 'Jesus, I'm looking forward to getting home and having a shower.' The good old spa had clearly now become too remote an idea in her mind for her to think of it any more. 'Can't we heat some water and rinse most of the dirt off ourselves? I'm getting sick of the smell of my hair.' She wrapped her arms around herself in the hope of increased warmth. 'And I don't want to be found looking like shit if we die here.'

Garðar snorted, but when he spoke he ignored her pessimism. 'If you're willing to go up to the house with me I can heat water there. It's no problem.' He pulled his trousers up over the woollen underwear he'd bought specially for the trip. 'The food is there so we need to go anyway, unless we're planning to starve to death. And when we go we can try to continue with some of the repairs. We're better off doing something apart from hanging around here getting freaked out. I promise you time will pass quicker that way. We know now that the child is just as likely to turn up here as there.'

Katrín reached for the woolly jumper she'd taken off before crawling into her sleeping bag, but missed very much when she woke half frozen. The garment was ice-cold to the touch. 'You want us to go and paint? I can't say I'm wild about the idea.' Putti looked as if he agreed with her. He probably didn't want to go out into the snow at all, and would happily have continued to lie on the mattress at her feet.

Líf was still shivering. 'I want to walk further up the fjord.' She finally looked as if she were going to put on more clothing. 'Maybe, maybe we'll find a boat that we can take to Ísafjörður. I'm not talking about going far, just far enough to give us a better view of the fjord. Remember the big chimney and the remains of the whaling station, or factory, or whatever it is, just near here, that we saw from the boat on the way? Can't we go there?'

'Do you even know how to pilot a boat?' Garðar seemed irritated by their negative reaction to his idea about continuing the repairs and Katrín found this rather silly; he could hardly have expected them to leap eagerly to their feet. 'I wouldn't want to risk it.' His voice was slightly shrill with agitation.

'If there's a boat here, there's probably a radio or a phone in it.' Líf wasn't giving up.

Not for the first time, the negotiator in Katrín stirred. 'I suggest we go up to the house, have something to eat, perk ourselves up a bit by washing our hair, work for a while and then go for a hike when it's light enough.' She had no idea if it was pitch-dark outside or whether the sun was shining brightly. Nor did she know whether she could walk for any distance, although the aching in her body had subsided somewhat. 'Of course it depends on the weather, but it sounds to me like it's quietened down outside.' They couldn't hear the wind moaning; silence seemed to dominate outside as well as in. 'Is that a plan?' She looked at Líf, who shrugged her shoulders, then at Garðar, who stared sadly at her. Why he should be sad, she didn't know; perhaps it was dawning on him that this was going to end badly. They would probably make it home okay, but then the struggle would begin all over again, not helped by their worsening financial problems. A guesthouse in an abandoned village, whether it was dilapidated or newly renovated, wouldn't change anything. She smiled sweetly at him but he looked away. Líf, however, seemed thrilled with her proposal; they could walk further up the fjord after all. In search of a boat that didn't exist.

The water was far too hot, or did it just seem that way in the cold out on the porch? Katrín felt her scalp contract as Garðar poured water from an aluminium pot over her head, and the throbbing of the bruise there nearly killed her. She was facing the mutilated woodwork and the black soil beneath the gaping hole that they still had to repair. She was surprised there was no snow on the soil, despite the area all around being covered in white. Maybe the black soil was warmer than the surrounding ground and had melted the snow as soon as it fell. Black objects were generally warmer to the touch than lighter-coloured ones on sunny days. Luckily Garðar had covered over the fox skeleton immediately after they found it, so she didn't have that staring up at her. That would have been the icing on the cake. Another wave of water cascaded over her head, getting soap in her eyes but diminishing the pain in her warm, sore scalp. 'Shit.' Katrín rubbed her eyes but that just made things worse. 'Hand me the towel.' She bent down, opened her eyes, and gasped when she thought she saw little filthy feet on the porch, directly below her face, as if a child were standing close in front of her. She shut her eyes again, but when she reopened them she saw only the wet planks of the porch. She straightened up so quickly that her head spun, and water from her hair flew in all directions.

'What's up with you?' Annoyed, Garðar used the towel to

dry off the water that had splashed on him, before handing it to Katrín. 'You two are so messy!'

Líf had been the first to wash and had managed to splash water everywhere when she also claimed to have got soap in her eyes. Putti had received an unwanted shower this way; he'd jumped off the porch and now didn't dare step back onto it. Katrín wondered now whether Líf had experienced the same hallucination but she didn't want to ask, since she didn't know what answer she was hoping for. Nor did she want to bring up the boy, since they'd managed to avoid talking about him for three whole hours as they worked on repairs. On the other hand, it was no secret that he was on their minds. They'd started working through the wooden planks on the lower storey that had been stacked there by the former owner, although he hadn't lived long enough to finish laying out the new wooden floor. This meant, they could all work in the same place and be comforted by each other's presence. Although the house wasn't big, none of them wanted to end up alone in a closed room. 'Let's see how you handle it.' Katrín wrapped the towel around her wet hair. 'How much water is left?'

'Not enough.' Garðar showed her what remained in the pot. 'I'm going to get more; the stove is still burning and it won't take the water any time to warm up. I'm tougher than you two, I don't need to have it that hot.'

'Sure. Sure you are.' Líf stood up from the kitchen stool that she'd dragged outside. She'd also wrapped her hair in a towel, like a white turban. She looked a whole lot better simply after a hair-wash and she seemed relaxed. 'You're so much tougher than us.' She took the butt of the cigarette that she'd just finished and stuck it back into the packet, frowning.

Her tobacco inventory seemed a greater cause for concern than arguing with Garðar over which sex was braver when it came to hair-washing. 'Did you see any more packs of cigarettes in the doctor's house?'

'No.' Although Katrín was unhappy that Líf had taken them, everything was a lot calmer since she'd been able to burn off some of her stress with cigarettes. She suspected that the atmosphere wouldn't be as relaxed once the pack was finished. 'We'll take a closer look through the cupboards tonight.' They'd already decided to spend another night in the doctor's house. 'Maybe we'll find more cigarettes.' Líf beamed, making Katrín worry that she was about to light up again and finish the pack in the expectation of finding some more. 'Don't get your hopes up, though,' she warned

Garðar had gone down to the stream, and although Katrín would have liked to wait for him on the porch she was too cold; the ends of her hair where they poked out from beneath the towel felt stiff and icy. 'Shouldn't we go inside?'

'God, yes. I'm frozen.' Líf shook herself. 'Can you imagine how cold it must have been when that woman and her kid fell through the ice? I wouldn't have thought it could get much colder here, but the fjord isn't even frozen over yet. How low does the temperature actually have to be for the sea to freeze?'

'I have no idea.' Katrín didn't want to know. She had the feeling that if they spoke too much about it they would somehow conjure up even colder weather. And then the boat wouldn't be able to dock at the pier – in fact, a rubber dinghy wouldn't even make it up to the beach.

Líf shuffled her feet on the porch, but made no move to go inside. 'Can you imagine her desperation when she realised she wasn't going to be able to save her child?' Katrín's goose bumps had returned. She wished Líf would change the subject. 'How she must have flailed around in the water, trying to get a strong enough grip on him to lift him out? I suppose she didn't give a damn about herself in the end, as long as he was saved.'

'Stop talking about it.' Katrín couldn't take any more. 'We both know it was a horrible way to die, without having to go into all the details.'

'Do you think the child we saw is the drowned boy?' Líf spoke so softly that she was almost whispering. 'Something hit the house from the outside when Garðar was telling us what had been written about them. If it's a ghost, it would explain a lot.'

'No,' said Katrín sternly. 'He's much older; the little boy who drowned was five. And this child is definitely alive, not dead.' Her voice wavered; she wasn't even convincing herself. 'Let's go in.' The warmth from the wood stove met them at the door. Putti came up as close to her as he could manage and lay down at her feet, delighted to get some warmth into his little body. The sensation of stepping in from the cold was the best Katrín could recall since their arrival in Hesteyri, and she was filled with indescribable longing for the warmth of her own home in Reykjavík. It didn't help that she had the sneaking suspicion something bad was about to happen, since they were all feeling so good. She felt like crying, but restrained herself.

'I really want to crawl in there.' Líf stood in front of the wood slot on the stove, holding her hands as close to it as she could stand. 'I'd forgotten how it feels to be warm.'

Katrín followed her example. She watched her hands redden, from her fingertips up along the backs until the redness disappeared beneath the arms of her jacket. Her pain seemed to have subsided; her body no longer ached. 'Me too. I've already started to worry about it cooling down again.' She didn't get any further, since a terrible cracking sound came from behind them, almost like gunfire. Líf screamed and grabbed Katrín. Putti had shot to his feet and was looking around, bewildered. 'What the hell was that?' Katrín tried to shake off Líf but in the commotion she'd bumped into the towel on her head, nearly knocking it off. She managed to get Líf off her and grab the towel before it fell to the floor. She could still see the child's filthy feet too vividly in her mind to dare turn around to look. The sound of Garðar's rapid footsteps came from the porch and she decided to wait and let him see what was in the room with them, since he thought he was such a great hero.

'What was that noise?' Garðar sounded breathless. 'I was so startled when I heard you two screaming that I almost lost all the water. What happened?'

There was clearly nothing weird in the room, since Garðar seemed calm enough. Katrín turned around and fought the desire to squint so that she'd be able to shut her eyes quicker if there was something there. She didn't tell him it was only Líf who'd screamed, as she wasn't entirely sure that was the case. It was quite possible that she'd cried out too, without realizing it. 'We heard some sort of terrible noise, like a loud cracking sound, inside the house. Then you came. I have no idea what happened.'

Garðar looked around and Katrín followed suit. Líf, however, was still facing the wood stove, her back to the room, her face buried in her hands. 'Tell me when you've figured out what it was.' Then she added: 'Just make stuff up if it's something awful. I really can't take any more.'

'No one needs to make anything up.' Garðar walked into the room and towards the rotten patch in the wooden floor. 'I can see what happened.' He leaned over and picked something up. When he straightened up he handed Katrín a broken floorboard. 'The parquet cracked.' He seemed puzzled. 'Maybe we nailed it down too forcefully and it expanded in the heat from the stove.' He reached down for another piece of wood that also lay against the wall. 'Or else it has something to do with this rot.' He examined the wood as if it held the answer. 'I guess we'll have to take out all the boards in this part of the floor. There are several there at the front that the former owner laid down.'

'Isn't that a really big project?' Katrín longed to toss the plank she was holding into the fire, and if she had her way, the leftover floorboards and the rest of it would all go the same way. 'We can't even finish what we've already started, let alone add new projects to the list.'

Garðar stared at his feet as if in a trance and didn't answer immediately. 'There's something about the state of this floor that's making me sure we need to fix it. I feel like it could spread throughout the entire house if we don't do something, and then it'll all be ruined.'

'The stain hasn't got any bigger since we last saw it. Why would it start spreading now?' Katrín peered at the mark. Was she right? To her it appeared not to have changed at all, although she hadn't exactly memorized its outline. 'Isn't it weird that it's so square?' Now as she looked at the floor she found the edges of the affected area abnormally straight, the corners almost sharp. 'Could something under there be causing it?'

'Like what?' Garðar knew about as much about damp and

rot as Katrín did. 'If that's the case, ripping up the floorboards will expose it.'

Líf came over to stand between them, staring at the spot. She hadn't said anything until now and it was clear that her interest in the topic was limited. 'I think we should hurry if we're going out for a walk. Let's bring the water over so you can wash your hair, Garðar, and then let's get going. Otherwise it'll be dark before we're even halfway there.' Garðar opened his mouth as if to say something, but Líf interrupted. 'You promised, Garðar. We're going to the factory.'

Instead of agreeing to this or mumbling a protest, Garðar looked for a second into Katrín's eyes before turning and going back out to get the pot he'd left behind. Despite the warmth, Katrín felt a familiar chill pass through her. She had the feeling Garðar also suspected something bad was about to happen. But who knew what it might be?

Chapter 20

Freyr fell asleep before the plane took off and didn't stir until an embarrassed flight attendant shook his shoulder lightly, after all the other passengers had alighted. He hadn't been very sleepy during the night; exhaustion and his vivid imagination had played games with him. He'd heard all kinds of noises in the house, as if someone were wandering around in the basement. He couldn't persuade himself to get up, dress and go down to have a look; it wasn't the cold outside that stopped him, but rather the image of his son he'd seen in the hospital corridor. He was convinced that something similar awaited him downstairs. When he forced himself to get up, he saw dark rings under his eyes in the mirror, and although a cold shower should have made him feel better, he looked worse than he would have liked. He'd toyed with the idea of saying hello to some old colleagues at the National Hospital or even dropping in to see Sara. He would have enough time to do so between his meeting with the forensic pathologist and the departure of the afternoon flight, even if he also met up with Lárus Helgason. Now he wasn't so sure this was how he wanted to spend the day; he flinched at the thought of his former colleagues thinking his unkempt appearance meant that he was losing his mind, and speculating that it wouldn't be long before they heard news of his taking indefinite sick leave. Anger, paranoia, slander; he could handle most things, but he couldn't bear pity. There was no way to respond to it; anything he did or said would only make matters worse, and possibly even serve to further convince them of his decline. No, it was better to avoid his colleagues and leave Sara be.

Now the forensic pathologist was telling him, 'The weirdest thing about it is that I vaguely remembered similar injuries in other cases, which led me to do a little research. And it appears that most of them were scarred on their backs in precisely the same way.' The man spoke through a white paper mask. Little could be seen of his face behind that and his clunky safety goggles. Freyr would have had trouble recognizing the man out on the street, since he didn't even know his hair colour; the doctor had greeted him with a green surgeon's cap on his head, and had then pulled the mask up from his chin and pushed his glasses down onto his nose. 'I find it very strange that this didn't find its way into the woman's medical records, since the scar seems to have been created over a long period of time. Although the cross is fully formed, it was made from many different wounds that healed at different times; the last one rather recent.'

Freyr stared at Halla's bluish-white back. He'd been asked to wear the same sort of protective garments as the pathologist and was finding it hard to resist ripping the goggles off his face, as he found it hard to see through them clearly. 'Did she do this herself, in your opinion? Inflict all these wounds to form a cross?' Up along her entire spinal column lay a tight row of white and pink vertical scars of various sizes. In some places they'd run together and many of the lines were far from straight, though they looked that way from just a short distance. Beneath her shoulder blades a similar collection of scars ran perpendicular to the other, forming a cross. It was clear which of these scars were the newest: those located at the end of the perpendicular line on Halla's left side were redder than the others.

'It's difficult to see how most of them could be self-inflicted.' The pathologist pointed with his gloved hand at the area in the middle where the lines of the cross met. 'She could have done it with some sort of sharp implement, but considering the precision – none of the scars lies outside the cross itself – she would have had to use two mirrors as well. It would be very hard to concentrate properly under those circumstances, I would imagine.' He removed his hand from Halla's back and stuck it in the pocket of his gown. 'I would guess that she had help, if you can call it that. Or maybe this was done against her will, but for some reason she didn't put up a fight.'

'How did it look in the other cases you mentioned? Did the victims inflict the wounds themselves, or did someone else?'

'They were never sure.' The doctor pulled the white sheet back over the body. 'It was two individuals, a woman and a man, but I didn't handle either of their cases so I don't know all the details.'

'Who were they?' Freyr looked at the white lump that now constituted Halla's earthly remains. She was to be sent back west on the afternoon plane, her funeral scheduled for two days later. He never failed to be struck by the sight of what a person left behind; where before a heart had beaten and a ceaseless torrent of thoughts had poured out, now there was nothing but dead flesh on white bones. And in time, only the bones would remain.

'The first was the body of a man who'd died in a car accident, and the second, the woman, came to light at the funeral parlour. I was on my summer holiday when the first one came up, so I first heard of it just recently when I started asking around for you, but photos were taken and reports were filed. Someone from the funeral parlour told me about the other case, but the coroner who autopsied the first one had also heard about it.' The doctor pulled off his rubber gloves and dropped them into the shiny steel rubbish bin. 'Counting our friend here, these three deaths occurred over a period of just over two years. It makes me wonder whether it was some sort of religious ceremony, some cult that keeps far enough under the radar for no one to have heard about it.'

Freyr pulled off his own gloves, rather clumsily. 'Halla was religious, but her husband didn't mention any cult. She helped with relief work for the church in her home town. I suppose there's no chance the other two lived in Flateyri?'

The doctor shook his head. 'No, the woman lived in Reykjanes if I remember correctly, and the man was from Ísafjörður. He paused as he leaned over to scribble something on a form lying on the desk. 'The three of them may not have lived in the same town but they did have one thing in common: they were all born in 1940. I don't know whether that means anything, but I made a particular note of it.'

Freyr licked his lips beneath his mask. 'What were their names, might I ask? Could the name of the man who was run over be Steinn?'

The doctor's safety goggles shifted slightly as he raised his eyebrows in surprise. 'How did you know that?'

It was a strange feeling to be a car-less visitor in the city where he'd been born and had lived most of his life, as well as to have no place to go and lie down for an hour or so. He didn't want to visit his family, since that would just make them worry about him more; it had been bad enough telling them he was moving out of town. Neither his parents nor his brother had understood, and had taken it as a sign that he was ill. They were probably right. So, instead of sitting over a cup of coffee with his family, Freyr found himself yawning in the back seat of a cab on his way to Sara's. He was determined not to have a repeat of what had happened in the plane, and fought to stay awake. Of course he would have preferred to walk the short distance to her place on the west side of town, but he was worried about being even more tired by the time he arrived. It would be enough of a trial as it was. Sara had actually sounded stronger than usual on the phone, as if this time she might not burst into tears. Hopefully this meant she was coming to terms with the past, but Freyr knew he mustn't get his hopes up based on one short phone call. Of course he should have told her his plans the night before, but things hadn't gone the way he'd intended. He hadn't wanted to call Sara while Dagný was there, and by the time she left after midnight he'd felt it was too late to do it. Nor had he known when, or even if, he could meet up with Lárus, who hadn't answered his calls. He'd called Sara when he'd exhausted his other options; not very courteous of him, which was probably the reason why she'd responded so unenthusiastically.

But his thoughts were mainly dwelling on his meeting with the forensic pathologist. Freyr had asked him to find out whether the other two members of the group who were already dead had exhibited the same wounds when they died. Of the five deceased he already knew three had been marked in this way, which made it plausible that the other two, Védís and Jón, had been too. This could easily be verified now that he had given the doctor their names. Once he had, the doctor had quizzed him concerning the relationship between the individuals and how Freyr himself was connected to the case. Freyr had answered his questions conscientiously and not held anything back, since he saw no reason to do so. He told him that he thought perhaps these people had believed in the prophetic power of dreams, or that ghosts had played some part in their lives – and their deaths. The man had listened attentively, and said finally that of all the branches of the medical sciences, Freyr's specialism was one of the few that were no better at diagnosing the dead than the living. He personally had little experience of mental illnesses; he saw only their consequences and never their causes, despite being able to work his way unhindered through the parts of the body and the organs that couldn't offer an easy diagnosis in the living. Therefore, he conceded, he was in no position to judge what Freyr said; he would simply have to believe him. When they parted, the doctor asked to be allowed to follow the progress of the case, hinting that he might consider writing a paper about the scars and their origins. Freyr had his doubts that a paper on such a peculiar case would be published in any self-respecting medical journal, but promised to stay in touch nevertheless.

The cab stopped outside the beautiful wooden house where

Sara lived. The apartment was on the middle floor and Freyr could see in through the living room window, where she was standing and watching him. He paid the driver and stepped out, but when he looked up again Sara was gone. He drew several deep breaths on his way up to the house and found he was walking more slowly than usual. He felt terribly apprehensive about seeing her, and asked himself why he was doing it; it would be best for them both if they ceased all communication. That was easier said than done, though, based to no small extent on the guilt he still felt over having abandoned her when she'd needed him most. Before he rang the doorbell he reminded himself that his hand had been forced by self-preservation, one of the strongest human instincts.

He'd barely rung the bell before the door opened and Sara stood in the entrance. She was even thinner than last time, down to nearly nothing. It made her head look abnormally large, like that of a PEZ dispenser. Yet even though her body appeared frail, there was something in her face that made her look healthier than he'd seen her in a long time: her eyes were sparkling and full of emotion, but not the one he'd expected. Sara seemed furious. 'Hi.' He leaned forward to kiss her on the cheek as usual, but she turned away and beckoned him in. Freyr tried to act unconcerned, though he felt uncomfortable. He took off his shoes and followed her inside. Everywhere he looked he saw familiar furniture and ornaments from when they'd lived together. To him they seemed lost in their new location, as if they were still waiting to be moved back to their original home.

'This is my friend, Elísa.' Sara indicated a woman sitting on the living room sofa, which they'd put so much effort into choosing. They greeted each other, and he suddenly thought that Sara was going to tell him she'd realised she was gay. 'Elísa is a medium, and she's been helping me recently. You can spare me the moralizing, because she's been much more use to me than you have, as a supposed expert in other people's well-being.' Following this introduction, Sara sat down on the sofa and patted it to indicate that he should sit as well. 'I'm glad Elísa was able to drop by, given it was such short notice. I wanted her to meet you.'

'Sorry, Sara.' Freyr chose a chair facing the sofa. 'I was only expecting to see you. It's not really any excuse, but I've had a lot on my plate, and I haven't exactly been at my best recently.' He turned to the medium, who was blushing, obviously wishing she could get up and leave. Sara probably hadn't planned this meeting in advance; she wasn't usually that organised. 'Just so you know, although I'm not much of a one for mysticism or spirituality, I think everyone is entitled to their own opinion – and it would be a boring world if everyone believed the same thing. If you've helped Sara, that's great, and I would never oppose any treatment that works.'

Elísa smiled at him, clearly relieved. She was dressed in very ordinary clothes: jeans, shirt and jacket. The garments were all clean and ironed, but on closer inspection had been worn a great deal: her shirtsleeves were threadbare at the edges and her jeans lighter-coloured at the knees. Nothing about her fit the stereotype of a medium; perhaps she took steps to counter this by avoiding long, colourful skirts and making sure to straighten any curls out of her long hair. 'Thanks. Sara and I are making good progress and I'm hoping that by working together we can help her get past what's bothering her.' She looked at Sara and gave a little smile. 'But from what Sara has told me, her problem seems to be connected to you somehow. I know this might sound strange to you, but I don't know exactly how or why it concerns you. Contact with those who are no longer among us isn't like a conversation between two people; there may be a few words here and there, but it's often more like a kind of . . . *effect* on a person, which that person might not necessarily understand.'

'Is that really so different from the kind of work you do, Freyr?' His ex-wife's voice had softened slightly, which woke memories of the Sara he once knew. 'Doctors might understand how muscles and organs work, but you actually have no idea what causes a person to be happy or sad. Do you? You can't explain what an emotion *is*, yet you assume they're there and don't doubt their existence.' Freyr nodded to acknowledge this, not wanting to irritate them by explaining psychiatry's theory on emotions. Science's investigations and definitions of well-documented phenomena were worlds away from the simplified explanations of occultists.

'What are you expecting me to say? Or do?' He felt even more exhausted as soon as the words were out; by asking this he'd become a participant in Sara's latest desperate attempt to cure herself, and given her the green light to continue on this course. It could only end one way, with more disappointment.

'You appear again and again, both in Sara's dreams and in conversation. It's no coincidence; it happens repeatedly, and even more frequently in recent days.'

'And what would you like me to do about that?' Freyr longed to lean his head on the soft back of the armchair, shut his eyes and ask to be left alone for half an hour.

'I don't know.' Well, you couldn't say Elísa wasn't honest. Freyr had to concentrate on not laughing out loud. The woman, who seemed to realize he didn't think much of her, added: 'When people die without coming to terms with their end, they get trapped between worlds. They can't move on to the next level of existence, because the ones they leave behind are still too connected to them and want justice to be done, or for a reckoning to take place. If that doesn't happen, these wayward souls try to find a way to tell their loved ones what happened, but that's not always achievable – often they can't manage to make contact with the living. This stage is most evident while family members or close friends of the deceased are still alive, and more often than not the dead give up when there's no one left with an interest in resolving the matter. The soul can get stuck in limbo, its demand for justice turns into an obsession and that's when you get hauntings in old houses or cemeteries.'

Freyr was finding it increasingly difficult to keep his attention on the conversation. 'Do you have any coffee, Sara? I slept badly, so I'm having trouble following this.'

She stared at him, her expression impenetrable, but then stood up and walked into the kitchen. Elísa continued: 'The longer the soul remains at this stage, the harder it becomes to deal with. In extremis, even the best and brightest soul can experience a total reversal and become extremely dangerous. We need to prevent such a thing from happening to your son. You wouldn't want to have to deal with him if things went *the wrong way*.' This last thing she whispered, to ensure that Sara didn't hear.

'And how do we stop that from happening?' Freyr wanted that coffee so badly that it took a huge effort for him not to get up, abandon the woman mid-sentence and run into the kitchen.

'Find him. Solve the puzzle of what actually happened to him and bury him with his relatives. Free him from the torment of knowing his mother is living in a hell of uncertainty, and you as well.'

Freyr couldn't play along any more. 'Don't you think we've done everything we possibly can, spirits or no spirits? Believe me, no stone was left unturned.'

'Nonetheless, you have to keep trying.' Elísa stared at him, her dark blue eyes steady beneath her overplucked eyebrows. 'If it's not too late.'

'Too late?' Freyr could hardly keep up. The only thing he knew for certain was that this woman wasn't helping Sara – quite the contrary. Her methods were working against Sara's recovery, enabling Sara to put off accepting the tragic fact that they would probably never know what happened. Maybe Sara seemed a bit better right now, but it wouldn't last long.

'I sense your son's presence. Very strongly. But I also sense a tremendous anger that is disproportionate given how little time has passed since his disappearance. I have no explanation for it, but I know there's not much time left.' Elísa glanced quickly towards the kitchen door. 'You simply must resolve this. If you think the situation's bad now, I can assure you you'll soon be looking back on this time as the best you had since your son disappeared.'

Sara walked in with coffee and Freyr was genuinely relieved to see her. It wasn't simply that he would now get his long-desired dose of caffeine, but also that he was saved from the medium's doom-laden prophecies. He didn't think he had the strength to argue with her or even comment on what she'd said, though he certainly didn't agree with her. He reached out to pick up the cup Sara had placed in front of him, but started when the medium placed her cool hand over his. He gave her a puzzled look.

'The devil's afoot. Keep that in mind,' she said. He smiled awkwardly, freed his hand and lifted his cup. Before he could take a sip, she added: 'I fear things are going to go badly for you. Very badly.'

Chapter 21

They'd waited too long to get going. It grew darker with each step as they walked along the narrow trail towards the old factory, which lay further up the fjord. But the sky was clear and there were no signs of it changing, or of the snow resuming. At times it was difficult to make out the trail beneath the snow, but luckily in most places it was slightly sunken, making it easy enough to follow. Katrín had lost count of the streams she'd had to jump over, mostly with Putti in her arms since he whined and fussed every time they approached even a small one. His short legs weren't made for great endeavours, and he feared being left behind on the other side of these fearsome rapids. Several of the streams were bridged with logs or planks of wood. For most of the way the path had run alongside the beach, but it had been sloping uphill for some time now and below them were sheer rocks over which the water gushed, in some places capped with silvery ice.

'How much further do you think it is?' Katrín was last in line, since she was in the worst shape and kept turning back to make sure Putti was still following them. He'd slowed down a bit, yet she still found it amazing how energetic he was under the circumstances; it was the equivalent of them having to wade through hip-deep snow. 'There's no boat to be seen. Maybe we should turn around?' She was afraid her aches and pains would make the return trip unbearable if they went too far.

Garðar had said nothing during their hike. He wasn't limping, which must mean that his heel was better, so his reticence wasn't caused by pain. Maybe he was nervous. He turned and looked back at Katrín but said nothing, just looked away again and kept walking. Líf led the group, and seemed to be ignoring Katrín's suggestion. 'We're nearly there. Garðar and I went there when we came to look at the house; it's half an hour away at most.'

Of course, that time everything wasn't covered in snow, but Katrín decided there was no point saying so. Líf would disregard all attempts to dissuade her. Katrín hoped her uncharacteristic cheeriness didn't mean she'd cooked up a plan to dupe them into going further and further, until they unwittingly found themselves walking all the way to Ísafjörður. But then again, Líf hadn't suggested that they bring food along, so it seemed unlikely, unless she'd completely lost her grip on reality and thought that they could live off the land along the way. The thought of forcibly dragging her back over slippery tree stumps and unbridged streams was less than appealing. 'What were you doing all the way out here?' Katrín almost lost her balance when she tripped on a bump in the middle of the path, concealed by the snow.

'Oh, it was just a ridiculous idea I had.' Líf's pace hadn't slowed even though she'd stumbled on the same bump as Katrín. 'I'd read about it and thought maybe we could buy the whole shebang and turn the factory into a hotel or something. Don't laugh when you see the state of the buildings.' She stopped suddenly and pointed ahead. 'See, we're just about there. You can see the chimney. It's just down here.'

Katrín paused at the top of the slope and stared down at the strip of low ground where the factory stood. The snow hadn't managed to cover the ruins, which stood out darkly, distinctly, against the otherwise snowy white landscape. A towering chimney captured their attention, apparently only days away from collapsing. 'Look, can you see the hole at the top of the chimney?' She pointed, and both Líf and Garðar stopped their downward progress to look. 'Is it safe to go near it?'

'That was the Coast Guard. They used the chimney for target practice in the Cod Wars. Shot at it with a cannon.' Líf resumed walking, and Garðar followed.

Katrín hesitated before following them. The light was steadily dwindling and she didn't want to lose her step as she descended, in case she fell and hurt herself. Every step down also meant another step up on the way back. Putti had stopped with her on the edge of the slope and seemed worried, whining and barking to dissuade her from going down. Then he gave up and followed. Now the entire fjord was visible and Katrín found the unnaturally calm sea incredibly beautiful in the twilight. 'I still can't see a boat,' she called down to Líf and Garðar, who were steadily increasing their lead, 'Shouldn't we turn back soon? It'll be dark before long.' They said nothing; they didn't even slow down. 'We came here to look for a boat, remember?' Still no reaction. Irritated, she considered scooping Putti up in her arms and heading back without them. She was even seized by the childish notion that it would teach the other two a lesson if she got lost and froze to death. But a frantic bark from Putti brought her back down to earth. 'What's wrong, boy?' She turned and saw that something in the sea seemed to be bothering the dog. She leaned down to him and tried to work out what he was staring at, before noticing two black humps sticking up from the surface of the sea just beyond land. At first she thought it was two wet, shiny stones, rocks on the seashore. But it wasn't long before she realized their movements were being watched. 'Seals!' At this Líf and Garðar did stop, and turned around to see what was up. Katrín pointed at the sea, where the seals' heads were still poking up, and smiled. Garðar smiled back at her but Líf simply shook her head and continued walking.

Katrín nudged Putti forward with her foot and made to set out after them, her mood now lighter. Putti stayed where he was, growling and staring at the seals. 'Enough of that nonsense. They're not about to come to shore, so you're safe.' Putti stopped growling and gave her a mournful look, as if he wanted to tell her something. He made do with licking her hand, and she tried to cheer him up by scratching him briskly behind the ear. 'Come on. Let's get this over with. Then we'll go home. I don't want to be here any more than you do.' She stood up and walked away, Putti right behind her. When she saw how reluctantly he was moving she picked him up, though that would slow her down even more. And in fact she was in no hurry; it would be dark on the way back, whether or not it took her a few minutes longer to make it down the slope. From time to time she looked towards the seals and was never disappointed; they shifted their positions slightly, but continued to stare in her direction. Of course they were too far away for her to get a good look at their faces, but she recalled the saying, 'seals have men's eyes'. Putti, however, was now carefully avoiding looking at the sea, probably because his primitive dog logic told him that if he couldn't see the seals, they were no longer there. When Katrín put him down at the base of the slope, he shook himself and seemed to perk up again, since the seals were no longer visible.

'Isn't it fantastic?' Líf was sitting on a low concrete wall tossing a cigarette pack from one hand to the other, as if wondering whether she should have one more or preserve them for later. 'What do you think?' She gestured around her with the pack.

'Well, I won't laugh at your idea about the hotel.' Katrín studied the ruins. Everywhere she looked she saw reddish-brown; rusted tanks and hulking lumps of iron in among half-collapsed brick buildings. A brick or two poked up out of the snow, as did twisted shapes of wrought iron. 'But God, this place is weird.' The factory must have been among the biggest in the country in its time, but it had truly seen better days. Katrín could see that the buildings were unrestorable. The roof of a large room located beneath the tall chimney had collapsed and now hung in strips from long iron rods, and none of the walls had withstood the ravages of time, though they had fallen into ruin in a variety of ways. 'Why did they need such a tall chimney?'

'I don't know.' Líf leaned her head back so she could look up at it. Unbelievably, it was in the best state of repair of all their surroundings.

'They were liquefying something. Making cod-liver oil, maybe.' Garðar had been silent for so long that he was slightly hoarse. He cleared his throat. 'But don't ask me about all this iron junk. I haven't got the faintest idea what it's for.' Rusting cranes, winches, bolts, pipes and tanks lay silently around them, revealing nothing.

'I'd like to know what this thing is behind me.' Líf peered into a long pit beneath the wall where she sat. A huge iron pipe supported by welded-on struts leaned over it, a short distance from them. 'There's all sorts of stuff in there that must have had some purpose.'

Garðar glanced into the pit and then looked speculatively up and down the pipe's length. When he spoke it was clear that he was just as clueless as they were about the factory's former activities. 'This had something to do with processing offal, I reckon.'

'Ugh.' Líf turned away from the pit, though without leaving her perch on the wall, where she was comfortable enough. 'You should look inside, if you think it's strange out here.' She pointed Katrín to a large opening leading into the darkened factory. 'But don't go in. Just look through the hole.'

Katrín felt ill at ease, but she said nothing. She thought she heard a noise from the beach below them. She checked to see whether Putti was still with them, or if the seals had come ashore and he'd perhaps gone after them. He hadn't; he was still standing next to her, looking dejected. Katrín glanced at the mountains across the fjord; they would soon be invisible in the dark. She found it isolating to think that across the huge span of territory lying before their eyes, there was probably not another single soul. She was momentarily struck by the question of what she would do if Garðar and Líf were gone when she turned around. She couldn't hear them; neither the scraping of their shoes nor their breathing. This was probably just because she'd pulled her hood over her head, but it felt as if she were entranced by the sea and the dark blue, white-capped mountains, just as Putti had been spellbound by the seals. If she didn't turn around, Líf and Garðar would still be there and would continue to be there until she pulled her eyes away from the sea and saw that they were gone.

'Katrín? What's up?' Líf stretched her leg out and kicked lightly at Katrín's bottom. 'Did you hear me? I said you should have a look inside.'

Although Katrín didn't like being badgered, the contact was a relief. Of course they weren't gone, she was just tired, both mentally and physically; her mind was playing tricks on her. She turned around and smiled at the familiar faces that looked back at her in surprise. Garðar seemed a bit jumpy, as if he'd heard a noise, though he didn't say anything. Líf was the only one who was acting normally, though her normal state would be considered abnormal by most people. She'd put the cigarette packet in her pocket and now rolled her eyes impatiently. Katrín decided to do as she suggested; perhaps they could head home after this total waste of time. 'Fine, I'll take a look, but then shouldn't we be getting back? I'm really tired and hungry, and soon there'll be no light left at all.' She walked off towards the building, which looked even darker than before. The opening, so intriguing according to Líf, was pitch-black, the bricks at its edges like stained, rotten teeth in a hideous mouth.

'Go with her, Garðar.' Líf was in her element. She had a talent for giving orders, and when Katrín heard the crunching of snow behind her, indicating that he'd obeyed, she could imagine Líf smiling from ear to ear. She was relieved he was there. Although she wasn't planning on spending much time here – she'd just stick her head in, say, 'Wow' and that would be that – it was better not to be alone. Putti followed her, of course, and although his faithfulness undeniably warmed her heart, it didn't provide the same security as Garðar's presence.

Once she was standing in front of the hole she no longer wanted to see what was inside. How interesting could it be? Adrenalin streamed through her veins without her understanding what caused it. It was as if her subconscious sensed some imminent danger that her usual senses weren't picking up. Did she catch a glimpse of something moving in the darkness? Could the boy be staying in there? They hadn't seen any tracks in the snow, but it was perfectly possible that he'd managed to cover them. Katrín peered as far in as she could without having to go any closer to the opening.

'What? Did you see something?' Garðar had come up next to her. He took one step closer to the wall and ran his hand over it. 'It's incredible that this is still standing.'

'Do you think the child could be in there?' Katrín spoke quietly enough for Líf not to hear. 'I thought I saw some movement.'

Garðar peeked in through the hole. 'No. There's no one here; no one would choose to stay in these ruins.' He took hold of an iron hook cemented into the stack of bricks and tried to move it, unsuccessfully. All he got for his efforts were rusty streaks on his gloves. 'Shit.' He grabbed a piece of rope hanging on the wall and tried to wipe his glove on it. 'Have a look inside and let's go. I have a bad feeling about this and I want to get back as quickly as possible.'

Katrín was glad to have finally found out what was bothering him. She moved up to the opening, feeling much more daring and happier given this new development. Soon they would be back at the doctor's house, eating at the dinner table by candlelight. But she'd barely stuck her head through the opening when she saw the outline of the boy inside, on the other side from her. Suddenly he looked up; in the darkness his skin appeared inhuman, grey, his eyes large and sunken in his fish-cheeked face. The boy stared at her, then opened his mouth and screamed soundlessly. Katrín started and fell backwards. At the same moment, a large chunk of brickwork from the section above the hole fell to the ground in front of her with a loud crash. Several bricks hit her, but although it hurt, the pain was nothing in comparison to her terror and the hammering of her heart. Putti yelped, scampered awkwardly over to her and huddled against her thigh. The dust now hanging over everything clouded her vision; she could hardly see a thing. 'Garðar! Garðar!' She couldn't form the words, but wanted to warn him before the boy did him any harm. Then all the dust drifted suddenly to the ground and she could see more clearly. She was hugely relieved to see that Garðar had managed to jump away when the wall collapsed, though he hadn't come out of it much better than she had. His face was bleeding and he limped as he tried to hurry over to her.

'Jesus. Jesus.' He seemed just as startled as she was. Frightened yells behind them told them that Líf had also been taken by surprise. 'Are you hurt? Where?'

Katrín felt the tears running down her cheeks, at first warm but then cold as they trickled saltily over her lips. Her body couldn't take this. Not now. She managed to moan: 'My legs.' She tried to lift herself up and managed it with the help of Garðar, who at first wanted her to stay still while he examined her injuries. Although her tears were still flowing, anger was her strongest emotion. 'I'm leaving. Even if I have to crawl.' She made the snap decision not to tell him about the boy for fear that he would rush into the death-trap of a building. The pain was awful when she finally got to her feet, but she paid it no heed; she had to get out of there. 'Líf! Come here and take Putti. I think he's hurt.' She leaned on Garðar, who winced despite trying as hard as he could not to let his own pain show. Some bricks must have hit his shoulder.

Together they hobbled up the slope, Putti still whining in Líf's arms. When they were halfway up, with Katrín on the verge of giving up because of her pain, she spied the seals, still dawdling in the same spot. The creatures appeared to be watching their progress with the same lazy interest as before. Maybe it was the poor light, or pain was confusing her, but suddenly Katrín felt sure that they weren't the heads of seals at all but of humans; the mother and son who had vanished beneath the ice sixty years before.

Chapter 22

Time went by slower on the flight back to Ísafjörður than it had on the way south. Freyr had barely been able to keep his eyes open when he'd needed to, but as soon as he fastened his seatbelt his fatigue vanished, or rather took a little break. There was no prospect more appealing than closing his eyes and forgetting everything, even if only for a short flight, but it was impossible: he had too much to think about. An odd discomfort and anxiety welled up inside him, and in the end he even ordered coffee from the friendly flight attendant. After that there was no turning back and he lost control of his thoughts. He felt like he did when he couldn't sleep at night. At those times, everything seemed hopeless and the tiniest problems became insurmountable. His trip south had yielded no real explanation for Halla's death, and he was surprised now that he'd ever thought the autopsy would provide a definitive answer. There were far too many unanswered questions for that, too many complexities. In addition he was disappointed, though not surprised, not to have got hold of Lárus, the only member of the old group of schoolmates still alive. The man had neither answered his phone nor been at home when Freyr finally took a taxi there. It was possible that he had been there but didn't come to the door; the apartment was in a block and it was equally likely that the doorbell was broken. Nonetheless Freyr rang it several times, and even circled the building in the hope of finding the windows to apartment 5.03, but to no avail. He thanked his lucky stars that he hadn't gone into architecture all those years ago, as he'd considered doing for a time; he clearly had terrible spatial awareness. But it didn't really matter, as Freyr had no idea what he would do if he saw a light or movement in the apartment. He'd hardly planned on bursting in on the man.

But he felt worst about Sara. His disappointment was even greater considering that he'd allowed himself to hope that finally she was showing signs of improvement. Of course he should have known better, evaluated the situation professionally instead of letting himself be influenced by optimism. But he wasn't the first psychiatrist in history to misjudge a relative's circumstances. Although he no longer loved Sara in a romantic sense, he was still very fond of her and that fondness would never go away, any more than he could stop loving his parents. Although their relationship had taken a different turn than they'd planned on their wedding day, they still stood in its shadow; in any case, the way things were at the moment they were still a long way from feeling able to look for happiness once more in the arms of other people. If Benni's fate were never explained, they might remain this way all their lives. His disappearance bound them with slender but strong threads, the web of their shared tragedy.

When the plane landed, he made it his first task to call his ex-wife. It was much colder in Ísafjörður than in Reykjavík and Freyr's coat flapped in the wind, allowing the cold to bite through his thin shirt. With his free hand he managed to button his coat loosely as he increased his speed across the tarmac. He was about to hang up when Sara finally answered.

She wasted no time on a greeting, and instead asked curtly: 'What do you want?'

'I just wanted to say goodbye to you properly. It was all a bit weird when I left and I found it difficult to discuss things properly with your friend there.'

'You don't have to patronize her like that to me. You made it perfectly clear what you think of people like her. However, you might want to think about abandoning your prejudices and listening to what she has to say. It's not just mumbo-jumbo.'

'Maybe not.' Freyr was striding purposefully through the airport. He lowered his voice slightly as he made his way through a group of travellers that had gathered at the luggage belt. 'But if I try to open my mind to this, would you at least be willing to look at it with a slightly more critical eye? Maybe we could meet halfway? How about that?' He was more than ready to play along and pretend to consider a Ouija board and other such nonsense if it would bring Sara a bit more down to earth.

'I've tried it, Freyr. It doesn't work. I'm still having the same dreams and I'm still haunted by the same feelings.' She took a deep breath before continuing: 'I can *smell* Benni sometimes. I see him at the shops, outside the apartment, everywhere I go. I'm not hallucinating, Freyr. He's still here. You've got to realize that.' Again she drew a breath. 'There's something bad in the air, something that's getting worse. If you choose to pretend it's nothing, then so be it. I wish I could say something or do something to get you to take this seriously, but I know I can't. But I felt obligated to you, which is why I took the chance of having Elísa talk to you and open your eyes to what you don't want to see. It didn't work, obviously.'

'Sara, I'm not sure you ought to have much more to do with this woman.' He said this as carefully as possible, for fear of her hanging up on him. 'If you dream about Benni, think you can see him and so on, it's perfectly natural and it doesn't have to have any psychic meaning. You must believe me, these things are more common than you think. Your mind is still tied to him, and because he's always uppermost in your thoughts he'll keep appearing like this for a long time to come, though it might eventually be less often. Do you think I haven't experienced these things myself?' He didn't want to tell her about the incident at the hospital, when Benni had seemed so real to him that he'd felt as if he could touch him.

'I can't talk to you about this, Freyr.' There was defeat in Sara's voice. 'And I know you lied to me. About what, I don't know, but you once lied to me about something that makes a huge difference in all of this.'

'What?' Freyr's heart skipped a beat. 'What are you talking about?'

'I wasn't going to mention it to you, but it's been plaguing me and it's best if I just say it. It's up to you what you do about it; you can tell me the truth, continue to lie or just say nothing. You decide.'

Freyr was silent for a moment. 'If you think I have information that could solve Benni's case, you're very wrong.' He was angry; at her and at himself. He'd reached his car, which he'd left in the car park outside the terminal. He allowed the wind to cool him down. 'Where is this coming from?'

'When I wake from the dream that haunts me every night, I know it for certain. You can't say or do anything to change it, so you can spare yourself the trouble.'

'What is this dream about, Sara? Maybe the feeling it gives you can be explained by its contents.'

'It's about Benni. What else? I'm chasing him; I never catch him, of course, but I'm always really close and get closer every time. Everything is green, even the air. It's difficult to explain but I wake up in a sweat, knowing that you were the cause of all of this. Because you lied.'

Freyr said nothing. The dream seemed startlingly similar to the last one he'd read about in Védís's dream diary. He was afraid to admit how much Sara's words affected him, especially the part about lying. There, he knew he was guilty.

'She wouldn't stop. I hope you don't mind, but I thought you would want to know about it even though you were on leave.' The nurse's anxiety was plain to see as she stood there with her arms crossed, deep wrinkles creasing her youthful brow. Freyr smiled reassuringly, realizing that his preoccupied state might have been taken by the woman as annoyance at having been called to the nursing home. Nothing was further from the truth; he'd been happy to receive the call, because it meant he could push his own troubles aside for a while.

'No problem, you were absolutely right to call.' He concentrated on sounding perfectly normal: 'You said Úrsúla had repeatedly asked to see me, but did she say why?'

The woman shook her head. 'No, you know how she is. Not exactly a chatterbox. It actually started on the morning shift but I didn't come in until the afternoon, so I don't know for sure whether she was any more lucid then. I doubt it. I thought I'd better get hold of you before we left for the night, in case she needed to be admitted to hospital and monitored.

You never know how well sleeping pills will work if a patient's having an episode.'

'I'd better see what's up.' Freyr put his hand on the door-knob to the woman's room. 'Has she been out today?'

'No. She wouldn't hear of it. She actually stiffens in fear if you so much as mention even going into the corridor. She's terrified of something but refuses to say what it is. In the meantime there's very little we can do to help her overcome her fear.' The woman stretched her back. 'I feel like she's deteriorated. The little progress we'd started to see seems to have gone into reverse, unfortunately.'

This didn't particularly surprise Freyr; in fact he'd been worried this might happen. For a long time all the signs had suggested that she could regress. 'I'll look in on you before I go.' He opened the door and the heavy air in the apartment was nearly palpable. 'Oof. Can't we open a window?'

'She doesn't want to. She gets very agitated.' Although the nurse didn't describe the woman's reactions in detail, Freyr was well aware that she was far from easy to deal with and it was unfair to expect the staff to have to insist on opening the window. He doubted he'd even be up to the challenge himself. At least not the way he felt now.

Freyr took a moment for his eyes to adjust to the darkness inside the room. He didn't want to turn on the light for fear of startling her, feeling it would be better to approach her first on her own terms and then see whether it were possible to convince her that she'd feel better with fresh air and more light. 'Hello, Úrsúla. I heard you wanted to talk to me.' He walked cautiously towards the woman, wary in case he fell over something on the floor. She was sitting at the window, as before. The dim light of a streetlamp shone through the thick curtains, making her appear in silhouette. 'So I decided to look in on you and see how you're doing. I would have come this morning, but I had to make a quick trip to Reykjavík.' No response. He was starting to think that Úrsúla had fallen asleep in her chair, even passed out from lack of oxygen, but when he went up close he could see that her eyes were open. She stared straight ahead at the curtains. 'Don't you want to open them to see out? Maybe it'll start snowing again. I always find it very relaxing to watch the snowflakes fall.'

Úrsúla shook her head slowly. 'No. Absolutely not.' Her voice was hoarse, almost as if it were dusty. 'I don't want to see.'

'Why not?' Freyr pulled a stool over. Úrsúla didn't look at him, but continued to stare straight ahead.

'Do you think there's something out there? If so, I can truly promise you that there are just a few cars, including mine.'

The woman suddenly snapped her head towards Freyr. 'There's more out there.' She stared at him, seeming angry, as if he'd tried to convince her of some sort of damned nonsense that she could see through easily. 'There's more out there than just cars.'

'Such as?' Freyr kept calm, having seen and heard a lot in his time. The woman turned back towards the curtains with the same speed as she'd turned towards him. 'The boy.'

'The boy?' Freyr frowned. 'Not this late, Úrsúla. Maybe there was a boy out in the car park today, but now all the children have gone home for dinner. And you don't have to worry about kids, they won't do you any harm.' Úrsúla pursed her lips and said nothing. Freyr watched her and considered the best way to keep the conversation going. It was unusual for her to express herself so much, and it would be a shame to waste the opportunity. 'Did you want to get me here to talk about kids? I can certainly talk about them, and even tell you stories about a little boy I once knew well. He was often naughty, but always good inside. That's what matters, as you know.'

'Stories about Benni?' The woman's face didn't change, leaving Freyr to drop his jaw in amazement. Where the hell had she heard his son's name?

'No, not about Benni.' Freyr was careful to keep his cool. 'But what do you know about him? Can you maybe tell me something about him?'

She shook her head as before, very slowly. 'No, I know nothing about him.' She swallowed. 'I don't know Benni.' She shut her eyes. 'Do you think the blind see things when they dream?'

Freyr had no idea. 'Probably those who could see at one point but were blinded later on, but not those who were born blind. At least that's what I'd imagine. Why do you ask?'

'I don't want to see any more. It's better to be in the dark.'

'You're wrong.' Freyr waited for Úrsúla to open her eyes again but she gave no sign that she would; she continued to sit there with her eyes closed, still as a statue. 'It's much better to see than not to see. Fortunately, there's much more beauty than ugliness in the world. If you went out more often for walks you would start to realize that, and to realize that I'm right. Don't you want to try? If I'm wrong, I'll stop pestering you about it.'

'I don't want to go out. Not here, in this place. I know exactly what I'll see.'

'And what's that?'

'The boy.' She screwed up her eyes so tightly again that her short, pale eyelashes were nearly swallowed up by her eyelids. 'I don't want eyes any more.' Freyr watched her hands whiten on the arms of the chair.

'Which boy is this, Úrsúla? Is he someone I know?' She shook her head and he tried again. 'Is he from here?' She remained silent and didn't confirm or deny it, either with a head movement or otherwise. 'What's his name? Or maybe he doesn't have a name?'

Her eyes opened and she looked at Freyr. The fear in her face was tangible, a sick hunger that had etched out a new, yet terrifying reality in which she was trapped. As if the true one weren't bad enough. 'Bernódus.' Tears ran down her cheeks. 'He's waiting for me outside.' She wiped her tears with her bony hand. 'He's angry at me. So angry.' She raised her hands to her eyes and stuck her fingernails into her eyebrows, so hard that blood sprang up from beneath them. Before Freyr managed to stop her, she'd scratched the skin open to the corners of her eyes.

Freyr grabbed at the woman and pulled her hands from her bleeding face, calling for help as loudly as he could. When he heard the rapid footsteps of the nurse coming down the corridor he relaxed his grip slightly. His voice even sounded completely calm when he asked her to fetch a tranquillizer immediately. After she'd run off again, he managed with some dexterity to move the woman's hands to her lap, and held them there. 'Calm down now, Úrsúla. Calm down.'

She laughed joylessly. It didn't last long, and afterwards she looked at him, her face streaked with both blood and tears, now running down in streams. 'He wants to hurt people. Did you know that? Hurt them, hurt them badly.'

She tilted her head as she stared into Freyr's eyes. 'Maybe you, too. But first he wants you to find Benni.' A pair of blood-tinged tears ran down her chin and dripped onto the tired old bathrobe she wore over her nightclothes. 'He tells me that in my head.'

Chapter 23

The pain in Katrín's foot was so piercing that she had no doubt whatsoever that it was broken. Her foot had swollen fast and it had hurt so much when Líf and Garðar tried to remove her shoe that they'd had to cut it off instead. For some reason she was also colder than she should have been, shivering terribly despite being dressed warmly and wrapped in a blanket. She constantly had to fend off the thought that now she was in the same situation as long-past generations who ran the risk of developing gangrene in wounded limbs, losing them or even dying of septicaemia as a result. She was so tired and beaten up that she had trouble forming an opinion as to which would be worse. Compared to her current condition, her injuries after falling down the stairs had been mere trifles. 'Coffee's ready.' Garðar handed her a steaming cup. 'Drink this, it should warm you up a bit.' His face was swollen around the cuts he'd received and in the eerie light of the torch he looked like a stranger.

'Why didn't I bring ibuprofen? I always have some in my bag, but now when I actually need it, it's not there.' Líf rummaged in a big, shiny black leather handbag and it wasn't clear to Katrín whether she was searching so frantically for the painkillers for herself or for Katrín. 'This is ridiculous.'

'I've got to go down to the doctor's. Maybe there's a

first-aid kit there with medicine and bandages.' Garðar spoke softly, his voice oddly distorted by the swelling in his cheek.

'You're not going anywhere. I'll survive until morning.' Katrín meant what she said. Although she was in more pain than she'd ever experienced, a terrible, sleepless night would be a hundred times better than Garðar going out alone into the pitch-black that had descended upon them as they inched their way back to the abandoned village. It was only a short distance to the doctor's house but Katrín hadn't been able to go any further than to theirs, and Garðar and Líf had actually had to carry her the final stretch. It had exhausted them, and Putti was tired as well. The plan had been to rest for a few minutes but then continue at a gentle pace to the doctor's with as much firewood as they could carry, and sleep there that night. Their sleeping bags were there, as well as candles and security: the three things they needed most. But after Katrín's shoe was removed, it was clear that she wouldn't be going any further for now. None of them had stated the fact; they didn't need to. It was only now that a trip over to the doctor's was mentioned. 'Why are you suggesting that? No one's expecting you to go off by yourself and there's no need to offer. We'll be fine until morning without you playing the hero.' Katrín's fear of him rushing off into the unknown burst out of her as anger.

'Nothing's going to happen to me and it'll take me half an hour at most to get there and back. We'll freeze to death tonight without our sleeping bags, and the torch won't last much longer. Do you want to sit here tonight shivering in the darkness?' Garðar spoke with almost no inflection or animation, as if he were a mechanical version of himself. 'I'm not *playing the hero*; this is just something that needs to be done.'

'Why don't you go, Líf?' Katrín's question was absurd, as Líf was the least likely of the three of them to go anywhere alone. 'The sleeping bags are light, and you could carry them here just as easily as Garðar.'

The yellow light from the torch illuminated Líf's face when she looked up from her bag in surprise. 'You're joking! Do you have concussion? I'm not going anywhere.' Her bottom lip stuck out a little, making her look like a sulky child.

'Stop this nonsense.' Garðar had stood up. 'I'm going and you wait here; I'll be back before you know it.' The torch dimmed and flickered. 'It's the only solution. The sooner I go, the more likely it is that the torch battery will last for the time I'm gone.'

Líf looked at Katrín, who found it difficult to tell whether her cheeks were so red from the hike or whether it was an effect of the faint light. They looked each other in the eye and Líf proposed a solution that at first sounded very much unlike her. 'Would you be okay here alone if I go with him?' She glanced at the dog sleeping at the foot of Katrín's chair. 'Putti's here too, of course.'

Katrín opened her mouth to answer unhesitatingly in the affirmative, but changed her mind in almost the same second and shut it again. Of course she would feel much better if Garðar didn't go alone; it wouldn't take them long, but the proposal was still better than his original idea, the only difference being that it would be she rather than he who would be entirely dependent on herself. Líf was the only one whose position remained unaffected: she would have company at all times either way. 'What if something happens?'

'I don't think anything worse could happen today. You were lucky to get out of that alive.' Líf held up a hand to silence

Garðar, who seemed about to speak, probably to say that he was going alone. 'If you hadn't jumped back, all the bricks would have hit you on the head, not just one on your foot.'

'Did you hear a noise before the wall fell, Katrín?' Garðar had tried to ask her this on the way back but Katrín hadn't wanted to answer, so afraid was she that he would leave them alone, go back and look the place over in the hope of finding the boy. Since Katrín was now convinced that this was no ordinary flesh-and-blood child, she didn't dare imagine what would happen if Garðar confronted him, let alone if the creature or whatever it was lured him into the ruins and killed him. 'Maybe you saw a movement out of the corner of your eye, in time for you to get out? Líf's absolutely right – your quick reaction saved you. It's pretty clear what would have happened if you hadn't moved.'

'I saw the boy.' Katrín remained stony faced. She was risking nothing by admitting it now; Garðar wasn't about to go all the way back to the factory with things as they were. 'I didn't hear anything; I was just startled and jumped away. He was in there.'

Garðar's expression suggested that he needed a moment to digest this. 'He was in the ruins?' He took a deep breath. 'Are you saying that he's staying there, that he lives there?'

'I'm not saying anything other than that I saw him. Or about as well as we see him in general. He was standing hunched over, far back in the darkness.' Katrín rubbed her knee; it had started to stiffen because of the unnatural position of her foot, which she tried to keep continually protected, even while sitting down. 'Who knows, maybe he pushed the wall down somehow, but he certainly wasn't anywhere near it.'

'We've got to get out of here.' Líf's voice grew louder with every word. 'Let's go, like I suggested. I'm not staying here tonight.' She stood up and Putti stirred at the screech of the chair as it was dragged across the floor. He lifted his head, looked at his owner and then went back to sleep, apparently accustomed to such disturbances.

'You can see I'm not going anywhere on foot, Líf.' Katrín moved her foot carefully and the pain shot up through her leg so forcefully that she winced. Of course this looked like a theatrical performance, but she felt so bad that she didn't care what Líf thought. 'Maybe you want me to stay behind and wait while you go to get help?' She spoke through clenched teeth, her leg still burning.

'Stop bickering.' Garðar walked off towards the door. 'You can argue as much as you want after I'm gone, but I'm in no mood to listen to this. I don't want to waste any more time.' He turned back towards them in the doorway. 'I'm going – you wait here. It's not safe for you to be here alone, Kata.' He didn't wait for an answer but left the room with a resolute expression, without turning around again. He'd hardly gone out of the door when Katrín made a snap decision that she knew she'd regret, yet also knew was right. 'Go with him, Líf. I'll be okay. Just hurry.'

The torch flickered again. At that Líf decided she didn't need to be told twice, sprang to her feet and ran after Garðar. She turned around in the doorway, went back to Katrín and gave her a big kiss on the cheek. 'Sorry. I'd forgotten about your foot when I suggested we get out of here. I didn't mean that you would have to stay behind. This situation is just driving me crazy and I'm dying for a cigarette.' She smiled at Katrín, who tried to smile back, although it came out awkwardly because of the pain, which seemed to be getting worse. 'Putti will look after you.' Líf ran out so as not to lose Garðar, who could be heard putting his coat on noisily in the dark front entrance. Katrín remained behind with Putti, who had opened his eyes to watch Líf leave the room. He closed his eyes again after the front door shut, at approximately the same moment as the torch went out.

The heavy, slow breathing of the sleeping dog granted Katrín little peace of mind. The torch refused to turn on again, despite her repeated attempts. The bulb had lit once but the light was barely noticeable and lasted only a few seconds. Time passed slowly and Katrín was painfully aware that under these circumstances each minute would feel like ten or a hundred or even a thousand. If she'd been out having dinner, in good company, the same amount of time would have gone by in a flash, but now she passed the time by repeatedly counting up to sixty, keeping track of every minute that passed. But she kept speeding up the count, ruining her timekeeping.

'I'm sure they'll be back any minute now, Putti.' Her voice sounded silly to her in the silence and emptiness. Yet it was better listening to herself than to no one. 'Don't you think so?' The dog didn't make a sound in response, and judging by his breathing he hadn't even woken. Katrín considered stretching out her uninjured foot and wiggling it a bit, but stopped for fear that the movement would somehow jar the injured one. Still, she desperately wanted to wake Putti; she found it a bit unfair that he was lost in his dreams. She might just as well be alone. Besides, he was a good monitor of the environment; his senses were better adjusted and more powerful than hers. If he were on guard and didn't utter so much as a growl she could relax in the knowledge that everything was all right. Now it would take an entire boys' choir to burst in and start singing to disturb him, since he was unused to long treks through heavy snow. Katrín hadn't even finished this thought before Putti's breathing changed and he gave a curt bark. What had she been thinking? It was much worse to have the dog awake and imagine terrible things at each noise that emerged from his throat. The bark seemed to hang in the air long after the dog had fallen silent again, and Katrín fought the temptation to cover her ears. When it came down to it, she wanted to hear it if there was anything to hear, not wait unknowingly for something bad to happen. Although she wasn't in a fit state to be any kind of action hero, she was fairly sure she could defend herself if necessary.

A soft rustling noise reached her ears, followed by a vague creak. Katrín was startled when she realized it seemed to come from inside the house. Putti growled softly and then barked, now at full force. 'Hush!' If the dog continued, she wouldn't be able to hear anything but his noise, nor would she be able to determine where the sound came from when and if it came again. The dog barked again, now much more quietly, before falling silent. Katrín listened carefully and then wrinkled her nose when she smelled an unpleasant odour, like rotting fish. Suddenly she felt as if someone were standing behind her. Again she heard a creak and the noise repeated itself almost immediately, as if someone were shuffling his feet on the rotten floorboards. Katrín swivelled very slowly towards the sound, certain that out of the corner of her eye she would see the expected figure standing behind her chair. But there was nothing to be seen in the darkness. She focused on the place she felt most likely, prepared for any movement.

But when the creak came again she wasn't aware of any and realized she'd miscalculated where it had come from. It hadn't originated inside, but rather outside on the porch, and she turned her head slightly to the right to look out of the window.

Katrín's heart stopped, only to start again so violently that her chest heaved. Although the darkness was black and thick as soot, her eyes had grown sufficiently accustomed to it for her to see a pale hand up against the glass, its fingers spread as if expecting a pen to draw the hand's outline on the pane. The short, skinny fingers suggested it was the hand of a child, and although it was difficult to distinguish colours, the fingertips were clearly darkened. The colour was unpleasant in some indefinable way that didn't seem related to simple dirt; she felt it was something different, and worse. Putti also appeared to have spotted the hand on the glass and he whined piteously. Katrín tried to breathe normally but her breaths felt too deep, and the air wouldn't leave her lungs when she tried to expel it. The disgusting smell of fish offal had intensified and she felt sick, then sicker still when she heard the owner of the hand start to mutter something outside. She wanted to cover her ears, shut her eyes and start counting down the seconds again until one of two things happened: either Garðar and Líf returned, or a cold little hand tore her back to full consciousness. But then she thought she could distinguish the words:

'*Run, Kata, run.*' She gave in, clapped her hands over her ears and shut her eyes. She didn't want to know what awaited her.

Chapter 24

The moon peeked briefly through the bank of dark grey cloud that would soon fill the night sky. As it did so, the leafless shrubs in the hospital grounds appeared once more – but even they wouldn't be visible for long. Snow was falling, covering everything, which for Freyr meant that there was little to see after staring for nearly an hour through his office window. He'd dragged his chair there and sat with his phone in his lap without knowing who he imagined he could call if he decided he wanted to get things off his chest. He was little nearer to figuring anything out after his conversation with Úrsúla, who'd withdrawn into her shell after opening up to him and hinting at things that might possibly explain what was going on and free him from his psychological torment. But instead of telling him more of what she knew – or thought she knew – she was now lying sedated in a hospital bed. Considering her condition when he left her room, it was unlikely that he would be able to get much out of her the next day; even worse, in the light of her medical history, she could quite easily not say a word for several years to come. What did she mean by saying that Bernódus, who disappeared half a century ago, wanted him to find Benni?

To make matters worse, he'd called Halla's husband to ask about the scars on her back and hadn't received the answer he was hoping for. Everywhere he looked there seemed to be dead ends. The man had been flabbergasted, though Freyr had only got as far as mentioning the word 'scars', and was angry at being called so late in the evening with what he seemed to consider a trivial question. Freyr had managed to apologize humbly enough for the man to calm down and answer his questions, though his replies hadn't been particularly informative. The only thing that was clear from the phone call was that Halla had kept her injuries secret from her husband, telling him that it was eczema when he asked about a little spot of blood on her nightdress or the bed. He said the skin condition had first appeared a few years ago, though he couldn't be any more specific than that. Freyr said nothing, but reckoned that it had been three years ago; it must have been at least that, given everything else he knew. Freyr didn't want to arouse the man's suspicions too much so was cautious with his questions. But he did find out for certain that Halla hadn't suffered from eczema until after her back had been injured, and that it was worst in the mornings, after restless nights. The man hadn't known how bad it had been; she'd always hidden her back from him, which he'd found very vain. Freyr said goodbye to him without mentioning anything about crosses or the doomed group of friends, feeling that the widower should be allowed to bury his wife in peace, but he did ask him how he was doing and was told that he felt awful, but was getting better. His daughter was looking after him and his sons were prepared to help as well.

After hanging up, Freyr could do little but scratch his head. So it seemed Halla must have inflicted the wounds on herself during the night, according to her husband's description. This pretty much ruled out the idea of anyone else having been involved; the man would have been aware of any nocturnal activity. But Freyr also felt certain that the husband hadn't had anything to do with it. He had been so convincing that anything else was unthinkable. The low voice of insanity that crept up and muttered in his ear when he let his guard down whispered that neither the woman herself nor any other living person had caused the wounds. They had been caused by other powers, worse ones. As Freyr agonised over these confused thoughts, another idea formed in his head: could Halla have made the wounds on her back without realizing it? They would have had to be caused either by her scratching in the night or without any external contact whatsoever, subconsciously; Freyr had heard of such things but had never really believed them. Stories about wounds of this sort mainly concerned people who claimed to have received so-called stigmata, wounds in their palms and on their soles as if from a crucifixion. No one had ever proved that people could make such wounds appear through the power of thought alone, although theories did exist for the phenomenon. It was a crazy idea, yet not as strange as that of some entity from beyond having inflicted the wounds on Halla's back.

The office phone rang. On the line was the nurse he'd dropped in to see on the way up to his office, in the hope that the old teacher was awake and in a good enough condition to speak to Freyr. He hadn't been, but she'd promised to let him know if he woke; he had a tendency to lie awake at night. She told him that the man was now sitting up and was even excited at the prospect of seeing Freyr, happy to have a visitor to help fill his sleepless night. As Freyr jumped to his feet he wondered what would have happened if she hadn't called. He probably would have stared out of the window until the morning shift staff drove their cars into the car park, then gone to work for yet another day with bags under his bloodshot eyes. Which was of course still a possibility; it wasn't at all clear whether he'd be able to sleep despite his overwhelming fatigue, which intensified by the hour. Hopefully he would feel the desire to go to sleep in his own bed at home after speaking to the old man.

He hesitated when he opened the door to the corridor. He was met by the familiar blinking and popping of the fluorescent light, despite the fact that the bulb had been replaced. The light fitting itself must be broken, and he determined to speak to the caretaker despite the man's undoubted opinion that Freyr was a compulsive complainer, and an extremely odd one at that. He took a deep breath, thinking of the vision that had plagued him here a short time ago. Now, when he was overcome by tiredness, was when he could expect all sorts of nonsense to enter his head. Freyr gathered himself and went out, feeling a surge of relief when he saw only the linoleum floor and white walls. Nonetheless he got goose bumps as he walked down the corridor, unable to shake the feeling that someone was watching him. He looked over his shoulder repeatedly to assure himself that this was not the case, but he never saw anything, although he thought he heard a soft snickering behind him as he continued on his way. Of course he was hearing things, wasn't he? Yet somehow he suspected that if he were to record the sound he would discover it was not a hallucination. He stopped, activated the recorder on his mobile phone and let it run as he walked slowly towards the staircase. When he reached it he turned off the device and sprinted up the stairs, taking them two at a time. It wasn't until he entered the wing and looked into the friendly, smiling face of the nurse that his goose bumps disappeared. It was obvious from her surprised expression that his relief was written all over his face, and, embarrassed, he resolved to act as normally as possible.

'He's in his room. There's no one in the other bed; we released the patient today.' The woman hesitated. Freyr had always liked her, but unfortunately they hardly ever worked the same shift. She was extremely sharp and usually went straight to the point, as she did now: 'Can I ask why you want to see him?'

'I'm investigating the case of the woman who committed suicide in Súðavík. He taught at the school she attended as a child.' He smiled at the nurse when he heard how far-fetched the connection sounded. 'Believe me, this story is so strange that it's too complicated to try and explain it coherently now. When it's all sorted out, I'll sit down with you over a cup of coffee and tell you the whole story.'

She smiled, revealing her even white teeth. 'It sounds as though a glass of wine would be better than coffee. Something a bit stronger.'

Freyr wasn't born yesterday and he knew she was flirting with him. He smiled back. She reminded him of a woman with whom he'd had a brief fling, which he had quickly come to regret. He'd had no business starting a relationship back then, but now he thought circumstances were not only different, they were better. Besides, this woman was a much more amiable version of the other one, and seemed to be a lot more grounded. It was high time he started living again, and Dagný seemed to be drifting away from him in terms of any sort of relationship, although their friendship was strengthening. This woman was gorgeous, smart and apparently willing. Maybe a decent relationship with a member of the opposite sex was what he needed to get him back on track. 'Wine would work, too. Let's do that.' Feeling slightly more cheerful, he walked off in the direction of the only room casting a light into the corridor. He hesitated at the doorway and his cheerfulness dwindled a bit when he saw that the old teacher seemed to have fallen asleep again. His bed was in the upright position, but the man was leaning back against his pillow with his eyes closed and an earphone in one ear, probably to listen to a repeat of the day's schedule on Channel 1. Freyr coughed softly to draw the man's attention, in case he wasn't actually sleeping but was just absorbed in the radio. Freyr was indescribably relieved when he opened his eyes. 'I wasn't sure if you'd fallen asleep again. I hope I haven't woken you.'

The man patted the edge of the bed. 'No, you didn't wake me. Come in. I don't sleep much any more without the help of drugs.' He took the earphone from his ear and lowered his voice as he did so. 'What else can I do for you? I gather it's connected to what we talked about the other day. I've been thinking about it a bit and recalling old times. It's odd how some of your oldest memories are so vivid, but you can't necessarily remember what you had for supper last night.'

'If that's something you want to remember, given the food here.' Freyr sat down by the bed. 'But you guessed my errand correctly. I've also been thinking a bit about the boy you told me about, Bernódus, who disappeared. His name keeps coming up in connection with a case that's unusual, to say the least, and seems to have ties to the past.'

The man nodded. There was hardly any flesh left on his bony skull, and his skin looked like soft wax, as if his face were melting. 'This thing with the boy was a great tragedy, but I can't understand how his story could be connected to anything now.' He looked at Freyr. Although his days were clearly numbered, the old teacher still had a gleam in his eye. 'Not unless you've found his bones – is that it?'

Freyr shook his head. 'No, nothing that simple, I'm afraid.'

'That's a shame. I've always thought that someone's death was never settled until his bones were buried in consecrated ground.' The little white bud of the earphones seemed somehow incongruous in his ancient hands. 'Maybe because my father drowned at sea when I was a boy. I thought constantly about where his bones might be lying, whether they would disappear under the seabed over time or whether someone would set eyes on them before they vanished completely. You have to remember that I was just a kid. As I got older of course it became easier to bear, but I would still leave this world more contented if his remains had been found. They certainly won't be now, any more than the bones of the other thousands lying in watery graves off these shores.'

'Do you think the boy perished at sea? Drowned?' Although Freyr was sorry for the loss of the old man's father, he wanted to stick to the topic for fear that the memories would overwhelm him; one old story would lead to another, and so on.

'Actually, I really don't know. All I know is that the sea-god Ægir rarely returns those who end up in his icy embrace. So it wouldn't surprise me. There's no other place around here that could hide such a secret for long. It's been nearly half a century since his disappearance, and no unidentified child's bones have been found in these parts. It's not as if the town is surrounded by lava and rocks, where no one can go to search.'

'But what if someone kidnapped him, murdered him and

buried him somewhere? His remains wouldn't necessarily be found.' Freyr had difficulty finishing the sentence. These same thoughts had run far too often through his mind in connection with his own son.

The old man shook his head sadly. 'I think the world was better then and I find it hard to believe that such a thing happened. No one lived here – and hopefully never will – who could have committed such a deed. At the time people gossiped that Bernódus's father might have beaten him to death, intentionally or unintentionally, and got rid of the body. He certainly had a free hand, if he was in that kind of mood. But I found it hard to believe and I never trusted those stories. The poor man didn't have it in him, in my opinion, to do such a thing. He would have let the boy lie there on the floor in his own blood until he was found. Alcohol was the only thing that mattered to him.'

'I got to see the old police reports on the case and it seems that an extensive search was made for the boy, all to no avail. The reports didn't reveal much but one thing caught my attention: the boy's mother was never mentioned. Was she dead, or maybe as much of a lost cause as the father? Did she just leave? I wondered about this particularly because it would have been typical for a child in his position to run off and try to find the missing parent, who his imagination had idealised. Then he might have died of exposure or in an accident. Wasn't it winter?'

'Yes, winter had certainly set in when it happened. But he hadn't run off to find his mother, because she was dead by then.' The man's eyelids half closed. 'She died several years before when she tried to save Bernódus's younger brother from drowning. The child had gone out onto the ice after the fjord froze over and fallen through it, and the woman waded out after him. They both drowned there, and they say that that's when Bernódus's father lost his grip and gave in to drink and debauchery. He couldn't cope with the loss and couldn't bear to look at his surviving son, who'd had to witness the tragedy unfolding. Someone told me he blamed the boy, thought that he could have done something about it – which was absurd, of course; the boy would never have been able to save his mother and brother. He would have just followed them under the ice and died with them. I don't know whether the drink gave the man this idea or whether the seed was sown when things started going downhill. But one thing is certain: he never showed his son any affection or treated him like a father should.' The old man shut his eyes completely. 'Believe you me, he had to live with his shame forever.'

Freyr needed a moment to digest this. In this respect it was easier to speak to the older generation; short pauses in the conservation didn't matter. 'So the boy was blamed by his alcoholic father for the death of his mother and younger brother,' he said thoughtfully, verbally putting the story together. 'What tragic circumstances to grow up in.' Freyr was even starting to suspect that the boy had committed suicide. 'Didn't he have a grandmother, grandfather, or other relative he could go and stay with?'

'The family wasn't from here and I never heard mention of any other relatives. I expect he had some, but to my knowledge no one knew who they were. The accident that killed the mother and younger son occurred before Bernódus and his father moved here, so I never knew the mother or even met her. They were living in Hesteyri in Jökulfirðir when the mother and her child died.' The old man lifted his head slightly from the pillow and turned to face Freyr directly. Blue veins stood out in his white skin, which was nearly transparent. 'I never taught him, so I was never involved in his case, but all of us were certainly aware of him, as his situation was so distressing. And he became even more memorable after his disappearance. It really affected us teachers. The break-in at the school occurred soon afterwards, so it really was a difficult term.'

'Remind me how much time passed between the two events?' Freyr had lost track of the dates.

'Ten days; a fortnight or so? I don't remember precisely.'

'Were they thought to have been related in any way?'

'I don't recall anyone ever suggesting it. I don't see how they could have been.' He turned away from Freyr and let his head droop. The depression that formed beneath it in the soft pillow was barely noticeable. 'And I wouldn't think it was likely.' His voice had faded and although their conversation hadn't been long, it was clear that he was tired.

There was little to add to this and Freyr prepared to stand up and leave. He hadn't really got anywhere, except that he was fairly certain that one way or another, the boy had followed his mother and brother and perished at sea. That was the most likely explanation, and more often than not the simplest hypotheses proved to be the correct ones. Before he stood up he asked one more question, partly in the hope that the man had recovered a little and they could talk for a bit longer. 'Do you know whether Bernódus's teacher is still alive? She might know something more about the case.'

The old man shook his head weakly. 'No, she died a long time ago. She died very prematurely, too. You're several decades too late to get anything out of her.'

'Did she die at around the same time that Bernódus disappeared and the school was broken into?'

'No, no. It was quite some time afterwards. Probably around ten years later. She'd had to quit teaching because she lost her sight.'

'Did she go blind from an illness?' Freyr recalled that the teacher in the class photo had been rather young-looking, and would barely have been middle-aged ten years on from then. It was extremely unusual for people to go blind at that age from glaucoma or degenerative diseases, but of course there were other conditions that affected the eyes regardless of a person's age.

'No, it was an accident. She slipped on the ice in the spring, landed in a peculiar way on some fencing and damaged both her eyes so badly that they couldn't be saved. She started acting a bit strangely afterwards, the poor thing; said that she'd been pushed, but numerous witnesses stated that no one had been near her. That was why I was asked to take over her class in the autumn. She had to stop teaching.' The man's hands twitched for no visible reason. 'You could say that the accident led to her death, in fact, because later she stepped in front of a car. She had a white stick, but either she wasn't careful or she became confused, and that was that. While I'm feeding you old gossip, I heard at the time that when they examined the body they discovered that she'd completely lost it, though I found it hard to believe. Just thought I'd mention it, since you're a specialist in matters of the head and heart.'

Freyr didn't find this any worse a description of his specialism than the traditional one, *psychiatrist*. 'Do you know what happened?'

'The story goes that she'd inflicted wounds on herself that couldn't be explained by anything other than mental instability.' Freyr's skin prickled unpleasantly. The old man yawned again, even more weakly than before. 'Actually, she always seemed rather odd, and that's maybe what started the rumours. She was moody, she favoured some pupils over others and was generally rather cold and uncaring.'

Fearing he knew the answer, Freyr asked what he'd decided would be his final question: 'What sort of injuries did she have?'

'A cross. She'd cut a cross in her back. And rather neatly, too, I understand, considering she was blind.'

Exhaustion finally overcame Freyr and the desire to fall into his own bed at home was overwhelming. He'd had enough.

Chapter 25

Katrín had never rejoiced so much at any sound as at the din that now came from outside. Líf's laughter at something Garðar said convinced her that the owner of the hand was no longer standing on the porch. She dared to open her eyes and felt her heartbeat slow down and her breathing become stable. The odour of fish offal seemed to have gone and she enjoyed breathing normally again, after the stench had filled her nostrils. Unlike other odours, she hadn't grown used to this one; instead it had intensified until Katrín felt as if she had a piece of rotten fish covering her nose. As her fear had increased, so the pain in her foot had diminished, but now that the terror seemed behind her, the pain returned in waves, both there and elsewhere on her bruised body. But most of all she felt like weeping with happiness when the vague outlines of Líf and Garðar appeared in the dark kitchen doorway, their arms full. 'Weren't we quick?' Líf placed two rolled-up sleeping bags and a plastic bag full of things on the floor without entering the room, then started untying her walking boots. The dull scent of cigarette smoke filled the room and Katrín was happy to breathe it in; it was much better than the newly vanished smell of rot.

As far as Katrín was concerned, they couldn't have been gone any longer, but she didn't have the heart to say so. 'I can't begin to describe how relieved I am to see you. Did you bring the candles?' Her longing for light was probably no less desperate than Líf's for nicotine. Her voice quivered to an embarrassing degree and after Líf put on her furry slippers, took a candle from the bag and lit it, Katrín knew that it was her own deathly pale face that caused Líf to take one step back and exclaim in surprise. 'My foot is killing me,' she muttered. 'And there was someone outside. Just before you came.'

'What did you say?' Garðar walked in, half limping himself. His sore heel was apparently playing up again after the day's walk and the trip down to the doctor's house. 'We didn't see anyone.' He sat down opposite Katrín at the kitchen table and placed a white medicine bottle in front of her. 'Take four. You should feel better afterwards.'

'Doesn't she get anything to drink with that?' Líf looked around for water or juice, but the limited light from the candle did little more than cast shadows beyond the kitchen table.

'It's all right.' Katrín took four white tablets from the bottle. They seemed unnecessarily large and when she put them in her mouth it was as if all the saliva drained from it, forcing her to make a real effort to swallow them. 'How long do they take to work?' She didn't ask what she was swallowing, nor did she feel like reading the label on the bottle. The only thing that mattered to her was to reduce her intolerable pain.

Garðar watched her take the pills. 'Half an hour. Something like that. Maybe less, since it's been so long since we ate.' His brow was furrowed with worry; there seemed little left of the cheerfulness that had accompanied him and Líf to the door. 'Tell me what you saw. We've got to take precautions before we sleep, if that little bastard is around.'

Líf's laughter also seemed remote when she said in a

trembling voice: 'What precautions? What can we do?' She pulled the chair closer to the table. 'Why didn't we go and stay at the doctor's again? We could just as easily have helped you down there, Katrín.'

'I can't go anywhere. Maybe tomorrow, but now I would have to hop on one foot and I wouldn't trust myself to do that. You two could hardly carry me and all the stuff back down. How would we cross the stream, for example?' Katrín's pitch continued to rise and she stopped before she started sounding like a banshee. 'We're not going anywhere now. My foot is killing me again.'

Garðar's frown had deepened. 'If the worst comes to the worst, we'll sleep in shifts. One child can't handle all three of us. His only weapon is surprise, and the only time he could really do us any harm is when we're all asleep.' Garðar pulled the candle closer to the centre of the table. 'We have enough candles now and it's easier to stay awake that way than when everything's pitch-dark. I'll take the first watch, and I suggest you go straight to bed. It's silly for us all to be awake if we're going to do it this way.'

'I wonder what he wants from us.' Katrín was too drained physically and emotionally to have an opinion on Garðar's idea, much less to suggest any other solution. She was immensely relieved not to have to make the decision and would even have accepted one of Líf's ridiculous suggestions, so long as she didn't have to walk anywhere. 'I mean, why is he hanging around here? He hasn't given the impression of wanting to steal anything; he's had enough opportunity to do that, and he's not looking for companionship or help.' She sighed. 'I just don't get it.'

Líf looked over her shoulder as if she expected to see the

boy staring at her through the window. On the other side of the pane was sheer darkness. 'The boy isn't alive. Why don't we admit that? It's not as if the situation would get any worse.'

'That's enough of that nonsense, Líf.' Garðar looked at neither of them as he said this. 'You don't know what you're talking about, and there's no reason to imagine the worst. Things are fucked-up enough as it is.'

Katrín was in agreement with Líf. There was something more than a little peculiar going on, and it couldn't be explained by the presence of any normal child. She was going to tell Líf this when a creak in the floorboards silenced them all. 'Was that one of you?' Katrín whispered, though there was no reason to lower her voice. 'That's how it started before.' The sound seemed to originate there in the little kitchen.

No one wanted to admit to having caused the noise. 'Putti?' Líf bent down and took the dog in her arms. 'Was it him, maybe?' She glanced around furtively and squeezed the little animal tightly to her chest. 'Is he heavy enough?'

'Are you kidding? He weighs as much as a cork. He wouldn't make the floor creak even if he started jumping on it with all his weight.' The creaking sound came again, now much more softly than before. Líf muttered something under her breath and in her attempt to move closer to them bumped the table; Garðar just managed to grab the candle before it toppled over. He held the candlestick aloft, illuminating the room better. Then he stood up and stared towards where the sound seemed to originate. 'Don't say anything.' He focused his eyes firmly on the spot and when the sound came again he walked with the candle away from the table, towards the internal wall of the kitchen. There was nothing to see besides the damaged floorboards and the ends of the broken planks. Garðar was only one step away from the damaged patch when the creak came again, now so softly that they would hardly have noticed it if they hadn't been completely silent. 'There's nothing here.' Garðar seemed surprised. He bent down and swept the candle along the wall and floor in search of an explanation. When he stood up he was much calmer. 'There must be something wrong with the foundations here. Do you remember the planks? Maybe the mould, or whatever it is, is damaging the wood and the house is shifting because of it.' He turned round, satisfied to have come up with an explanation, but also quite worried since he knew he was the only one of them who hadn't given up on the house. 'Damn it.' He walked back over to them. 'I think there's nothing we can do but tear up the floor and see what's underneath.'

'Not now. Please.' Líf had loosened her grip on Putti slightly and he struggled weakly in her arms, desperate to get back down to the floor. 'What if there's something under there?'

'Like what? A ghost?' Garðar grimaced and shook his head.

Líf let Putti go and rearranged her jumper, which had been pulled out of place by the dog's wriggling. 'Or maybe a perfect breeding ground for an infestation of some disgusting fungus. I read online that you can become horribly ill breathing in that kind of fungal growth. It occurs precisely in old houses like this one. If I remember correctly, the spores float around in the air; they're so small you can't see them.'

'If that's the case, then we're already affected, Líf.' Garðar placed the candle back on the table and sat down.

'Was there anything in the article about the fungus causing hallucinations?' Katrín wondered whether what she'd seen and heard when she was alone in the house had been due to skewed perception from toxic poisoning. That would explain a lot of what had happened since their arrival at the house. If it was life-threatening, the fungus could also explain why the former owner had left the house and died outdoors somewhere. 'Maybe we're getting high without realizing it.' A stab of pain that went all the way up her leg when she moved slightly in her chair didn't suggest that she was all that doped up.

'There was nothing about that, but it wasn't a very scientific article.' Líf seemed to cheer up at this weak hope that everything had a logical explanation, but she hadn't thought it all the way through: if they were on some sort of mushroom trip, they were probably seriously ill. 'Wow, that would be awesome! Then there's probably nothing wrong here and we've just been imagining all this shit.' She looked at Katrín's leg, resting outstretched on a chair. 'Except maybe this. I think you're seriously injured.'

'I think so too.' Katrín leaned back as far as she could in the hope that a different position would make her feel better until the painkillers took effect. 'How long has it been since I took the pills?'

'Ten minutes. Fifteen. Not even that.' Garðar yawned widely, after trying unsuccessfully to suppress it. 'They won't have started working yet, but they will.' They all fell silent for a few moments, unsure whether to expect more unwelcome noises. However, nothing could be heard but their own breathing. 'I think we should stick to our plan of going to sleep now, and I'll keep watch until I can't keep my eyes open. Then you'll take over, Líf.'

'Me?' Líf sounded shocked. 'Am I supposed to sit here in the dark, alone?'

'There's just the three of us, Líf, and Katrín is injured. It makes by far the most sense for her to sleep while the medication is working, and then take over from you when it fades. Then you just take another dose, Katrín, and keep watch as long as you can. After that I'll take over again and hopefully by then it'll be morning.'

Katrín found his plan over-optimistic; judging by Líf's reluctance to take her shift, she wouldn't last long. They would probably each take two shifts before daybreak. 'I can't make it up the stairs. I'll have to sleep down here.' No one said anything; they were all too tired to ponder what this meant. In the end Katrín broke the silence: 'If anyone wants to bring a mattress down, I'll just sleep in the living room. It won't be any worse for me than sleeping upstairs.' She pushed aside the thought of how many windows there were, windows through which it was easy to enter, unlike the ones upstairs.

'We'll all sleep there.' Garðar stood up. 'Come on, Líf, let's bring the stuff down.'

'But . . .' Líf said nothing more. She stood up, looking shattered. 'I don't want to go to sleep.'

Garðar sighed, his patience long since exhausted. 'What now? Are you going to keep watch by yourself the whole night?'

'No. I don't want to sleep precisely because of this stupid arrangement. As soon as I fall asleep I'll forget everything, and I'll be happy, and then you'll wake me up and I'll remember all over again, and then I'll have to be awake and alone. I might as well take the first watch and get it over with, see?'

Katrín suddenly felt indescribably weary. She'd been in too much pain and too frightened to feel tired, but now it rushed over her. 'Why don't you just do that, then?' she snapped.

'We'll see.' Garðar pulled Líf along with him to go and get

the mattresses before she had the chance to respond to Katrín. The face she made from the doorway as Garðar stopped to take another candle suggested that Katrín's sarcasm hadn't pleased her. After they'd gone, Katrín looked at Putti and wanted very much to bend down and scratch the poor dog's ears. She didn't, however, for fear of moving her foot before the medication kicked in. Instead she listened to Líf and Garðar's footsteps on their way up the stairs, and to their muffled conversation, which seemed brusque but friendly, fortunately. If there was ever a time that they needed to make peace, it was now. She personally had to make quite an effort to put up with Líf, even on a good day. They didn't need to put up with her much longer, because soon the nightmare would be over, and it would be best if they could get through that short time without bickering or fighting. She resolved to make an effort not to say or do anything to upset Líf.

'We're back.' Líf stood in the doorway, looking extremely pissed off. 'Garðar's spreading out the sleeping bags.'

Katrín started. 'Wow. I fell asleep.' She stretched and yawned. 'You know what I thought? If you want, we could take our watch together. Isn't that the simplest solution? We'll keep watch while Garðar sleeps and try to hold out a little longer. Of course it'll be easier if it's the two of us, and we can look after each other.' She smiled at Líf in the hope that she would accept this diplomatic compromise.

At first Líf frowned, apparently wondering whether Katrín was trying to trick her. But then her face brightened and she smiled back broadly. 'I really like that idea. Do you want me to tell you some gossip? I know so many stories that it'll be morning before you know it.'

'Yes please! I don't have any at all, so I hope you know as

much as you say!' Katrín stretched properly and prepared to move over to the living room. 'I don't know what I'll do if I have to pee in the night.'

'Oh, I'll just go with you.' Líf was so thrilled with Katrín's suggestion that now she was clearly capable of anything. She walked into the kitchen and bent down to Putti. 'I guess we're just hallucinating. Do you think Putti's tripping as well?'

'I don't know whether I'd rather we were high or crazy. I'm not sure which is worse.' Katrín watched as one of Putti's hind legs jerked back and forth aimlessly as Líf scratched his side. He'd closed his eyes and rolled onto his back, perfectly relaxed. It had been a long time since he'd appeared so calm and Katrín was happy about this small sign of normality, which she took as an indication of a quiet night ahead.

She stirred in the night when Garðar shook her shoulder lightly and said that he was going out for a piss. The drugs might not have worked miracles, but now her leg felt more tingly than as if it were being crushed. She smiled sleepily at him, yawned and said that she would get up when he came back in. Then she slept again, without knowing that next time she woke, the night would be at an end. And Garðar would be gone.

Chapter 26

The strange fog that had lain over the town had seemed to subside. Freyr watched it creep away from Skutulsfjörður out into the sea. He took a heavy cardboard box full of old medical records from the back seat of the car and shut the door behind him with his foot. He'd got the records through the sheer goodwill of the hospital archivist and doubted he'd have met with the same helpfulness in Reykjavík, where everything was less personal and more formal. Of course people sacrificed a lot when they moved away from the capital, but they got a great deal in return, like mutual trust. When it came down to it, Freyr found the comparison favoured the rural areas.

The hospital's equipment technician held the door open as Freyr entered and tried to take a furtive peek into the box. He seemed a bit disappointed to discover that it didn't contain any new devices. Freyr saw from the clock hanging in the foyer that he'd been away much longer than he'd told his colleagues he would be. He cursed himself for not having set aside more time when he realized that such old files were kept here. There was little he could do about it now but drop off the box at his office and head back to the wards, though he was well aware that it would be hard to keep his mind on his patients until he could start examining the reports.

On the wards everything was calm, business as usual, despite Freyr's lateness. He immediately got down to work on the few items of business that awaited him, went over some test results that had come back that morning, ordered further tests for one patient, changed prescriptions where necessary and updated medical records. Afterwards he went and checked whether there was anything more to do, and when there turned out not to be, he informed his colleagues that he was going to his office and that they should call him if something came up. Before leaving the ward he dropped by the old teacher's room, but walked quietly back out to the sound of the man snoring. It didn't matter really, he'd probably told Freyr everything he knew.

The box sat in the middle of his desk, which was otherwise nearly empty. Freyr couldn't stand clutter and couldn't concentrate when everything was a mess, which Sara had never understood. He suddenly recalled how he'd been irritated by things that he now saw hardly mattered, and he longed to pick up the phone and ask Sara's forgiveness for his behaviour while everything had still been fine. Long ago he'd realized that it was much simpler to believe that everything had been all right between them before Benni disappeared. The tragedy and sorrow that had followed simply overshadowed everything else. If he looked honestly into his heart, he knew that their relationship would probably have ground down slowly but surely, in the end leaving them wanting nothing to do with each other, even if Benni hadn't gone missing; the only difference would have been that they each would have had half-custody of their son, instead of both having full custody of their separate memories of him. Freyr decided not to call Sara; there was no point digging up details from the past that made no difference in the present. Or at least he hoped not.

As he opened the box he was met with the smell of old

paper that had lain undisturbed in closed containers. It was remarkable that these medical reports should still exist; for a time they'd obviously been important sources of information on the patients concerned, but after these patients had died their importance diminished rapidly. He took one stack of paper after another out of the box before placing it on the floor. He opened the first report and began reading.

'You were so mysterious on the phone that I decided to come straight over.' Dagný had declined Freyr's invitation to hang up her jacket before she sat down. He understood why; he'd opened the window wide when the dust and odour of the papers had started to get on his nerves, and he'd been so absorbed in the contents of the files that he hadn't noticed it was as cold inside as out. Now that he was a bit calmer he also felt the cold draught and shut the window.

'I hope you didn't misunderstand me and think that I've managed to tie all these threads together. Far from it.' Freyr sat down. 'On the other hand, I did find one or two curious details that reveal unexpected connections.'

'Let's hear it.' Dagný unzipped her jacket now. She leaned over the desk and stared at the old reports, before wrinkling her nose. 'Is that smell coming from the papers?'

'Yes, I'm afraid so. But I can put them back in the box if you want – I pretty much remember everything that's in them.'

Dagný declined the offer. 'If my suspicions are correct, this case is going to look very strange, so it's just as well that I have the papers here. I'm not saying I doubt your word; it's just that I've got to see it with my own eyes if it turns out to be something weird.'

Freyr left the papers lying on the table. 'That's precisely the right word to describe it: weird.' He pushed some documents aside in search of the first report he wanted to tell her about. He found it and handed it to her. 'This is a letter from the school nurse to the hospital's chief physician in 1952, in which she expresses her concerns about a new student, Bernódus Pjetursson.'

Dagný took the letter, along with a copy of the nurse's report on the boy. She glanced over the letter. 'Oh God. That's horrible.' She put down both of the papers without reading the report. Freyr didn't blame her; the descriptions of the boy's scars didn't exactly make easy reading. The reason that the nurse had decided to write to the doctor was because two crosses had been carved and burned with a pocket knife and cigarettes on Bernódus's back.

Freyr picked up the papers. 'I couldn't agree more. The boy's father must have been very, very ill, either from some progressive mental disease or some problem that was initially triggered, when his drinking got out of control. The old teacher said he'd heard that the man blamed the boy for the death of his wife and his other son, and him having marked the child in this way, to my mind, confirms that this could have been the case. Two crosses, two dead loved ones. It's a terrible tragedy, and you have to wonder whether he didn't simply murder the boy, although who knows how he then disposed of the body.'

'I don't remember being called in for that kind of medical examination at school.' Dagný crossed her arms and leaned back from the desk, as if wanting to keep herself as far as possible from the horrific reports. 'I had various vaccinations, but that was it.'

'The report states that the nurse was asked to speak to and

examine the boy. He'd refused to go to his P.E. class and when they once forced him into it he didn't want to change his clothes, saying that he didn't have a P.E. kit and refused to take anything other than a pair of lost property shorts. Then he wouldn't have a shower after the class. He and the shower attendant argued and the kids in the class teased him, winding him up even more and causing a huge disturbance; it all ended up on the school nurse's desk after the shower attendant removed his clothes by force and pushed him under a shower, to the delight of his classmates. He was ashamed of his back and didn't want others to see it, so you can imagine how traumatic this was. He was only twelve years old.'

'And how come nothing was done? This letter was sent a month before the boy disappeared, which meant it would have been possible to intervene and help him.'

'I don't know.' Freyr had been just as angry as Dagný when he'd read the report, but he was calmer now, though overwhelmed by a feeling of sadness at the boy's fate. Lying on the table was the copy of the class photo that he'd taken from a drawer, and he found himself staring regularly at the boy's sad black and white image. His position apart from the rest of the group was even more noticeable now that Freyr had discovered his awful misfortune. The withdrawal of love and support from those who were supposed to care most always deeply affected children, and there was little hope of rehabilitation without intervention – which appeared not to have come quickly enough in Bernódus's case. 'It was a completely different time then; child protection was much less advanced. Probably some sort of process to help him was set in motion; maybe the authorities here had to contact the child protection authorities in Reykjavík, and that chain of communication took place at a completely different speed than it would do today.'

'That's no excuse.' Dagný bit her lip. 'She says that he claimed it was an accident, but she rules that out. Was she right?'

'Yes, it's out of the question.' Freyr took back the report. 'The wounds are a combination of knife cuts and cigarette burns. He couldn't have made them himself, according to her description.' He handed Dagný the papers and pointed at the relevant part. 'She got him to directly admit that his father had done it, after ruling out other explanations by asking him over and over and evaluating his reaction each time. This woman was really excellent. She was able to coax him out of his jumper and get him to open up, without expecting him to tell her everything immediately. Not everyone's able to reach children who have suffered that kind of violence. The saddest thing is that her efforts came to nothing.'

'Are these reports all about him?' Dagný pointed at the stacks of paper, which Freyr had put in order of importance.

'No. I also gathered data about others involved in this case and learned various things. It's remarkable that no one's put it all together, but that's probably because it all happened over such a length of time.' He reached for the bottom stack. 'I received an e-mail just now from the doctor who autopsied Halla. I asked him to find out whether the other two classmates, Jón and Védís, also had scars in the form of a cross on their backs. It's easier for him as a forensic pathologist to get hold of that kind of information.'

'And?' asked Dagný, though it was clear from her expression that she knew what would come next. Freyr handed her a printout of the e-mail. 'They had crosses too, which means that all five of the dead classmates had almost exactly the same scars as Halla. A large cross scratched on their backs. Actually, Jón died in a fire, so information about him isn't conclusive, but nonetheless signs of a cross on his back were noted in his autopsy.'

'I see. But what exactly does this mean?' Dagný skimmed the text. 'Bernódus's father died years ago. He couldn't have done this. Unless . . . are these scars from when they were little? Did the man attack other children besides his own son?'

'Not according to what I understand from this. The scars were formed after the victims were fully grown, maybe even when they were already elderly. Since it was possible to estimate the age of the scars, the oldest one had been made less than five years ago. So I understand this to mean that it all began in 2007, or three years ago, when most of these strange events seem to have started; this completely rules out any involvement on the part of Bernódus's father, since he was long dead.' Freyr paused for a moment. 'To my mind, this means one of two things: either it wasn't the boy's father at all who did this to him, but someone else who lived longer; or else someone replicated the original injuries, but for what purpose I have no idea. I have even less idea how this could actually have happened, because the scars were formed over a long period of time in all instances.'

Dagný appeared far from convinced. 'Who do you think could go around cutting people like this all over the country without anyone pressing charges? They didn't all live in the same place. And how did this person go about it? You said that these people were getting on a bit, but the men at least could have put up a fight. I find it more than a little bit bizarre.'

There was no denying this, and Freyr made no attempt to come up with a rational explanation. 'The same lesions were found on the class teacher's back when she died.' Freyr handed her the copy of the photograph. 'It was about a decade after Bernódus went missing.'

The picture lay on the edge of the table for a few moments before Dagný picked it up to have a better look. 'Is it possible that Bernódus survived and that he was responsible for the attacks? That he might even still be alive?' She stared dumbfounded at the picture; to Freyr the boy seemed to absorb all her attention. He understood this well. It was hard to imagine a more poignant image, particularly knowing the boy's story. 'He could just as well be the one who broke into the preschool.'

'I can't believe that.' Freyr looked out of the window at the cold environment. 'Where is he supposed to have lived all this time? And how has he been supporting himself? Someone would definitely have noticed him over all the decades that have passed. Unless he took someone else's name and lifestyle, though that's also pretty far-fetched considering how young he was when he disappeared.' Freyr took back the picture and placed it on the table before him. They'd wandered into yet another blind alley. He decided to tell her about his visit to Úrsúla and what she had said about the boy she 'didn't want to see', and who wanted Freyr to find Benni. When he'd finished he waited for her to respond but Dagný said nothing, just sat and stared at the papers on the desk. When the silence grew uncomfortably long, he spoke up again. 'For the moment I don't see any other option than to wait for Úrsúla to recover and try to speak to her again in the hope that she expresses herself more clearly, as well as keep on trying to reach Lárus, the only surviving friend. He hasn't answered my calls and I've actually started to think that he must be out of the country.'

Dagný looked up. 'I'll see to that. I think it's time I got my colleagues down south to help us find him. Hopefully he'll have something to tell us.'

When Freyr said goodbye from the doorway shortly afterwards and watched her walk down the corridor, he remembered the recording he'd made on his mobile phone the night before and the words that he thought he'd heard behind him. When Dagný turned the corner he shut the door and sat back down at his desk, mobile phone in his hand. He found the recording after a short search and listened.

At first he could hear little more than a buzzing sound and his own irregular footsteps. But then he heard something else that he couldn't distinguish until he'd rewound it and turned the volume up fully. Although he'd never swear to what words he thought he heard, personally he was convinced that they were: 'Tell the truth. Then you'll find me, Daddy.' Nor was there any question that it was the voice of his son. It was Benni.

Chapter 27

It wasn't pain in her foot or elsewhere in her body that woke Katrín, but simply the fact that she'd had enough sleep. At first she was confused, blinking slowly while the dream that had been so vivid a few moments before faded and slipped steadily away as she tried to recall it. After finally waking fully, what remained was only a hazy and uncomfortable memory of a nightmare in which she'd done a terrible job as a teacher, turned a blind eye to the poor treatment of her students and been forced to pay for it. She couldn't place any of the students or remember the conclusion of the dream or whether she'd been punished. In fact she was relieved to wake up; she was supposed to be feeling rested, but her rapid heartbeat suggested that the dream had ended badly. Katrín turned on her side and looked at Líf, who was sleeping soundly. Only her eyebrows and a bit of her hair poked out of her sleeping bag. She turned on her other side to look instead at Garðar. As she wriggled in her sleeping bag she felt as if something were wrong, though she couldn't grasp what it might be. As soon as she laid eyes on Garðar's empty sleeping bag she realized what was bothering her and jerked herself upright. A terrible pain shot up the front of her calf from her injured instep, but that was nothing compared to the anguish that the abandoned sleeping bag stirred in her.

It was too bright inside for it still to be night. 'Garðar!' Her hoarse voice broke the silence. No answer. The house was absolutely still. Putti jumped up from where he'd been lying at the foot of her sleeping bag and looked no less bewildered than she did, newly awake as he was. Katrín tried to breathe more calmly; Garðar had probably gone upstairs to sleep. Her sleep-intoxicated mind struggled to recall whether she'd woken at some point in the night to take over from him, but to no avail. It could be that Líf had kept watch alone, and Katrín turned and shook the lump lying motionless beside her. 'Líf! Líf! Wake up.' A vague murmur came from inside the bag. Katrín shook Líf's shoulder even harder. 'Wake up! Garðar's gone.'

Líf sat up, not quite with the same energy as Katrín and Putti, but almost. She peered bewilderedly through the tousled hair hanging in her face, then clumsily pushed it aside to see better. 'What time is it?'

'I don't know.' Katrín gritted her teeth. 'Late enough for the sun to have risen.'

'We've slept an awfully long time.' Líf yawned without covering her mouth, subjecting Katrín to a vision of her rows of white teeth. 'Where's Garðar?' Putti seemed to understand the question. He circled the room and sniffed the floor. When he encountered a dust ball he sneezed comically, stopped his search and sat down self-consciously.

'I don't know; it looks like he's gone.' Katrín's voice was still hoarse; she realized that she'd spoken far too loudly in her agitated state. 'He didn't wake us up in the night. Not me, anyway.' A hazy memory of him nudging her appeared in her mind but vanished before she could fix it there. Maybe it had happened in the dream that was now lost to her.

'Me neither.' Líf looked around in confusion. 'At least I don't think so.'

Katrín reached for Garðar's sleeping bag and ran her hand down its interior. 'The bag is freezing cold, so he hasn't just left.' Putti misunderstood the message, leapt up and wagged his tail happily as he stepped onto the soft bag, where he curled into a ball, contented. 'Maybe he's outside working on the porch. Or making us breakfast.' Líf never changed; her mood turned cheerful at the thought of someone pampering her.

'He didn't answer when I shouted, so he could hardly be in the kitchen. And you can hear for yourself that there's no one working outside.' Katrín tried to restrain her resentment. If someone had to go missing, why couldn't it have been Líf? She pulled herself together. 'Maybe he's gone down to the doctor's house to get something.'

For the first time now they felt how cold it was inside and Líf pulled her sleeping bag back up over her shoulders. Katrín did the same and they sat there like that for some time without saying anything, both praying silently that the sound of footsteps would come from the porch. But the only thing they heard was the soft ripple of the stream. 'Shouldn't we go and see if he's outside?' Líf gave Katrín an anguished look, but then her face brightened. 'Maybe he went down to the beach because he heard a boat!'

Although Katrín didn't believe this for a minute, she found it more comforting to have a possible explanation, no matter how unlikely it was. She clenched her jaw and stood up in a rather roundabout way in order to protect her foot. The heavy throbbing in her swollen instep intensified with each minute. Her foot was the only part of her body that felt burning hot.

The question was no longer whether it was broken, but just how badly. Yet in the end she managed to get herself out of her sleeping bag and was then able to hop on one foot towards her jacket, which she'd put in a corner of the room the night before. Luckily she hadn't wanted to remove her trousers because of her foot; it would have been impossible now for her to put them back on, considering how much the swelling had increased. Katrín put on her jacket and supported herself on the wall as she walked to the door. She wanted to scream in pain every time she attempted to put weight on her injured foot. Putti, sensing this, or reading it in her screwed-up face, jumped off the sleeping bag and came over to her, uncertain about how he could help her.

Líf realized she would be alone if she didn't get up, so she jumped up and dressed in a hurry. Líf's bustle made Katrín feel dizzy and she held on tighter to the doorframe for fear of toppling over. Even Putti moved away slightly, to be safe. When most of the racket was over Katrín hopped on one foot ahead of Líf, determined to get Garðar to help her make a crutch when he returned.

There was nothing to see in the kitchen, and although that might have been clear to Katrín before she limped there, she was deeply disappointed not to see Garðar standing there preparing breakfast for them all. The air was stale and terribly cold, even colder than in the living room. The kitchen table looked exactly as they'd left it the night before: on it were only the candlestick, matches and the medicine bottle. A stack of dirty dishes waited patiently on the counter for someone to take them, along with the cups and glasses, out to the stream and rinse them off. That was hardly likely to happen any time soon. Katrín hadn't looked at anything else before

Líf appeared in the doorway. She pointed at the damaged floorboards. 'Look.' She tapped Katrín's shoulder and pointed. 'Garðar's started repairing it. Maybe he's gone to look for tools or materials.'

Katrín looked around and saw the traces of the repairs made in the night or the morning. She couldn't recall having heard Garðar pottering about when she fell asleep, or having woken to those kinds of sounds. She hopped towards the broken floor in the hope of finding something there that might suggest what had happened to Garðar; as ridiculous as it was, she simply couldn't think of anything better to do. Supporting herself on the wall, she leaned forward to get a better look at the part of the floor he'd been concerned with. Surprisingly, Putti didn't follow her, but went and stood by Líf.

'Do you see any mould or fungus? Maybe Garðar was poisoned and ran out to throw up.' Líf sounded quite frightened. 'I told you to leave it alone. I told you.'

There was no nasty fungus to be seen, however. Instead it looked as if another layer of floorboards, much older in appearance, lay beneath the ones that had been removed. 'There's no fungus here. I'd need a candle to get a better look, but I can't see anything special.' She frowned. 'But there's an awful smell coming from down there, probably from opening up the space that's been closed for so long.' She took care not to breathe in too deeply. The area might contain bacteria that modern-day people couldn't handle. Including Garðar.

'This floor isn't that old, Katrín. The last man who owned the house installed it, remember? That was only three years ago.' Líf had moved as far away from the area as the confines of the kitchen allowed. 'If it smells bad, it's because of the fungus. Even though you can't see it, it could still be there.'

Instead of arguing about this, Katrín pulled herself away from the wall and the half-finished repairs. She hadn't found Garðar under the floorboards. Putti greeted her enthusiastically when she reached Líf, as if he were seeing her for the first time after several days' absence. Under normal circumstances she would have enjoyed the dog's behaviour, but for the moment her mind was occupied with something entirely different. 'Garðar!' Katrín shouted as loudly as she could. No reply. 'Maybe he's sleeping upstairs, Líf. Would you mind looking?'

'Why should he have gone up there? The mattresses and sleeping bags are down here. And he would have answered if he were there.' Líf's expression gave no indication that she was about to go upstairs alone. 'He would definitely have woken up with all your shouting.'

Katrín breathed in and counted to ten in her head. 'Not definitely, Líf. You didn't wake up when I called out to him before. Besides, he was probably up all night; he didn't wake us, remember? And if he's been messing about with the floor all night, he could very well just be completely out of it.'

'But what if he isn't upstairs? I don't want to go up there alone. Can't you go, or at least come with me?'

'I can hardly get from one room to another. How am I supposed to go up the stairs? Believe me, I would if I could.' Katrín knew she would have to do better than this to get Líf to do what she was asking. 'I'll come and stand by the stairs, where I can see you at all times, and the only thing you need to do is open the door to the bedroom and peek in. Putti can go with you if it would make you feel better.'

'But what if we both go and stand by the stairs and shout

as loudly as we can? If Garðar doesn't answer, then we'll know he's not up there.'

'But what if he's there and can't answer? Or he's been knocked out or something? What then?'

Finally Líf was persuaded to go up while Katrín watched from the bottom of the stairs and urged her on. Líf took Putti with her but had to hold onto him, since he tried to turn around at every step and go back to Katrín. 'Open the door, nothing will happen.' Katrín tried to sound encouraging, but couldn't suppress the thought that she was glad she wasn't in Líf's shoes. There was no window in the stairwell, making it dark and cold. Katrín regretted not having brought a candle.

'Garðar?' Líf's weak voice wouldn't have disturbed a conscious person, never mind a sleeping one. 'Are you there?' She grabbed the doorknob and pushed the door open. Putti stared straight down at Katrín, his eyes telling her that he didn't have a clue why he couldn't be downstairs with her. Líf turned to Katrín with a look of relief. 'Nothing.' Then she went to the next door and did the same, and again there was nothing to see in the room. The third and final door was a little too far down the hall for Katrín to see all the way. When Líf realized this she went back and stood on the top step. 'I don't want to open any doors unless I can see you.' She made ready to come down. 'I'm not kidding. I'm not going to do it.'

Katrín sighed and grabbed the handrail. With great effort she managed to wriggle up the steps high enough to see the third door. It led to the room where they'd previously been sleeping. 'Try it now. I can see you clearly.'

Líf turned around and walked down the hallway, but looked back twice on her way to reassure herself that Katrín could still see her. Finally she came to the door and stood there awkwardly before looking nervously at Katrín, who signalled to her to hurry up and get it over with. At that Líf grew bolder and opened the door, more firmly and confidently than she had the other two. Which was a shame, considering how startled she was by what she saw. Líf let Putti drop without thinking. The dog landed more or less on his feet and ran immediately back to Katrín, leaving Líf behind by herself.

'What's there?' Katrín was preparing herself mentally to have to clamber all the way up to see what Líf was staring at. 'Is it Garðar?' She felt burning tears forming in the corners of her eyes while part of her brain constructed all sorts of images of her husband dead in the empty, ice-cold room.

Her question roused Líf. 'No, no. It isn't Garðar.' She turned from the door, crossed the hallway in a few large strides and took two stairs at a time to get down to Katrín. When she got there she hung trembling onto Katrín, who just managed to keep her balance by supporting herself against the wall. She didn't want to tumble down the stairs again, though the fall would be shorter than last time. 'There's nobody in there, I swear.' Katrín stared at her open-mouthed. 'The floor is covered with fucking shells and I felt someone breathe in my face.' She looked at Katrín and seemed to be irritated by how indifferently she reacted. 'There was nothing there last night when we went to get the sleeping bags. Not one shell. And I'm not making it up about the breathing; I'm sure that disgusting stench is still sticking to my skin.' She glanced sidelong down the hallway. Katrín smelled a putrid odour as she turned her head. 'Is this some sort of misguided joke on Garðar's part? Do you think he's hiding here somewhere to see our reactions?'

'No.' Katrín knew in her heart that this wasn't the

explanation. Garðar wouldn't be wasting time collecting shells at the beach just to scare them, especially not when he was exhausted in the middle of the night. But there was something else that convinced her that Garðar had nothing to do with this, which was a soft, sad voice inside her telling her that he was gone for good; that she would never see him again.

That voice faded as they went outside to continue their search for Garðar. Although Líf supported Katrín, they made slow progress and realized almost immediately that they wouldn't get far and would never manage to comb the entire area. They spied tracks in the snow going from the porch towards the sea, a route they couldn't recall any of them having taken before. The tracks were recent and large enough to convince them that they were Garðar's. They looked around the house without any success and then decided to try to follow the tracks, at least for some distance. Along the way Líf regularly called Garðar's name loudly and shrilly, until Katrín asked her to stop. She found it uncomfortable to hear the silence return after every shout, each time more painful to her than the last. Katrín was at her wits' end when they came across another set of tracks, looking as if whoever made them had fallen from the sky and landed next to Garðar. Putti sniffed at them but jumped back immediately with a soft whine. 'Come on, Líf. Let's go back inside and lock the door behind us.' The voice inside her head now sounded louder than before as it kept on repeating the familiar refrain, causing Katrín's head to spin. *Garðar isn't coming back.* She watched three distant seagulls flying in circles over the sea and plunging downwards to snatch the food that was waiting for them below. She couldn't rid herself of the horrible feeling that Garðar was floating there half submerged, with the seabirds pecking at whatever was left of him.

She stared sadly at the tracks and watched a tear fall from her cheek. It landed in the snow, between two prints made by a barefoot child.

Chapter 28

The northern lights danced in the black sky. The long ribbon expanded and retracted dynamically, powered by forces that Freyr didn't understand, sometimes looking as if it reached the ends of the earth. Occasionally pink waves passed through it but the green aura always returned in full force, holding Freyr's attention. He was near the harbour, in the Lower Market, the oldest part of town, whose origin could be traced back to merchants operating under the Danish trade monopoly in the mid-eighteenth century. Most of the buildings dated from that period and if he ignored several modern memorials, he felt as if he could be a destitute farmer from a former time coming to make a deposit with his merchant. He sat on a large stone outside Tjöruhús, a charming restaurant in an old renovated warehouse that was more reminiscent of Denmark than of Iceland. Freyr had only managed to eat there once before the place had closed for the winter, but he would certainly be among those waiting on the doorstep for it to open again in the spring. It had been during one of his first evenings in Ísafjörður. Two colleagues of his from the hospital had suggested they have dinner together to get to know each other better. Freyr had been so taken by the ultra-fresh seafood that he'd added little to their conversation apart from compliments about the food. They hadn't asked him to hang out with them outside work again, which was actually fine by him. He had little in common with these family men who had lives outside the hospital.

However, it wasn't the memory of the excellent meal that had brought him down to Lower Market. An aimless walk had led him by coincidence to this historical spot; maybe he'd wandered here instinctively because of how few people were out and about in the area, assuring him peace and quiet to ponder things and compose his thoughts. He was amazed he'd managed to complete his working day without embarrassing himself. His hands had trembled so much that he could barely do anything requiring any kind of dexterity and he could hardly follow the thread of a conversation when speaking to others. The recording from his mobile phone had thrown him completely off balance, and although he'd previously thought he'd heard his son's voice, and in the same place, it changed a great deal that now he had a recording confirming it. Maybe because it made it much more difficult to ascribe the incident to hallucination, stress or imagination. That alone, however, wasn't enough, because of course he could still be convincing himself that he was hearing things that weren't there. For this reason, when he'd heard the caretaker busying himself with changing the faulty fluorescent bulb, he'd rushed into the corridor and asked the flabbergasted man to tell him what he heard on the phone. '*Tell the truth. Then you'll find me, Daddy*,' the man had replied. The words had affected Freyr so strongly that he couldn't care less about the bewildered look on the caretaker's face. He'd received confirmation that he hadn't misheard it, and he didn't care if this injected new life into the gossip in the break room about the strange, antisocial psychiatrist from the south.

With his mobile phone in his hand, Freyr continued to stare at the northern lights, which had spread out even further and now covered most of the sky. The green colour fascinated him in some incomprehensible way; he had never pondered colours much and didn't even have a favourite one. But there was something about this greenish flickering in the sky that captured his attention, and like everything else that day, the colour prompted a familiar feeling of sorrow. Sorrow over what had happened and what could have happened. He pushed aside all the 'what ifs' that would never find an answer and was surprised at how hard it was turning out to be, to follow the advice he gave to patients who remained stuck in *if onlys*. Until now he'd been able to hold these kind of thoughts at bay, largely by simply not letting his mind drift that way and refusing to allow regret to gain the upper hand. He was realistic enough to know that it would only have made things worse to be honest with Sara. On top of the sorrow that was already overwhelming her he would have added bitter anger, which would have done nothing to improve either her situation or his. The truth wouldn't have changed Benni's fate. So there was no justification to increase Sara's burden or take the risk that she might seek revenge, which could have led to his being suspended from work or even fired.

By this rationale he'd managed to live more or less at peace with his own dishonesty for nearly three years. But after listening to the recording, this shaky reasoning had collapsed and guilt burst forth. He was probably reading more into the soft voice in the faint recording than he should, but it didn't matter; he was convinced that his son expected him to come clean. Perhaps the point of Benni's strange appearance was to help Sara and enable her to get on with her life. And in order for this to happen, Freyr needed to tell her the truth.

The phone rang and he answered it without looking to see who it was. He simply stared, hypnotized, at the green colour that refused to stay still long enough in his eyes for him to remember or work out what meaning the colour had or to what memory it was connected. 'Hello.'

It was Dagný. 'Lárus is dead.' She waited for Freyr to say something, then continued when all she heard was silence. 'He was found at home. The police in Reykjavík called and informed me. I don't remember whether I told you, but I asked them to help find him.'

'What happened?' Freyr shut his eyes in order to tear himself from the aerial display and focus on the conversation. 'They don't know, but it looks as if he ingested poison. Maybe accidentally, maybe deliberately, though that has to be considered unlikely.'

'Do they know what type of poison it was?' The question actually didn't have anything to do with the case, but Freyr needed time to digest the news and to think.

'I didn't ask. I'll probably get better information tomorrow. They'll call back for sure; I didn't go into any detail when I asked them to find him. It took me so much by surprise that I didn't have a decent story ready, I just told them that I needed to reach him regarding an old case for which he could possibly provide information, and that he wasn't answering either his home phone or his mobile. I didn't need to explain any further, since they just assumed that the man simply didn't want to be contacted.'

'Was his back scarred?'

'No one's said so. I assume that it still hasn't come to light.

The police don't undress people; that's left to those who handle the dead.' Dagný sighed softly. 'It certainly won't reduce the barrage of questions waiting for me.'

Freyr had nothing to add to this; he wasn't in any condition to consider what it meant, and whether all speculation about the relationship between this doomed group of friends and the disappearance of his son was now invalid. Now there was no one left who could inform them of this first-hand, it felt pointless to ponder the matter further. Maybe that was a good thing. Until he'd got dragged into this he'd felt all right; not great, granted, but he could make it through the days without any particular mental anguish. But now it was as if he were returning to the same emotional rollercoaster as he'd been on when Benni had disappeared.

Freyr said goodbye, his tone of voice so sad and distracted that Dagný asked how he was feeling before ending their call. But instead of taking a load off his mind and telling her about the recording, he said she needn't worry, he was just tired. He didn't feel able to describe recent events well enough for her not to think that he'd completely lost the plot. That story would have to wait until he could hand her his phone and allow her to listen to Benni's distant voice. A voice that Freyr had managed to capture despite the fact that it was made without vocal cords, tongue, central nervous system or any of the other things needed to form words. But in the sky there was nothing evident that Freyr considered necessary to ignite the northern lights. Who was he to judge what was possible and what was not?

In order to guarantee himself peace and quiet for what remained of the evening, Freyr was careful to turn off the ringer on his phone before he stuck it in his jacket pocket.

Despite his sadness he smiled at the futility of this gesture; almost no one called him after work apart from Sara. But better to be safe than sorry. Freyr stood up and stared for the final time at the northern lights before setting off for home, still certain that the colour green mattered. A great deal.

The area was like a graveyard. He'd chosen to go there precisely for the quiet, but suddenly he felt uncomfortable at seeing no one else there. His every exhalation was accompanied by a hazy cloud that vanished almost as soon as it appeared, but in the second that the haze passed before his eyes and evaporated Freyr thought he noticed movement in places where there was none. He quickened his pace but refrained from running, which he thought would be a sure sign that he'd lost all control of the situation. What, in fact, did he have to fear? If the unbelievable proved to be true and Benni's spirit was haunting him, that could only be good. Benni was his child, no matter whether he was alive or dead. Freyr wasn't especially concerned by all the medium's talk about the dead growing malevolent over time. And even if they did, what would be the worst that could happen? That he would die? He had no desire to sleep the long sleep but had to admit that he didn't fear it either; his life wasn't worth much now and his future didn't look very exciting. This simple fact made him stop. He looked up the alley that lay ahead; the streetlights and the strange glow from the sky weren't able to illuminate it properly, and long shadows stretched up it from the streetlights as if they were pointing him to the shortest yet most hazardous way home.

Freyr was startled by laughter from a solitary great black-backed gull. His heart made its presence known with a dull pounding and he forced himself to breathe calmly in the hope of regaining his composure. Standing stock-still, he peered ahead, trying to spot any movement, but saw nothing except the deathly still buildings staring at each other with big black eyes. Freyr cursed himself for having felt the need for peace and quiet and wished he'd gone through the centre of town instead. Again he heard suppressed laughter, now more clearly. It sounded desolate, originating in malice or pleasure over others' failures. Even though Freyr could never have described Benni's laughter, could not even recall it in his mind, he knew that this was not his son. In his short life, Benni had never made such a spiteful sound. Freyr looked in both directions and wondered whether he should avoid the shadowy alley and walk along the sea, or take the next street along, which was much wider and brighter. He didn't expect to be attacked, but neither did he want to go looking for trouble, and he wanted least of all to come any closer to the source of the laughter. Without pondering it any longer he chose to walk along the sea, turned right and set off slowly.

The lapping of the waves welcomed him as he approached the sea wall and Freyr's mood lightened with each step that brought him closer to this pleasing sound and further from the alley. He sped up and distracted himself by guessing how many steps it would take him to reach the wall. The count fluctuated – but at least the task absorbed all his attention in the meantime. Then he heard the giggling again. Now it sounded as if it was coming from the other side of a nearby fishing boat propped on trestles, awaiting repairs and the spring. The sound was clearer than before, the voice bright and sharp, like a child's. But not any ordinary child, that much was certain. His estimated step-count evaporated and he stopped some way away and looked at the area around the boat. There wasn't a soul in sight. Freyr bent down and tried to see if there were any feet beneath the boat, but saw none. If the laughter came from there, whoever made it must be hiding inside the vessel. Freyr grew angry at the thought that this was maybe just a trick, some kids who'd decided to make fun of the strange man from the south who'd lost his son. Maybe the same little sods had been at work in the hospital. Before he knew it he was storming towards the boat and didn't slow down when the same horrible giggle came from behind it.

When Freyr reached the side of the boat he realized it was higher than he'd thought and that it would be no easy feat to clamber into it. He leaned up against the gunwale and looked over the deck, but saw nothing except for rusted iron, decaying ropes and pieces of netting that appeared so badly tangled they would never have posed little threat to the lives of any fish. He walked around the boat and knocked on its sides, in case that would succeed in scaring the kid or kids up out of it. Heavy, hollow sounds, each blow taking its toll on Freyr's bare knuckles. But no one stuck his head out or emerged from the boat; all that happened was that some yellow paint flaked off and fell to the ground. The outline of the boat's name and registration number were still visible: Gígja Ólafsdóttir ÍS 127. Finally the drumming had a result when the laughter rang out again, now clearly from within the body of the boat. Freyr needed no more encouragement; he went to where the gunwales were lowest and swung himself up on deck.

The first thing that struck him was a strong smell of sea salt. Everything here had been so thoroughly drenched by the waves that the boat would have to remain on shore for many years before it lost the smell of the sea. The odour might also have come from the puddles of water lying here and there along the deck, gleaming softly in the moonlight. Freyr stared at them; it was so cold outside that such shallow puddles should have frozen, even if they were seawater. Probably whoever was on board the boat had brought the water with him. The deck creaked under Freyr's every step and he hoped fervently and sincerely that the kid's heart was now in his throat at the thought of being discovered. But what was he going to do after catching the snake by its tail? He could think of no sensible answer. He would probably drag him out into the open by his jacket, ask him what the hell he was doing and then give him a vigorous shake before letting go and allowing the kid to run home, scared out of his wits. The only thing he had to be careful of was giving in to his anger or taking revenge for the injustice of the past few years. The temptation to do so would be great.

Although the laughter had come from below deck, Freyr decided to look first in the little pilothouse to make sure that any possible accomplices didn't take him by surprise from behind while he scared the shit out of their friend. But luckily no one was there, and Freyr turned to the wooden hatch at the prow. He stomped towards it as heavily as he could to increase the impact of his steps, which must be echoing throughout the enclosed space below deck. Then he waited a moment before loosening the latch, in order to heighten the kid's nervousness even further.

Freyr bent down and took hold of the latch. His fingers had only just begun to loosen it when the giggle came again, now clearly beneath the hatch; the kid seemed to be trying to hold back his laughter. So he was less scared than amused, although his tone seemed as brutish as before and his laughter completely joyless. Freyr found the sound so unpleasant that he abruptly let go of the latch; his bravado had left him. But when anger was no longer the driving force behind his actions, common sense took over and Freyr stared at the latch. It was on the outside of the hatch. So whoever was down there hadn't entered through this opening. He looked back over his shoulder but couldn't see any other way in.

'Open it.'

Freyr froze. It was a child's voice, but nothing about it reminded him of Benni.

'Do you want to play hide-and-seek?'

Freyr was breathing so fast that he didn't know whether he was inhaling or exhaling. He leapt to his feet and stood there as if nailed to the spot, staring at the hatch. He took a step backwards as the woodwork shook and the voice repeated: 'Open it. Let's play hide-and-seek.' Then the giggling began again and it followed Freyr as he leapt over the gunwale, it was at his heels as he stood up again after landing in the snow-covered shingle and it followed him as he sprinted towards the centre of town. When he got there he slowed down and breathed easier, free of the echo in his mind.

What had Sara's psychic friend said? That he was in danger? He didn't doubt it and suddenly realized that he had no desire to end up suffering some unspeakable fate. Freyr headed towards the hospital, determined to go over every scrap of paper, every record and every single tiny detail that could possibly help him solve this puzzle and find his son. He took out his mobile phone and selected his ex-wife's number. Without apologizing for how late he was calling and how breathless he was, he went straight to the point. 'You need to send me the computer files the police gave us dealing with Benni's disappearance. Every single one of them; the video recordings from the petrol station as well. Send them to me a few at a time; the files are large and they won't all fit in one message.'

'I'm not a complete idiot, Freyr. I know how to send e-mail.'

Freyr exhaled resolutely through his nose. 'And I need to tell you something, Sara. I wasn't working when Benni disappeared. I was with another woman. That's why I arrived so late. You probably don't want to hear how awful I feel about it, but—'

Sara hung up. Freyr prayed to God that she would still send him the files.

Chapter 29

Katrín found the fact that Líf was a giant bundle of nerves helped her stay calm. While everything was focussed on preventing Líf from completely losing it, she had something to think about and could keep the depression hovering over her at bay. She badly wanted to crawl into her sleeping bag, pull it up over her head and wait for whatever awful thing might come. She didn't think for a second that they were going to find anything good, which dragged her down but carried with it the advantage of preventing unrealistic expectations from getting in her way. There was also a peculiar comfort in knowing that although tragedy was around the corner, she would face it with her head held high; she was broken but not defeated. Obviously, it wasn't as though she had any choice in the matter; one of them had to take charge, and it certainly wasn't going to be Líf. Let alone Putti, who seemed to have given in to depression and slept curled up on Garðar's sleeping bag more or less all day.

'We should eat something.' Katrín adjusted her position where she sat on a mattress in the dining room. Her foot was troubling her less and less; the pain was just as bad but she'd grown used to it, and the painkillers took away the worst of it. She suspected that this was a bad omen and that under normal circumstances what was most dangerous for her now was lack of immediate medical attention, not falling prey to the unfathomable and the unknown. 'Aren't you hungry?' They hadn't had anything to eat since waking up; the day had passed without them paying any attention to their appetites. Now it was evening. Katrín didn't particularly feel like eating, but knew it wasn't wise to sleep on an empty stomach. She was afraid of waking up hungry in the middle of the night and having to stumble to the kitchen alone in the dark. That was out of the question.

Líf stared at the open doorway as if wanting to say something to someone standing just inside it. 'Do you think if someone does something bad, they always get punished for it?' She fiddled listlessly with the tattered cigarette packet. There was only one cigarette left inside.

'What are you on about now?' Katrín prepared to pull herself to her feet. If she knew her at all, Líf would follow her. 'Some people get what's coming to them, others don't. Somehow my instinct tells me that the mess we've ended up in isn't payback for past sins, if that's what you mean. I can't imagine we've done anything awful enough to deserve this.' Her battered nerve endings sent her brain a desperate message to keep quiet. Putti seemed to sense this; he raised his head and looked at her with dark, melancholy eyes that seemed to tell her that there was nothing to be done. This was bad, and it would only get worse. Yet the pain in her foot told her that she was still alive; soon she would feel nothing.

'I think this is revenge on us. Maybe the dead will work together and help each other carry it out. What do you think?' Líf sounded half-dead herself.

'I think that doesn't make any sense. I mean, what could Garðar have done to deserve . . .' She couldn't complete the sentence; she didn't want to, and indeed she didn't know how to. What *had* happened to Garðar? Líf looked at Katrín and opened her mouth as if to say something, then closed it again. Katrín turned back to the dark doorway, which the flickering candlelight wasn't strong enough to illuminate properly. 'Come on. Let's eat. You'll feel better afterwards, and maybe you'll see how ridiculous this is when your blood sugar level rises. We mustn't give up on ourselves completely.' Putti stood up and hobbled on sore paws towards Katrín. His breed wasn't meant to live under these conditions, and they were starting to take their toll on him.

'Some people die of blood sugar levels that are too high.' Líf didn't look as if she was about to move. She laughed dryly and her shoulders shook beneath the blanket she'd wrapped around herself. 'And others, too low.' Again she laughed, but stopped without completing the laugh normally, laughing for one second and then staring straight ahead as if in shock the next.

'We're in no danger of either. I can promise you that.' Katrín supported herself on the wall as an intense pain in her foot passed up her leg. Líf made no indication of either saying anything or getting up. 'If you don't come with me you'll be here alone in the dark. Putti's coming with me, and I'll take the candle as well.' There was no reason to take Líf's candle; there were enough of them in the kitchen. This was a desperate attempt to get Líf to stand up and come with her. Katrín would never admit it out loud, but she simply didn't have the nerve to go alone, whether Putti went with her or not. 'You decide.'

Líf turned her head slightly to face Katrín. The dancing candle flame was reflected in her pupils, making it look as if something were squirming in her eyes. 'I don't want to die, Katrín. Not alone.' She stood up. When she walked away her gait was like Putti's, suggesting surrender and hopelessness; the steps of a doomed prisoner going to his execution.

'You're not going to die.' Katrín's words sounded to her like a lie, or a bad joke. 'We'll feel better after we've eaten.' She didn't want to say more, but she knew she would have to get Líf to understand that they needed to go out before nightfall. It was best to wait to tell her this until after they were full and hopefully feeling a bit braver. A ghastly smile crept over Katrín's lips; as if food could overcome the dread that possessed them both! But they needed firewood, and they all had to go out to relieve themselves. Besides, they could call out for Garðar, send his name out into the darkness in the faint hope that he would hear it and follow it back. How ridiculous. 'Take the candle with you, Líf. We need to be able to see.'

The shadows the orange light cast over Líf's face gave her a terrifying aspect; her eyes sunken into black pools and her bones jutting out as if the flesh had retreated. The ghostlike effect wasn't lessened when she spoke. 'What do you think happened to Garðar?' she whispered, as if not wanting anyone to hear her.

'I don't know, Líf. Hopefully he just ran into some difficulty and had to take shelter in another house. Maybe he's unable to get back here – if he got injured or knocked out or something.' Katrín bit her lip, hoping she wasn't right to think that Garðar wasn't anywhere inside, but rather lying in the open air with the cold snow as a mattress and nothing but the merciless wind as a blanket. 'He's probably at the doctor's house.' Katrín felt as if she could influence reality just by saying this. As if the universe was waiting for her to dictate his fate. 'That must be where he is.'

'Then why don't we go there?' The hope that filled Líf's eyes was nearly enough to balance out the shadows from the candle and make her face look human again. 'I could help you, and it would take us no time at all. Please.'

'I can't make it, Líf. We'd need to cross the stream and my foot is worse. I can't make it over on one foot, and it would be risky for you to carry me piggyback. What if you slipped and we fell into the icy water? We'd freeze to death before we made it back inside. You could go alone, of course, but I'm not sure you have the nerves for it. Am I wrong?' Katrín held her breath for fear that Líf would suddenly offer to go. It would probably mean the end for both of them if they parted.

'He won't be there either.' Líf's tone was once more full of surrender; the spark of hope that had been audible when she still clung to the illusion that if they got out of this house, things would be all right had been extinguished just as quickly as it had ignited. She looked at Katrín. 'But you should know one thing. It's better to lose your husband because he died than because he left you for another woman.'

'Stop it.' Katrín felt a surge of desperate anger envelop her and she had the urge to slap Líf in the face. She didn't want to hear her potential fate put into words, and certainly not from Líf, like this. It was unfair to compare her relationship with Garðar to the one that Líf and Einar had ripped to shreds between them. But then her anger vanished, and sorrow was waiting to take its place. Katrín knew that if she gave in to tears it would be difficult to stop them; she forced down a huge lump in her throat and cleared it. 'We should talk about something else. Garðar will come back. You can be sure of that.'

Líf didn't reply, and they said nothing until they'd got into the kitchen and lit a new candle. Their stock had been dwindling rapidly but the need for light overcame common sense, and just to be able to see reasonably well perked them up enough for them to eat something. Neither had any appetite, so they made do with taking whatever they found in the boxes and laying it out on the kitchen table. Putti was given a slice of liverwurst, in which at first he seemed to have no interest, but then started to eat slowly and steadily.

'I hate milk biscuits.' Still, Líf didn't let that stop her from taking another bite of biscuit number two. 'There's no point in eating them somehow. They taste of nothing, they're hard and dry, and you'd think they'd been made in a cement factory.' She took a drink from the milk carton and frowned. The milk wasn't off, but since she had no appetite it was difficult getting anything down.

Katrín smiled and hoped it was a good sign that they were able to talk about something besides their situation. Maybe soon she could suggest that they go out for some fresh air. They had to fetch firewood and Putti surely had to pee, though he wasn't showing any signs of it. She didn't feel she wanted to let him go out by himself, in case he ran off and never came back. In case the child got him as it had got Garðar. She swallowed a dry mouthful of the flatbread she'd been nibbling. 'I hate flatbread.' Neither of them smiled.

The floor creaked sharply and they looked at each other, their pupils wide in the dull light. 'What was that?' asked Líf, through a mouthful of biscuit. 'It sounded like it was right behind me. Is someone there? Is that fucking child standing behind my chair?' Líf's voice sounded like she was on the verge of a nervous breakdown. Her eyes bulged and she hadn't blinked since their terrified gazes had met.

There was a certain security in looking only into Líf's eyes and Katrín had no desire to turn her gaze elsewhere, least of all in the direction from which the sound had come. But she did just that, shifting her eyes slightly to the side without moving her head so that she could let them flick back to their place if she saw something bad. But she saw nothing in either direction. 'There's nothing there.' Neither of them found much consolation in this and they continued to stare distraught at each other, waiting for the inevitable second creak that would surely follow. Despite their anticipation, they were startled nevertheless when it came, especially Líf as she turned her back to the sound.

This noise was followed by a low whine from Putti, which had little effect since the floor creaked again, now slightly more softly. This was followed by a whisper, just like the one that Katrín thought she'd heard before but hadn't wanted to mention. Since she was always alone when it came, she hadn't wanted the others to think she was hallucinating or deranged. But despite her hope that the others would hear this unbearable voice, she took no comfort in the fact that Líf was hearing it now. Katrín actually felt even worse on seeing her look so frightened. Now she could no longer flirt with the idea that she'd just been hearing things. 'Who said that?' Líf seemed on the verge of tears and Katrín didn't feel much better.

'I don't know,' Katrín whispered, so softly she could barely hear herself. 'I don't know.' The words sounded better the second time as Katrín's courage rose again, but it was rising and falling like ocean waves. 'What did you hear it say?' She leaned closer to Líf, making sure not to look past her for fear of seeing the outline of the boy deep in the darkness of the kitchen.

'O-o-op-open it.' Tears were pouring down Líf's cheeks. They gleamed, making it look as if she was weeping gold.

Katrín had heard the same thing. 'Open what?' She asked the question softly, without expecting an answer. Again the words sounded behind Líf. Katrín felt goose bumps spring up on her arms and she clamped her eyes shut as Líf let herself slump forward onto the kitchen table. She didn't want to see what was behind her friend, but her eyes immediately snapped back open, making her flight from reality last only a second. It hadn't been intentional; Putti had stepped on her injured foot as he sought shelter between her legs. The pain was unbearable and Katrín cried out. This earthbound, vivid feeling of pain cleared a path for her back to common sense. It also helped that there was nothing to see behind Líf, besides a crowbar propped up against the wall near where Garðar had been working in the night. Katrín got up. 'I'm going to see whether there's a hole there where this whispering could be coming from.' Líf shook as she lay face down on the table and said something inaudible. But Katrín had made her decision.

She hopped to the wall where the sound had originated from, concentrating on taking care with the candle flame. There was nothing strange to see, although Katrín was seized with the vague feeling that something was sharing the immediate vicinity with her. She half expected to feel a warm breath creep beneath her neckline, but nothing happened. The only thing she sensed was an unpleasant, powerful smell ascending from below, not unlike the one that had emanated from Líf after she'd come down the stairs. She let herself sink to her haunches to better view the floor, with all her weight on her good foot. It was difficult and the intensifying pain strengthened her resolve. Damn it, nothing could happen that wasn't going to happen anyway. It was only a question of taking it kneeling down or standing on her feet, boldly. She tried not to think that Garðar had probably gone missing because of his boldness, and they had escaped the same fate by being cautious. 'Jesus.' She raised the hand not holding the candle to her face and stuck her nose and mouth into the crook of her elbow. The fungus or mould had actually spread, nearly hiding the wood beneath the new planks under its green patina.

'What?' Líf had risen and turned in her chair. She clearly found it better to have what she knew in the foreground, rather than in the darkness that could hide anything at all. 'What's there?'

'A disgusting smell and a disgusting growth, like what we saw on the floorboards, remember?' Katrín's voice was muffled as she spoke into her arm, but Líf seemed to understand every word. 'Only much, much more of it.' Katrín moved the candle closer and spotted a little area next to the wall that the green slick seemed not to have reached. She brought the candle flame as close to it as she could, having to use both her hands to do so.

'Don't breathe in that stuff!' Líf stood up and covered her mouth. Putti moved over to her and stood pinned against her legs, from where he stared dejectedly at Katrín. He whined softly, once.

'I'm dead anyway if this is dangerous. Both of us are.' Katrín squinted in order to see better. 'There are hinges here.

It's probably an old trapdoor.' She turned to Líf. 'There's something under the floor. Maybe we'll finally get an explanation for all the disturbances in the house.'

It didn't look as if Líf were desperate for an answer. 'If that bloody child is under there, do we really want to be opening it for him? Have you lost your mind?' When Katrín didn't reply, but instead shifted herself enough to be able to reach the crowbar, she added: 'Why do you think the man who lived here before laid a new floor over this trapdoor? He knew that there was something bad under the floor. Don't open it, Katrín.' She was commanding, pleading and horror-struck all at once.

'He probably never saw these hinges. I didn't notice them until now, after the mould spread through the wood and uncovered them. They're all the way up against the wall so they could have been lying partly under the old skirting board. Plus there's not much light in here, in case you hadn't noticed.' Katrín tried to find the outline of the trapdoor, without success. She took the crowbar and tried to stick it between the planks where she thought the end of the trapdoor might be, but nothing happened, so she tried the next ones with the same result; the same went for the two other pairs of remaining planks before the new floor material took over again. She hesitated and realized that there were perhaps other hinges on the side opposite to where she'd been trying and that the end of the trapdoor was on the other side. She shifted awkwardly again to apply the crowbar to that spot.

'Katrín. Don't do this. What will you do after you've opened it? Stick your head into the hole? It was impossible to determine whether Líf was concerned mainly about Katrín's head or her own safety if it were cut off. 'Please. Don't do this. At least wait until morning.'

It was too late. The floor broke open when Katrín finally found the right spot. She was terribly scared, and what Líf had just said was weighing heavily on her mind. If she let go of the crowbar the hatch would probably drop down through the opening. The latch that held it up, as well as the old hinges, had creaked; all three had probably given under the force. But what then? *Was* she going to stick her head down there? Hardly. 'Hand me your camera, Líf. Isn't there still some life left in its battery?'

'What?' Líf stared dumbly at Katrín, but then came to her senses and nodded. She looked around and spied the camera where she'd left it. She grabbed it and walked over to Katrín but before handing it over, she hugged the pink device to her chest as if she had changed her mind, but then changed it back again and extended her hand. 'Please, be quick about it and then shut that sodding hatch tightly again.'

Katrín took the camera and let go of the crowbar, causing the hatch to fall with a drawn-out creak. She didn't tell Líf, but there was no way that she could manage to put it back in its place. A cloud of dust nearly suffocated the candle flame. Katrín leaned away from the opening to avoid inhaling it, but found from the dry taste in her mouth that she was too late. She looked at Líf and read everything that needed to be said from her terrified look. If this was a mistake, it was too late to regret it. Putti neither whined nor barked, but looked almost disappointed in her. Katrín turned her eyes away from the two of them and stared at the black hole now gaping before her. She shook herself and turned on the camera, her hand trembling. Then she reached out as far as she dared. She was still trembling uncontrollably when she stuck the hand holding the camera down through the hole, her index finger prepared to snap a photo. In fact, she half expected to lose her hand and so had chosen the left one. When the camera had gone far enough down she pressed the button, the bright flash sending a blaze of light up through the opening as if a bomb had exploded beneath the house. She turned the camera slightly and pressed it again, then turned it around and pressed a third time. Although it was impossible to know how successful she'd been or if she'd managed to capture whatever lay below, she didn't have the nerve to continue and pulled her arm back up with a speed that she didn't know she was capable of.

'Show me the photos!' Líf held her hands to her chest as if she expected to have a heart attack as soon as Katrín revealed what she'd captured.

Katrín said nothing. She slid herself on her bottom across the floor and away from the opening as she brought up the first photo, and as soon as she felt her back hit the kitchen cabinet she peered at the screen. When her eyes had taken in what appeared to be lying on the dirt floor in one corner of the frame, she swallowed and looked at Líf. 'They're bones. Human bones. A dead person in the crawl space beneath our feet.'

Líf grabbed her mouth. 'Garðar?' It hadn't even been twenty-four hours since they'd seen him last, but nothing was logical any more in this place.

Katrín didn't reply, and instead pressed the arrow button she thought would bring up the next photo. Another photo did appear, but instead of it being another shot from the crawl space, she'd gone in the opposite direction and was now viewing the oldest photo on the camera. She looked at it in exhaustion and felt her lower jaw slacken. She pushed the button again and saw the next oldest, then again and again and again until she realized this was no misunderstanding. She looked up and stared at Líf.

'What? Is it Garðar?' Líf seemed terrified, but also uncertain, given Katrín's impenetrable look. 'Is he dead?'

Katrín didn't reply immediately, and instead scrambled to her feet. The pain plaguing her foot didn't touch her; it simply didn't matter. After standing up she threw the camera at Líf, who caught it in surprise. Katrín suppressed her longing to spit, and made do with hissing: 'You know what?' Her voice was as cold as the ice that now enclosed her heart. 'I really hope he is.'

Chapter 30

Freyr felt as if he'd just shut his eyes when the alarm clock demanded that he open them again. Yet he'd managed to nap for four hours, which wasn't too bad. The sleeplessness he'd feared hadn't manifested itself, nor had nightmares stopped his sleep being restful. He'd gone to bed much later than planned and had been absolutely exhausted when he finally laid his head on the pillow. He'd intended to turn in early but the e-mails from Sara – with the files that he'd asked her to send – had started coming in just as he was about to turn off the computer. Maybe she'd hoped to interfere with his sleep that night, and he wouldn't blame her. She was furious with him and would no doubt stay that way for some time, possibly indefinitely. He would have to live with that, and maybe that was a cleaner separation than a friendship built on sand, or lies. Every e-mail ended with the same line: *Fuck you, you fucking bastard, you monster.* Fair enough, he thought.

As it so often did, sleep had helped to order Freyr's thoughts. Once he'd gone through most of what Sara had sent and set it alongside what he had already gleaned, everything felt like it had merged into a mess of confusion. It was impossible for him to draw any conclusions or even discern a coherent thread in the swarm of reports he'd gone through, nor could he find anything useful by fast-forwarding through the CCTV recordings from the petrol station forecourt. This hadn't particularly surprised him – why should he, all these years later, spot something the investigative team had overlooked? He'd been a fool to think he might. Nonetheless, he'd viewed all the clips diligently, though at high speed; it was like watching a cartoon in which people didn't walk, but waddled like penguins in a hurry, and cars seemed to appear and disappear at random. But Freyr had no choice; he couldn't watch four hours of recordings of a garage forecourt at normal speed.

The reports, however, he read word by word. Of the dozens he went through, Freyr set only one aside for further perusal; the others told him nothing new. The one that captured his attention had sparked something indefinable in his mind. It was the testimony of one of the boys who had taken part in the game of hide-and-seek, a boy who Freyr had noticed never looked him in the eye the few times that their paths had crossed after Benni's disappearance, the one who'd mentioned the submarine. At that point he'd been too burdened by grief to wonder why the child was behaving that way, but now time and distance granted him sharper vision. Freyr didn't know whether he'd worked through his reading while half awake or asleep, but by the time he'd woken up he'd realized that certain details in the boy's statement didn't fit; they weren't glaring errors, and only the few people closest to the situation could have spotted them, so it was understandable that the police had overlooked the inconsistencies. If that was indeed what had happened; it was perfectly possible that they hadn't had all the reports to hand, and that further conversations with the boy had shed better light on the case. Either way, Freyr was going to sort this out before the end of the day. How, he didn't know, but he had enough time to find out.

He'd also realized some other things during the night, concerning his accident at Ártúnsbrekka the day that Benni had vanished. In the recording, only the car he'd hit was visible, not his own, and not the trailer that the man had removed and positioned in a third parking space. They'd parked on the edge of the forecourt, in the only place where there had been spaces. The other driver could be seen stepping out of his car and walking out of the frame, and Freyr knew they'd been talking during the time that he was gone. Then he returned, took his insurance papers from his glove compartment and disappeared again while they filled them out. Just over a quarter of an hour passed before he appeared again, stuck the papers back in the glove compartment and then walked into the petrol station, where he stayed for half an hour, probably having something to eat. Freyr had known all of this beforehand, yet he'd woken wondering what had happened to the insurance papers. The claim had never been followed through; he'd neither lost his no claims bonus nor received any notice that he'd been in the right. His car hadn't really needed repairing; after Benni disappeared, a dented bumper hadn't been high on his and Sara's list of priorities. Nothing but Benni had mattered and the accident had been forgotten, like so much else at the time. But now this struck him, without his understanding why; maybe it irritated him that there was a loose end that had been overlooked.

It was still dark outside. Freyr emptied his cup only to refill it with more flavourless instant coffee. Double the amount this time, to help him wake up properly. He was off today but had still set his alarm clock as if he needed to go to work. Of course, he realized now, he could have slept a little longer; he couldn't get hold of anyone so early in the morning, which meant there was nothing to do other than pace and drink coffee. And yet. He could call Sara, who never slept in, and try to apologize. She deserved both the apology and the chance to yell and hurl obscenities at him.

'Don't hang up,' Freyr said hurriedly, in case she'd only answered so she could tell him to piss off. 'I've got some stuff to tell you. Then you can shout at me as much you want.'

'You're not worth it.' Her voice was so cold, there could be no doubting her conviction. 'Just fucking say it and then leave me alone.' Sara paused for a moment before adding: 'For the rest of our lives.'

'Sara, I was an idiot. I'm not going to try to make excuses for what I did; it was despicable of me; I couldn't withstand temptation, but I should have. I failed you, my job, and maybe Benni too, but the worst thing is that I let you down in such a horrible way.'

'So you never went to the hospital, and that's why there was so little insulin in the box? Was it just some old left-over stuff you had lying around? Did you falsify the data in the hospital pharmacy, you bastard?' Sara spoke so quickly that it reminded Freyr of the fast-forwarded recordings he'd watched the night before.

'I went to the hospital, Sara, and got the insulin. That's the truth. But I didn't stay there to work like I told you; instead, I was with this woman. That's why I was late. She'd called, and since I was going to get the insulin I had an excuse to see her.'

'Where did you meet up with her?' There was pain in her

voice, which he found harder to bear than anger. He might gain some absolution for his sins if she just bawled him out, but seeing the raw wounds in her heart was a different matter.

Freyr cleared his throat and hoped that she wouldn't now ask where precisely they'd had sex. But if she did, he would lie to her, for the very last time. He didn't think the awful cliché of adulterous sex on his desk would make things any easier. 'At my office. She suggested it.'

'Classy.' There was a brief, bitter silence. 'Where did you meet this whore of yours? Didn't she know you were married?'

'Yes. She knew. She was married, too.' Now it was Freyr's turn to hesitate. If he told her the whole story, he would be placing his job in her hands, to some extent. He let it out. 'She was one of my patients. She wanted help with marital problems, and with life in general. Her husband had had an affair with another woman, and she felt as if everything was falling apart around her.'

'So she thought it was a good idea to mimic his behaviour.'

'She has a mild personality disorder, Sara, which is why her treatment lasted longer than the several meetings that it took for her to reconcile herself with her marital issues. Heightened sexual aggression is a common complication in her disorder. She instigated it, though I'm well aware that's no excuse. When I discovered that she was attracted to me, I should have immediately referred her elsewhere, rather than started an affair with her. But that's not what I did, and now I've got to live with it. I haven't seen her since that day at my office, nor have I spoken to her. She never made another appointment, so I didn't have the chance to break it off, as I'd resolved to do, I swear.' He declined to mention that the woman had been exceptionally beautiful, with a fantastic figure; it would have been nearly impossible for any red-blooded man to resist her advances. Sara didn't need to hear that.

'That's the most pathetic apology I've ever heard.' Sara was angry again, which made Freyr feel almost relieved. She hadn't said a word about reporting his transgression, though she might well do so later. 'Utterly pathetic. You're a fucking loser. I mean it, never call me again.' She took a breath. 'There's just one thing I want to know so I don't accidentally end up speaking to this mad tart of yours.' Again she breathed in sharply, as if gathering the courage to ask the question. 'What's her name?'

'Líf.' Freyr cleared his throat again. 'Her name is Líf.'

The insurance company had no record of a damage report for Freyr's car on the date in question. The service representative obviously couldn't explain why the other party hadn't sent in the information and suggested that Freyr speak to the man's insurance company, but Freyr couldn't remember which one it was. He had no idea what had become of his copy of the report, which he remembered shoving into the glove compartment of his car before driving home from the petrol station. Sara had got the car when they divorced and since they last spoke, true to her word, she was refusing to answer his phone calls. This particular trail would lead nowhere unless something changed.

Freyr's conversation with Sara had brought up memories of his meeting with Líf that fateful afternoon; memories that he'd long since pushed aside. At first Benni's disappearance had crowded everything else out and as time passed he'd tried to forget about the affair, which was made simpler by the fact that he hadn't heard a peep out of Líf. But now he remembered everything. When she came to the office, she'd been quite interested in the insulin in the little paper bag. Freyr had taken it out and shown it to her, explained what it was without mentioning Benni, as he preferred not to discuss his son with a woman with whom he was having an affair. Her first question had been whether it was possible to get high from it, in case they could spice up the sex. When he'd told her that no, the drug was dangerous to anyone other than diabetics, she'd asked all sorts of questions that he'd thought arose from stress, assuming she'd simply welcomed the chance to have something to talk about. *Would you die from it? Could it cause a heart attack? What about an irregular heartbeat? And could that kill someone with a bad heart? God, I'm glad I didn't try it for fun.* He recalled how later that same day, when the police had wanted to see confirmation that he'd gone to get the insulin, it had come to light that there was only one pen left in the box.

Now that he could face up to his own failings and his thoughts about all this were unencumbered by the fear of Sara finding out about his affair, it occurred to him that Líf might have seen what had become of the drug. Maybe she'd noticed at the time that the pens had fallen out of the package as she handled the box, or had taken them out to have a look while his back was turned and then put them down somewhere, after which the cleaning staff would have removed them or thrown them away. It was a long shot, but not inconceivable. Yet another irritating loose end. He decided to call Líf and simply ask her about it, to go straight to the point even if it was uncomfortable. But she didn't answer her home phone, which was listed in her name only; her husband was apparently out of the picture, no great surprise, and her mobile was either out of range or turned off. He'd hit another wall.

It might help if he called the boy he suspected of having lied; he would still be at school, but ought to be home shortly. The hypothesis he had in mind was a little crazy, but he knew he had to speak to the boy without him being able to hide behind his parents. Of course it was just as likely that the kid would hang up on him, but that was a chance he would have to take. As he waited for the right time to call, he read the report on his statement and compared it to the statements of the other children. He made notes on the printouts so he'd have what he needed to hand when he reached the boy, particularly on the details he felt didn't make sense.

With the papers in his lap and his phone in his hand he sat on the couch and tried to think of something useful to do while waiting. But he couldn't think of anything, and despite all the caffeine he'd consumed he dozed off, starting several times when his chin dropped to his chest, though he always managed to make himself comfortable again and fall back to sleep. It wasn't until his phone rang that he woke, annoyed with himself at having wasted his time. It was Dagný. 'I've come across some information that will probably surprise you.'

'Oh?' Freyr couldn't force himself to sound interested or alert, and she didn't bother asking whether she'd woken him.

'Úrsúla, that patient of yours who started talking about Benni, was in the same class as Bernódus, Halla and all the others. She wasn't in the class photo; maybe she was off sick the day it was taken.' Freyr sat up, his sluggishness vanished like dew in sunlight.

'How did you find that out?' Of course, of course. She was born in the same year, 1940, so it made sense that she'd gone to the same school, being a resident of Ísafjörður.

'I finally got my hands on some old records from the school, which I searched for when the similarities between the break-ins at the primary school and the preschool became clear. There's more: it seems that she and Bernódus were good friends. I found a report by the teacher in which she describes her surprise that Úrsúla had finally formed a close friendship; it appears that she was something of a social outcast. She'd probably been bullied by her classmates, but that's not mentioned explicitly, since no one gave much thought to such things back then. The teacher's statement is a bit brusque – harsh, even; she definitely sides with the class as a whole at the expense of the other two, who were obviously weaker personalities. It makes for very peculiar reading, and I didn't feel particularly sorry about what happened to the teacher after I'd gone over it. But in any case, the connection between the two kids is clear.'

'Is there any way I can have a look at it?' Freyr rubbed his sore neck as he tried to imagine this. Úrsúla, the girl everyone loved to hate, forging a relationship with the new member of the class, who is also a weirdo, an outcast. 'Do you know what usually happens in this kind of situation, when two children excluded by the remainder of the group join together?'

'No, what?'

'The group senses that there's strength in not being completely isolated, and an unconscious decision is made to sever the bond between the two excluded individuals. It's probably one of the most vicious forms of bullying, and those who experience it seldom or never repair their friendship afterwards.'

'Are you suggesting that the kids killed Bernódus so that they could keep bullying Úrsúla?'

'No, not necessarily. It's just a very interesting angle. Finally something that connects all of this, and that might help me crack Úrsúla's shell once she's feeling more like talking.'

'Should I drop by?' Dagný asked, then sounded embarrassed, as if she feared he would read too much into her words. 'I'm actually finished for the day; I worked a double shift yesterday and I'd rather not be here any longer than I have to, so it would make more sense for me to come over than for you to put yourself out by coming to the station.'

'Sure, see you soon.' Freyr hung up immediately, aware that he mustn't waste any time if he were going to call the boy before Dagný arrived. He doubted she would approve of his methods. He dialled the number, his foot jiggling nervily as the line rang and rang. When he was almost convinced that he'd have to try again tomorrow, the phone was answered and a child's voice greeted him. 'Hello, is Heimir there?' Freyr felt as if he were making a prank call.

'Uh, yeah.' The voice sounded surprised. 'That's me.'

'Hello, Heimir. My name is Freyr, you might not remember me. I'm . . . I was . . . Benni's dad. Do you remember Benni?'

'Yeah.' The boy was on his guard. 'Why are you calling me?'

'The police gave me some old reports to go over and I saw a little something in them that I wanted to ask you about. It's nothing terrible and it should be easy for you to answer my questions. I don't even have to come to your house, it's such a small thing.' Freyr was barely breathing. 'Is that all right with you?'

'Um, yeah. I don't know.'

Freyr rushed on. 'In the report it says that you hid behind the garage in the garden next to mine, so you didn't see where Benni or some of the other kids went. Then you realized you were late for your cousin's birthday party and left before you were found. Is that right?'

'Yeah, I think so. I don't remember really. It was a really long time ago.'

'I know, but we should just assume that the police wrote down correctly what you said. But now two other kids say they also hid in the same garden; one says that he hid behind what he thought was a shed, and the other behind the bushes. They could see each other, but neither of them remembers seeing you. The thing is, that garden only has a garage, no shed. So either you were in the same hiding place as another boy, or somebody's lying, or somebody remembered incorrectly. Which is it?'

'Um . . . maybe I hid somewhere else. I'm not sure.'

'Heimir.' Freyr tried not to let anger get the better of him. 'It's all the same to me where you hid. I just want to know whether you have any idea of what happened to Benni. And I'm not concerned about why you didn't tell us before; you were so little, and everyone can make mistakes. I won't mention this conversation to anyone else and you'll feel so, so much better if you tell the truth, exactly as it happened.' Freyr drew a deep breath and calmed himself. There was little more he could say now; at least nothing that he could live with saying to a child. 'Benni needs to be found, Heimir. He wants to be found, and I'm sure you want to ease your mind.

At first you said that Benni wanted to hide in a submarine, didn't you?'

'Uh . . . uh . . .' The boy sounded on the verge of tears. 'You promise not to tell anyone . . . especially not my dad?'

When Dagný arrived, Freyr opened the door to her without saying a word, then turned and walked to the kitchen like a ghost, without checking whether she was following. He sat down at his laptop and resumed staring at the screen. 'Is something wrong?' said Dagný. She repeated the question, and Freyr finally found his voice.

'Benni. I think I've found Benni.' He kept staring at the screen. 'In a manner of speaking.'

'What do you mean?' Dagný's tone suggested that she thought he'd lost it. 'He ended up here. Just out of frame. You can't see him.' Freyr pointed at the edge of the laptop's screen, where it met the black plastic casing. Dagný went over to him and bent down to see what he was talking about. She raised her eyebrows when she saw the freeze-framed image of the petrol station forecourt. The car Freyr had hit was visible in the lower right-hand corner. 'Unfortunately, I don't know what became of this car or its driver.'

'In other words, you think Benni ended up in this car? Was he kidnapped by the driver? How do you work that out?' Dagný was extremely calm, as if speaking to an inebriated member of the public who needed to be calmed down.

'He didn't get in the car, and I don't think the driver did anything to him.' Freyr was struggling to find the right words. 'But if I could find him, I would find Benni.'

Dagný peered more closely at the screen. 'Move,' she said gruffly, taking Freyr's seat as he obediently stood up. She fiddled with the keyboard a bit, enlarging the part of the image that showed the cars. At first Freyr thought she was going to try to read the licence plate number, which he'd tried to do many times, but before he could say anything she turned to him, frowned, and said: 'I know all about this car. And nearly everything about the driver.' She held his gaze. 'Unfortunately, we believe him to be dead.'

Chapter 31

It stopped hailing as unexpectedly as it had started; one minute it was hammering the windowpanes, and the next everything was absolutely still. It had sounded as if someone had been standing outside tapping a rhythm with his fingers, but when the noise ceased, the silence was just as unbearable; the feeling was very much like being underwater, with the water playing softly about your ears, letting in no sound. The house, which had previously moaned in the wind, complaining bitterly of its harsh treatment, was now silent as well, which magnified the silence between Katrín and Líf. They were reflected in the black glass, and anyone arriving now would surely have chosen to abandon himself to the ravages of nature rather than tackle these furious women. Even Putti, who was used to sticking close to Katrín's legs, had slunk off to a corner, as far from them and the hole in the floor as possible. Now and then he looked up, tilted his head and stared at them alternately, as if to check whether they were still in conflict. Then he stuck his nose back into the little twisty bun formed by his body.

Katrín sat with her feet up on the kitchen chair, resting her head on her knees and favouring her wounded foot. It was terribly cold inside; better for her to maintain her precious body heat. Although she knew little about the limits of the human body, she suspected they were in danger of freezing to death in the night if they didn't do something soon: fetch firewood or at least get into their sleeping bags, which were waiting for them in the dining room. But her foot hurt more than ever. She wouldn't be going out to fetch so much as a stick. And she would sooner freeze to death than ask Líf to do so. Her anger overpowered her instinct for self-preservation, which was positive in a way, since it left no room for fear. She'd never had a reason to arrange her feelings into any sort of hierarchy, but she now knew that anger was the mightiest of them all; fear and sorrow came somewhere below it, retreating as they did before rage which revealed itself to be a cruel master. No doubt these feelings would fade to be replaced by weaker ones, but Katrín was going to enjoy every minute of her fearlessness and take pleasure in observing how bad Líf felt, though actually she'd been slightly disappointed in that regard so far.

Líf actually didn't seem as distressed as one might have expected after she was found out. She seemed more upset that Katrín couldn't see her side of the story. It was as if she wasn't quite right in the head. Katrín had suspected this for some time, but had always attributed it to her own imagination or to her jealousy over Líf's ability to coast through life's little traumas. The only emotion she actually seemed capable of was fear. Fear of her own demise.

'I hate you, Líf.' The thought of Líf not feeling as miserable as she should prompted Katrín to say this. She was determined to put all her efforts into making Líf's usual escapism impossible. 'I hope you freeze to death tonight. Or just disappear. That would be the best solution; then I wouldn't have to see your dead body.'

Líf's frown deepened, but then she smiled as if Katrín

had been joking. 'We should try to be friends. It's all in the past.'

Katrín felt like shouting, but held back. The woman before her was capable of anything. There was no help to be had for dozens, if not hundreds, of kilometres. There was a skeleton beneath their floorboards and some sort of entity haunting them, apparently wishing to do them harm. The situation couldn't get much worse, yet there was no point moaning and complaining. Katrín bit her lip and buried her face in her knees again. She could feel the pain trying to break through the screen of rage. She forced herself to block it, pushing aside images of Garðar, naked, sleeping in Líf's arms. It wasn't easy. Although she hadn't had the nerve to examine the photos in any detail, they'd burned themselves into her mind and she could imagine the tiniest specifics without any effort. They'd been lying together in a large bed; the impersonal yet tidy environment suggested it was a hotel room, probably in Ísafjörður. Garðar's eyes were closed; he was either fast asleep or absolutely exhausted from what they'd been doing. Líf's face was anything but tired as she smiled, bare-breasted, at the camera, which she was holding. Garðar looked exactly the same in every photo, but Líf arranged herself in a variety of positions, looking just like a hunter on safari with photos of his prey. How she could have thought of taking photos under these shameful circumstances was a mystery to Katrín, but she couldn't imagine asking about it; the reason was doubtless yet another manifestation of Líf's unbalanced state of mind.

The dim light flickered. Katrín saw fear appear in Líf's eyes and a wave of satisfaction passed through her. If she'd had the nerve to sit with her in the darkness, she would have leaned forward and blown out the candle in order to cause her the greatest anguish possible. But the thought of being alone in the dark with an insane person held little appeal. On the other hand, the way the candle-stub was jutting just above the candlestick, she expected the light to be extinguished at any second. 'The candle will go out soon, Líf. What are you going to do then? You can't seduce the dead. Maybe Garðar's roaming about now too.' Líf's eyes widened, but only for a second. 'You're disgusting, Líf.' Katrín spat out. 'Disgusting.'

'I've said I'm sorry. What else do you want me to do?' Líf seemed hurt, sounding as if she felt she were the victim in all of this. 'Garðar and I were always attracted to each other, even from the beginning. It just happened. We couldn't do anything about it.'

'Shut up!' shouted Katrín, without meaning to. She couldn't bear to listen again to the account of Líf's relationship with Garðar. Although Líf had already told Katrín the story from beginning to end, it was from such a biased, narrow perspective that Katrín had to read between the lines to get to the truth. If her intuition was correct, her entire existence since her relationship with Garðar started had been staged. She alone had been unaware that her closest surroundings had been merely props and scenery. Maybe at the time she hadn't wanted to see what had been revealed now that the poison had poured from Líf's beautifully shaped mouth; maybe she'd been too in love with Garðar even to glimpse the now crystal clear reality in front of her. Garðar had never loved her. She'd simply been the next woman available once it was clear that Líf had chosen Einar rather than him; maybe he'd thought that seeing him with someone else would change Líf's mind.

But he'd been very wrong. Líf had enjoyed watching him squirm, knowing she could have him whenever she pleased. Líf probably hadn't loved Garðar any more than he'd had feelings for Katrín; she'd just found it handy to have him as a kind of safety net, a life preserver that you don't use daily but can reach out for when you need it.

This was all so incomprehensible that Katrín's head was spinning. For example, she thought that Líf was telling her that she had simply chosen Einar over Garðar after weighing it all up. She hadn't put it quite so explicitly, but it was impossible to interpret what she'd said any other way; Einar had seemed more financially driven than Garðar and likely to make more money, which meant that he got Líf and she would get him and his riches.

But then Einar had sought company elsewhere too. He'd probably realized that there was something missing in his wife's character, some capacity for love. Maybe he hadn't come right out and asked for a divorce because Líf was so devoid of emotion and he was afraid that she would come up with some way of getting back at him; maybe she knew things about him that he didn't want to come to light. She'd responded in kind and the only thing that Katrín could console herself with was the fact that Líf's affair with Garðar hadn't begun then, although she suspected that Líf had tried to make it happen soon after learning of Einar's infidelity. No doubt it would have been perfect for her – to cheat on her husband with his best friend and rub his face in it at an opportune moment. Garðar had probably resisted the temptation precisely because of his friendship with Einar, not having been able to imagine going behind the back of his childhood companion and best friend. The same didn't apply where

Katrín was concerned, however; she clearly didn't matter, since he'd taken the first opportunity to jump into bed with Líf once Einar was dead. But however it had all happened, Líf appeared to have also found herself an earlier victim, a shrink who'd been supposed to help her patch up her marriage. What a joke.

And although Líf hadn't said anything to suggest that she'd played a part in Einar's death, she didn't have to. Einar had left her, doubtless after arranging things so that most of their money would remain with him and Líf would be left empty-handed. Not to mention the humiliation of the situation. Katrín knew Líf well enough now to realize that she would never have accepted such a thing. So Einar had had to go, and somehow she'd made it happen. Katrín simply knew it; in the same way that she didn't need to be told that it was dangerous to stand too near the edge of a cliff, it was perfectly clear to her that the same went for Líf. A person who seemed unable to repent or to express regret for their actions was much less predictable than the edge of a cliff, which could easily be avoided by keeping a safe distance. But a safe distance from Líf wasn't an option here. Katrín promised herself that she would never, never, ever again be under the same roof as this woman, if they made it safely back to Reykjavík. Never.

Neither of them said anything for a while. In the meantime it continued to grow colder. Their breath ascended frostily from their lips and Katrín felt that she didn't have as much control over her fingers as usual. She pulled her sleeves over her hands in the hope of keeping them warmer, without producing the desired result.

'What is that in the basement?' Líf stared at her, and no matter how much Katrín wanted to look away, she couldn't help but meet her eyes. But she didn't answer. Líf persisted anyway: 'You can see a bag in the photo. An old-fashioned schoolbag.' She leaned forward conspiratorially and whispered, as if they were trusted friends sharing secrets: 'And there are seashells all over the place.'

Katrín said nothing, but turned away from her and rested her head on her knees again. She had no idea what bones were down there, but she couldn't rule out the idea that they might belong to the boy they'd seen. It seemed to her that the material partially covering the bones resembled the jacket the boy was wearing when he appeared to them.

'It's probably the ghost, Katrín. His bones. It looks to me as if he's missing some fingers on one hand, so I suppose the fox under the porch got to the body and the ghost killed it to take revenge for the loss of its fingers.' It was as if Líf had already forgotten their conflict. Katrín couldn't see her face, but she was speaking as if nothing had happened; no doubt Líf had grown tired of Katrín's attitude and was determined to pretend everything was the same as before. 'Maybe he'll disappear now that we've opened up the floor. I'm sure that was what he wanted the whole time – for us to find the bones. Maybe that's why he killed the previous owner; he accidentally blocked the hatch, making the likelihood of the bones being found almost non-existent. We've fixed the problem, so everything should be all right now.' Líf hadn't actually had a hand in any of it, but naturally claimed a share of the credit. 'I hope so, anyway,' she whispered.

Katrín felt as if she were in a dream, or rather a nightmare. She didn't look up, but spoke into her knees. 'Why were you messing around with this house at all? Why didn't Garðar just leave me for you, without dragging me into this madness?

You have all Einar's money now. I don't understand you two. Was Garðar just as crazy as you?' Líf muttered something that Katrín didn't hear properly. She didn't ask her to repeat herself, however; the little she'd understood was enough. 'Ah, you didn't want Garðar with all his debts? Is that what you're saying? Despite your having so much money you wouldn't have to lift a finger for the rest of your life?'

'I'm not going to pay someone else's debts. It isn't fair.' Líf was clearly a great proponent of fairness where it concerned her. Unfairness was for other people, in her world. 'It was Garðar's idea and I tried to dissuade him. That's why I came along, to stop him.'

'Stop him from what?' Katrín pressed her face so tightly against her knees that her closed eyes hurt.

'From hurting you. Killing you, actually. He was the one who pushed the wall onto you. He'd already set it up. He just needed to tug on the rope that was there and . . . Boom!' Líf sighed. 'I tried to prevent it but I couldn't. Maybe it's for the best that he disappeared.'

Katrín said nothing, just let the tears flow; they didn't fall, but soaked into her trousers. She wasn't sure whether they were tears of anger or sorrow. She cleared her throat to get rid of the lump in it; she couldn't bear the idea of Líf knowing she was crying. 'What's *wrong* with you?' Garðar wouldn't have been better off with her dead; if they'd divorced, he would only have been responsible for half of their debts, but as a widower he would have been left with all of them. Then she remembered their life insurance. The money that was supposed to ensure that if one of them died, the other wouldn't need to struggle with financial difficulties on top of everything else, or their parents if they both died at the same time. What a joke. 'You slammed that door into me. Didn't you?' Líf didn't need to answer this; her embarrassed look was proof enough. Katrín was sure her sick mind was racing to find a way to explain this, probably by saying that Garðar had forced her into it. She didn't want to hear it. 'Did you kill Einar, Líf? Maybe Garðar as well?'

'No, how could you think that? I was telling you that I tried to stop Garðar. I tried to save you. We're friends.'

Nausea overwhelmed Katrín. How could Líf think that she didn't remember how the collapse of the brick wall had occurred? It was Líf who had urged her to peek in through the opening in the wall, and wouldn't take no for an answer. If Garðar had pushed down the wall it had been with Líf's full support and probably her encouragement. And when Katrín fell down the stairs, no one but Líf had been standing behind the door. 'Liar.' Katrín didn't dare say more. The tremendous rage that had been keeping her going was diminishing rapidly, to be replaced by sorrow at her situation, the betrayal and the injustice. Adding in the pain in her foot and the biting cold, it all became a perfect cocktail of grief and misery. Katrín had never felt so powerless.

'I'll pretend you never said that.' Líf's teeth were chattering. 'In the morning, after we've slept a little, everything will be better. Believe me, I can feel it. We've hit rock bottom and now the only way is up. The boat's coming tomorrow and everything will be just like it was. Well, almost.' She looked at the tattered cigarette packet on the table. 'I'm thinking of smoking the last cigarette. I know you can't come with me to the doorway, but I should be all right since everything's gone quiet and the scary stuff seems to have stopped now.' As if on cue, a creak came from a door hinge upstairs. Startled, they both stared wide-eyed at the ceiling, which revealed nothing. The creak came again, as if a door were opening slowly but surely. Then it was slammed with so much force that Katrín half expected to hear it fall to the floor. But this didn't happen; instead they heard a malevolent chuckling and then the footsteps of someone running down the hallway. The ceiling trembled and loose flakes of paint fell onto the kitchen table and the packet of cigarettes.

Líf grabbed her chest. 'He's upstairs.' As soon as she said this, a loud knocking came from the crawl space below. Katrín was so startled that her neck cricked painfully as she looked down. Adrenalin rushed through her veins and the pain in her fingers disappeared. Even her foot seemed to benefit from the shock, since the throbbing lessened, though without disappearing completely. Líf stared wide-eyed at Katrín. The knocking came again, now slightly softer, followed by a noise as if something were being dragged along the floor beneath them towards the opening. Neither Katrín nor Líf dared so much as breathe, and Putti made no sound. The noise grew clearer the closer it came and was accompanied by a vague mumbling that was impossible to make out. Katrín drew a deep breath and looked towards the window; her only thought was to get out of there and that was the shortest way out. She recoiled in horror, feeling hope drain away, for outside stood a boy who didn't seem to be the same one they had seen before. This one, who was smaller, stared in with glazed eyes, his greyish face infinitely sad. Outside or inside. It didn't matter. They were dead.

Líf followed Katrín's gaze to see what had made her go so pale, and her scream was so forceful that it snuffed out the candle. She fell silent and started snivelling. Overwhelmed by darkness and despair, they had no choice but to listen to the scratching sound coming from the hole as something seemed to drag itself up through it. Then the floor creaked as the creature made its way over to them. The footsteps stopped behind Katrín, who sat nearer the hole. She felt an icy breath hover around her neck, accompanied by the familiar rank smell. She moaned involuntarily, though she'd resolved not to emit a sound in the hope that the creature would disappear or move on to Líf. In her anguish it didn't cross her mind that if Líf and Garðar had been behind the attacks on her, the ghost might be good after all and wouldn't do them harm. Two little hands, cold as ice, closed around her throat.

Chapter 32

It was as if Freyr were finally free from a drug-induced haze. He looked around his home, which he'd done nothing to brighten up the entire time that he'd lived in Ísafjörður. The outlines of everything had become sharper, and now for the first time the mismatched fittings got on his nerves. He clutched a photo of his son to his chest, as if he didn't want Benni to see how his father lived now. He felt a certain consolation in holding his child so closely, even though the photograph in the frame was only ink on paper, a two-dimensional image of one moment in his far-too-short life. Freyr squeezed his eyes shut again and wished that the next few days and weeks would show him some mercy and pass by in a flash. Now when it seemed his sincere wish that Benni's earthly remains be found was going to be fulfilled, he realized that despite all his attempts to be guided by logic he'd always held onto the faint hope that Benni was still alive. That hope was now gone. He was scared to tell Sara the news and so hadn't even tried to call her; she wouldn't answer him anyway, and he felt it would be useless to hit her with something that hadn't even been positively confirmed. Which it would be shortly.

'Drink this.' Dagný had come into the room with a glass half full of golden liquid. 'I found a bottle of whisky in the kitchen. I hope you don't mind that I opened it.'

Freyr relaxed his grip on the photo frame and took the glass. He'd brought the bottle with him from Reykjavík; a parting gift from colleagues of his who didn't know he wasn't much of a whisky fan. The strong liquid stung his throat. 'Thanks.' He took another, bigger sip that went down more easily. 'Is there any news?'

Dagný sat down in a chair facing him. 'This is the car. I had the old case files looked over, and the driver bought himself something to eat at this petrol station. It was the last charge on his credit card before he used it again in Ísafjörður. The receipt was even in the glove compartment when we went through the car. The date and time fitted with the recording from the security camera.'

Freyr nodded numbly. He took another sip of whisky, hoping that he wouldn't start feeling its effects until later. 'No one knows what happened to him?'

'No. He disappeared around the same time as your son. Three years ago.' Dagný leaned back, but still seemed just as anxious. 'After we were informed about a car that had been parked for more than two weeks at the harbour here in Ísafjörður, we made enquiries about the owner and subsequently initiated a search. He owned a house in Hesteyri and had gone over there along with the supplies he needed to renovate it, which were in his trailer. The skipper of the boat that took him over said the man was meant to call when he wanted to be picked up, but he hadn't done so yet. He wasn't worried about it, but from his description of the provisions that the man had taken with him, we thought it best to go over to Hesteyri and check on his situation. It was autumn and growing colder, so we had every reason to worry about him. As it turned out, he was never found.'

'What could have happened to him? It's not a big place, is it?' Freyr refrained from asking what he longed to know most. It would take him a few more drinks to work up the nerve to do it.

'We don't know. Even though Hesteyri is a small, abandoned village, there are vast areas all around it where he could have got lost. He probably went for a hike or set off thinking he could walk to town. His phone was found there, dead. Of course you never know; the battery could have drained after he disappeared, but it could be that his phone hadn't worked when he'd needed it to and he thought his only choice was to try to walk back.'

'That seems likely.' Freyr took another sip of whisky, then threw his head back and downed the rest.

'Yes and no. There were at least two days' worth of provisions in the house. He could hardly have started panicking before he left it.' Dagný pressed her lips together. 'Are you tipsy enough to tell me how you got the information on your son's whereabouts?'

Freyr wanted to smile at her but couldn't. The muscles in his face refused to obey. 'No. I promised not to tell, and I can't betray that.' He didn't need to refer to her job. It would be impossible to expect her not to disclose the information when it came to writing a report on the conclusion of the case. He wanted to maintain confidentiality between himself and the boy, whose only mistake had been being young and reading the situation wrongly. He'd probably felt bad enough for deciding not to say anything. Of course it might turn out that when and if the discovery of Benni's remains made it into the press, the boy would tell his parents, but he would have to decide that for himself. Not Freyr. He himself wasn't certain if he would tell Sara the whole story, though she was entitled to hear it. There was a risk that she might view the matter differently to Freyr and consider the boy responsible for Benni's death, which would be unfair, but at the same time very tempting. There was no way of knowing how she would react to the shock.

Freyr put the glass on the table and leaned his head back. How long had it taken Benni to die? An hour? Two? Three? He didn't want to know the answer, yet the question burned inside him. It was completely pointless, as it would never be answered. He might just as well wonder what might have happened if this and that had been different. What if the boy who'd gone with Benni down to the petrol station in search of a hiding place hadn't suddenly remembered that he was late for his cousin's birthday party and gone home? What if the boy had stopped to talk to some of the other kids and let them know that Benni was planning to hide in the green container that they thought looked like a submarine, which was sitting on a trailer at the petrol station? What if he'd actually known what a septic tank was, and had said that instead of submarine? And then what if the driver hadn't detached the trailer from the car to check for possible damage to the coupling; would Benni have found himself a different hiding place, realising that the trailer might be leaving soon? But none of this had happened. It was a series of coincidences. What if the kids hadn't grown tired of their hiding places in the safe parts in the neighbourhood and decided to expand the hiding area all the way to the petrol station? And what if they'd decided to tell the police or their parents about it? What then? Would death have claimed Benni in some other way, and if so, how?

Freyr tried turning his mind to something else; he had so many questions. But it was difficult. Over and above all this speculation and regret, he was plagued by images of the final moments in Benni's life. There was no room for any doubt; as the moment the car had driven off, it had been too late. The only thing that could have happened differently was that Sara might have learned the truth about Benni's fate earlier if Heimir had told anyone what had actually happened. It would still have been too late to save Benni's life, since the boy didn't hear of his friend's disappearance until the next day. When he heard from the policemen who came to his house that they were searching for Benni, he had tried to tell them, but the men looked so stern and disbelieving that he had second thoughts. He'd misread the situation and thought he might get into trouble for planning to hide with Benni in the petrol station. The children were strictly forbidden from crossing the street that lay between the neighbourhood and the garage. When the policemen's faces turned serious at what he said, his child's mind had been quick to tell him that Benni had probably left his hiding place before he vanished, and he'd changed his story.

Freyr told himself there was no point going over this endlessly; it was clear that Benni would already have been dead by the time the other boy finally heard the news. Had he been conscious he would have made his presence known when the septic tank was taken off the trailer and put on the boat that brought it over to Hesteyri. He'd probably had a diabetic seizure when he realized his situation as the car drove off, his panicked state calling for insulin that his weakened bodily functions were unable to supply, and after that there had been no hope. Why he hadn't made his presence known when the trailer was hooked back up to the car was a question that would never be answered; maybe he'd considered it but feared a tongue-lashing from the trailer's owner. But really, if there were anyone to blame, it was Freyr himself. If he hadn't gone to meet Líf he wouldn't have hit the other car, and then the trailer wouldn't have been there when Benni and the boy turned up. Then Benni would have hidden behind something fixed, been found, and life would have continued as it was supposed to. 'I'm such an idiot, Dagný.' He didn't explain this, and she didn't press him.

'I think we should get going. If you're sure you want to come along.' Her tone was embarrassed, as if she worried that their conversation would take a personal turn. He didn't blame her. 'I found a skipper who's willing to take us over. Veigar's coming too; I'm not on duty so it's better for him to be there. But the sea is rough, so if you suffer from seasickness I'd advise you to think twice about it.'

Freyr looked at her. He hadn't the slightest idea whether he suffered from seasickness, since he'd rarely ever been to sea. Nor did it matter; he was prepared to puke his guts out to get to Hesteyri. 'I'm coming with you.' His voice contained all the conviction that was lacking in his soul.

The torch was of little use against the dark, but from the boat's deck Freyr could see the outlines of houses on the low ground between the beach and the mountains, whose upper reaches couldn't be distinguished from the heavily clouded night sky. 'I tried to warn them.' The captain pulled tightly on the rope with which he'd tied the boat fast to the pier. The sea was choppy and it was best to make sure that the boat would definitely still be there when they turned back.

'I didn't want to scare the life out of them, so I didn't go into too much detail, but I can tell you that this house doesn't have a great reputation. You can see over the fjord from there and probably a lot of people have died looking across at it, the last thing they ever saw in this life. It must have had some effect. There's nothing like the desperation of a drowning man; maybe it's contagious.'

Veigar snorted. 'We'll look in on them; it's their house we're heading up to. Their phones are off and they haven't called, you say?'

'No, but I didn't expect them to. We'd already agreed that I would come and fetch them tomorrow evening. I'm hoping they'll be ready to leave right now, so I don't have to make the trip tomorrow. The forecast is pretty bad, so they could be stuck here for another day or two. It isn't strange that they've turned off their phones; I asked them to save the batteries in case anything came up. They probably took me at my word.'

Freyr turned off his torch to conserve the power. 'The house looks empty. It's as dark as the others.'

The skipper shot him a patronizing look. He didn't need torch-light to see how little the man thought of him. Freyr had sat there pale and silent the entire trip, though it had had nothing to do with seasickness. He'd concentrated on listening to his travel companions chatting back and forth, sometimes lowering their voices to say things he didn't manage to grasp. In this way he'd managed to keep his head together, not fall apart at the thought of what lay ahead. He prayed to the God in whom he didn't believe that the septic tank would still be disconnected, that the man had gone missing before he'd got it in working order and that the three people from Reykjavík who were here for the same purpose had started on some other project than getting it set up. His child deserved much better. He felt nauseous – but not from seasickness. 'There's no electricity here, mate. They're probably there, even though the house isn't as lit up as the houses down south.'

'I understand.' Freyr was happy that the man seemed to have no idea who he was or what he was doing there. This ensured that the way he acted towards Freyr was motivated by something other than pity, which was fine by him; it meant less risk of him breaking down.

They stepped onto the pier and went ashore. The pier creaked loudly beneath their feet, but only silence and stillness awaited them at the top of the beach. Houses that had once been surrounded by vibrant life now either stood empty or had been converted into summer cottages. Freyr felt as if the buildings were gazing hopefully at them, wondering if the residents had finally returned. He half expected to hear a soft sigh when the houses realized they hadn't. But of course no such thing happened; there was only the silence, and it was so oddly heavy that none of them wanted to break it. So, saying nothing, they simply set off. For everyone but Freyr, the walk was nothing more than a necessary part of getting to the house; to him, every step was an important stage in an inevitable reckoning with the tragedy he'd caused for those he loved most.

Maybe the alcohol was finally starting to have an effect, or else depression was beginning to grip him, but Freyr felt as if he could hear a whispering in the dead vegetation that bordered the path leading from the pier. Their torch beams cast peculiar shadows, making it look as if something were moving on both sides. The cones of light swung irregularly to and fro, making it difficult for them to focus their eyes on anything. In one place Freyr thought he heard footsteps a few metres away, as if someone were walking beside the path, a silent escort who didn't want to be seen. He stopped and swung his torch round, pointing it left and right and then at the high, uncultivated ground, but saw nothing. He also tried to shine the light into the wall of vegetation surrounding the path, but saw nothing except darkness between the yellowed stalks.

'What?' Dagný had turned and walked back to him as he stood and stared at the light.

'I thought I heard someone, but I can't see anything.' He straightened up.

'Probably just a fox. There are lots of them here.' She looked at him as if searching for signs that he'd lost his mind. 'You can wait here or down at the pier. I'll come and get you when we know whether your theory is right. It's not necessary for you to be with us the whole time, and probably not wise.'

'No, no, I'm fine. Don't worry.' Freyr tried to appear confident. Of course he should wait and let them call for him when everything was finished, but he couldn't. He wanted to witness with his own eyes every step that revealed the whereabouts of his son, rather than sit alone in the darkness, waiting for whatever might come.

'Okay, then.' Dagný didn't sound convinced. 'You go in front. I don't want you lagging behind and getting lost. We have enough to worry about as it is.'

Freyr raised no objection to this, since it was simpler and would speed up the process. Nor could he deny that he'd been at the point of pushing the vegetation aside to see what lay beyond it when Dagný had interrupted him. As they trudged onwards in the cold he was careful not to look over his shoulder or aim the torch anywhere but straight ahead, so that Dagný wouldn't realise that he still felt as if something were following them. He desperately longed to turn around and ask whether she could hear whispering or a crackling in the brush, but was afraid she would send him straight back down to the boat. So he bit his lip and pushed back the desire to flee, despite his body shouting at him to stay alert and run away from this strange threat. When they'd crossed a little stream and come to the house, their destination, Freyr realized that he was drenched with sweat despite the still, cold air.

'It's like a graveyard.' Veigar immediately regretted his choice of words and tried to make up for them. 'I can't hear a thing. Not even snoring.'

Dagný frowned and her expression seemed exaggerated in the light from the torch. 'Are you sure this is the right house?' She turned to the captain.

'Yes. Definitely. They brought all this stuff with them on the boat.' He pointed at a stack of timber and something unrecognisable under a sailcloth. 'Shouldn't we just knock?'

They stood silently, side by side, staring at the house. No one responded to the skipper's suggestion, though it was a sensible one. Freyr took this to mean that he wasn't the only one to feel something odd was going on; the sounds had disappeared as they stepped off the path but that didn't change the fact that there was still something unpleasant in the air. Even the house, which was in every way a charming old-fashioned Icelandic wooden house, seemed oppressive to him as it stood there silently, daring them to knock on the door. The torch beams managed to illuminate only a portion of the gable facing them, and the long wall, which should have been visible, receded into the darkness. It was Dagný who cut to the chase. 'Veigar, come with me. You two wait here while we go and see whether these people are all right.'

'Suits me.' The captain gave Freyr a hearty clap on the shoulder. He didn't seem to mind having to wait outside. 'We'll just wait quietly out here, eh?'

Freyr staggered a little – the old man hadn't spared his strength, perhaps intentionally. Freyr had no business in the house; the septic tank was outdoors and maybe already down in the ground. He might even be standing on it. The thought caused him to take two instinctive steps sideways, but when he aimed the dull beam of his torch at the ground there was nothing to see but a thin layer of snow. He wondered whether he should walk around the house but couldn't bring himself to do it; it would be better if Dagný and Veigar were there. A loud knocking broke the silence and hung in the air. 'Is anyone home?' Veigar's voice resounded and Freyr thought it impossible that anyone could sleep through such noise. The knocking began again and Veigar called out: 'This is the police. We're coming in.' The screech of the doorknob was piercing, but it wasn't followed by a creak suggesting the door was being opened. Dagný and Veigar then came round the corner and said they were going to check whether the back door was unlocked. Otherwise they would have to break in.

Freyr and the skipper followed them automatically, keeping far enough back to give no impression of wanting to go in with them, but close enough to see what was happening. Dagný and Veigar stepped up onto an old porch that was in a rather sad state of repair and went straight to work, knocking hard on the door and calling out to those who were supposed to be inside. 'Of course they might be down at the doctor's house,' the captain shouted to Veigar just as the old, stocky police officer was about to throw himself against the door, shoulder first. 'I remember now that I let them have the keys so they could move there if they encountered any . . . inconvenience.'

Veigar and Dagný turned to them. Their faces weren't visible, but it was clear they were less than happy with the skipper. 'Was there any light there? Or smoke coming from the chimney?'

'Uh, no.' The old man took one step closer to Freyr as if to enlist him as a team-mate.

'All right then. If they're not here, we'll go and check that house.' They both turned back to the door and Veigar threw himself against the tired old wood. It gave a loud crack but didn't budge. He tried again and at the third attempt the door flew open. 'Oh, Christ!' Dagný and Veigar turned aside and a second later the stench reached Freyr and the skipper, forcing them to cover their noses and mouths. 'That's fucking disgusting!' Veigar spat on the porch and Freyr was tempted to do the same. The stench was unlike anything he'd ever smelled, and he'd encountered some rank odours in medical school. This one most resembled the smell that he remembered from forensic medicine when they'd opened the belly of a man who'd drowned and been found after several days in the sea. A salty, rotten stink.

Something shot out through the door and they all gasped. 'What the hell was that?' The captain now stood so close to Freyr that Freyr had to step slightly aside to avoid losing his balance. They waved their torches, searching silently for an explanation. Finally they saw a small creature trembling near Freyr, a little dog that had certainly seen better days. Its coat appeared sticky and had formed clumps in several places on its scrawny body. 'I'd forgotten him; they brought this dog with them.' The skipper held one hand to his chest. 'Scared the shit out of me.'

'Is there anything else you've forgotten to tell us?' Dagný walked angrily past them to the dog. 'It would be great if you'd share it with us before we go in.' She bent down to the little animal, which initially took a few steps back but then went to her and allowed her to pick it up. 'God, he's shaking, poor thing. Do you remember his name?'

'Hvutti, Patti, or something like that.' The captain stared at the dog, not particularly kindly. 'What a wretched little scrap. Call that a dog . . .'

Dagný didn't answer him, but handed the dog to Freyr. 'Keep your eye on him. I'm not planning to chase him around all over the place before we can go back.' Freyr took the dog, which looked into his eyes as if to check whether he was trustworthy. Its little body felt like no more than skin and bones and it would probably be easy to forget he was holding it at all if it weren't for the trembling that shook it from limb to limb. Freyr used his free hand to stroke the poor thing's head, unafraid that it would bite. It really didn't matter to him, and it might even make Freyr feel better. But the dog gave no indication of wanting to bite him and instead shut its eyes and relaxed slightly. Then it turned its head towards the house and growled softly, recovering its courage in the security of Freyr's embrace. As he adjusted the creature in his arms he noticed that his hand was stained with something after touching the dog. He couldn't see clearly what it was, but when he smelled his hand he realized it was blood. Instinctively he held the dog away from his body, then called to Dagný and Veigar: 'The dog's covered in blood!' They turned to look. 'But he's not injured, so it must be from someone else.' They nodded, their faces grave, and turned back to the house.

'What?' The captain shone his torch on the dog and stepped back when he saw what Freyr was talking about. 'What the fuck . . . ? This doesn't look good.' He turned towards the house. 'I'm glad *I* don't have to go in there.'

They watched Veigar and Dagný cover their noses and mouths in the crooks of their arms and walk in. Freyr and the old man said nothing, but through the curtainless windows they watched the torch lights move through the house. The lights stopped suddenly and moved up and down and back and forth in the same place. A few moments later one of the beams set off in the direction it had come from and Dagný appeared at the door, calling for Freyr.

'Can you come inside? We've found a woman. She seems to be injured, I think you'd better look at her before we move her.' Freyr handed the dog to the skipper, who was less than happy about taking the filthy creature and being left alone outside. But Dagný forbade him to move, and the seriousness in her voice made the man obey. In their haste, Dagný and Freyr neglected to defend themselves against the stench that met them like an invisible curtain in the doorway. But they forgot about it as soon as they were in. The little that Freyr could see of the house's interior appeared to be much as he'd expected: everything rather old and battered, though in several places the owners' attempts to renovate the place were visible

– and even the dull light couldn't hide how badly they'd done. 'She's here.' Dagný made way for Freyr to enter the kitchen. 'Watch out for the hole in the floor back there. You don't want to fall down it; the smell seems to be coming from there.' Veigar was hunched over a person lying face down on the floor, her head in a dark pool that Freyr hoped wasn't blood, but suspected almost certainly was. That could explain the state of the dog.

Freyr searched the woman for signs of life. He ran his hands down the back of her neck. It was uninjured. He asked Veigar to pass him a knife, and used it to cut away the woman's clothing. With her pale back exposed, he examined the remainder of her spine, which appeared undamaged, and couldn't find any other injuries. Her breathing was irregular and rattly. 'Help me turn her over, carefully.' Veigar hurriedly obeyed and together they turned the victim onto her back. Veigar started in surprise when he saw her injuries. Bloody red crosses had been cut into her face, and she could count herself lucky that she hadn't lost her eyes, the cuts had come so close to them. Freyr reached for Veigar's torch and aimed the beam to get a better view. It took all his powers not to let the woman's head fall back to the floor. Freyr could have sworn that he heard low, nasty, childish laughter coming from the hole in the floor behind him, but he was too flabbergasted even to be frightened.

It was Líf. Or what was left of her.

Chapter 33

Either the stench inside had gone or they'd become so impervious to it that they no longer smelled it; at least, none of them pinched their nostrils or wrinkled their noses any more. They'd been too busy searching for the other two people who were supposed to be in the house and looking after Líf to let the disgusting smell bother them; the group grew increasingly dismayed at each empty room they checked. The couple seemed to have vanished, and Veigar and Dagný's trip to the doctor's house in search of them had revealed nothing.

The old sea dog, now installed on a kitchen stool, let out frequent gusty sighs, shaking his head and muttering that he tried to warn people but no one ever listened, not even now. Freyr wasn't certain how well Dagný and Veigar could hear him, since they'd gone into the crawl space through the hole in the floor. Veigar had taken a look in there first, stuck his head down to follow his torch beam but raised it again immediately, his face pale, delivering the news that down in the crawl space was a skeleton. Probably a child's. Freyr had stood up from attending to Líf, whose condition was worsening slowly but steadily, and said that he was going down there, but Dagný had grabbed his arm and stopped him. She'd then followed Veigar down herself and soon afterwards stuck her head out to tell Freyr that it wasn't his son. Then they'd both come up and gone to the kitchen to have a word in private. As they moved out of sight, Freyr had positioned Líf's head carefully on his rolled-up jacket and gone over to the hole to see with his own eyes whether it was Benni. The barbed wire surrounding his heart tightened, and until he looked down into the dark, low space he felt as if he couldn't breathe for grief. But Dagný hadn't been lying – this couldn't be Benni; the body had clearly been lying there for too long.

When Dagný and Veigar returned, he was still lying on the floor with his head in the hole, transfixed by this sad sight. There was a tired-looking, dusty schoolbag next to the pile of bones that had once breathed, laughed and played without the slightest suspicion of where he or she would later die. Only the skull and delicate bones of parts of the fingers of one hand were visible, the remainder of the skeleton hidden beneath the clothing that the child had been wearing the day it had died. Shells were scattered over the earthen floor, covered with fine dust like everything else down there. Freyr had the sudden feeling that this must be Bernódus, who had vanished all those years ago. The boy to whom life had shown little mercy, and death even less. But this would no doubt be confirmed later. Freyr decided not to voice his thoughts to Dagný when she got him up off the floor by saying he mustn't disturb the area. She was most likely thinking the same as he was.

'Do you have much left to do?' Freyr turned his head and shouted the question at the hole, to which Dagný and Veigar had returned, and which looked very much like an entrance to hell. Yellow light from their torches illuminated the stream of dust that was rising from the hole, as if a fire was burning beneath their feet. Now and then there were powerful flashes as they photographed the scene. 'She's got to get to the hospital as quickly as possible.' It was hard to say what was afflicting Líf apart from the cuts on her face; those were hardly life-threatening, though they would change her life completely and permanently. As well as being boiling hot with a weak pulse, she was also coughing up blood regularly but weakly. She was probably suffering internal injuries and if nothing were done about it they could gradually lead to her death. And that wasn't out of the question even if they did get her to a hospital immediately.

Dagný and Veigar wriggled dustily up through the hole, looking tired and not dissimilar to the little dog that was still curled up in the skipper's arms. Dagný was holding the schoolbag and laid it gently on the kitchen table as if she were worried the leather might fall apart. 'We're ready. What's the best way to take her to the boat?'

Freyr looked from the bag into Dagný's eyes. 'We've got to make some sort of stretcher. The best thing would be to call a helicopter, but I think we'll be quicker going by boat; her condition is critical.' He cleared his throat. 'If you could take care of that I'd like to walk around the house and look for the septic tank. I can't leave here without knowing whether I'm right or not.'

Dagný stared at him but then made her decision. 'Come on then. No one's going out alone here.' Then she turned to Veigar and the skipper. 'Can you two handle the stretcher?' They nodded and Dagný and Freyr went out into the night, each armed with a torch. The feeling that Freyr had had before of someone following them returned as soon as he stepped out of the door, but then faded as they set off. Perhaps it was because he was focused on the surroundings and gave no thought to anything else; he found he actually didn't remotely care what or whether anything was sharing the night with them. He had other things on his mind. Dagný, on the other hand, seemed tense, as if they'd changed roles from when they arrived at the house. She constantly jerked her torch to and fro as if searching for a lost cat. 'Do you think we'll find the other two?' Freyr wanted to say something, had to say something to calm her nerves. He felt as if he were riding a giant rollercoaster that climbed steadily higher and higher until it reached its peak, then plunged down from there. 'I was able to get Líf to tell me that the man, Garðar, went missing yesterday or the day before. She didn't know what day it was or how long she'd been lying in the kitchen. I actually think it hasn't been that long since she was injured. A few hours at most.'

Dagný seemed relieved by his chatter; the jerky movements of the beam from her torch slowed a little. 'Did you ask her what happened, who attacked her?'

'I'm not certain she knew what she was saying but she mentioned a boy. I couldn't get a name from her or any more details. She said that he took Katrín; killed her and dragged her out. The cuts have severed the nerves that control facial movement, on both sides. Her face is paralysed so it's difficult for her to speak.' He decided not to mention the questions he'd asked Líf about the insulin when she came round. Because of the uncertainty of her condition this was his only chance to clear this up, and although it actually didn't matter, it was still churning up his insides. Otherwise, if the worst were to happen, she would take the answer with her to the grave. When Freyr witnessed her like this, deprived of her beauty, he finally saw through her. Of course he also bore the blame for their having been together, but he still felt hatred fasten its claws into him. If he hadn't met up with her after fetching the drug, Benni wouldn't have died. Not in that way. His hatred was primitive, like that which Adam and Eve must have felt for the serpent after they'd been driven from paradise. For this reason Freyr didn't feel sorry for Líf, however unfair that sounded. His heart and soul had hardened against her. So he didn't shield her from difficult questions, as he should have, but instead pressured her until she tried to answer weakly. The answers had been vague, yet she said that Einar, which he recalled was the name of her husband, had deserved it. Freyr had then stopped his questioning immediately; he suddenly didn't want to have his suspicions confirmed. Her questions about insulin, after finding out that it didn't cause intoxication, had been far too specific, and probably hadn't been asked just to fill the silence as he'd thought at the time.

They rounded the corner of the house to the gable end, facing away from the village. Freyr stopped as his torch beam revealed signs of an excavation. In the darkness he could make out the upper part of what had to be the septic tank, along with the little riser on top of it. Freyr walked slowly over to it, having to remind himself to breathe. The closer he got, the more the green colour stung his eyes, the colour that had plagued him both awake and asleep. When he reached the edge of the dug-up area he saw the tank in its entirety, though the lower part of it was covered in snow. A submarine. A green submarine. If he squinted, he had no trouble seeing the resemblance. A broad, cylindrical body with a little house on top; the only thing missing was the periscope. 'Hold on a second, Freyr. I'll have a look inside.' Dagný pushed him back from the edge. 'Don't fall in. You could twist your ankle or something even worse.' It wasn't a long fall, but Freyr knew she was right. He wouldn't even raise his hands to stop his fall in the condition he was in now. So he watched her step into the hole, clamber up onto the tank and inch her way towards the opening through which Benni must have entered. She easily unhitched the latch holding the lid tight and once again Freyr felt a sting in his heart; in all likelihood, the man whose car Freyr had hit had noticed that it wasn't fastened before he drove off, and secured it. Yet another 'what if' to add to the list. What if he hadn't done that? Would Benni have managed to open the lid from the inside and stick his head out? Would other drivers have seen him and stopped the car?

Dagný put the lid down and shone her torch into the little tank. At that, the empty space inside became like a lantern; the green light not unlike the borealis. Inside the tank a shadow appeared. The pain was worse than he could ever have imagined; it was like standing near to a huge fire, except that it burned inside him and it was useless to turn away. To Freyr it looked as if a tiny, skeletal hand formed part of the outline. Benni.

The sea did what it could to make Freyr's trip home even more unbearable. His stomach moved in tandem with every dip and rise of the boat, but his body was unable to relieve his discomfort by vomiting. He sat on a bench in the little passenger area behind the pilothouse and stared out. Although his eyes could see what was in front of him, his brain wasn't able to put together the information; he would have had trouble describing what he saw. Líf was dead; she'd passed away shortly after they sailed out into the Ísafjörður Deep; she'd asked for a cigarette, sighed softly, and then her head sank slowly to the side. His attempts to resuscitate her had been useless. Feeling her lips against his once more under these circumstances, lifeless as they were, had been almost too much for him.

'Freyr.' Dagný sat crouched in front of him. 'We're just about there. How do you feel?'

'All right.' This was a lie, clear to both of them.

'Your son will be brought back first thing in the morning. I'll see to it.' He didn't reply, since it wasn't necessary. 'I looked in the bag. It belonged to Bernódus.' A large, powerful wave nearly toppled her over, but Dagný managed to keep her balance by grasping Freyr's knees. 'The contents are practically undamaged and I found a notebook that he wrote in after he went missing.' He didn't react, and she continued: 'In it he describes what happened to him. It's pretty shocking. I'll have it photocopied for you later if you want.'

Freyr nodded. Maybe he would read it, maybe not. At the moment he just wanted to be alone. Completely alone. He no longer felt Benni's presence and he was fairly certain that the boy would no longer appear in Sara's dreams. He couldn't avoid the thought that in the end she would miss it. Just as he did already.

Úrsúla wept silently. The salty tears flowed over the wounds beneath her eyes, still unhealed. It must have hurt, but she didn't show it. 'He's gone.' She rubbed her veiny hands. 'He isn't here any longer.'

'Is this an accurate description of what happened, Úrsúla? Do you remember it?' Freyr put down the paper from which he'd been reading aloud. He'd got it from Dagný the day after they'd returned from Hesteyri, having contacted her first thing the next morning after a sleepless night. He'd wanted to read it before she returned to Hesteyri with back-up to search for the missing couple and transport the physical remains of both Benni and Bernódus back to town. Unfortunately the search had been postponed by a day because of bad weather and so the group was there now, probably working diligently to complete their mission before darkness fell. He hoped they would show his son respect and handle his little white bones gently; he would have preferred to be able to deal with them himself and had tried to go with them, had done everything but fall to his knees and beg Dagný, but to no avail.

'They didn't want to be my friends; they just pretended to be. After Bernódus disappeared they treated me as they had before. Cruelly.' She twisted her hands together more fervently, as if trying to plait her fingers. 'He was my only friend and they made me betray him – tricked me into thinking I could be part of their group. The popular ones. The pretty ones.' Her hands stopped moving. 'They didn't mean it; they lied. When he was gone everything went back to the way it had been.'

Freyr didn't know what to say. He hadn't read the complete text to her; he'd left out the final statement, where the boy vowed revenge, asking whoever found the text to see to it that they all, but particularly Úrsúla, got their just reward. It had certainly come true; all the kids that he'd named had suffered as adults, and the teacher who had turned a blind eye to his problems was the first to suffer. The father was the only one the boy had spared, which was typical of a child's loyalty to his parents. But apart from the avenging spirit and the fury of a dying child, which the handwritten text described, the resemblances to Benni's fate were striking.

So striking that Freyr couldn't bring himself to think about them, not immediately. Perhaps he would do it later, after reconciling himself to his life again, which at the moment seemed like a distant dream. 'Kids can be so ruthless, Úrsúla. But they grow out of it. Who knows, maybe you would have become friends again if you hadn't got ill and moved to Reykjavík.'

'I should have told someone about it. I just didn't dare. They threatened to beat me up, tell the police that I was responsible for it, not them. Who would have believed me against all of them?'

Freyr prepared to leave, folding the paper and tucking it into Úrsúla's medical history file, which he had with him. The story of Bernódus, kept with ECG readouts and descriptions of drug dosages for an old woman who had long since lost her grasp on what was considered reality – perhaps not surprisingly. Undoubtedly her disturbed mind had had trouble coping with what had happened. Watching her new companions bully and tease a boy who had given her his friendship, calling him awful names, saying that he was ugly and dirty, the insult they chose for him because he never wanted to have a shower after P.E. But now they'd found something new to tease him with. They mocked him for being so poor that his dad couldn't afford crosses for the graves of his mother and brother, and had to carve them on his son's back. When he tried to flee their taunts they followed him, chasing him down to the harbour where he found himself at a dead end, with his best option for getting out of it to clamber on board a boat that was releasing its moorings. The group of kids had stood at the end of the pier and watched the boat sail away, while the boy hid beneath a sailcloth and tangled mess of netting for fear that the sailor would see him, return to the pier and leave him there. From his description, what had hurt him the most was looking out from his hiding place at Úrsúla standing among his tormentors, and having to face the fact that she was a willing participant in their teasing and wasn't going to do anything to help him.

The boat had ended up in Hesteyri and when the man left it to do whatever it was he needed to do there, which was never clear to the boy, he decided to sneak ashore and fetch the crosses from the grave of his mother and brother, show those bastard kids that they were wrong. While he was busy pulling them out, the boat had sailed away and left him behind, alone in the abandoned village where he used to live. In the winter, in a place almost no one ever came to.

For a long time he held out hope that someone would come and get him; that one of the kids who'd watched him sail away would let someone know and that the police would find out where the boat had sailed and come to find him. He lived on the contents of shells from the beach, since he had no fishing gear and didn't know how to make any. He'd gone to stay in his old home, not daring to break into any other house for fear of getting into trouble when they came to fetch him. As the cold got more and more severe he was forced to seek shelter in the crawl space, where it was warmest, but it was all for nothing. The cold found him and didn't let go until he was dead. Naturally, there was no description of this, but his description of the fingers of his left hand turning black indicated that the boy had suffered from frostbite; without medical assistance, septicaemia and death generally followed shortly afterwards, as the empty pages following the description strongly suggested.

'Why wasn't he found sooner?' Úrsúla's voice was broken and hoarse; it had been a long time since she'd spoken for so long or so much to another person. It was as if a heavy burden had been lifted from her shoulders. Perhaps she meant: *What if he'd been found thirty years ago? Or forty? Would I have had a more normal life then?*

'The house was empty, no one stepped through its door for the next few decades. From what I understand, some people who came there one autumn to secure their own houses for the winter decided to board up its windows and doors, but it wasn't until three years ago that anyone lived in it even for a short time. The man who went there to renovate it probably couldn't see very well since he laid a parquet floor over the hatch, nearly ensuring that the boy would be hidden from the world for much, much longer.'

'He broke into the school the night that he died. Revenge from beyond the grave. Then I knew he was dead, because that's when he appeared to me for the first time. Ever since then I've been seeing him. And hearing him.' She looked into Freyr's eyes and seemed surprised not to find in them the same disbelief she must often have met with over the years. 'But now he's gone and he won't be back. Maybe he wanted to be found.'

'Maybe.' For the first time since he'd started treating her, Freyr didn't feel like interrupting the woman's story, which was finally making sense. If, and only if, this extraordinary explanation for the first break-in were true, was it the same dead boy who had gone berserk in the preschool? And why? If Freyr gave his imagination free rein for a second, he might conclude that the break-in was connected to the arrival of the trio at the house in Hesteyri, but there was no point pondering this. The mystery would probably never be solved. Neither would the question of whether Bernódus had pushed to have Benni found in the hope that his own remains would be discovered in the search, and that he would gain the peace he had so long desired. In any case, it was a satisfactory ending to a great tragedy. With the exception of Úrsúla, everyone who had hurt Bernódus was now dead and there were no longer any ties binding the boy to this world. Freyr allowed himself the faint hope that this dark night was now at an end.

'I'm tired.' Úrsúla closed her eyes. 'I think I'll sleep well tonight.' She rested her head on her pillow, facing away from Freyr. 'Won't that be strange?'

Like so many things. Freyr said goodbye and left. He was too tired, sad and distracted to pay any attention to the low giggle that came from the room after he shut the door.

Freyr drove away from the nursing home, his window wide open. The cold winter air invigorated him a little. He knew the boat bringing Benni home was expected shortly, and he wanted to be waiting for it on the pier. He might very well have to hang around in the car, but that was all right; nothing was more important to him just then. He drove down to the harbour and angled his seat back to make himself comfortable. Then he looked out over the sea and hoped that the black spot against the sky at the horizon was the boat, even though it was bringing him final confirmation that all hope was gone. Once all the formalities had been taken care of, there wouldn't be too much to think about. Work, eat and sleep were the only things he could come up with, apart from possibly taking care of the dog, who no one seemed to want to claim and whose name might be either Patti or Hvutti. It seemed to respond to both.

Maybe he would go on a long holiday; take some unpaid leave and settle down far from everything, both people and civilization. He thought of the house in Hesteyri, watched by all the people who'd drowned in the nearby fjord over the years. Maybe he could acquire it cheaply. The owners were either dead or gone and it would give him something to think about; he could try to get it back into a decent state and maybe then the negative aura that seemed to surround it would disperse.

He watched the boat as it approached. Surprisingly, the sea was mirror-smooth, as if in honour of Benni. A warm tear ran down his cheek. With it, the sharpest of the pain seemed to leave his soul, and he felt a bit better. He resolved to make it happen, this thing with the house. He could bring the dog with him and even invite Dagný to come along; her or the nurse who resembled Líf, though only in appearance. Maybe Sara would also like to see the place eventually, and could make her peace with it and with life. Her tears when he had told her the news had sounded like the right kind; the healthy grieving process had finally begun. Although they would never be married again, it was possible that they might become friends once more, and perhaps Hesteyri was the perfect place for him to go for a more peaceful, happier life. Maybe that could be the one good thing that came out of all this. They had beautiful, bittersweet memories of Benni that could never be taken from them and if Sara visited him there they could remember him together, calmly, in between arguing and resurrecting all their old issues. One thing was certain, it would do them both some good.

He decided to buy the house and get it back into shape.

Katrín had watched the waves rock the boat out in the fjord as she stood at the top of the beach, unnoticed by anyone. She felt a bit odd, as if she were drunk – not very drunk, just a bit light-headed, and as though everything was suddenly very simple. Water dripped from her clothing onto the snow-covered ground, its trail following her past the doctor's residence, over the bridge and in the direction of the house, her house. There was a rustling sound and the dry, yellowed undergrowth cracked behind her, but she ignored it. Nothing else mattered now except the anger that boiled deep inside her. This was her home and nothing would disturb her here again. She would make sure of it.